COLORS

David Berardelli

COLORS

GRAVESTONE PRESS

PART I - FRIDAY NIGHT
The Old Woman

Chapter 1

As the solid wall of traffic roared past, Maisie coughed wetly and waited for the light to change.

The lights had always been her friends. They told her things, warned her of impending danger. They'd give her enough time to cross. Once she reached the mall at the intersection of Colonial and Maguire, she could use the restroom in one of their stores to wash up. Then she could find shelter behind a dumpster to get through another long, muggy night. Since the other homeless had chased her away from the Presbyterian Church, Maisie had to find some other place to rest. It was getting harder and harder to find empty nooks these days.

Thankfully, eating was not an issue. She no longer enjoyed the leftover food she found in dumpsters or the few eateries she went into with quarters she'd earned from panhandling. Burdened with crippling arthritis and the nagging wet cough that had been building up in her chest the last few months, she didn't know how much longer she could manage.

The cigarettes had done this. The many years of smoking were going to kill her. She'd given them up years ago – mostly from lack of money – but the heavy wetness in her chest remained. The uncomfortable condition had gradually developed into a hacking cough. It raged mercilessly through her, keeping her awake at night and exhausting her during the day.

Central Florida scared her nowadays. It was much too crowded, too hectic, and too loud. Much like the merry-go-round at the circus she'd watched from her tiny booth years ago, before her special gift faded with the passing years. The city had become a huge merry-go-round packed with screaming kids and adults rushing around like a dog chasing its tail.

Many years ago, before Disney came in and brought along its own strange civilization, a body didn't have to put her life in danger just to cross the street. Back then there wasn't as much traffic and not as many people. The pace was slower, and the anger not as heavy in the air.

Modern times had made people crazy. They'd trample somebody without a second glance, everyone always wanting to be somewhere else. Modern mentality wasn't much different than it was in the camps, where people who'd been herded into a barbed wire pen wandered around in a daze, living out what was left of their existence until the uniformed monsters came to take them away forever.

The hacking fit came suddenly, without warning. She doubled over, clutching her stomach. It had come from a deeper place this time. The expulsion was heavier. She hawked out a thick mass of brownish-red into the storm drain and wiped her mouth with the filthy handkerchief she hadn't been able to wash since yesterday.

The light changed. She stepped down from the curb and hobbled across, her failing eyesight focused on the cracked pavement straight ahead. Headlights aimed at the intersection sliced through her path, clouding her vision. The moaning and growling of the stilled traffic sounded so much like the bulldozers far off in the hills, cutting into the earth to create the next mass grave.

She ignored the searing catcalls and the insults as she crossed. Ugliness, bad manners, and foul language posed no problem. She'd endured insults and rudeness most of her life. Folks no longer respected one another because they no longer respected themselves. They looked down on others to make themselves feel better, their misery oozing from their souls like bleeding sores. In their eyes she was just some dirty old woman making them late for their dinner or their trip to the 7-Eleven for beer and cigarettes.

In front of the endless line of cars, a long-haired prissy sat in a convertible, tapping the wheel impatiently while glaring at Maisie for making her late for her date or some appointment at the nail salon.

Soon it will all be gone, Maisie wanted to tell her. *Long before you realize it, that beautiful long hair will turn brittle and break off. Your smooth skin will peel away and form pouches of tired flesh beneath the liver spots. Your bosom will fall. You'll no longer be gorgeous or desirable. Time will become your enemy. But if you remain patient, you will see that time has also become your friend. It will let you see things you were unable to see in your youth, and feel things you were unable to feel as a young, self-centered girl.*

With a deep sigh of relief, Maisie reached the end of her journey. Stiff and tired, she climbed back up onto the curb. It took a little time to catch her breath. In the midst of it, another cough tore from her throat. This one was not as intense. The sputum, mildly brown and not as thick, barely stained her handkerchief.

The light changed. The angry wall of metal screamed past. Maisie resumed walking. One more block and the light would enable her to cross Colonial. This journey would take much more time and greater care. Colonial consisted of many lanes. She'd have to proceed with utmost caution.

A few yards down, two skinny figures approached. They were male, around eighteen, wearing the baggy clothes all the kids wore nowadays. Their pants were pulled down, exposing their colored undershorts. The glaze in their eyes pierced the approaching darkness.

Maisie had seen this type often. The anger flowed freely, possibly because they had no one to guide them into adulthood. Their arrogance had run rampant. They were stupid and confused, could not speak correctly, and respected no one. They seemed to be the result of some laboratory experiment gone bad, ending in an evil mutation.

"Hey, old woman," one of them said, sniffing.

"You smell like an old couch."

She made no comment, veering right, into the grass.

The other one blocked her way. His friend came up behind her to prevent her from turning around. Both reeked of weed and BO. Maisie wondered if they lived with their parents. Few of them did anymore. Usually one parent and a steady stream of boyfriends or girlfriends occupied the household. The mother produced the kid, ran the man off, and let the government support her.

In Maisie's day, the family shared one household, food, chores, laughter and tears. But that took place in another world.

"Got money?" the one facing her said.

"Yeah." His friend nodded eagerly. "They bum quarters all day. Bet she's got a stash!"

The one who'd just spoken shivered. Maisie could smell their fear. She knew they wanted to do something they could tell their friends. Kids loved showing off in front of one another. It was a status sort of thing. America was a great country with all its freedoms, but over the years its children had become savages no better than those working the death camps a lifetime ago.

These two didn't seem to care about anything. They didn't even care about the traffic roaring by. Or that someone might stop or call a policeman.

Darkness had already settled in. With darkness came anonymity. To the passing traffic, Maisie and the boys had become a blurry, strange-moving shape along the sidewalk.

The one facing her held out his hand. "The money, bitch."

Maisie shook her head.

"Got my blade right here." The boy patted his trouser pocket. "No money? You're gonna see my blade."

"I wanna see *blood*," his friend said, giggling like a girl. "Lots and lots of *blood*."

Maisie studied the first boy's face. The pale white glow of fear emanating from the hollow spots beneath his glazed eyes had changed to blotches of red. She'd seen this same color change thousands of times before. Even though her gift had been failing her, it still told her what she needed to know. It didn't fail her now. And when she saw the boy's colors, she couldn't hold back the snicker.

"You *laughing* at me, you old cow?"

"Go home to your mother, sonny," she said. "Both of you."

"Listen here, you stupid ugly old bat–"

"You don't have a knife in there, sonny. Just that crap the two of you are smoking."

"What the–"

They both froze.

"Your mothers should be ashamed of *both* of you."

Neither said a word as she passed.

Chapter 2

Her feet sore and tingly, Lindsay Foreman finished up her cashier duties at Sarah's Shirts 'N Stuff. Leaving the store, she walked back to her two-bedroom apartment just west of Semoran Boulevard, where she and her mother had been living the last six years. It usually took less than fifteen minutes to make the trip, but longer when she drove because of traffic. So, most of the time, she walked. It was just a couple of blocks and gave her a chance to restore circulation to her legs after standing behind that cash register for eight painful hours.

The apartment was empty except for Marvin, Lindsay's turquoise-blue Crowntail Betta, obsessively patrolling his territory in the small tank on the third shelf of the living room hutch. Momma wasn't home yet, probably still at the office, running late again. Ever since she'd started dating her boss, Momma came home late almost every night. At least Marvin was home to greet her, in his own cold, detached way.

Lindsay had bought Marvin a year ago at the pet store three doors down from the tee-shirt shop just before Sam, the owner, went bankrupt and vacated the building. Marvin was beautiful but slightly sociopathic. The one and only time she brought home a companion for him turned out to be a huge mistake. When Marvin savagely attacked and killed the intruder in just minutes, Lindsay realized she should've left well enough alone.

Lindsay fed Marvin his usual miniscule ration of dinner, then went into her bedroom. She laid her purse on her desk, changed into her Florida State jersey and frayed jeans, freed her long brown hair from its confining barrette, and trudged barefoot into the kitchen. She was a little hungry, but decided to wait until she'd heard from Momma. Momma wouldn't like it if she came home with supper and saw Lindsay eating a sandwich.

A cold drink would hit the spot. She dropped an ice cube into a glass and popped open a can of Sprite, then plodded back into the living room and picked up the remote. *Charmed* blazed onto the screen. She flipped through the channels. A group of giggling teens tried out for cheerleader practice. On another station, a trio of giggling teens painted their toenails and complained about their boyfriends. Lindsay wasn't in the mood. She spent eight hours a day working in a store that sold tee-shirts, jeans, and posters of rock stars and rappers. Most of the store's customers were between twelve and twenty, and she had absolutely no incentive to waste her evenings watching that same oftentimes annoying age group on TV.

She switched to the Discovery Channel, where a group of rough-talking guys risked their lives on a boat, searching for giant crabs. She watched the show for about five minutes, gripping the arm of the couch when one of the fishermen tripped on a trap line and nearly fell into the ocean. During the commercial break, she got up and went back into

12

her room, sat down at her computer desk, and looked out the window.

The street was heavy with Friday night traffic, everyone hurrying to get to restaurants or movie theaters. She picked up the partially read newspaper lying on her desk. The advertised giant summer sale ended this Sunday. Those large rose-tinted sunglasses she had been wanting appeared on the list. They were twenty percent off, which translated into a savings of ten bucks.

Her cell buzzed. She picked up, hearing the familiar breathy voice saying, "Lindsay, baby, it's Momma."

"Everything all right?" Lindsay asked quickly.

"Something came up. I'm gonna be late. Okay?"

Lindsay sighed. Dinner was probably going to be deli chicken or roast beef again. "Any idea how long?"

"Maybe an hour. Have you eaten? I'll stop at a chicken place—"

"I'm okay."

"Later, maybe?"

"I'm really not in the mood for chicken," Lindsay said sullenly. It wasn't that she didn't want her mother to have fun and enjoy her life. Momma and Dad had been divorced for years, and Momma, at forty-four, was still a great-looking lady with a terrific figure. It was just that Lindsay didn't care for Momma's boss. He flaunted his wealth and let Momma dote over him. He also had a way of staring at Lindsay that made her uneasy.

13

"How about pizza, then?" Her mother offered. "Sausage and pepperoni?"

"And mushrooms."

"I'll be about an hour – two, tops. Love ya, baby."

"You too, Momma." Lindsay ended the call. The last time Momma said 'two, tops,' she got home at ten that night.

Best find something to do. It was Friday night – nothing interesting on the tube. She wasn't in the mood to log onto her computer and waste time checking out the stupid things people were doing on YouTube. Deciding to head on over to the mall and check out those sunglasses, she slipped on her tennies, brushed her hair, and tied it in a ponytail. Then she snatched up her keys, grabbed her purse, and left the apartment.

***

As Lindsay walked to the mall, the muggy night air swelled with a mix of traffic exhaust fumes, whiffs of charbroiled beef, and the sound of kids yelling from the open windows of passing cars. Colonial was lit up and bustling, lined with stores, fast food places, and a few fancier restaurants. Most of the activity was focused at the mall, and the theater megaplex.

Lindsay reached the end of the block. The wait for a break in the steady stream would probably take forever. She was used to it. She'd grown up in this area, seen it expand from hectic to total insanity in just a few years. She'd been dodging fast-moving traffic since she was little.

The squealing of tires directly ahead pierced the night. A loud thump resonated, followed by the screeching of brakes, then more squealing.

About a hundred feet farther down, a dark muscle car stormed loudly away from the motionless figure lying just off the curb.

Her pulse thundering, Lindsay ran over and knelt beside the still form. An old woman in wrinkled, foul-smelling clothes lay on her back, her head turned at an awkward angle. In the haze of the streetlamp, Lindsay saw that the woman's face was rough and covered with wrinkles and liver spots. Her curly white hair, dirty and matted, poked out beneath a brown-and-red checkered scarf. Her veiny gray eyes stared blankly at Lindsay. She stirred. Her small, dirt-smudged hand lifted awkwardly.

The traffic behind Lindsay slowed but didn't stop. She wondered if anyone even noticed them – if anyone even cared. *I do. I guess that's enough.*

She covered the weak, cold wrist with her hands. No pulse. She didn't know if that was because of her own trembling or because the woman's heart had already failed. "Stay with me, okay?"

No reply.

"I'll get help. I promise. We'll get you out of here."

The woman's eyes closed. Lindsay held the old woman's wrist with her left hand. With her right, she fumbled for her cell.

***

Lindsay waited on a hard bench while workers

15

in scrubs rushed up and down the long corridor in front of her. Some pushed gurneys while others carried clipboards, each focused on his own assigned emergency. She barely noticed. She was too busy trying to forget the horrible thumping sound of the muscle car slamming into the old woman.

Why was that the only thing she could think of? That, and the nagging fear that Momma was going to freak when she got home and found the message Lindsay had left on the answering machine. Momma wasn't the most collected person in the world. She'd come home, put the pizza on the kitchen table, yell for Lindsay, then check the machine. When she heard Lindsay's voice, she'd imagine the worst. But that wasn't important right now.

Why couldn't she remember anything else about that awful moment? Aside from the sickening thump and a brief glimpse of the car zooming away, her mind had gone blank. No license plate. No bumper sticker. And since it was dark, the make and color of the car had blurred into emptiness.

Even if she *could* remember, what would it accomplish? How could it help the old woman? She was a bag lady and probably had no identification or health insurance – or relatives, even. Lindsay didn't know much about such matters, but did know a little about how the system operated. *They'll make her comfortable but won't waste any meds on her because she has no money.*

Lindsay earned fifteen thousand dollars a year

16

working at the tee-shirt shop, plus what little medical insurance Sarah, the shop owner, provided. How could that help this situation? Lindsay had very little savings. Because of her parents' divorce, Lindsay's college education was halted right after her sophomore year. The divorce, the therapy Momma needed when Dad left with his secretary, and the care needed to help get Momma back on her feet became a full-time job. Lindsay tried attending the local community college part-time, but even that was too much. With nothing else coming in but the monthly pittance Momma obtained from the desertion decree, Lindsay had to support them both. It had been a rough couple of years, but she'd managed. She just couldn't afford to go back to school at this point in her life. And, since she couldn't complete her education, she couldn't begin a professional career in anything that would afford her a good income or sufficient medical coverage.

Lindsay looked up, spotting Momma, still in her business suit, rushing down the hall toward her. Her sharp-featured face was pale, her makeup unable to hide the fear in her eyes. Lindsay realized she should have waited a few minutes before leaving her message.

"Baby, what *is* all this? Are you all right?"

"A lady was struck by a car on Colonial, in front of the mall."

"My *God* ... But ... why are you *here*? Your message said–"

"The car hit her and kept on going." Even as she said it, she couldn't believe it had actually

17

happened. "The poor lady ... she didn't have a chance." Lindsay could feel a sob working its way up her throat.

Momma shivered. "Baby ... I thought *you* had an *accident*..."

"I'm sorry, Momma. I was upset and rushed when I left the message. I didn't know when the medical unit would–"

"Why didn't you come straight home? You don't *know* this lady, do you?"

"No..." That didn't seem to matter.

"You can't do anything else, can you? If it was a hit-and-run–"

"She's *alone*, Momma."

"Listen, baby." Momma moved closer. "I know how sensitive you are. That's a wonderful thing, it truly is. But you've done all you can do."

A medium-sized guy in scrubs pushed open the swinging doors. He was about thirty, with his black hair brush-cut and a two-day growth of beard. He glanced at them. "Either of you call this in?"

Lindsay got up from the bench. "I'm Lindsay Foreman. I–"

"It was a nasty accident. She's barely alive."

"Will she ... I mean..."

"She's very old. There's internal damage. And a tumorous growth on her left lung."

"See, baby?" Momma gently tapped her shoulder. "You can't do anything else. They'll take care of her and see to it that–"

"Is it ... malignant?"

"The results haven't come in yet, but we

suspect so. It's very large."

"Lindsay, baby, we need to–"

"Momma, the lady's *alone*." Lindsay kept her anger in. Momma always seemed to be wrapped up in her own little world. That was okay most of the time. But right now, it seemed cruel.

The man said, "She wants to see you."

It took Lindsay a second to realize what he meant. "The *lady*?"

"The sooner, the better."

"She *said* that? She wants *me* to–"

"She keeps asking for someone to come back. I can only assume she's asking for you."

"Baby, there's nothing more you can do for that woman," Momma insisted.

"Please, miss. We'd better hurry."

Chapter 3

The colors cascaded before her in a blinding spectacle. Maisie forced her eyes shut. It had been dark before the heavy stone wall of bright pain slammed into her. The flash of images mixing in with the colors became so strangely familiar. Images she hadn't seen since she was a little girl, when she and Mikka, the family sheepdog, were playing in the woods that dreary afternoon, just moments before the world turned black with death.

Her father and her five older brothers worked the fields while her mother, her aunts, and her two older sisters bustled about in the kitchen, baking bread and biscuits. Maisie, finished with her chores in the barn, had retreated to the woods with Mikka.

Mikka caught some animal scent and scurried into the underbrush. Maisie quickly lost him, despite the bright sheen of his brilliant white fur. *A pheasant,* she decided. *Or a rabbit.* Once Mikka caught a scent, it was impossible to distract him.

The sounds of sirens shrieked up the valley. Gunfire. The abrupt heavy silence, like the slamming of a metal door, echoed wildly. Screams suddenly broke out. The smell of fire scorched the afternoon breeze.

Maisie ran back down the hill. Soldiers, their faces seared with death, surrounded the house. They came in trucks, the sounds of their machinery and gunfire deafening. They broke into the house, dragging out the screaming women. The inside walls were torched along with the few sticks of furniture. The men were dragged from the fields and tossed in the back of a flatbed truck.

The sky over the village turned cloudy, then hazy, then finally black with thick columns of smoke rising from the flames.

The shadows faded ... then changed. Swirling bright colors dissolved the blood of the dead lying on the frozen ground in the camps, the sky made black once again by the smoke stacks of the busy ovens, the yellow decay of the walking dead ... everything turning into a clear darkness encrusted with twinkling lights – stars, evening.

The angel appeared. She was tall and slender, with large almond eyes and brown hair covering her shoulders. Her eyes, like the stars, sparkled in the night, then dimmed, growing sad as she knelt before Maisie. The angel's lips moved, but the deafening roar directly beside her drowned out her words.

What *was* the roar? The ocean? A storm? It was the train that had come to take them to the camps.

I've got to get away...

Her limbs had gone numb.

I'm so old, so tired...

A throbbing blister of hot pain swelled beneath her, somewhere deep in her lower back, where the screaming stone wall had slammed into her.

Fight the pain. Ignore it. Concentrate on the angel.

The angel could help her, hide her from the soldiers. The angel could help her family get away as well. That's what angels did. She'd read about that in her Bible studies, heard about it in the stories her grandparents read them at night, everyone comfy and warm in front of the glowing fireplace. Angels helped all sorts of people.

With the angel to guide her, Maisie wouldn't have to worry about being crammed with the hundreds of others in the boxcars, where everyone would remain until they reached the camps. She wouldn't be forced to watch everyone die a second time. She wouldn't have to be alone, spared only because of her strange gift, which had proved useful among the superstitious wives of the Nazi officers.

Maisie tried to speak but couldn't. She could barely raise her arm. The angel grasped her hand. The angel's hands were warm and strong – much like Maisie's were when she was a young girl, working in the fields. So very, very long ago. Before the camps. Before the endless deaths.

I can't go back there … can't...

Blackness.

Maisie opened her eyes. The woods had faded, grown dark. *Mikka … where is Mikka? Where is the angel?*

"Where … *is* she?" she asked the darkness, in a tiny voice that trickled fearfully out of her throat. "She must come *back*..."

A hazy light appeared from the center of the darkness, where the woods had once been. A room. A cold room with no color. The walls were white. The ceiling, the door, the sheet covering her – all bland, devoid of color. White – the color of fear. Tubes and clear containers marked with white labels hung off to her side.

A haze formed in front of the door. A mix of white and deep blue, turning into a lighter shade of blue, the white dissipating... Two figures appeared from the haze. One, a man. The other – the angel, the one who'd held her hand beneath the stars.

She was beautiful, with smooth alabaster skin. The inner beauty radiating from her delicate, innocent face glowed in a bright flash of turquoise. She had come to give Maisie the peace she'd been seeking all these many years. Turquoise – the color of beauty, of warmth. Of kindness.

With the angel's help, Maisie would find the others and free them before the soldiers came back. But then she remembered. *I'm old now. Old and dying. The great death has long since passed.* The soldiers were probably all gone. The others were probably gone as well. Her father. Her mother. Her aunts. Her brothers and sisters. All of them, taken to the ovens, never to return. So long ago. A lifetime. And the angel standing beside her bed would take her to see them. Peace had finally come.

Maisie gestured for her angel to come closer. It was an effort – her arm weighed a ton. The tubes made movement even more difficult.

Maisie opened her mouth to speak. The words – heavy, jagged rocks deep inside her throat – wanted to stay right where they were. She made a conscious effort to force them out. "You've ... finally come ... for me ..."

***

The old woman lay in the bed, her withered

23

face strangely peaceful, her glazed gray eyes focused on Lindsay standing in the doorway. A little frightened, Lindsay followed the doctor in. He went over to the cluttered row of monitors beeping softly from the long shelf bolted to the wall behind the bed.

Lindsay dreaded hospitals. Fifteen years earlier, as a little girl, she'd visited her grandmother in this same building. Granna could barely see or talk, but wanted to hold Lindsay's hand. Lindsay took it, shivering at its coldness, its frailty. Granna tried talking, but in the middle of her sentence closed her eyes and went limp. Lindsay was afraid Granna had died. She was also afraid that since she was holding Granna's hand, Lindsay would also die. She put Granna's hand gently back down on the mattress and backed up quickly, knocking over the food cart. The accident woke Granna and brought in two nurses, an orderly, and a nurse's aid to see what had happened, turning Lindsay's panic into a huge embarrassment that gave her nightmares for weeks.

The old woman's hand raised a few inches, gesturing for Lindsay to come closer.

Lindsay felt so sorry for the poor soul. This lady might have been on her way to church to find shelter for the night. No one should be struck by a car and left to lie in the gutter amongst the tossed food wrappings and cigarette butts.

It just wasn't fair. She wasn't *always* an old woman. At one time, she was a little girl. At one time, she was Lindsay's age. She'd probably had a husband and kids. Who knew what happened to turn her into someone no one cared about? Who knew what injustices, what horrors, this poor old lady had endured to turn her into the broken creature living her last agonizing moments in a hospital bed?

Hesitantly Lindsay took the old woman's offered hand in hers. It was just as cold as it had been earlier, when she lay beside the busy highway. But right now Lindsay felt a strong, fast pulse. It pumped through the woman's brittle veins with bursts of energy from reserves that probably hadn't been used in a long time.

"You've ... finally come ... for me," the woman whispered weakly.

Lindsay could hear sharp clicking sounds in the woman's throat. They sounded wet, almost bubbly, in her labored breaths. The old woman was probably hallucinating. *Best agree with whatever she says and make her last moments pleasant.*

"Please ... come closer..."

Lindsay bent, forcing herself to ignore the woman's sour breath, the urine smell emanating from beneath the sheet, and the dirt and sand in the damp matted hair. The woman's eyes were now very clear. They closed, and she smiled, showing yellow teeth with some missing. "Thank you ... for coming back," she whispered.

"You shouldn't be alone," Lindsay replied. "Everyone else–"

"They have ... all gone."

Confusion, obviously. It was no wonder. Her head had whacked the pavement, cracking her skull and causing major trauma and possible swelling in her brain. Lindsay could only imagine how hard it was for the poor soul to think coherently.

The doctor remained watching the monitors. He must have sensed Lindsay's gaze. His slight grimace told her the worst.

"Are you in a lot of pain, ma'am?" Lindsay asked.

"I am ... at peace."

"Is there someone ... someone I can–"

"They're ... all gone."

"I'm *so* sorry..."

"Everyone is happy. I will be with them again. I might even see Mikka again."

*Mikka. Her husband? I need to find out her name, who she is. Where she's from. If she has anyone. She has to have some*one. *She can't really be all alone.*

The old woman began staring at Lindsay as if seeing her for the first time. Confusion and fear cast shadows over her ancient features.

My God... She's going away...

"Is ... everything okay?" Lindsay instantly realized how stupid that question was. "I mean, is there something I can do?"

No reply. The old woman tilted her head as if she was listening to something. Or somebody.

She's hearing voices. There was *brain damage.*

"Ma'am?"

"I must ... give you something..."

Lindsay choked down the sob filling her throat. This poor soul had nothing, yet wanted Lindsay to have something. There was no one else. She'd even said so. Maybe she kept a trinket or a memento

26

from her childhood, and wanted Lindsay to have it for helping her. But it wasn't necessary. Besides, Lindsay would feel funny accepting such a gift from someone she didn't even know. "You don't have to give me anything."

The veiny gray eyes narrowed. "Yes. I do."

***

The angel had vanished.

The turquoise colors radiating from the slender figure gradually faded, becoming a pale white. The alabaster skin changed to pink. The beautiful face turned plain. The dark-brown almond eyes, too large for the narrow face, filled with sadness. The figure standing before her was the young girl, the same sweet thing who'd stopped for her, held her hand, and called for the ambulance.

Where is my angel?

Then Maisie heard the voice. "*I am here, child...*" The silken voice drifted very close to her ear. The room had grown warmer. The hot, intense pain consuming her only moments ago vanished.

Where are you? Maisie wanted to know.

"*I am right here.*"

Am I going with you?

"*Very soon.*"

"*I'm ready.*"

"*You must do one thing first. You must give this girl a lasting gift for her kindness.*"

The angel was right. Because of this girl's compassion, Maisie would die in this bed – not on that filthy pavement beside the road. *She's the first person who did something nice for me in a very*

27

long time.

But Maisie had nothing to give. Everything had been taken away. Many years ago, when she came to this country with the others who'd escaped, she had nothing but the dirty, well-worn clothes on her back. And, of course, the gift...

"That is it, child ... your gift."

Give it away?

"Yes."

It had been both a blessing and a curse, destroying Maisie's chances for romance, for happiness, for a normal life. It had made her an oddity. An oddity she remained all her long, lonely life.

This girl is very sweet. And sensitive – much like I once was. Perhaps she is too sensitive to handle my gift. She appears very troubled. I shouldn't burden her...

"Give it away, child ... you no longer need it."

It could ... destroy her.

"Maybe ... and maybe not."

But how will I know what it does to her?

"If you do not give it away, I cannot take you with me."

Her family waited for her in their wonderful new place. A place without soldiers, without camps, without barbed wire. Without ovens. Without monsters masquerading as children. Or faceless fiends that ran over old women and left them to die along the road.

"I must ... give you something," she told the young girl.

"You don't have to give me anything," the girl replied, and Maisie could feel the sadness emanating from her.

"Yes. I do."

The colors. The only thing Maisie had left. The only thing no one could ever take from her.

This girl wasn't like the others. She was shy and humble, much like Maisie once was. Everyone was like that back then – quiet, hard-working folks providing for their families, hurting no one.

The colors might help this girl as they'd helped Maisie during those long, bone-chilling nights in the camps. As they'd helped her escape. This girl was restless, insecure. The white halo framing her young head burned clear and bright. The darker slivers hovering near her eyes eclipsed whatever light attempted to escape. The fear, the confusion – everything clung to her like a suffocating shroud. The hazy pink aura surrounding her slender form told Maisie this girl feared people and hid her innermost feelings from them. The colors might even give her the courage to face life – as they had for Maisie.

Using what little strength she had left, Maisie grasped the girl's warm hand in her own and squeezed. *Go to your new home, little ones...* They raced down her arm like frightened ants, mingling with the girl's hand.

The warmth disappeared. Maisie's hand, depleted of all life, dropped to the mattress like a chunk of concrete. She no longer felt the girl's hand, or her own arm. The room grew dark, the white turning gray, then darker, until it became the gaping mouth of a tunnel. The haze disappeared.

The angel's voice drifted out of the darkness. *"Now we can go, child..."*

A thick sphere of glimmering turquoise appeared, floating just above the mattress. The angel, bright and beautiful in her long white robe of shimmering satin, stood within the sphere. The angel's hand, a flawless masterpiece of alabaster, reached for her. Maisie, young and happy once again, rose from the broken husk on the mattress, took the angel's hand, and hopped into the sphere.

Chapter 4

While Momma started up the BMW, Lindsay closed her eyes and surrendered to the heavy waves of darkness enveloping her. Luckily, Momma didn't want to talk. She probably suspected Lindsay didn't want to, either. Lindsay was content to concentrate on the insides of her eyelids and the steady hum of the BMW. The smell of pizza hung heavily in the air but she barely noticed it. Images of the old woman kept coming back in hazy waves. *If I'd driven to the mall instead ... if I'd gone straight up Maguire instead of turning right on Colonial ... the poor soul would have lain there in agonizing pain, unable to cry for help while everyone drove on by.*

Momma suddenly stopped the car, put it in park, and switched off the engine. Lindsay opened her eyes. They'd reached the apartment complex. Moths fluttered about in the haze of the street light.

Strange. The last thing Lindsay remembered was holding the woman's hand in the hospital room. Everything else had become a blur. A collage of colors that wouldn't stop unraveling.

The old woman's coarse, leathery hand felt very warm. Lindsay experienced a tingling sensation – probably from the sudden pressure. The tingling immediately moved farther up, near her shoulder. Then, as quickly as it had appeared, it vanished. The old woman's hand turned ice-cold. Her grip loosened. The wrinkled forearm dropped to the mattress. The blinking of the monitors became a steady hum. The hectic white lines jumping up and down turned flat. The old woman lay still.

Someone tapped Lindsay's left shoulder. "Baby?" Momma's voice. "You all right?"

"I *think* so." She felt as if she'd just crawled through a dark tunnel, guided only by the bright colors flickering in front of her. Colors that diminished as soon as she reached them.

"You're kind of pale."

She needed air. Momma's strong perfume and the pungency of the pizza had created a throbbing pressure on Lindsay's temples. She opened her door and immediately pulled in great gobs of muggy, exhaust-laden air.

Momma got out and shut the door. "I'd hate to have to take you to the doctor at this time of night. Especially after I just bought fresh pizza."

Ignoring Momma's comment, Lindsay followed her up the walk. "She wanted to give me something."

"Who?"

Sometimes Momma's shallowness infuriated her. Lindsay let it pass. "She died before she had the chance to say more."

"Baby, she was homeless, wasn't she?"

"Yes, Momma." As if that had any bearing on the subject.

"If she had anything, the hospital would have found it."

"It seemed really important to her."

"I'm sure it was. To her."

It was probably the most important thing the

poor lady could think of. Fear had filled the old woman's eyes when she mentioned it. Her last important act in life, no doubt.

"It might've been an old locket or something she carried with her," Lindsay said, mostly to herself. "She probably had a lot of memories. Don't you think she might have saved *some*thing from her childhood?"

"She was *homeless*, baby."

Momma's insensitive statement rankled Lindsay like fingernails screeching on a chalkboard. Momma made it sound like homelessness was some sort of disease. Momma obviously decided being homeless made owning anything – or having memories – impossible. "She wasn't *born* that way," Lindsay objected.

"That's not what I meant, baby."

"That's how you made it sound."

"I certainly didn't mean it that way."

"One day a long time ago, that lady was a baby. An infant. Like all of us once were."

Momma squinted. "Baby, are you *sure* you're okay?"

"She grew up just like you and me and everyone else. She might have had a much rougher life than either of us could know about. Maybe that's what forced her into the streets."

"Baby, don't you know that most homeless people are that way because they actually *want* to be? A lot of folks can't stand pressure or failure or responsibility. Many don't even know how to deal with *success*, for God's sake. Look at those movie stars, those music divas – especially the ones who are famous in their teens. By the time they're twenty, they're so out of control, they need a straitjacket and a padded cell. People have weaknesses. You know nothing about that woman."

"I know she was nice. At least she was to me."

"Wasn't she ... out of it? Didn't they have her doped up?"

"She held my hand. She wanted me to have something."

"You got her to the hospital. Of course she was nice to you. Without your help, she would've died right there on Colonial."

How could Momma be so cynical? She had always been somewhat of a snob, but Lindsay never heard her talk so badly about the poor. "I just think she once had a normal life. We don't know what happened. And just because she died homeless doesn't mean she was always that way. She might have been well-off. Like I said before, she might have been carrying around an old locket or something from her childhood."

"The hospital didn't say anything when we left. If there was something, they would have let you know. You were the closest she had to next of kin."

"I would have liked knowing what she meant – especially since it seemed so important. If it was a locket or something, I hope no one at the hospital took it."

"You're overreacting, baby."

"I know how mean and selfish people are."

"She probably found something lying on the

34

road somewhere, or in the trash. Those people are always looking through dumpsters."

They went inside. Momma slipped into the kitchen, opened the box on the table, and got some plates. "It's cold." She found a knife and set about separating the slices. "We'll need to nuke it."

"I'm not very hungry."

"It'll be here for you later on. You like it better when it's cold anyway, right?"

Lindsay opened the fridge. "I guess so..."

"Tell me something, baby."

Lindsay took out a can of Sprite. "What's that?"

"Why'd you bother?"

"Bother?"

"Stopping for her. Calling it in. Riding to the hospital."

Lindsay couldn't believe her mother had asked that question. It probably had something to do with her boss. Derek Tanner wore Italian suits and Italian shoes and drove around in sports cars. Momma acted differently when she was around him. Her obsession with belonging to a man, no doubt, had fueled this. She still hadn't gotten over the humiliation of Dad leaving her for a younger woman. Momma probably considered it sweet revenge that, at over forty, she'd attracted a thirty-six-year-old man.

"Why, baby?"

"She was all alone."

Momma smiled. "You always were a caring kid. Not many people would've done that."

Lindsay didn't feel so special. The incident still angered her. "The jerk in the muscle car kept on going."

"That was horrible." The microwave bell went off. Momma pulled out her steaming slice of pizza. She put the plate on the counter and got a beer from the fridge. "I hope they find whoever did that and nail his ass – or hers, since females can be even crazier than males." She got the bottle opener from the top drawer. "You didn't, by any chance, *see* who did it, did you?"

"No..."

"I'm *so* glad." She popped open her beer and poured it into a glass.

"What do you mean?"

"You don't want to be involved in something like this. Anyone who can do that is probably a psycho."

That wasn't what bothered Lindsay. "She lay there so *helpless*. I guess I thought she wouldn't be lonely if I was there with her. I ... just didn't want her to die alone."

"Baby, we *all* die alone."

"You honestly believe that?"

"Of course I do," Momma said. A tiny red sliver, glimmering in the kitchen light, appeared beneath her left eye.

Lindsay stared.

"Something wrong, baby?"

Lindsay walked over and gently touched her mother's cheek in the hollow just below the eye.

Momma pulled back. "What was *that* for?"

"I thought I saw a smudge."

37

PART II – SATURDAY
The Colors

Chapter 5

After a long, restless night, Lindsay forced herself out of bed. She'd spent most of the night wrestling with weird dreams ... patchy gray images of the old woman beckoning to her from some dark place. The woman's voice was far away, barely recognizable. Sometimes it sounded like laughter. Other times, sobs.

As Lindsay dressed, she wondered once again about that red sliver beneath Momma's left eye. At first it looked like blood, but when she moved closer, she realized it was just some strange reflection from the kitchen light. Momma's eye shadow, mixed with a glint of perspiration, had cast a red glint on her skin. Surely there was nothing mysterious about that, but it certainly had looked like blood at first glance.

Lindsay followed the smell of bacon and coffee drifting into the hall from the kitchen. Facing the stove, Momma cracked an egg and dropped it into the sizzling skillet. "You're up early."

"Couldn't sleep." Lindsay padded barefoot across the linoleum.

"It's no wonder. I'd have nightmares for weeks if I'd done what you did last night."

The coffee maker gurgled quietly on the

counter. Lindsay poured a cup, added milk and sugar, and took her brown mug to the table. "I'm going out a little later. The Police Department."

Momma flipped the eggs with the spatula. "Why?"

"I ... want to find out a few things."

"About that bag lady?"

"She must've known *some*one."

"And what'll you do if you find someone who knew her?"

Lindsay sipped the hot coffee. "I just think someone should be told what happened."

Momma picked up the eggs, slid them onto a plate, and brought them over. "Next, you'll be telling me you want to find out who ran the old woman over."

Lindsay nibbled on a piece of toast. She did want to find out something. The police might be able to help. They probably had a list of people the rescue missions or soup kitchens had provided. But she surely didn't want Momma worrying about her. When Momma was worried, she made everyone around her nervous. Best keep things to herself. "I won't be gone long."

Momma speared a sliver of egg with her fork. "I'll probably be at the office."

Lindsay suspected Momma wanted to spend time with Derek Tanner. "Anything important?"

"Just some work I didn't finish yesterday."

That same faint red smudge Lindsay had seen the night before had reappeared, this time directly below Momma's right eye.

Big and bulky, his coppery hair reduced to short stubble, the desk sergeant looked more like a retired prizefighter.

About fifty, he had a ruddy complexion, a large bulbous nose, and a perpetual scowl. His nametag said *Rossen*. He didn't glance at Lindsay at all as he typed loudly on the keyboard. She wondered if he considered her a little crazy, asking questions about a bag lady.

"Yep, a Jane Doe," he said in a low, gruff voice. "Get those all the time."

"She had no ID at all?"

"She was a bag woman." He'd said it just as disdainfully as Momma had. "They don't carry ID. Just something else that can be taken from them by their cronies, or juiced-up punks. What's your interest, anyway?"

"I ... helped her."

He blinked. "You *saw* the hit-and-run?"

"I called nine-one-one and went with the ambulance to the hospital." Lindsay looked down at her lap. "I was with her when ... when she died." The sadness rushed back.

Rossen's face softened a little. Apparently he wasn't as cold-hearted as he'd first appeared. "Most folks wouldn't have bothered."

"I couldn't let her just lie there."

"Most folks wouldn't have gotten any closer. They're turned off by the homeless. They can look right at them without even seeing them."

"She wasn't *born* homeless." Her gut tightened.

40

Having to explain this again was taking its toll.

"Many spend their lives making themselves that way. At least yours died in a hospital bed."

Yours. He'd made the old woman sound like personal property.

"Why do some people end up like that?" she asked.

"Some can't handle life. Some don't know how to make the right decisions. Many can't take pressure, stress. Responsibility."

Momma had told her practically the same thing. But it didn't make this any easier.

"You didn't by any chance get a tag number, did you?"

"I'm sorry. It was some kind of muscle car, and it was dark. I couldn't see much of anything else."

Rossen scratched his large square jaw. "Nothing at all?"

"I was too far away."

"No light above the plate?"

"I didn't see any."

"Broken tail lights? Spoilers? Bumper stickers? Fancy hub caps?"

She shook her head.

"Not even a glimpse of the driver? Male or female?"

Nothing would come. The only thing that registered was the screeching of brakes and that horrible thump. "I'm really sorry."

"Like I said, this kind of thing happens."

"It shouldn't."

"A lot of things shouldn't, miss. We can't be

everywhere."

"Maybe if there were cameras..."

"Folks are already whining about their privacy. Cameras have been around a while but it'll be years before we can get them installed everywhere they're needed. Don't forget – more cameras, more taxes. And we all know how everyone feels about more taxes."

"But the poor woman was–"

"Just try and forget about this. She's in a better place now."

"You really think so?"

"Sure I do."

A faint haze of red appeared just above the cop's large square head.

My God. What's happening? Lindsay rubbed her eyes.

"Miss? You all right?"

She sat stiffly, eyes closed. When she was reasonably sure her vision had cleared, she opened her eyes. The haze was gone.

***

According to Officer Rossen, an old Presbyterian Church sat a couple of blocks north of Colonial, across the street from one of the strip malls.

Vagrants were often seen in the area. Many slept near the church building or in the park behind it. The church boasted a large cafeteria that provided meals for the homeless five days a week. If the old woman needed a free meal, she would have gone there.

Lindsay parked her tan Honda Civic in the gravel lot behind the large brick building, between an older BMW and a light-blue Saturn. Uneasy and confused, she sat behind the wheel, trying to convince herself her nerves were making her think she was seeing things – strange colors. She'd spent a restless night filled with weird images and sounds.

She had to snap out of this. She couldn't learn anything by sitting here worrying. She got out of the car and followed the cobblestone walk leading to the open doorway.

The sanctuary was huge, cool, and nearly empty. Thick columns of morning sun filtered in through the stained glass windows on the eastern wall, dusting the pews and the marble aisle with a golden haze. Two scruffy men in tattered jackets lay in pews, snoring peacefully. She followed the signs indicating the church offices were located up the winding staircase in the foyer in back.

A slender, attractive lady in her mid-fifties with curly auburn hair and large hazel eyes wore copper reading glasses perched low on her nose as she sat behind a desk, talking softly on the phone. She put down the phone when Lindsay walked through the doorway. "May I help you?" she asked pleasantly.

Despite the lady's sweet demeanor, Lindsay shifted nervously. *Focus*, she reminded herself. "Could I possibly talk to one of the ministers?" Her voice sounded strange. "Is anyone in right now? I don't have an appointment–"

"Reverend Allen is in his office. May I ask what this is about?"

"An old lady was run over last night near the mall."

"My goodness. How terrible."

"The police said she was a bag lady. I want to find out if anyone here knew her or saw her around."

The receptionist picked up her phone. She whispered briefly into it, then put it back down and pointed to the open doorway. "If you'll just go down that hall, it's the first room on your right."

***

Reverend Allen was about forty-five years old, tall and slim. He had curly black hair, small blinking brown eyes, and an easy smile. His gaunt cheeks swelled up at the top, covering his sharp cheekbones and causing two long dimples to extend to the jaw line.

He closed the door and invited Lindsay to sit in the tan armchair facing his desk. It was a small office, very warm and comfortable, and smelling faintly of vanilla-flavored coffee. Hardcover books filled the shelves covering three of the four walls. Books also cluttered the desk.

"Your name is...?"

"Lindsay Foreman."

"Stella tells me you want to talk about someone who could have been one of our walk-ins."

"This lady died last night in a hit-and-run. She was about seventy, I guess, maybe older. She was so ... alone. She didn't even tell me her name."

"Tell me what happened."

He sat quietly, his large hands clasped together

44

on the desk blotter. He remained this way, not moving, barely blinking. When she finished her story, he sat back. A shadow wafted across his eyes. "That was a very nice thing to do, Lindsay. It is very unsettling that terrible tragedies like that happen at all. This lady was very fortunate you could help her."

"I'm not here to make myself look good. I'd like to find out something about the lady. There was something ... special about her."

"Special?"

"She was obviously more than just a bag lady. She wasn't that way all her life."

"None of them are."

"I may be young, but I know how cruel life can be. Who knows what actually destroyed her?"

"They usually don't confide in anyone, unfortunately."

"Why *is* that?"

"They've reached bottom. Life has beaten them. They've given up. They no longer trust anyone."

"Maybe that's why she wouldn't tell me anything. I tried helping her, but..."

"It probably wasn't that at all. It might have been the medications the doctors gave her."

"Even so, I still felt something. It seemed almost as if her spirit was trying to show me who she really was."

"How so?"

"When she touched me, I felt a tingling rushing up my arm. Her hand grew really warm. I felt like ... like I knew her. I mean, really *knew* her." She hoped she wasn't sounding weird. Reverend Allen might not understand any of this. She didn't know if he'd ever held someone's hand while they died. Or helped someone no one else cared about. He obviously saw an actual *person* beneath the tattered rags of the homeless, but she supposed all clergymen thought the same. But the tingling thing ... that was totally bizarre. "Does that make any sense?"

"Sounds like you were experiencing a special bond few people experience. She was probably already in transition when you two connected."

"Transition?"

"Her spirit was in the process of ascending, and you felt it."

"I didn't think of that."

"Most people think death is the simple act of the spirit leaving the body. It's much more complex, especially when someone else is involved – as in your case. You helped her, showed her compassion. When you held her hand, you became part of her, of her final departure. It was only natural that you experienced the sensation of her spirit leaving her physical body."

"Would that explain ... the colors?"

"Colors?"

"I've been seeing strange colors since I left her."

Reverend Allen went silent.

Lindsay feared she'd gone over the edge. The man's guarded expression told her she should've stopped while she was ahead. The tingling thing was more than enough for anyone to handle. Telling him about the colors probably ruined everything, and now he thought she was a nut.

"There are many things in this life we don't understand," he said. "Many things we never will." He smiled. "I personally think it's the Almighty's special way of keeping us humble."

"What do you think the colors mean?"

"You might be experiencing residual aspects of the woman's last physical event. The colors might even be a kind of manifestation of what she herself saw the moment she left this life."

"You mean–"

"She might have given you a glimpse of what she saw the moment she passed."

***

Behind the church, a tiny graveyard, its tombstones cracked and darkened with age and the elements, hunkered inside a black iron fence. The sidewalk beyond it extended straight to a small grove of trees and benches before veering around a row of three-story stucco condominiums at the end of the block.

A man and woman, both in their seventies, sat on the bench, smoking cigarettes. Lindsay walked up to them and smiled. "Hello."

Neither spoke.

"An old woman was killed last night trying to cross Colonial. She was homeless."

Still no reply.

"I went with her to the hospital. She wouldn't tell me her name."

"Why'd ya wanna know her name?" the woman asked in a loud, raspy voice.

"She was all alone," Lindsay said. "I thought maybe I could find a son somewhere, a daughter–"

They both laughed. Lindsay bristled at the sharp cackling. Was she the only one who cared about this woman? "No one should be alone," she said, forcing the anger away.

"What's a *name* gonna do?"

"You might have known her."

The woman shrugged and puffed on her cigarette.

The man squinted. "Got money, missy?"

Lindsay sighed. She found some ones in her purse and handed them over. "I'm sorry I bothered you." She turned to walk away.

"This woman." The man carefully counted the bills. "What'd she have on?"

"A flowery dress. Tennis shoes. A long black frayed coat with large red patches. And a brown and red checked scarf."

The two looked at one another.

"You knew her, didn't you?"

The old man pocketed her money and took a deep drag of his cigarette.

"*Please* tell me who she was."

"What good's it gonna do?" the woman asked.

Lindsay shrugged. "I don't know. At least I could remember her better."

"Why?"

"Everyone should be remembered."

Again the two laughed.

Accepting defeat, Lindsay turned to walk back to her car.

"Maisie," the woman said.

Lindsay spun around. "What?"

"We called her Crazy Maisie."

Lindsay's pulse hastened. "*Maisie*?"

They nodded.

"Why'd you call her crazy? She seemed all right to me."

The man said, "She was from Europe, said she was a gypsy."

"Said a lotta things," the woman added.

"What did she do? When she was younger, I mean."

They both shrugged.

"She never talked about herself?"

"In the past," the woman said. "Everything's dead, like she is. Like we'll all be. Nobody cares. It just don't matter."

The man chuckled. "Woman was whacky, always saying she could see things. Could read people." He shook his head.

"Crazy," the woman said. "Crazy as a bedbug."

"Because she could read people?" Lindsay asked.

"*You* wanna cuddle up to a body, says she can peek inside your head?"

"Loony," the man said. "We all stayed away."

"Now you know," the woman said. "Now you know why Crazy Maisie died alone. Remember her. Crazy as a bedbug."

Chapter 6

The apartment was empty when Lindsay got back. Momma was probably still at the office – which was good.

Lindsay didn't feel like answering any questions. She supposed it was because she had no answers – at least not the ones she wanted. All she'd learned was the old woman's first name, and some gossip about strange powers that had alienated everyone who knew her.

Lindsay filled a glass with ice, picked up a can of Sprite, and flicked on the TV. *Animal Planet* came on with a show about veterinarians operating on a little dog that had been hit by a car.

People just don't care. They run over dogs. They run over old women. Disgust throbbed low in her gut as she sat down in the recliner.

The name of the woman no one cared about was Maisie. She was from Europe. She could read people. She was *touched*.

And she touched me...

The scene flashed before her like a movie image. *"I must ... give you something."* But she'd merely grasped Lindsay's wrist, squeezed it, and died – as if her gift to Lindsay was the squeeze itself.

The tingling. Was it the result of the sudden pressure? Or something else? Was there some weird element in Maisie's touch? Something other than what Reverend Allen had said? The colors could be what Maisie had glimpsed when leaving her physical body ... but they could also be something else.

Lindsay sipped her Sprite thoughtfully. Last night, Momma's statements about believing everyone died alone, and the reason she was working today – Saturday – was because she needed to finish some things at the office, had caused slivers of red to appear beneath her eyes. And at the police station, a faint red haze had appeared above Officer Rossen's head when he'd said he was sure Maisie was in a better place now.

Lindsay frowned and leaned against the couch back. How could people read other people? Did they look at them and see things? Sense things? Hear things? Could Maisie sense things about to happen? Could she tell the future? Hear thoughts? See images? Predict things? What powers did she *really* have? And what did her powers have to do with these colors Lindsay was suddenly seeing around people?

Lindsay drank some Sprite. Gripping the glass with her left hand, she held her right hand straight out – the same hand Maisie had touched in her last moments. It no longer tingled, but it somehow felt different. Warmer than its partner. Warmer and more sensitive.

It feels warmer because you're holding a cold drink in your other hand.

She was being plain silly. Her right hand was just like her left. She was making something totally ridiculous out of all this. So ... why did she think that whatever she touched, something strange would result?

**

Momma, carrying two bags of groceries, returned home just before four and immediately set about putting things away.

Lindsay came in just as her mother set a bottle of expensive Glenfiddich Scotch whiskey on the table. Momma didn't drink Scotch; she only kept it on hand for Derek Tanner.

"So, what did you find out about that old woman?" Momma asked.

Lindsay sat down at the table, deciding it would be wise not to tell Momma too much at this point. "I went to the Presbyterian Church down the corner from the theater megaplex off Maguire. Some of the other homeless people knew her. They said her name was Maisie."

Momma went over to the coffee pot and emptied it, rinsing it out and pouring water for a fresh pot. "I don't know about places like that. They let just anyone bum meals and beg for change at the corner when everyone else is trying to go inside to worship. Isn't that what soup kitchens and rescue missions are supposed to do?"

"Churches do that, too."

"The more freebies there are, the more these people will take advantage. This country actually rewards bums, vagrants, and all those other worthless folks who don't want to work."

Lindsay couldn't believe how cold her mother could be. "Maisie had a rough life. She–"

"Who *doesn't* have it rough? Tell me one single

52

person who's having an easy, problem-free time, and I'll personally pay serious money to find out their secret."

Lindsay didn't reply. Momma had been with Derek – it was no wonder she was acting like this. It was a shame that even at her age, she let someone else's snobbish opinions rub off on her. "You don't know anything about her, Momma."

"And you do?"

"Actually, no one did."

Momma got the coffee going. "Doesn't that tell you anything?"

"Like what?"

"She obviously had no friends. Making friends isn't all that difficult. Everywhere you go, you'll see some young jerk walking around without a job but with an entourage of females following him around. Granted, the females are just as worthless. When you see something like that, you'll agree that having no friends at all is quite an accomplishment – but not in any *good* way."

"She might've had friends when she was younger."

"If she did, don't you think you would have found out by now?"

"Her friends could be out of the state. Or dead. She *was* pretty old."

"Everything's kind of pointless now, don't you think?" Momma began unbuttoning her blouse.

"Going somewhere?"

"Derek's coming over later. Make sure we don't sour the evening with all this silly talk.

Okay?"

"I usually don't get to talk much when he's here."

"Baby, Derek always speaks to you. Look, I know you don't care for him, but he's been good to me, and he's good *for* me. I have a really good setup with him."

Lindsay shrugged. This wasn't the time to start another argument. "He's all right, I guess."

"He likes you, you know. Derek's a little strange, but that's only because he's an executive. He has to be tough in his profession. Otherwise, he wouldn't have been successful building up his software brokerage firm. To be your own boss at thirty is quite an accomplishment, don't you think?"

"Sure, Momma." Lindsay frowned, feeling resentful that she wasn't able to finish her own education when she'd wanted to.

"You okay, baby?"

"I'm fine."

"You sure? You haven't really been yourself since ... since that godawful accident."

"It just bothers me that someone ran over another person and no one seems to care – not even you."

Momma hugged her, then kissed her on the forehead. "I care, baby. I really do."

"Really?"

"Of course." Momma patted her shoulder, turned and crossed the room.

Lindsay watched her in silence. The red haze just above her mother's thick brown hair glowed

54

brightly.

***

Derek Tanner came over a little after eight and sat on the couch while Momma fixed him a drink in the kitchen.

Tall and boyishly handsome in a Pierce Brosnan sort of way, Derek Tanner wore expensive jewelry and drove a red Corvette convertible. Momma loved to ride in it with the top down, even though it made a mess of her hair. But she wouldn't think of complaining. Momma never complained to Derek about anything.

Tonight he wore red and gold checkered shorts, tennis shoes, and a dark-blue polo shirt. He always wore his gold necklaces, bracelets, and his Rolex so people would see that he was rich, even though his look was what he'd call 'casual.'

Lindsay sat curled up in the recliner, an old Cary Grant movie playing on Turner Classics. She could tell Derek was watching her, but at least the movie kept her mind off him.

"So how're things at the tee-shirt shop?" he asked.

Lindsay shrugged. "Same as always."

"Making a lot of money?"

She wondered if his conversations with Momma were just as irritating. "Me? Or the shop?"

He laughed his usual understated chuckle – which Lindsay suspected he'd practiced because he thought it made him sound cool. Derek Tanner considered himself the king of cool.

"Anyone interesting come in lately?"

55

"*Interesting*?"

He shrugged. "Any cool guys?"

"I really don't pay much attention."

"A girl your age? Not interested in *guys*? Doesn't seem natural, does it?"

It seemed perfectly natural to Lindsay. Only arrogant, sloppy-dressed teens with studs, tattoos, and obnoxious attitudes came into Sarah's. Besides, she just wasn't interested in anyone right now. Her two-year relationship with David had ended abruptly when she found out about his other girlfriend, who lived in Winter Park, worked in a bank, and showed up in his apartment on the wrong day and at the worst possible moment.

Lindsay rarely drank, never went to clubs or bars, got bored at the beach, and was afraid to meet someone on the Internet. People were shallow and cold. Lindsay surely had no interest in men like Derek Tanner, whose materialistic ways were a huge turn-off. She wanted someone who liked music and art and old movies. Someone who might even open a door for her. She hadn't met someone like that yet, but remained hopeful.

"Well?" Derek was apparently waiting for an answer. "Seem natural to you? A girl as good-looking as you are? Not interested in guys?"

She turned to see if he was putting her on.

His face showed curiosity. But a dim red haze framed the top of his professionally-trimmed brown hair.

Thankfully Momma came in with the drinks and sat down beside him. He sipped the Scotch and

56

nodded his approval. Momma smiled, had a sip of her own mixed drink, and cuddled closer to him.

Lindsay turned back to the Cary Grant movie. Cary was a chemist, working on a fountain of youth formula. He and his team were trying out the formula on some lab monkeys. It was a cute movie, one of Lindsay's favorites, but right now she couldn't concentrate. Derek kept whispering things to Momma that Lindsay could hear.

"Bedroom..."

"Not *now*..."

"Why not?"

"*Later*, Derek..."

Lindsay got up. She suddenly needed fresh air. "I think I'll go down to the 7-Eleven for a paper."

"Now?" Momma frowned at the clock on the wall above the TV. "It's getting late."

Lindsay shrugged. She wanted to tell Momma that she'd give them half an hour to themselves but decided that would be tacky. "I need to stretch my legs. I won't be long."

Chapter 7

The 7-Eleven parking lot was nearly deserted, with only one gas pump in use. Three sloppy-dressed teen boys were obviously in a hurry. After all, it was Saturday night. They swiped a card at the pump, chattered away as they pumped the gas, got back in their beat-up Toyota Supra, and hastily joined the passing flow of traffic.

Lindsay went inside the brilliantly-lit store. A tall, gawky black kid around twenty faced the line of refrigerators in the back. He wore loose-fitting dark clothing and a black baseball cap turned around, with the bill pushed up. He was staring at the shelves of beer, but Lindsay could tell he was watching the store activity in the reflection of the glass doors.

Another black kid around the same age slumped beside a comic book tree, leafing through an issue of Spiderman. He wore wraparound shades. His Gators cap was mashed down, the bill hiding his forehead. Only his lips, a broad nose, and some facial hair were visible.

The desk clerk, a large, beefy man with a brush cut and the look of a former Marine, leaned over the counter, working a crossword puzzle. His reading glasses were pushed down to the tip of his large fleshy nose.

Lindsay picked up a paper from the rack and glanced at the kid at the book tree. A spire of black haze erupted like billowing smoke above the Gators cap, and an image of a switchblade being snatched from a trouser pocket blipped brightly in her mind. The flash of that image was followed by a flash of black. *What's going on?*

"That it, miss?" the clerk asked.

Snap out of it. She suddenly realized she stood at the counter, cradling the paper in her arms as if it was an infant. *Idiot. Remember where you are.* A little embarrassed, she nodded, put the paper on the counter, and found some bills.

He took her cash and opened the register.

Lindsay glanced at the convex mirrors bolted to the ceiling at each corner of the long room. The first kid had moved away from the refrigerator and strolled nonchalantly toward the coffee station. Like the other boy, black haze clouded his head. The switchblade image remained crystal-clear in Lindsay's mind.

The clerk carefully dropped her change into her palm. After he'd closed the register, she continued staring at him. Her pulse pounded.

"Something wrong?" he asked.

Lindsay wondered if he could hear her heart thumping. She glanced at the mirrors again. "I think ... you're about to be robbed," she whispered.

He stared at her. She let her eyes return to the mirror. The clerk followed her gaze. He nodded slightly, then leaned closer and shifted his weight. He'd probably stepped on a floor alarm switch. He said, "Thanks, miss, and stop by and see us again, okay?"

***

Lights flashing, two squad cars jerked to an abrupt stop in front of the pumps. A third cruiser slammed to a stop around the corner, blocking the rear exit.

Lindsay had just passed the pumps when they appeared. They must have been close when they received the alarm. One of the uniforms jumping out of the second car grabbed her by the arm and pulled her behind the cover of the cruiser while two other cops, guns drawn, rushed inside the store.

No gunshots followed. Cuffed, the two teens were escorted out of the store and shoved into the back seats of the awaiting cruisers.

The clerk came outside with a cop, answering questions. He spotted her and waved. She waved back. The clerk went back inside. The cop walked over to her. "You're the young lady who reported this?"

"Yes..."

He asked her name and address and recorded it in his notepad. "How'd you know what was happening? Did you see a knife?"

She wanted to tell him what happened but knew better. He'd ask her questions she wouldn't be able to answer. Or worse – he'd think she was a nutcase. "One of them was acting really nervous and kept watching the counter."

"But ... did you see a knife?"

"He was gripping something in his pocket." She hated lying but couldn't see any other way out of this. "I saw something glisten in the fluorescents."

"Good call. You saved everyone a lot of trouble."

"I just thought he should know."

He stared at her. A faint wisp of gray appeared an inch or two above his service cap. Lindsay suspected he was probably trying to understand why she was downplaying her role in this. She didn't want to tell him it had been just a matter of spotting the strange black colors and picking up on their restlessness. No big deal, right? Anyone could have done it.

"Would you mind stopping by the Station tomorrow or Monday for a statement?" the cop asked. "Merely routine, but it'll help keep those two off the streets for a little while."

"No problem."

The cop put his pad back into his shirt pocket. Then, still watching her, he pulled off his service cap and scratched his brush cut.

"Is something wrong?"

He put his cap back on. "This was just about the easiest collar I've ever made in my fifteen years on the Force."

More wisps of gray emanated above his cap. Something was obviously bothering him. "You sound disappointed," she said.

"I was just thinking, with more people like you, our job would be so easy, a grade school kid could do it."

***

Derek was gone when Lindsay got back to the apartment. Momma was straightening up the

61

kitchen. She'd combed her hair and changed into her bathrobe that partially hung open. Momma's black bra and panties showed underneath. Momma and Derek probably raced to her bedroom the moment Lindsay had left.

"You were gone a while," Momma said.

Lindsay grabbed a glass from the drainer and poured some water. "The 7-Eleven was robbed."

Momma's face paled. "While *you* were there?"

Lindsay nodded.

"What happened? I mean ... are you ... all right?"

As with the cop, Lindsay knew she couldn't explain what happened. She'd seen two guys, picked up on their nervousness, and visualized dark colors. But how did she know the place was about to be robbed? What *were* those colors?

"I'm fine," she said. "No one got hurt."

"Those robberies can be *horrible*, baby " Momma's cheeks flushed. "Are you *sure* you weren't hurt? Did anyone ... touch you?"

"The police got there in time."

"Now *that's* something that doesn't happen very often." Momma pulled her robe closed, then sat. "The police usually get there *after* someone is shot or stabbed. They actually got there *before* anyone was hurt?"

"That's what happened."

"They must've been tipped. They were probably really close."

It was time to change the subject. "Why'd Derek leave?" she asked. "It's still early."

62

Momma shrugged. "He had things to do."

"On a Saturday night?"

"He has to be at the airport early in the morning. Apparently one of his clients is coming to town."

Lindsay watched uneasily as a faint reddish halo appeared above Momma's head.

PART III – SUNDAY
C.C. Cross

Chapter 8

After another restless night, Lindsay got up shortly before ten, showered, dressed, and made some instant coffee.

Momma always slept late on Sundays. She probably wouldn't come out of her bedroom for another hour or so. Lindsay took advantage of the peace and quiet by having her toast and coffee in front of the TV, trying to concentrate on the dog show on *Animal Planet*. But she couldn't stop thinking about Maisie.

The old woman's words replayed in her mind. *I want to give you something.* And then she recalled what the two homeless people outside the church had told her. "*Everyone called her Crazy Maisie. She said she could read people.*"

Read people. Momma had said something that didn't sound true, and a red sliver appeared below her left eye. She said something else that sounded untrue, and a red haze appeared above her head. The same thing happened with Officer Rossen. *Then, two kids plan to rob a store ... a black haze appears, and I see the image of a switchblade, and sense something bad is going to happen.*

Her pulse thundering, Lindsay sat bolt upright in the recliner. She shook so badly, she nearly spilled her coffee. *My God. I was wrong.*

Maisie *had* given her something. It wasn't a locket, an heirloom, or something found in a dumpster. It wasn't some tarnished memento Lindsay could put away in her dresser drawer or her jewelry box. Lindsay suspected the colors had nothing to do with what Maisie had glimpsed the moment she'd left her physical body. These strange colors Lindsay was seeing weren't from another world or state of being. They were the manifestations of emotions.

***

Lindsay reached the Police Station at around eleven.

It was important to begin functioning again. Moping around the apartment, avoiding Momma's questions, would not be very bright. She should continue living her life.

So what if she saw colors? How much harm could it do? Her strange feelings and suspicions – how often could *that* happen? It might not have even happened in the first place. It could have been her imagination. She was upset even before she'd reached the 7-Eleven. Derek Tanner wanting to mess around with Momma had released negative vibes. When Lindsay went inside and saw the black blur over the kid's head, who knew *what* was going on in *her* head?

Even if the colors and suspicions were real, Lindsay suspected such a gift wasn't such an unusual thing. Surely others saw colors, felt things. Those with the same abilities probably went about

65

their daily lives normally, living among other people without fanfare.

Maisie obviously hadn't handled her own situation in the most sensible way. She most likely had discovered her strange gift many years ago. In those days, people were superstitious, less informed, and much less sophisticated. There was no Internet, no cell phones – probably not even television. Education wasn't as important or refined. Maisie would not have been able to talk to anyone about her gift because she had nowhere to research it. She wouldn't know that the best way of handling it would be to not make a big deal out of it. Telling people about it would certainly alienate her.

It was never smart to tell anyone you were special. Lindsay found that out in grade school, when she made terrific grades and excelled in things without much effort. Earning excellent grades, along with being the tallest kid in the class, was more than enough to brand her an outcast.

At least she'd stopped growing in her sophomore year. Once she'd eased slightly past five-ten, she didn't think it would be much of a problem to reach the dreaded six-oh. But when the growing suddenly stopped shortly after her sixteenth birthday, she breathed a deep sigh of relief.

While driving to the Police Station, she carefully went over the scenario in her mind. She'd make her report as unexceptional as possible. She knew better than raise anyone's suspicion – especially in a building filled with law enforcement officers, detectives, and psychiatrists.

The man handling the case – a tall, thin man in his late thirties, the name *Stark* stamped on his nametag – asked her routine questions. Basically the same stuff the cop outside the 7-Eleven had asked, plus Lindsay's home address, age and occupation. The man typed everything in his report. When he finished, he asked if she wanted to add anything else. She said no. He smiled, thanked her for her cooperation, and told her to have a nice day.

She was genuinely relieved, knowing that as long as she didn't volunteer anything requiring a detailed explanation, she'd be just fine.

Officer Rossen was getting coffee from the station in the front alcove as Lindsay crossed the lobby. "Miss ... Foreman?" Obviously remembering her from the previous morning, he walked over, carrying a cup of steaming coffee. He was much larger than he'd appeared sitting behind his desk, at least half a head taller than Lindsay, making him around six-six. "Heard you had some excitement last night. The 7-Eleven just off Semoran. Robbery in progress."

"It ended up all right."

"I also heard you handled the whole thing yourself."

She couldn't help blushing. The way he'd said it made her sound like Xena the Warrior Princess. "I was just lucky."

"Scuttlebutt says you took one look at one of the suspects, spotted a knife, then quietly alerted the clerk."

"It was really nothing..."

Rossen blinked. "You risk your life to help a hit-and-run victim on one of the busiest stretches in Central Florida. The next day, you put yourself into even graver jeopardy by sticking around with two armed felons close by. No small accomplishment, believe me. By the way, they both had priors."

Lindsay was afraid to say anything else.

"Nowadays folks just don't bother. They see something along the side of the road? If it doesn't slow them down or block their way, they buzz right on by. In a store, they grab their beer and cigarettes and they're on their way."

It was time to change the subject. "Any progress on the person who ran over the old lady?"

He sipped some steaming coffee. "Not much, I'm afraid. But don't count on anything. In cases with no evidence, unless someone makes an anonymous tip or steps forward–"

"It was a Dodge Charger," she blurted out, totally shocked when she heard herself saying it. The image appeared briefly but clearly from her consciousness, a scrap of debris quietly surfacing from the bottom of the lake, then floating back down to the dark depths.

Officer Rossen lowered the cup from his face. "*What* was that?"

"The vehicle that hit her was a sixty-eight Dodge Charger. Black, with a personalized plate."

Rossen gawked at her. "A sixty-eight Charger."

"Yes."

"You're sure about the year."

"The same model they used in that old Steve

McQueen movie."

"And you say it was black?"

She nodded.

"With a personalized plate?"

Another nod.

Rossen shrugged. "Anything specific on the plate?"

"Sorry, but it's a little blurry."

Rossen went silent. A mix of colors appeared, smearing his reddish brush cut. White, gray, and yellow. Even some pale green floated around in there as well. He was obviously confused. And why shouldn't he be? She was also confused. If someone had told her such explicit details about a fast-moving car lurching into heavy traffic at night, she wouldn't know what to think, either.

"Why didn't you tell me this yesterday, when you first came in?"

Her cheeks grew warm. She fought hard to overcome her confusion. She had to focus, keep calm. Forget about the colors, the image in her head. She had to come up with some explanation that might ease his mind. Anything that would convince him she wasn't a fruitcake. "I think maybe my subconscious caught something and didn't want me to know about it before now."

"Really?" His colors faded slightly.

Lindsay shrugged.

"Anything else in there that wants to come out?"

"That's about it for right now. Will it help?"

He chuckled. "There can't be *that* many black

sixty-eight Chargers with personalized tags out there. I'd lay good money that one of them's sitting in a shop right now, having a dent or two pounded out near the front panel."

Chapter 9

Charles 'C.C.' Cross poured boiling black coffee into a Styrofoam cup and added three sugars. He frowned at it, then added another sugar. Hopefully, it wouldn't melt his stomach lining.

These cops really made lousy coffee. That just didn't make any sense. Anyone with a working brain cell could make a decent pot of coffee if he paid attention to what he was doing. Hell, McDonald's made better coffee than these bozos.

C.C. added cream just to take some sting out of it, then crossed the large, well-lit area where uniforms and plainclothesmen hauled around papers, briefcases, and cell phones from one cubicle to the next, each looking irritated and overworked.

C.C. had been an undercover DEA agent the last several years, working Orlando's strip club district off South Orange Blossom Trail. A former officer of the DEA Mobile Enforcement Team program, he spent three years in Kissimmee before being transferred to Orlando to handle the heavy influx of crystal meth flowing into northern Florida from Atlanta for mass distribution throughout the state. C.C. has been directly responsible for nailing dozens of local crystal meth dealers and closing down their labs. Not an easy task these days. Dealers, getting more educated, were acquiring the most expensive surveillance systems, booby traps, and alarms. Anyone who went after these guys was literally taking his own life in his hands.

71

Having a good snitch was half the battle. This was why he'd stopped by the station. His most reliable ear, Ernesto 'the Blade' Medina, had disappeared, most likely since he'd been causing problems for Giuseppe 'Jo-Jo' Lanza, Orlando's most powerful crime boss.

Medina had serious personal and mental issues. He was brought up by his prostitute mother and heavily addicted to blow by the time he was fifteen. He also had an obsession for strippers. Since Jo-Jo's clubs used the sweetest chicks in town, Medina probably got all juiced up and did something stupid in one of Lanza's clubs.

C.C. hadn't seen or heard from Medina in nearly a week – a sure sign that he'd probably taken his final dip in one of Orlando's lakes.

C.C. decided to see if anyone from Uniform Drugs was hanging around. Finding snitches could be a drag when you had a history of losing them. C.C. had lost three in the last year. That wasn't bad, considering the type of work he did. But finding a good one always presented a major problem.

He passed the front desk and headed down the long, busy hall, where the Uniform Drug guys usually hung out. Lou Rossen was standing in front of the desk, talking to a tall, slender chick with long brown hair. C.C. heard Rossen say, "Sixty-eight Charger," and stopped in his tracks. Trying not to be conspicuous, he took a tiny sip of his coffee and grimaced at its bitterness. Street Patrol made this batch, no doubt. But that wasn't the issue right now. He blew on it again, focusing not on its bitterness,

72

but on Rossen's voice.

"...and one of them's probably sitting in a shop right now, having a dent or two pounded out near the front panel."

Rossen shouldn't be discussing such sensitive issues in a crowded police station. But Rossen obviously didn't *know* the issue was sensitive.

C.C. strolled over to the bulletin board. He stood in front of it, every few seconds glancing nonchalantly to his left to make sure Rossen was still talking to the chick. When she finally slipped through the glass doors leading out front, C.C. followed the big cop back to his desk. Rossen was logging on when C.C. came over. "How goes it?"

Rossen had a slug of coffee. "See you're still around and kicking."

"No one's been able to get me in their sights yet. But the day's still young."

Rossen chuckled softly. "So what brings you here? The scenery?"

"You got it. Who was that cute chick you were just talking to, and does your lovely wife Ida know about her?"

***

Five minutes later, C.C. left the OPD Building and got into the silver Mustang GT parked out front.

As he slid behind the wheel, he pulled out his cell. He had two calls to make. The first, to DMV, would be a quick exchange – just a couple of routine questions. However, the second wouldn't be so simple. He needed to tread lightly. The man he'd be talking to was not known for his diplomacy, patience, or self-control.

C.C. quickly made the first call. Billy Briggs had been employed with DMV for more than twenty years and really knew his job. He was fast and accurate, good with computers, and could retrieve anything in minutes.

"How goes it, C.C.?"

"Just great. And you?"

Billy let loose with a huge sigh. "Job's giving me a giant ulcer, my wife's on permanent PMS, the kids wanna go to Ivy League colleges, the mother-in-law wants to move in, and I've got a boil on my ass the size of a golf ball."

"Glad things are going so well for you."

"That why you called? To ask about my utopian life? Or do you happen to have a remedy for the boil on my ass?"

"I suggest a lengthy session with an S&M chick who knows how to use a whip. Or maybe one with nursing experience."

"Sounds like a plan. Shame Sandy wouldn't go for it. You know how antsy wives get whenever the old man wants to try something new."

"Why do you think I'm not married?"

"Could it be because they keep divorcing your sorry ass?"

"That might be a primary reason. Third time around, and I'm not even forty."

"What's your problem? More choice babes in this town than anywhere else in the country."

"My alimony payments are keeping me poor."

"That's not what *I* heard."

74

C.C. blinked. "Oh?"

"Just got wind of your new ride. Nice. Real nice. Things can't be *that* bad..."

C.C. shoved a hand through his short brown hair. "Actually, the bank owns it. For the next three years, anyway."

"I hear ya..."

Time to move on. "You busy right now?"

"Just sitting on my ass, listening to my boil fussing about the seat."

"I need an address, a plate number – anything you can get for a young female who lives in Orlando."

Billy started clicking. "Got a name?"

"Foreman. First name, Lindsay. She's a brunette in her early twenties. Tall, around five-ten, maybe six feet. Slender. One-ten, soaking wet."

"How fast you need this?"

"Now."

PART IV – MONDAY
Changes

Chapter 10

The shop was already open by the time Lindsay got there.

Sarah sat at her desk in her tiny cluttered office, her reading glasses perched on the tip of her nose. The enclosed space smelled strongly of her gingery perfume and the sanitizer she used to spray her keyboard and phone as she pored over sales receipts. Slivers of bright early morning sun whispered through the blinds, forming slender bars on the tile floor in front of the desk. Sarah's thick, raven-black mane appeared no different. No hint of color hovered near her face or head.

Lindsay wondered if Maisie's gift had suddenly vanished. Had the incident with Officer Rossen the day before jinxed it forever? Or had Reverend Allen been right about the colors being a residual image that would gradually ebb into the darkness with time?

"Good morning," Lindsay said, breaking the silence.

"How was your weekend?" Sarah asked.

"Pretty boring." Lindsay wondered if a splotch of red had appeared above her own head. "And yours?"

"So-so."

Still nothing. Lindsay attempted a quick experiment. "How's Edward?" she asked, referring to Sarah's live-in boyfriend. "Has he found a management position yet?"

Sarah's cheery aura dulled. "He's had a couple of offers, but nothing definite." A red haze appeared lazily above Sarah's head.

***

The workday trudged on like a turtle trying to climb a steep hill. Lindsay found it impossible to concentrate. After the exchange with Sarah, she'd expected the store to disappear in a storm of color whenever the customers flowed in.

A foursome of chattering young females rushed in, two of them checking out tee-shirts, the others the bargain bin. No colors appeared while they were talking softly amongst themselves. Lindsay sighed in relief. She'd been worrying about nothing. It was no wonder. The last couple of days had done her in. What she'd experienced might have been a fluke – one of those weird phenomena that couldn't be explained.

The foursome approached the register, still chattering away. The colors formed a thick haze above their heads.

"These prices seem high." *Red.*

"I'll bet I can find this at the mall cheaper." *Red.*

"This shirt reminds me of Teddy." *White.*

"I'm gonna tell my friends about this place." *Red.*

Then they left, taking their colors with them. Sarah had closed her office door – possibly to talk to her bank or argue with Edward – and Lindsay's thoughts automatically went back to her last conversation with Officer Rossen. He probably considered her a space cadet. Her explanation for her sudden burst of memory sounded feasible, but she'd clearly seen his confusion, and the wash of colors hovering above his head.

If *she* couldn't believe what happened, how could anyone else? Why did she blurt out something like that in the first place? Even if it was true, she should've thought it over before telling a police officer. She'd never done anything so impulsive before. What had changed? The fact that she'd helped a lonely old woman? Had some spirit taken possession of her? Was Maisie speaking to her from the dead? If Maisie *had* come back, would she be able to take over Lindsay's thoughts? Her vocal chords? Unlikely. At least she *hoped* so.

But what if she was wrong about the Charger? What if the image was something she'd seen on TV? The brain was a strange, wondrous thing. It responded to every conceivable form of stimulus, turning hopes and desires into dreams, fears and neuroses into nightmares. Something from the past could pop up during the day and reappear in some other form in a dream. The brain was perfectly capable of taking a thought or image it hadn't recalled for days or even weeks and convert it into something else. How could she know for sure that it was the same Charger from the Steve McQueen movie? Why not the Shelby? Or James Bond's Aston Martin?

The incident had taken place in approaching darkness. She was a hundred feet away when it happened. Traffic was horrible. The sounds of engines, horns and crazy, hyped-up people had transformed the night into deafening bedlam. But the image she'd seen remained clear.

***

For a change of scenery, Lindsay drove to the mall at lunchtime. As part of the wandering crowd, she was able to focus on other things. It was much harder to feel sorry for herself at a busy mall.

She'd been reluctant at first, expecting to be engulfed in a sea of color floating above the crowd like a strange fog. But she realized that the idea made no sense. Judging by what happened in Sarah's store, Lindsay could only see colors when someone was talking to her and sending out strong emotions. How could it happen otherwise? The concept was ridiculous. Although she'd sensed strong emotions at the 7-Eleven and was reasonably sure they belonged to the would-be robbers, she hadn't yet been able to read other people's thoughts.

She had enough problems of her own. And she knew enough about people to realize that she didn't want to wander into strange territory. Lindsay loved her mother, but shuddered to think what was going on in the woman's head. And she knew enough about Derek Tanner to realize she didn't want to know what *he* thought.

It was the same with everyone else. The two homeless people outside the church were exaggerating. People exaggerated all the time –

especially when they were frightened of someone or only knew half the story.

Maisie was able to read people's *emotions*. If she actually *could* read minds, she wouldn't have been able to cope and might have even committed suicide. The fact that she'd lived a long life suggested her powers were manageable. Closing her eyes would eliminate the colors, therefore nullifying the power and the aggravation that went along with it. Things wouldn't be as simple if she could read minds. Closing her eyes would do nothing – the thoughts would just keep coming. Lindsay could endure the colors. Closing her eyes at crucial times was a small price to pay for being different.

On her way back out to the main entrance, something caught her eye in the jewelry store at the corner. Their glass display case, spanning half the length of the store, glittered with diamond rings, studs, and necklaces spread out on green velvet. To her right, a short, red-haired lady in her sixties purchased a gold necklace. The tall, slender saleslady took the slip and tag, marched over to the register, and rang it up.

The saleslady brought back the woman's change. She counted it out and put the bills on the counter. The woman smiled and reached for them. Lindsay stared at the saleslady. A smear of red wreathed her professionally colored gold-and-brown highlighted hair. Lindsay's gaze switched to the customer's money, now gripped in her small pudgy hand. *Not enough there...* The tiny whisper drifted lazily from the back of her mind.

"You're short ten dollars," Lindsay said.

The woman blinked. "Pardon?"

"She gave you sixty dollars," Lindsay said. "Unless that necklace is marked wrong, the store owes you another ten." Lindsay smiled at the clerk, noting the woman's nametag. "Isn't that right, Brittany?"

The clerk acted genuinely surprised. Her red smudge brightened. "My *gosh*!" She rushed back to the register, opened it, and snatched out another bill, then hurried back. "That was *so* careless of me!" She handed her customer the bill with shaky fingers. "Honestly ... I don't know where my mind is today!"

The woman smiled. "Thank you, young lady."

"You're welcome." As the sales clerk went back to her register, Lindsay lowered her voice. "Be careful. People are really dishonest nowadays."

"Thanks again." She shuffled away.

The clerk turned away from the display case. Her large green eyes twitched as they focused on Lindsay. Her bright red halo turned a smoky black.

Chapter 11

Hidden by the heavy lunchtime traffic, C.C. Cross followed the Foreman girl from the tee-shirt shop off Semoran Boulevard to the mall on Colonial Drive.

For the next half-hour, he watched her as she strolled down the thoroughfare, gazing at store windows. According to Lou Rossen, the girl was a little strange. She'd helped the old woman who'd been hit by the Charger, then stopped a robbery-in-progress the night before. She gave Rossen the impression it was her civic duty. And it bothered her that no one else shared the same philosophy.

But she didn't seem the hero type. Totally opposite, since she blended so well into her environment. Maybe that was her thing. If he hadn't been watching her, she'd be one of those people no one noticed.

She was quietly attractive but played it down in a plain sort of way. Her long brown hair fell well below her shoulders. No ringlets or expensive swirls. No tint, no glitter. She didn't wear bright clothing. She wasn't large-breasted. She displayed no jewelry, studs, or tattoos. She was tall, giving one the impression she was a lampshade, or corner post. In other words, part of the furniture.

Briggs at DMV said Foreman had turned twenty-three on July 1. She lived with her mother and worked full-time at an independently-owned tee-shirt shop in the strip mall facing Semoran

82

Boulevard, one block south of Colonial. The girl's mother, Dorothy Hilliard Foreman, age forty-four, drove a three-year-old black BMW. The mother worked as a personal secretary for Derek Tanner, President and CEO of TannerSoftSystems, Ltd., a software brokerage in Industrial Park. The mother had been divorced for four years, suing her ex-husband, Alan L. Foreman, for desertion.

As evidenced by her soft, unassuming manner, Lindsay apparently led a quiet life for a kid in her early twenties. Her driving record was clean – no arrests, no charges, no warrants. No history of alcohol or drugs. No recent purchases of guns, ammunition, or explosives. No history of reported abuse, domestic or otherwise. A nice, quiet girl.

If only she hadn't IDed that Charger Friday night...

C.C. was still smarting from the second phone call he'd made outside OPD the day before. The man had answered on the second ring, after the usual anti-bugging clicks. "I'm in the middle of something right now," he said flatly.

"It's important." C.C.'s pulse hammered as always whenever he talked to this man. "You need to know."

"All right." Another click. "Talk."

"It's about a certain sixty-eight Dodge Charger that just came up in conversation."

"It's a good car. Good year, too. I liked the late sixties. Less complicated. People weren't as fucked up." He paused. "You mentioned conversation."

"It took place in the police station just five

minutes ago."

Another pause. "Who was discussing this car?"

"An eyewitness to a recent hit-and-run."

Another click. "Lots of Chargers out there. They've got shows in Central Florida almost every weekend. There's one next weekend at the fairgrounds. I believe this one is sponsored by Dodge. There should be at least a dozen Chargers there."

C.C. sighed. The man was being slippery, as usual, and he was good at it. He had to be slippery to be as successful as he was. "I'm sure we both know what we're talking about."

"We both like things black and white. Now tell me what's going on."

"Black and white is right." C.C. was getting perturbed by all this sparring. "The vehicle being discussed was black, with a personalized tag."

"Black's a popular color. And it's common knowledge that classic car collectors like personalized tags."

"I'm afraid the Charger being discussed is one you're personally familiar with."

Silence. C.C. knew he'd twanged a nerve.

"Are you saying someone IDed this *particular* car?"

He loosened his collar. He needed a drink but hadn't brought along his flask. As he sat in the Mustang, gathering the courage to continue, his thoughts shifted to his favorite watering hole – the O-Town Café off Orange Avenue. A strong drink would really hit the spot. He promised himself one right after this unpleasantness. "I heard a girl talking to one of the cops in the lobby."

"Go on."

"I believe this young woman saw a Charger that can be traced back to–"

"Is *that* why she was at the station? To ID this car?"

C.C. didn't want to tell this man too much. It was bad enough he had to deal with him in the first place. "She went there for something else."

"So you're not absolutely sure she reported it already?"

"I was told she couldn't ID the tag."

"See that she doesn't."

Icy slivers slid down his back. He knew what that meant. "I can't ... get any more involved in this."

"You've cut corners before. That's why you're useful to us. For right now, anyway."

C.C. wanted to tell this asshole where he could shove it, but he had to keep his temper in check. The other man had too many connections. "Doing anything about this will be more serious than cutting corners."

"What's involved?"

"Any number of things. Tailing. Wiretapping. Interfering. Putting my ass on the line."

"I'm not interested in your ass. I only want you to prevent this female from IDing that vehicle."

"I can't *possibly* do that unless ... unless I do something to her *personally*." C.C. waited for a response but heard only silence. He knew what that meant. "I ... *can't* ... do something ... like *that*..."

"Try the other stuff first – tailing, wiretapping, interfering. If that doesn't work..."

"She might not even remember that tag."

"Good for her."

C.C. had been in tight spots before, but never something like this. He loosened his collar even more. It felt like he'd just had his neck fitted for a noose. "I'm really uncomfortable about all this."

"You're uncomfortable? Get drunk or drive to one of the Pleasure Palaces on the Trail. Tell 'em your drinks are free, then take one of the lap dancers to a room. My treat."

C.C. frowned. "As great as that sounds–"

"That new ride you've got? The baby-blue one?"

C.C. wiped his glistening forehead with a shirt sleeve. "What about it?"

"Where is it?"

He squirmed in his seat. "It's parked outside my apartment."

"Why aren't you driving it?"

He hardly ever drove it. It reminded him of the things that had gone wrong in his life. It also reminded him of how low he'd sunk in the last six months. "I only drive it on special occasions," he said flatly.

"When you go home tonight, look at it. It's pretty, yeah?"

"Yeah."

"You remember how you got it?"

"Only too well."

"Just remember – we all have to do things we're not comfortable with. Some do it for nothing, while others – like yourself – earn a pretty, shiny, free car for their troubles. Yeah?"

"Yeah."

"I don't care what you have to do. Find out about this female and how much she knows."

"She saw the hit-and-run."

"That bag lady?"

"Yeah."

"Who the fuck cares about a bag lady?"

C.C. took a deep breath. "It's *still* a homicide."

"Homicides happen all the time. Sometimes they happen on the roads because of all the traffic. Other times, bad things happen to nice people in their own homes. You never know what's ahead. You step out of the tub and trip and hit your head on something – the edge of the tub, a corner of the toilet. Who knows? All sorts of accidents – understand?"

"Totally."

"Find out who she is, what she knows, and what she wants."

"What if she doesn't want anything?"

"Everyone wants *something*."

The call went dead. C.C. pocketed the cell and sat in his car for the next ten minutes, hating himself for what he'd become and for what he'd been forced to do with his life. He'd started out in law enforcement, trying to make things right for the little guy. Horror and disgust slammed through him when his best collars beat him out the front door with the help of their high-powered, fast-talking defense attorneys.

He reminded himself what he had to do. The man he'd just talked to was right – everyone had to do certain things they didn't want to do. It was life. And everyone knew life sucked.

At 12:35, the Foreman girl spent a few minutes in the jewelry shop, talking to a customer and the saleslady, then made her way for the exit. She stopped beside the tan Honda Civic parked halfway down the crowded aisle. According to Briggs, she'd bought the car two years ago from an Altamonte Springs Honda dealer and had been driving it ever since.

As the Honda pulled out, C.C. realized just how bad the next few days were going to be.

Chapter 12

After helping Sarah close up for the day, Lindsay decided to stop at the Corral, a bar and grill sandwiched between a shoe store and a furniture distributor.

It sat in a strip mall, about a mile east of Semoran Boulevard on Colonial Drive. Besides foreign and domestic beers and alcoholic drinks, the Corral served hoagies, pizza, and man-sized cheeseburgers. It didn't attract large crowds until the evenings, when the drinking customers showed up. Since it didn't specialize in fancy gourmet meals, it was the perfect place to enjoy a quiet drink after work. Sarah had mentioned the place once or twice, which told Lindsay it might be okay. Sarah, like Lindsay, hated crowds. Lindsay seldom drank, but after such a particularly taxing day, she figured one drink might help her relax.

Once inside the bar, Lindsay selected a booth near the big picture window overlooking Colonial Drive and ordered a strawberry daiquiri. Outside, traffic roared by, reminding her Momma would probably be coming home now. She'd wonder where Lindsay was and would check the machine. If there were no messages, she'd call Lindsay's cell. In anticipation, Lindsay pulled it out of her bag and placed it on the table just as the waitress set her daiquiri on a napkin in front of her.

She sipped and began thinking about Maisie again, wondering how old she'd been when she'd first discovered her special powers, how she'd discovered them, and if she'd kept quiet about them. She visualized a skinny little girl with pigtails running through a hilly field with her dog, laughing and giggling. The dog, a black and white sheepdog, quickly caught a scent and disappeared amongst the trees. Little Maisie called for the dog, then proceeded to enter the woods after it. But before she reached the tree line, something made her turn back toward the hill leading back to the village.

Lindsay had more of her daiquiri and mentally scolded herself for letting her imagination run wild. She'd seen too many *Little House* reruns as a child. She'd imagined Maisie as a young girl and immediately turned the situation into a romp with Half-Pint and Jack.

It was easy to imagine Maisie as a young girl, discovering the colors for the first time, becoming frightened, then rushing home to ask her mother about them – or her grandmother or an aunt. Realizing how different people were so long ago, Lindsay suspected they would have been taken aback by this revelation, fearing it and thinking little Maisie was touched or cursed in some way.

Lindsay knew this was one of the reasons she hadn't told her own mother. Lindsay loved Momma but found it difficult to confide in her. Lindsay, like most other young girls, had gone to her mother to talk about her first period, her first boyfriend, and her first bad grade. Momma was sympathetic about some things, brutally frank and tough about others. She wouldn't understand her baby daughter suddenly possessing a strange power. She wouldn't accept it.

"Want company?" The man had come directly from the bar. He was about forty, of medium height, and fairly slim. He was neatly dressed in black slacks and a light-blue polo shirt, and held a drink in his hand. He smelled strongly of Aqua Velva. His dark-brown hair was combed straight back and treated liberally with mousse, and his brown goatee was impeccably trimmed. Gold rings decorated three fingers on each hand. A gold necklace sparkled around his neck.

Lindsay guessed he was fastidious, but the vibes coming from him – as well as his burnt orange cloud – made her uncomfortable. She suspected he might have been in prison or a drug treatment center. "Not really," she said pleasantly. "But thanks anyway."

"You look lonely."

"I'm all right."

"Hi."

She blinked. "*Hi*?"

"It's my name. Everyone calls me Hi."

"Hi ... uh, Hi..."

He grinned. "See there? Now you know my name. What's yours?"

"I really didn't come here to–"

"You look like an ... Anne? Alicia?"

Lindsay frowned. Why couldn't guys accept it when a girl wanted to be alone? "Listen ... I just came here for a quiet drink and some think-time."

"Barbara? Beth? Brittany?"

Lindsay just sighed.

"You're not gonna make me run all the way down the alphabet, are you?"

The colors floating around him turned red and orange, with white strands. Despite his jocular approach, he was giving off flashes of fear and irritation.

It was time to leave. She couldn't relax with someone leaning against her table, invading her space. After one last sip of her daiquiri, she collected her cell phone and purse, left her change on the table, and got up.

He stiffened. His colors darkened. "You don't have to *go*. I didn't mean—"

"I really need to get home." Forcing herself not to gag from the heavy miasma of his cologne, she squeezed by him and hurried outside. She pulled out her car keys as she rushed to her car. She sincerely hoped he took the hint. The last thing she needed was—

Footsteps clacked on the sidewalk behind her. Her heart sank as she looked over her shoulder. Apparently Hi didn't handle rejection very well.

"Listen..." He grinned sheepishly, a swarm of bright colors moving around him. "I didn't mean to upset you, I just—"

"I understand." She was feeling a little lightheaded. The daiquiri? Or was it fear? Or nausea? "I just wanted to be alone, okay? And you know what? I still do."

He shrugged. "Can't blame a guy for trying, can you?"

Lindsay sighed. Now she felt horrible. "I'm really sorry. You're probably a nice guy and all..."

"I am." His colors turned a deeper red. "I really am. Ask anyone who knows me."

She opened her car door. "I believe you. Honestly. But I need to get home."

"Do me a favor first."

"What's that?"

He reached into his pants pocket. "Just write down your phone number. Maybe we can get together another time."

"I'm sorry. I don't think–"

He grabbed her wrist. His hand was hot, scorching her as it encircled her skin. The air around her grew warmer. A hot bubble surrounded her head, making it difficult to breathe. She forced out a weak gasp.

A shadow moved toward her left.

The man was about thirty-five and moved quickly, pulling Hi away, tripping him and forcing him to the cracked pavement. Hi gasped, rolling away and crawling on all fours toward the narrow walkway between the shoe store and the Corral. Her rescuer rushed him. His leg lashed out, his foot connecting with Hi's butt. Hi let out a high-pitched wail. With one last burst of energy, he scrambled away frantically, like a frightened mouse, disappearing in the shadows of the walkway.

"You okay?" her rescuer asked.

"Thanks to you." The sudden iciness covering the back of her neck made her shiver.

"I take it you met him inside?"

She nodded. Her heart was thundering, her wrist hurt, and her knees trembled. She felt stupid for letting this happen. And she felt bad for Hi, who just got a bit over-friendly.

"He's nobody to worry about. Just had too much to drink."

"He was nice enough, I guess, but he wouldn't leave me alone."

This man was good-looking, but his eyes were cold. A deep blue with flecks of black inside. He was giving off tiny tufts of white. *Fear?* He certainly didn't mind physical confrontation. And he appeared to be anything but frightened. She was obviously reading him wrong. Maisie hadn't left a book of instructions.

"Well, since you're okay..." He waved.

She wanted to tell him how much she appreciated his help, but found herself at a loss for words. Something like this had never happened before. It was right out of a romance novel, almost. She seldom saw kindness these days. "Thanks again," she managed.

He crossed the lot and disappeared behind a row of tall bushes.

***

The Foreman girl pulled out of the lot and turned right, heading west. Possibly going home. Once she was out of sight, C.C. squeezed through the bushes and cut through the walkway between the eatery and the shoe store.

Hiram 'Pockets' Sheldon leaned against a dumpster, gingerly rubbing his ass. C.C. knew he was in for a lengthy dialogue of whining. Pockets was the absolute king of whiners.

"Why the hell'd you have to kick me so hard?" he demanded. "I ain't a *dog*, ya know."

"I never kicked a dog in my life. I like dogs."

"I ain't a kid anymore, either."

"Hey, all I did was pull you away from her and–"

"I'm *forty*, dammit. I don't *bounce* like I used to."

"Is that why you don't ride car hoods for the insurance money anymore?"

Pockets huffed. "You ought to do standup comedy."

"That would deprive me of the pleasure of dealing with sweet ex-cons like yourself."

Pockets continued massaging his butt. "Yeah, a real comedian, all right. But it still don't give you the right to kick me like a dog."

"Like I said, I like dogs. Matter of fact, if I ever *see* someone kicking one, I'm liable to shoot the bastard and take the dog home."

Pockets frowned. "How about that? A regular Lancelot."

"Can the self-pity. I had to make it look good." C.C. reached into his pocket and pulled out a slim wad of twenties.

"And why the damn rush?" Pockets brushed himself off, grumbling at the scuff marks and dirt stains on his trousers. "I had an appointment at Naomi's in an hour. Did her a favor a while back, and she's gonna give me a free tattoo. She was supposed to put it on my left butt cheek, but since I'm probably gonna be hauling around a *bruise* there for six weeks–"

"Last I heard, we've all got *two* of those." C.C. peeled off three twenties. Pockets could be a genuine butthole when things didn't go his way. But there hadn't been anyone else available in the area. And since Pockets always seemed to be pulling some sort of scam, he was elected. "Tell her to carve up the right one."

"Not the point." Pockets took the sixty bucks and frowned at it.

"Problem?"

"Sixty bucks for getting my ass kicked? Doesn't seem worth it. These threads cost me a hundred."

"Ever hear of dry-cleaning? There's even a tailor in the area."

"Still doesn't seem worth it."

"Sixty bucks for two minutes' work." C.C. couldn't believe these guys. They did you a small favor and wanted a windfall. "That's eighteen hundred bucks an hour. Who the hell makes that much jack?"

"Celebs. Athletes. Politicians. Porn stars. Movie directors."

"You direct or star in a movie, get picked for the Magic, or run for office, I'll make sure you get an extra grand."

"You're an asshole, Cross."

"Tell me something I don't know. And tell Naomi I asked about her."

"She doesn't like you."

"A damned shame. I *love* chicks carrying the tattooed names of ex-boyfriends over their tits. It's a real turn-on. Now get out of here, or I'll call OPD and tell them about that new tourist scam you've been running outside these restaurants."

Pockets stiffened. "After I did you this favor?"

C.C. smiled. He loved pressing Pockets' buttons. The boy had so many of them.

"You really *are* an asshole."

C.C. went back out to the lot and got in his Mustang. His cell buzzed. The display said *Unknown Name, Unknown Number*. With a deep sigh, he flicked it on and hoped it wasn't who he thought it was. But when he heard the familiar clicks, he knew he was in for more grief.

"How's this latest irritation going?"

"I'm working on it."

"You don't have the time to tell me such a stupid thing. The cops may be slow, but they also have the nasty habit of getting there just when you don't want them around. You've been on this, what? Eighteen hours, now?"

"I haven't been counting."

"I have. And you know what else I'm doing?"

C.C. knew better than ask.

"I'm thinking of sending someone to make sure you do this properly."

That was the worst possible thing he could think of. This man employed some dangerous figures. If any of them were involved in this, a lot of people would be hurt. "I've been a cop for fifteen years. Believe me, something like this should be handled delicately."

"You find out what you can about this female. If it looks like she'll become a threat, buy her off or get her out of the picture."

"Buy her off? With what?"

The man sighed. "That's why you need to find out what she wants."

"What if she doesn't want money?"

"You just answered your own question."

The call went dead with a click. C.C. shoved the cell back into his shirt pocket, sat back, and pulled the metal flask from his jacket pocket. The fiery whiskey burned its way down his throat. He closed his eyes. A wave of warmth eased through him.

He couldn't ignore the obvious. He was caught between a rock and a hard place once again, only this rock killed, and the hard place shattered bones.

***

Lindsay crouched in her Honda parked between Momma's BMW and Derek's Corvette, waiting for her nerves to settle down.

The scuffle outside the Corral had been too much. At least it had nothing to do with the colors. Besides, it had turned out well. If not for the nice guy coming to her aid, it could easily have gone in the other direction. But there was no reason to worry about what *might* have happened. Best get past it and get on with the rest of the evening.

Momma and Derek were relaxing on the sofa when Lindsay walked through the door. *Law &*

Order was playing on the TV. Momma loved *Law & Order*. She'd obviously been too busy with Derek and the show to call and ask where Lindsay was.

Momma glanced at the wall clock. "You're late."

Derek pulled his arm free from around Momma's shoulders. "Hi, Lindsay."

"Hi. I stopped by the Corral for a drink."

Momma looked surprised. "What's the occasion?"

She shrugged out of her jacket and hung it in the entrance closet. "I just felt like having a drink." She went over to the fish tank. "Did you feed Marvin?"

"You know I won't ever do that again."

"Just checking."

"Last time I did, you yelled at me."

"Only because you gave him too much." She picked up the orange fish-shaped dispenser, doled out three miniscule pellets into her palm, and dropped them into the tank. Marvin immediately appeared from behind his little blue castle and snatched them up. "I didn't yell, just said you gave him too much."

Momma muted the volume on the TV. "Meet anyone?"

Lindsay knew better than mention the scuffle. Momma would scold her right in front of Derek for getting into such a predicament. "I had one drink and left."

"You went to a bar and didn't even *meet*

99

anyone?"

"I didn't go there to *meet* someone. I just wanted a drink."

"You need to quit being so picky, baby. There are a lot of guys out there. They're not gonna wait forever."

"I'm not *looking* for a guy right now."

"I realize you're still smarting over your fling with what's-his-name–"

"David. David Ellington."

"Whatever. He did you bad and all, but it happens. I know that better than anyone. Besides, that was *two years ago*."

"I know when it was."

"Listen, no guy's perfect, but–"

"*No* guy?" Derek asked, grinning.

"Very few," Momma amended, giving him a quick kiss on the lips. "But you're a sweet kid, baby. You shouldn't close yourself off just because of one bad experience. You can't be by yourself all the time."

"I like being by myself."

"You've been doing that since grade school, you know."

"It helps me think."

"Why do you have to *think* so much?" Momma picked up her drink.

Lindsay just sighed. Sometimes Momma made no sense whatsoever. Lindsay wondered how many drinks she'd already had.

"It's not healthy – is it, Derek?"

He drank some Scotch. "Not healthy."

100

"Take my word for it, baby. Being by yourself is okay for now. But one day you'll find loneliness a drag. Then you'll *want* someone."

It was time to change the subject. "What's for supper?"

"It's on the counter in the kitchen. We brought home Subway. Hope that's okay."

"Subway's fine." Lindsay went into the kitchen. Her nerves were still jittery, but she knew she'd better eat something. She hadn't eaten since breakfast. That little bit of daiquiri on an empty stomach had made her sleepy as well as light-headed. Or maybe it was a combination of the daiquiri and the excitement.

She opened the fridge, got out a can of Dr. Pepper, and found a clean glass. Her sandwich sat in the white bag on the table. She pulled it out. A strange image flashing in her mind made her stop cold. She shrugged, put the sandwich on the table, and rubbed her eyes. She was obviously more tired than she thought.

What had she seen? A bunch of letters that made no sense. *K-L-M-A-N-J-K*? The picture ignited a flare of bold, black lettering on white, with a palm tree and an orange silhouette flanking it. It appeared in her mind's eye in a bright flash, then slipped away in darkness.

Lindsay knew what that image represented – a license plate ... on the back of a dark muscle car. She trembled so badly, she nearly knocked over her Dr. Pepper. She'd just glimpsed the personalized tag on the Charger that ran over Maisie.

PART V – TUESDAY
Stirring the Pot

Chapter 13

Strips of morning sunlight peeked through the kitchen window blinds as Lindsay ate a piece of whole-wheat toast. She hardly noticed anything as she focused on what had happened at this very table the night before. The image of that license plate remained prominently in her head as she finished breakfast, drank her coffee, then left for work.

Even though she soon found herself busy with customers and the usual flurry of store activity, she barely noticed her customers as she rang up their purchases. There were too many other things to consider.

She knew she should call Officer Rossen, but had no idea what to tell him. Should she stick with her original story, that her subconscious had been picking up things since the accident? Could she convince him details were trickling into her memory like grains of sand through an hourglass? Would he believe her or think something was wrong with her?

Something *was* wrong, but she had no idea what it was, or what she should do about it. She couldn't tell a doctor about the strange colors, the images, or the feelings. She couldn't tell anyone she suspected a dead woman had somehow slipped her important clues about the man responsible for her death.

But no matter how she felt, she had to tell Rossen. It didn't matter what he thought. The police needed all the facts to solve the case. They *had* to check it out – it was their job. If she was right, they could find Maisie's killer and bring him to justice. If not, Lindsay would have to face the possibility that she might be losing her mind.

At twelve o'clock, Sarah took over the register, and Lindsay went out to her car. The Honda was parked less than twenty feet from the front entrance, but the short walk turned out to be surprisingly difficult. Her feet were unsteady, and she almost lost her footing. She dropped her keys twice before she could unlock her car door. She cracked her head on the door frame getting in. Her hands shook as she made the call, but she forced herself through it. It was the right thing to do. Honest people did stuff like this all the time. Anyway, it was for Maisie. Whoever killed her should be punished for it.

Officer Rossen answered on the first ring, and Lindsay quickly forged ahead. "Hi, this is Lindsay Foreman. Do you remember me?"

"Miss Foreman. *Course* I remember you. In fact, I was gonna call and let you know how the case is going."

Her spirits lifted. Maybe it wouldn't be necessary to volunteer the plate number. "You've *found* something?"

"Seems there's a classic car show scheduled at the Fairgrounds this weekend, and they're expecting no less than two dozen vintage Chargers to show up.

Many will be coming from out of state, of course, and some aren't the right year, but we'll have a few to pick from. We won't have a plate number, but we might be able to narrow it down."

She sank in her seat. Her pulse fluttered. The words, thick and as heavy as mud, found their way out. "I think ... I remember ... the plate."

A short pause. "Didn't you tell me you couldn't see it clearly?"

"Yes..."

"And now you're telling me you know what it is?"

"It came to me last night. I don't know how it came to me or why, but there it was, as clear as glass."

"Miss Foreman. You didn't mention a light above the plate, did you?"

"I don't *remember* mentioning it..."

"Then how could you possibly tell what you saw? It happened at night, didn't it?"

"Yes..."

"And you weren't exactly right where it happened – am I correct?"

Her heart pounded. Yes, this was a lie, but it was the only thing she could think of. "My subconscious ... it must have picked up the plate when the vehicle behind it shined its headlights on it."

"That's possible, I guess." She heard him sigh. "That subconscious of yours. It does go on, doesn't it? Well, let me have the number. No matter how you got it, it's evidence."

She gave it to him.

"Just so we have this right... Kilo-Lima-Mike-Alpha-November-Juliet-Kilo?"

"That's it."

"We'll go with this, then." He paused. "Anything else coming to you I should know about? I know I asked you that same thing before–"

"Nothing. And I'm really sorry I can't remember everything all at once."

"Things come to me like that, too. Anyway, I'll run this and see what we can find. Appreciate your help."

Lindsay sat in a daze for the next few minutes, staring at the MiniMart across the highway, where a young Hispanic man in tan shorts and no shirt pumped gas into his low rider. A feeling of dread filled her, and she shivered. Despite everything she believed, she feared she shouldn't have made that phone call.

Chapter 14

Active Files, a relatively new branch of Unsolved Cases, was hastily assembled two years earlier to handle Orlando's rapid population growth.

AF consisted of a dozen or so college grads with law enforcement background and computer technology proficiency. Active Files received new cases, logging them and prioritizing them before distributing them to the appropriate channels. It was an efficient new way of keeping with the workload, which had more than tripled in the last five years.

Steve McGuire had been with AF since its inception. McGuire graduated from the Police Academy ten years ago and walked a beat in Miami for almost six months before being shot in the leg with a .44 Magnum in the hands of a twelve-year-old Cuban punk high on crystal meth. The high-powered slug shattered his thigh bone and promptly ended his career as a beat cop. The traumatized bone eventually mended and didn't bother him, as long as he didn't stress it. However, since then, he hadn't been able to pass OPD's annual physical qualification test – his leg gave out after just one lap around the track. He'd resigned himself to the fact that the rest of his career would be spent behind a desk.

Steve received each case as it first entered the database. He was the one responsible for redirecting it to the proper department. Like everything else in the computer field, the process quickly became monotonous. However, once in a great while, something interesting popped up. Like right now.

He set down his coffee cup and stared numbly at the screen. *No fucking way.* "This'll definitely make someone's sphincter pucker," he muttered. "In fact, when this gets out–" He stopped abruptly and glanced to his left, to see if Sanderson had heard him from her desk. *Not there. Good deal.* It was also good that most of the other guys hadn't come back from lunch yet. He didn't want people to know he talked to himself. *Or* what had just come through.

He studied the data in front of him. Were his eyes deceiving him? Hardly. Especially after what had come over the other morning about the black sixty-eight Charger involved in the hit-and-run on Colonial. A classic car guy himself, Steve had done a double take on that bit of data.

This was bad. This was the ball game. License plate KLMANJK. Owner of vehicle: John Anthony Santella, age twenty-six, six feet tall, weight one-seventy. Brown hair, brown eyes, Caucasian. Unmarried. Casselberry residence. What the report didn't say was that John 'Cool Man Jack' Santella had bought the classic car six months ago, for cash, and could easily have bought half a dozen other classic cars with the money he made working for his daddy.

Jack Santella was the only son of John 'Big John' Santella, a major investor largely responsible for the development of shopping malls in the Central Florida area. Big John also boasted political as well as governmental ties. Most important, he was a very close friend and associate of Giuseppe 'Jo-Jo' Lanza, one of Central Florida's major crime bosses and owner of six of Orlando's most successful men's clubs, eight of its best restaurants, one of its tallest buildings and two of its most prestigious golf courses.

Being obsessed with classic cars since his early teens, Steve went to a show about eight months ago and met a friend of one of his managers, a man calling himself Mr. Smith. When Smith learned what Steve did for a living, he took him aside and quietly explained that if he wanted to earn a few extra bucks, all he had to do was let someone know how things were going in AF from time to time. If something of a sensitive nature came up, one carefully directed phone call would cause a sizeable check to appear like magic in his personal bank account.

Being honest, Steve originally balked at the idea. But a few weeks later, when suddenly forced to come up with several grand to replace the transmission in his ancient TransAm, he reassessed the situation.

This latest bit of information could definitely be classified as sensitive. And it created very little risk. It involved a Jane Doe. A bag lady. Someone without family, ties, or resources. Someone nobody even cared about.

He glanced at his watch – 12:46. He was overdue for lunch anyway. He logged off, left the office, and went out to his brand-new black Lexus, where he could make his call in total privacy.

***

His muscular body already lightly seared by the early afternoon sun, Arthur P. Radner adjusted his shades just as Jenna, tastefully-tanned in her microscopic black bikini, brought over his drink. Half orange juice, half cranberry, a slice of lemon and lime, two maraschino cherries, and a straw. The perfect drink for a healthy bladder and good kidneys – two very important organs most people overlooked nowadays.

Jenna handed him the glass. Her large silicone specials pressed tightly against the thin scrap of material holding them at bay. Her delicious lavender scent gently brushed his face. He took the glass and sipped, watching her as she sashayed back toward the French doors leading to his comfortable air-conditioned two-bedroom apartment.

No one splashed in the pool at the moment. A few oldsters sat at a table on the other side, just outside the rec room entrance, chattering away beneath their straw hats. He thought about spending the next hour in the weight room. Yesterday was 'chest and back' day. He was still somewhat sore after those repeated bench presses with two-fifty on the rack. Today he could work his arms. A few sets of pushdowns, heavy curls, and several sets with the wall pulleys, blasting the hell out of his delts.

He needed a shower more than exercise. Jenna had given him enough strenuous activity for the rest of the day. He decided on a massage. It was up to Jenna if she wanted to earn the extra cash. A grand a day was a lot of money, but a guy just couldn't put a price on *some* things.

He decided to soak up the rays for another half-hour and have a long, cool shower before enjoying one of Jenna's body massages. For added enjoyment, he'd pop Tchaikovsky's *1812* into the CD player. Then, after a small steak tartare and a bowl of sliced peaches, it would be time for bed.

He hadn't had an assignment in weeks and found himself getting antsy. He didn't like being antsy because it gave him too much time to think. When he spent his time thinking, he grew depressed. No one should think that much. He began realizing just how many mindless dregs inhabited the planet, and it made him claustrophobic and uncomfortable. But he couldn't help it. The only thing that eased his mind was that he knew the time would come when he'd be getting paid big money to eliminate some of the dregs.

Still, an intelligent, active guy had to find ways of getting through the dry spells. Pumping iron worked out some of the tension, but there was nothing like the real thing to get the adrenaline flowing. If he didn't land an assignment soon, he was going to have to resort to a little S&M, or find some worthless teens fouling up the city. He enjoyed beating up teens. They were serious dregs, contributing nothing to society. They wandered around, showing off their underwear, robbing people so they could buy drain cleaner to shoot into their systems.

S&M – especially with the right female – also

provided a pleasurable respite. Jenna wasn't a good candidate. She liked rough sex but laid down specific guidelines. No rope, just scarves or tape. And no slapping. She bruised easily. Slipping her an extra grand for each session made no difference. Carrying around bruises and welts was bad for her business.

Art drank more juice and considered his options. The Pleasure Palace and Babes Galore provided a hefty assortment of hookers. However, they were both on the Mob's payroll. And since Art had a good working relationship with that crowd, he didn't want to offend his employers. The Fox Trappe used decent girls, but he'd already entertained two of their most popular ladies, and they knew his face. They'd submit again, but the price would be triple. Some new clubs had opened closer to downtown. He'd heard that a few of the Pleasure Palace's older ladies, no longer the lap-dancing age, had gone to the new places to hook. He could drive on over tonight or tomorrow night and proposition one of them.

Jenna came out carrying his cell phone. She handed it to him.

"Who is it?"

"Wouldn't say." She went back inside.

He put the cell to his ear. "Radner." When he heard the clicks, his face stretched into a wide grin.

"Are you available?" the familiar voice asked.

"Yes."

"We'd appreciate a small favor."

"I'm listening." He remained smiling. A 'small

111

favor' often earned him five large.

"One of our employees is giving us trouble. We'd like to remind him who he's working for."

Radner could hardly contain himself. Chills washed down his limbs, making him shiver in the ninety-degree heat. He took a deep breath. *Keep the energy contained.* "How hard would you like him to be reminded?"

"Make him uncomfortable."

***

Sitting in the Mustang, his eyes on the slim, brown-haired figure in the store window a hundred feet straight ahead, C.C. Cross once again grew impatient.

He'd wanted to call Lou Rossen and ask more about the hit-and-run. But if he sounded too eager, Rossen would be suspicious. This wasn't his case, so why was he interested? C.C. had already gone out on a limb asking Rossen about Lindsay Foreman. It was a smart tactic, making it a guy-thing. Otherwise, Rossen would have asked questions. Rossen was the honest Abe sort – he didn't approve of cops getting down and dirty with scum. Rossen, like everyone else, realized cops couldn't get anywhere unless they lowered themselves to the same level of the people they were trying to put away. He just didn't like it. And if Rossen ever discovered just how down and dirty C.C. had actually gone, the big cop wouldn't hesitate to pull strings to have C.C. investigated by IAD.

Down and dirty. That's what it was in the

beginning, anyway. C.C. couldn't help it if the case he'd been working last year had turned sour. Working undercover put him waist-deep in scum. He'd had to take the chance that his sources were reliable and his snitches were trustworthy. C.C.'s lead had taken him dangerously close to the Lanza cocaine pipeline when the bottom fell out. One of his snitches was tortured and killed before he could report his latest discovery. The snitch talked before he died, implicating C.C. The next night, C.C. went looking for him. His tip took him the Pleasure Palace, one of Lanza's strip clubs. He had one drink and one drink only – which turned out to be the worst mistake he'd ever made.

He woke up the next morning in a motel room bed with a dead hooker lying beside him, and a collection of incriminating snapshots spread out on the dresser. The pictures, presumably enhanced with some photo software, clearly showed him strangling the hooker as well as dumping the body of his snitch. The negatives, he was told later, were locked up in a safe place.

C.C. soon discovered how thorough these guys really were. Ten thousand dollars had been deposited anonymously into his checking account. He was then contacted anonymously and told to supply sensitive information about a certain drug sting. Otherwise, copies of his bank records – as well as the photos – would be sent to OPD, the FBI, and the *Sentinel*.

After much regret and inner turmoil, C.C. supplied the information. The next day, another ten thousand was deposited in his account. This same procedure happened on a sporadic basis during the next few months, until the new baby-blue Audi convertible was delivered to his front door just weeks ago. He couldn't believe how low he'd sunk. He'd started out trying to be the best cop he could and ended up on the Mob's payroll.

For the last few months, he'd made the best of it. He'd supplied them with the necessary information, altering a crucial fact or two to keep them from being too successful. Several of his tips had resulted in arrests. When questioned, he claimed that his information, at the time, was totally accurate. He'd been beaten up because of it, but enjoyed the satisfaction of knowing he'd gotten back at them – at least in a small way.

But now he'd come to the very worst place of all. Down and dirty didn't even begin to describe this one. He had to shadow an innocent young girl and do what was necessary to get her out of the picture. How was he supposed to tell a nice person that she'd jeopardized her life by helping an old woman? How could he convince an honest young lady that the good deed she'd done might get her killed?

Lindsay Foreman stood behind the register, doing her job. Nice kid. Sweet, shy. He could sense all that when he'd peeled Pockets Sheldon off her the day before. He hadn't expected those large almond eyes to zero in on him. It had been a long time since a woman looked at him that way. Her gaze and her smile actually made him feel like he *wasn't* dirty. A miraculous accomplishment, to say the least, and one that hadn't happened in ages.

This was by far his toughest job, and certainly the most distasteful. He'd rather go unarmed into a den of crystal meth cookers than do anything to this girl. He didn't kill people, but revealing information that resulted in a death, in his view, was the same thing. It would happen to this girl, and he wanted to shoot himself for getting her involved. It was bad timing for both of them, his being right there in the station at that particular moment. If he had it to do over, he would have kept his mouth shut. But if the monsters pulling the strings of his life had found out where he was during the initial report, they would have nailed his ass.

C.C. knew they'd find out. They always did. Cops chattered away like old ladies. C.C. was certain a handful of cops, perhaps even more, were tied to a secret 'dark side' of the Department owned and operated by a network of politicians, attorneys, and high-powered businessmen that had snatched up large chunks of Central Florida since the mid-seventies. One phone call would be all it took to stop his clock.

He had to invade Lindsay Foreman's life again. The staged scam at the Corral had, as intended, made him the good guy. She wouldn't be wary of him and might even open up to him. This made him feel even dirtier. Rock bottom. The worst place to be. He knew he couldn't possibly go lower, but it sure didn't make him feel any better about it.

He decided to let the air out of her front tire.

That tactic would take about a minute and could be done without drawing attention to himself. Her Honda was parked off to the side, at the end of the store. An older model Volvo was parked next to it, on the driver's side. It would hide him from view. When she came out of the store, she'd see the flat. He'd be coming out of the Savings & Loan right then and would happily assist her. She'd be grateful enough to have a drink with him, and he could get to know her and find out what she wanted out of all this.

They'd given him forty-eight hours to do this, but if they didn't see sufficient progress in the first twelve, they'd swoop down. He actually expected a call any time now. If he didn't give them what they wanted, he'd have something to worry about.

He opened the car door, then noticed movement directly behind him. A cold gun barrel pressed firmly against the back of his neck, turning his skin hot. "Get back in," a soft deep voice said.

***

The information his employer had given was correct. The address in question showed the target's tag number on the silver Mustang in the parking lot. Art Radner didn't know the name of the target, but that didn't matter. The description was enough.

A heavy rush of excitement shimmered down his limbs when the target opened his car door. It had been much too long since his last assignment. He was relieved to discover his reflexes were as lightning-quick as ever. The S&M sessions and the iron-pumping kept his senses sharp and clear, but

116

there was nothing like the real thing to keep the mind alert, the reflexes sharp, and the energy level high. He enjoyed the moment – which, for him, had always been on the same level as an orgasm.

This was strictly a scare tactic, but it didn't matter because the hunt always eclipsed every other aspect of the game. As an added bonus, he was allowed to damage the target a little. He *loved* the perks that came with his profession.

He climbed in directly behind the target and kept the unregistered Beretta .25 pressed snugly against the man's neck – just in case he decided to get cute. "Close the door."

The target did as ordered, and watched him in the rearview, but that wouldn't help him figure out who he was. Art's black baseball cap, large-rimmed shades, and fake stash concealed his bleached buzz cut and most of his face.

"What do you want?" the target asked uneasily.

"I was told to pay you a little visit."

"I'm in the middle of a job."

"Apparently you're taking too long."

"I had forty-eight hours. That gives me until–"

"Well, judging from my surprise visit and the gun kissing the back of your neck, I guess you could say there's been a change in the game plan."

The target stiffened. Strands of his neck muscles quivered beneath the Beretta. Art could sense the fear emanating freely from the man's pores as he said, "I ... have to go easy with this. Otherwise–"

"You've got twenty-four hours."

"I can't *possibly* wrap this up in twenty-four hours unless–"

"I don't care. I'm only here to remind you that if you don't get it done, I'll be taking over. And believe me, I work fast."

The target swallowed hard. "Some things *can't* be done fast."

"Like I said, I don't care. If I step in, that's when you'll know your time is up."

No reply.

"Did you hear what I said?"

"I'm not deaf–"

Art slapped him on the back on his head. "Wrong answer, jackass."

The man sighed. "All right, we'll play your little game. I heard you. Is that better?"

"Much." Art loved it when they upped the ante without realizing it. It was almost like they were giving him permission to hurt them. "And since you want to play a *game*, let's make this fun. Are you left- or right-handed?"

The man cringed.

"I asked you a question."

"Why do you–"

"If you don't answer me, I'll make the decision for you."

"I'm ... right-handed."

"Good. Now hold up your left hand."

"What the–"

Art swatted him again. "You're *not* making me a happy camper."

Trembling, the man raised his left hand. An

118

onyx pinky ring covered nearly half the little finger.

Damn. Complications. "Take the ring off."

The man half-turned. "This ring was a birthday gift. It was–"

"I didn't ask where you got it, did I?"

With a deep sigh, he pulled it off. He held it in his palm for a moment before handing it over.

"I don't *want* the ring, jackass. What do you think I am? A common *thief*?" Some people just didn't have a clue. "Put it in your pocket."

The man complied.

"Good boy. Now hold up your hand." Art took the little finger between his thumb and forefinger. With a lightning twist of his wrist, he snapped the little finger at the second joint. Arching his back, the man stood up in the seat and howled. His head thumped the roof. He doubled up and gasped in pain.

"That should help you remember. Understand?" Moaning, the man cradled his wounded hand. "I'll take that as a yes."

Art rapped him on the back of the head with the butt of the Beretta. With a grunt, the man collapsed, bumping his forehead on the rim of the steering wheel.

Art got out of the car, crossed the lot, and returned to his van. He got in and pulled off his mustache, shades, and cap. A wide grin covered his face in the rear-view mirror. Working for the right people made life *so* invigorating.

Chapter 15

At six-thirty, Lindsay closed and locked the shop door. She flipped the *OPEN* sign around so *CLOSED* could be seen from the street. She returned to the register and emptied the cash drawer, then carried the white sack of uncounted money into the office. Still doing her bookkeeping at the computer, Sarah looked up and asked, "How'd we do today?"

"Pretty much our usual business." Lindsay placed the sack on the counter and sat down.

"Really? It seemed a little slow to me."

"It picked up as soon as you went to lunch." Lindsay opened the sack.

"Figures. By the way, you don't have to count that." Sarah smiled behind her reading glasses. "I'll do it. Go on home."

"I really don't mind. Anyway, it's my job."

Sarah drank some coffee from the white mug with *WORLD'S GREATEST AUNT* inscribed in brown lettering on the side. "I have some paperwork to finish, anyway."

A dark gray cloud tinged with flecks of red floated directly above Sarah's head. Even without the colors, Lindsay could tell something was wrong. Sarah wasn't the most happy-go-lucky person in the world, but didn't usually let much bother her. Edward was the only person who really pushed her buttons.

Lindsay figured her boss might actually *want* to

120

be by herself. But she felt she should at least offer. "Couldn't you use the company?" she asked.

"It's all right. Tell your mom I said hi."

Lindsay walked out of the shop into another warm, muggy evening. She unlocked her car door, slid in, and put her lightweight jacket and purse on the seat beside her. Before firing up the engine, she decided to give Momma a quick call and ask if she should stop on the way home to pick up anything. Flipping her cell open, she glanced in her rear-view mirror and stiffened. A dirty silver Mustang was parked about five spaces behind her, in front of the short chain-link fence bordering the lot. The driver's door was partly open. Even from her vantage point she could see someone slumped over the wheel. The figure didn't move.

Her cell gripped in her hand, Lindsay got out of the Honda and crossed the lot. A man in faded jeans and a loose-fitting light-gray tee-shirt sat bent over, cradling his left hand. When he noticed her approaching him, he sat up sharply.

Lindsay gasped. He was the man who'd helped her outside the Corral yesterday evening. The little finger on his left hand was black, swollen and twisted outward almost perpendicular to the ridge of his hand. "You're hurt," she said, quickly realizing how stupid her statement was.

His deep-blue eyes filled the sockets. The colors around him swarmed like a starburst – red swirls, washed-out orange, gray, black and white. An avalanche of emotions. "I'm ... fine." His voice was hoarse and weak – a mere whisper barely audible over the rush-hour traffic roaring down Semoran.

She couldn't leave him like this. He needed medical attention, and he needed it quickly. "Your finger ... looks pretty banged up. Is there something I can do to help you?"

"I ... need to get ... away." He glanced behind him, then struggled for the ignition. His body trembled. He could barely grasp the key. In the process, he bumped his injured finger and howled in agony. A burst of black appeared brightly amidst his colors.

"I have to get you to a doctor."

"No!" His eyes grew even larger. His colors deepened, especially the tufts of white. "*Please* ... I'm fine. I just–"

"You're *not* fine."

"You ... don't understand–"

"You're coming with me."

He tried protesting, but was in too much pain to make much of a fuss. *Why is he being so stubborn?* She gingerly grabbed his left arm and helped him out onto the pavement. His knees buckled. He could barely stand. She shifted to his other side, took his good arm, and draped it over her shoulders for support. Then, with a swing of her hip, she forced his door shut and directed him carefully back to her car.

***

Outside the ER, slouched in a chair three seats down from an elderly man in a wheelchair, Lindsay could not stop thinking about the man's broken

122

finger. It looked as if it had been caught in something and snapped like a twig. She had to stop thinking about it – she was getting queasy.

In an attempt to focus on something else, she glanced in the old man's direction. A swarm of filmy black tendrils flickered above his shiny bald head.

He grinned weakly. "Family?" he asked.

"Pardon?"

He pointed to the ER door. "In there."

"Just a friend." Her thoughts shifted back to the man she'd brought in, but this time she wondered who he was – how he'd gotten hurt and why he'd refused help. Was it a macho thing? Judging by how he'd acted outside the Corral, he was definitely the hero type. Such men all acted in the same fashion – brave and stupid around women, reckless and arrogant around other guys. He could have tripped on a crack in the pavement and fallen, landing on his hand. A stupid accident, to be sure ... but why refuse someone's help when he needed it?

He obviously felt foolish. In the eyes of such a man, clumsiness could be a sign of weakness. Macho men were strong, well-coordinated machines oozing testosterone. Any macho man worth his salt wouldn't admit to something 'unmanly,' like falling on his butt. And he certainly wouldn't admit to pain.

But what about those colors swarming around him? A flurry of them, with thick strands of white mixed in. Fear? Maybe. But why was he afraid? And why did he keep looking around in his car, then hers as she brought him here? His colors yesterday had also been tinted with tufts of white. Had he been afraid while he was pulling Hi away from her?

She still wasn't totally sure of her interpretations. She hadn't done any research on colors of emotions and moods. But this man definitely seemed frightened and uneasy.

Down the corridor, everyone scurried around, pushing gurneys, carrying files, meds – just like Friday night when she'd been here with Maisie. This was the second time in four days that she'd brought someone to the ER. Had this same strange phenomenon happened to Maisie when she'd first discovered her special gift? Was the gift itself a kind of metaphysical magnet, drawing certain types of people directly into its path?

The man in the wheelchair had lowered his head. He looked like he'd fallen asleep. *Had* he? She immediately got up to make sure. He stirred, yawning. Lindsay sat back down.

Her cell buzzed. It was Momma. As usual, she sounded anxious. "Where *are* you, baby? It's after seven."

Lindsay took a breath and decided to just come right out with it. "I'm at the hospital."

"My God. What *happened*?"

"I found a man outside the store."

"Whaddya mean, you *found a man*?"

"He was sitting in his car in the parking lot. His finger was broken."

"How'd he break his finger?"

"I don't know."

"Who is he?"

"I don't know."

"Baby..."

"I know, I know. I should've found out more about him, but he wasn't very talkative. He was in a lot of pain. His finger was all twisted and black and blue. I thought it would be better if I got him to the hospital."

"Why are you still there?"

"I thought it would be less stressful for him if he saw me when he came out of the ER. I was going to drive him back to his car so he didn't have to spend money for a cab."

"Baby, you're *much* too nice for your own good."

"I know how I'd feel if I was in his shoes. I'd really appreciate it if someone helped me."

"You don't know anything about him."

He helped me yesterday when I needed it, she wanted to say. *He pulled a weird guy off me and didn't even want anything in return.* But she knew better than mention it. "He seems like a nice guy."

"You just said he didn't talk much."

"I can tell he's nice."

"How?"

"I have this feeling."

"Baby, you're not only too *nice*–"

"I know. I'm naïve."

"We've discussed this before. How long do you intend to stay there?"

"He should be coming out pretty soon."

"Let me know if you need me."

"I will."

"And be careful."

"I'm in a *hospital*, Momma."

"I'm talking about *him*. He's a *man*. You can't trust people these days – especially men."

Suddenly tired, she said, "I'll be careful," and hung up.

Momma was right about some things. Because of Dad, she'd probably always be bitter. Lindsay couldn't blame her because she also resented Dad leaving them. Momma was right – you just couldn't trust anyone these days. Nevertheless, Lindsay had a good feeling about this man.

***

Hospitals always made C.C. queasy.

This one was no exception. But at least the stuff they'd just given him had eased the thumping in his hand to a distant hum.

The nurse carefully wrapped the bandage over the splint on his little finger. She was about fifty and attractive in a Barbara Bush sort of way. She kept giving him the same sort of look his mother gave him years ago, when he'd done something stupid.

He'd told them he'd caught his finger in the car door. He couldn't tell them what really happened. As an undercover cop, he was accustomed to lying and had learned to be quite convincing. He could tell something was on this woman's mind. "Go ahead and say it," he said.

She got out the tape and cut two slender strips. "What do you want me to say?"

"Tell me how stupid I was to catch my finger in a car door."

"What makes you think I was going to say that?"

"Those looks you've been giving me."

She blinked. "I thought I'd spare you."

"From what?"

"Judging from the looks you're giving *me*, I'd say you're beating yourself up more than enough for the both of us."

He supposed his expressions and body language had been giving off bad vibes, but she was absolutely right. He wanted to kick himself for letting someone sneak up on him. He was a cop. Being alert was a requirement for survival.

"Is that your girlfriend out there in the hall?"

Damn. He'd hoped Lindsay had already left. "She's still there?"

"Since you came in." Her slim black brows bumped together. "You expected her to drop you off and leave?"

"I don't know her."

"She brought you in."

"She just happened to be walking by when I caught my finger."

"I should've suspected you two weren't a couple."

"Why's that?"

"She's too young for you."

That was something he didn't need to hear. "Thanks."

"You're what? Thirty-nine? Forty?"

He groaned. Whoever said women were sensitive didn't know what the hell they were talking about. "Thirty-four, thanks very much."

"Sorry." She smiled sheepishly. "You ... look a little rough around the edges."

"I lead a hard life. Ask any of my ex-wives."

"I'm sure they'd tell me. But it *is* a good thing the young lady happened by. You'd have trouble driving like that. The doctor said it was a simple fracture, but could have turned nasty if you'd waited longer to come in."

"It feels pretty bad."

"You saw the X-ray. You did a fine job breaking it."

"Thank you." He stared at the bandage. The man who'd done this was very dangerous. If he could calmly break a man's finger as just part of a 'game,' he wouldn't hesitate to do something worse to Lindsay Foreman.

"Whoever that girl is, she's very nice – especially for someone you don't know. She asked me about half an hour ago how you were doing."

He had to keep Lindsay out of this. Which meant going out there as soon as he was finished here and telling her thanks for the ride, but now she could drive back home. But he knew he couldn't leave her alone. They'd sent someone to remind him of what they wanted. All that did was remind him how hard they played. In their eyes, they'd done him a favor by giving him the option of clearing this up. If he didn't succeed, they'd handle it themselves. He had to somehow convince Lindsay to forget about the hit-and-run and get it off the books. They didn't care how he did it; they just wanted it to go away. How the hell was he supposed to make that happen without hurting Lindsay? He had no idea; he just knew he had to find a way. Since he'd put her in jeopardy in the first place, it was up to him to see she got out of this safely.

The man they'd sent was obviously a pro. He'd used a disguise. The black hat, black sunglasses and fake black mustache suggested he was probably fair in complexion. C.C. didn't see the gun but could tell by its small barrel size that it was probably a .22 or .25. Pros always used small calibers for close work. The small size made the gun easy to conceal and dispose of. Small calibers also did extensive damage. And when the slugs fragmented, they were almost impossible to trace.

What frightened him most about all this was the man's attitude. He stayed exceedingly calm and almost sounded like he was having fun. That told him the man was mental. Anyone who enjoyed hurting people definitely had a few screws loose.

The nurse was behind him. She didn't seem to be doing anything. He turned to look at her. "Something else on your mind?"

"You did say you caught your finger in your car door?"

"Yeah..."

"Did you happen to fall down and hit the back of your head when you pulled your hand out?"

Shit. He'd forgotten about that. Now he had to think up some safe way of pacifying her until he could get out of here. Otherwise, she'd want to report this to the police. "If you must know, I was mugged."

"Mugged?"

"You know. Somebody hits you over the head and takes your wallet."

Her face squeezed into a collection of wavy wrinkles. "You were *mugged*?" For some reason, she didn't seem able to wrap her mind around that one. "So ... they took your wallet?"

"Didn't have enough time."

"How much time does a mugger need to take your wallet?"

She was becoming annoying, but he knew he should be used to this. After all, he had been married three times. "Someone was probably walking by right after it happened. It was outside a strip mall. Customers, you know."

She straightened, moved behind him again, and applied something cold and medicinal-smelling to the bump on his head. A bright flash of pain made him wince and pull away.

"Sorry. The swelling's not so bad. I'll just clean it up and put a small bandage over it–"

"It's all right." He got up and staggered in a warm wave of dizziness. "I've ... been hit in the head before."

"You all right?"

He leaned against the table until the dizziness passed. "I'll be fine once I can get away from that evil nurse and her tray filled with implements of torture." He blinked. "Oh. That's right. It's you, isn't it?"

"So, you fancy yourself a comedian."

130

"Almost. I'm a cop."

"Cops don't usually get mugged, do they?"

"They do if they don't have an extra set of eyes in the back of their head."

"What do you do? I can't help noticing you're not in uniform."

"It's laundry day."

She just sighed.

He lowered his voice. "I'm undercover, all right?"

"I guess that explains the attitude. Now let me get something to cover that bump."

"It's all right. Really." He held up the Vicodin prescription the doctor had scratched out for him. "This'll take care of that."

"You sure you don't want it covered?"

"I'm fine. I've got a hard head."

"I'll agree with you on that..."

***

The Foreman girl smiled at him from her chair out in the hall. C.C. cursed under his breath. *Damn. Anyone else would've been gone by now.*

Still smiling, she stood up and came closer. "How are you?" she asked, glancing at his bandaged hand.

C.C. instantly grew uncomfortable in her presence. Her softness and innocence made him feel despicable. He hated himself for setting her up with Pockets. Now things had changed so drastically. The people calling the shots wanted him to finish this quickly. He knew exactly how they operated. They'd already sent someone after him – a definite sign they were desperate. And when they were desperate, they didn't like waiting.

He had to get away from her and work on some other way of handling this. The less she knew about all this, about him, about what she'd actually done, the better off she'd be. She was a sweet kid. He had to do whatever he could to see she didn't get hurt.

"I'm fine," he said. "Thanks for the ride." He started walking down the hall, toward the exit sign.

"Wait." She caught up to him. "Are you done here?"

He kept walking. "All done. Yep. They fixed me up good. Even gave me a prescription for some dynamite meds."

"You need a ride back to your car, don't you?"

"I'll catch a cab."

She stopped walking. "What's wrong?"

"Nothing." He kept moving, forcing his attention from her – from those big brown eyes. Her softness. Her innocence.

"You're making me feel like I've done something ... *wrong*," she called after him.

Shit, shit, shit. The hurt in her voice tugged at him. He stopped walking and turned. He couldn't leave her thinking she'd done something wrong. She hadn't – not really. In a sane world, she'd done something anyone with a big heart would have done. But from what he'd seen during the last twenty years, the world was anything *but* sane. "Why do you think you've done something wrong?"

She approached him slowly, the sadness in her eyes pulling him in even more. "You were sitting in your car with a broken finger. You fought me when I tried to help. You didn't want me to bring you here at all. Now you're fighting me again. All I want is to drive you back to your car."

This was turning sour quickly. Her eyes bored into him. He felt helpless, immobile, unable to move away, yet not wanting to. He had the feeling she'd penetrated his spirit. But his practical side hastily stepped in. She couldn't possibly have penetrated his spirit. No one could do something like that. No one would *want* to. It was his guilt working. His guilt, and his fear of what could happen if the bad guys decided she was a major threat.

"Is it *me*?" she asked.

"It's not you."

Her eyes lifted for a moment. He suspected she'd glanced at his forehead. "Why are you lying?"

He cringed. Somehow she *did* know what was going on. But that wasn't possible. She didn't even *know* him – how could she tell he was lying? His feeling of helplessness grew, causing a surge of warmth flowing down his body. "I'm ... not lying," he said firmly.

"Yes you are."

"Listen, miss, I–"

"My name is Lindsay. Lindsay Foreman."

"Listen, Miss Foreman–"

"And your name is...?"

"Pardon me?"

"You have one, don't you?"

"Of course."

133

"What is it?"

"My name's not important."

"Don't you use it once in a while? To sign checks? Identify yourself on the phone?"

"Of course I use it."

"Then it's important."

"Not to *you*."

She shrugged. "You know *mine*..."

"You volunteered it."

"You helped me yesterday, and I'm grateful."

Once again, he felt like a heel and an asshole for causing all this. "That was nothing. I was in the neighborhood anyway."

"Not many people help one another nowadays." Her eyes grew, glistening in the fluorescents. "When someone helps someone else, don't you think they should at least find out each other's name?"

This was getting *way* out of hand. He wanted to tell her to forget about what happened yesterday. He wanted her to forget about him entirely.

"*Please* tell me and I'll shut up and–"

"Cross. Charles Cross."

"What do people call you? Charles? Chuck?"

"Everyone calls me C.C."

"Hello, C.C." She held out her hand.

It was large for a girl, but delicate and warm. His entire mood softened as he took it. And despite his efforts, he found himself smiling. She smiled back. Her eyes relaxed. Tiny clefts appeared at each corner of her mouth. She had a very pretty smile. Her whole body seemed to give off a warm glow.

Even after she'd released his hand, her warmth remained in his palm. His hand closed into a tight fist to keep it there.

"My car's outside."

His practical side made another abrupt entrance. *You'd better start treating her badly. You have to make her hate you. You've had plenty of practice making women hate you. Act like the asshole you really are and get out of this girl's life while there's still time.*

"I'll get a cab." He turned away again. It was much harder this time, but he imagined her lying in a ditch somewhere, the victim of a drive-by engineered by the same people who'd sent the sadistic pro after him earlier. He hurried for the exit, this time with a fresh urgency.

"It's really no trouble," she called after him.

He didn't reply.

"It *is* me, isn't it?"

Dammit! Dammit to hell. Dammit, dammit, dammit...

***

Lindsay sat in the driver's seat, waiting at the light just beyond the hospital entrance, trying to be subtle about peeking at the colors hovering above C.C.'s head.

His bandaged hand in his lap, C.C. stared straight ahead. Even in the darkness of the car, his colors blurred the top of his head. Shades of light red, gray, and a little pink. He was obviously very edgy.

He'd lied to her back at the hospital. His colors

135

– deep-red, with wisps of black drifting through it – cried out strongly, passionately. But his eyes also gave him away. He couldn't focus on her and kept turning away.

Something about her troubled him. She wondered if it had anything to do with what had happened outside the Corral. He was upset then, too. Was it because he hadn't wanted to help? That didn't make sense. He could've just walked on by, as everyone else would have done. But he hadn't. He'd come to her aid.

So what troubled him? The fact that she'd helped him, taken him to the hospital? She knew she'd been pushy, but was concerned about his injury, about helping him. And in his weakened condition, he couldn't fight her sufficiently. Maybe the situation intimidated him, and bringing it up right now might make things worse. But she had to start up a conversation. She was uncomfortable with the silence. It wouldn't hurt to ask about his injury, would it? It might even clear the air. "You never said how you broke your finger."

He didn't reply.

"You don't have to tell me if you don't want to. I know I ask too many questions. It's just that, well, I don't like to see anyone hurting, and–"

"Caught it in the damned car door," he said, still looking straight ahead.

The red mist above his head deepened. She could hardly see his short, wavy brown hair beneath it. Why would he lie about all this? And why was he so angry?

He turned and watched her. Even though his blue eyes were just glints of light in the darkness, she could feel their intensity. "Something wrong?"

"What?"

"You were staring."

She stiffened. "Sorry."

"Is my hair messed up?"

"It's ... fine." Feeling flushed, she turned back to the road ahead. *Better watch it*. She didn't want to give herself away. She needed to concentrate on her driving. The white van behind her nearly tapped her bumper.

"Is the lump that noticeable?"

"What lump?"

"Now you're being cute."

"You mean ... on the back of your head?"

"That's the one."

She'd noticed it at the hospital when he'd turned away from her but hadn't mentioned it. Now that he'd brought it up, she was curious, but knew better than start another argument. "A little."

"I lost my balance after I pulled my finger out of the damned door and fell on my ass."

"And hit your head?"

"You're good," he said sourly.

He was obviously sensitive about all this. But why did the red mist thicken? She couldn't visualize a man like him getting his hand caught in a car door, pulling it out, and falling on his butt. Judging by how he'd handled the drunken guy the day before, she considered him much too coordinated for an accident as silly as that.

He turned his attention back to the road ahead. "How'd you know?"

"How'd I know what?"

"How'd you know I was lying to you?"

She swallowed. "When?"

"Back at the hospital. You asked if something was wrong, and I said no, but you knew I was lying."

Lindsay pushed a shaky hand through her hair. She could barely keep from trembling. She couldn't possibly tell him what was going on – he'd think she was crazy. But she had to tell him something. "Sometimes I can tell when someone's lying to me," she said, her voice unsteady.

He sat back in his seat and shook his head.

"What's wrong?"

His laugh was anything but humorous. "You get into a guy's head – someone you don't even know – and ask what's *wrong*?" The red mist had dissipated, replaced now by shards of white mixed with gray and flecks of black.

Fear again. Fear and something else – something she wasn't sure she wanted to know about. Was he afraid of her? Most guys didn't like it when they suspected a girl could do something to their mind.

"I ... didn't get into your head." If she was convincing enough, she might be able to make his colors disappear. "I guess it's intuition. You know, good old *women's* intuition."

"Women don't have any more intuition than men."

"You don't think so?"

"If they did, they wouldn't keep falling for dorks and assholes, would they?"

She stopped at the next light. She certainly couldn't argue with that.

"You know what I mean, so don't act like you don't."

"How do you know *that*?"

"You're a woman, aren't you?"

"Last time I checked, I was."

"I don't know any female older than twelve who hasn't fallen for the wrong guy at least once."

Yep, he definitely knew what he was talking about.

"Who'd *you* fall for?" His eyes searched hers, making her even more uncomfortable. Though the feeling wasn't exactly unpleasant, she forced herself to concentrate on the heavy traffic straight ahead. But at least his colors had ebbed into the darkness.

The good times she'd shared with David flashed before her eyes. The special evenings they'd spent in front of the TV, watching their favorite movies. The times they'd gone flea-marketing. David's minty smell after a shower. The tender way he held her. His touch. That special way his cheeks flushed whenever he wanted sex. Her mouth opened, and before she even realized it, she was talking about him. "He was good-looking and bright and sensitive and spontaneous. He could make me laugh and cry. Sometimes he made me forget what time it was, what day it was. Even *where* I was."

"What happened?"

She didn't reply. The throbbing in her heart and the coldness in her limbs had started up as soon as she went back to that time in her life. The heavy feeling of cold emptiness returned quickly, clinging to her like a suffocating blanket just like the day he'd walked out on her. She wondered if it would ever go away completely.

"I shouldn't have brought it up," he said.

"I can't even talk about this with my mother. Why should I talk about it with a total stranger?"

"Mothers aren't good for stuff like this. Strangers can see things more objectively. You can't talk about that guy to your mom. She already thinks he's an asshole for what he did – right?"

Momma said she never cared for David because of his thick black beard. She said she hated beards because the only bearded men she'd ever known weren't trustworthy. Lindsay had always thought Momma actually liked him and didn't appreciate it that David didn't show *her* any interest. Finally Lindsay shrugged and offered lamely, "She never liked him."

"So what can she tell you that'll actually help?"

"What can *you* tell me that will help?"

"You haven't told me anything, so how should I know?"

"He ... David ... grew tired of me." It was the first time she'd said that to anyone and was surprised she could blurt it out without falling apart or crying. Maybe it was because C.C. was a stranger and wouldn't judge her. And he seemed interested. But it still hurt. She supposed it always would.

"Been there," he said. "Several times."

"Wives?"

He held up three fingers on his right hand. "You're looking at a three-time loser."

She gaped in surprise. That didn't make sense. A good-looking guy like him, obviously bright, fit, and knew how to talk to women. "What happened?"

"Which time?"

"Start with number one."

He shrugged. "Said I was too frightening to be around sometimes."

Lindsay had already experienced that. Those eyes could turn to ice with a glance. Even without the advantage of seeing his colors, his attitude and body language spoke strongly. "How about your second?"

"That woman could make a guy ready for the nuthouse without even trying."

"I take it she was ... complicated," she said.

"She wanted sex when I didn't, and when she didn't, I did. But when she wanted it, she always got it."

"I don't understand," Lindsay said cautiously, not quite sure what he meant. Men were usually more straightforward about sex, giving it so much importance in their lives, while women oftentimes viewed sex differently. It was something they did to get attention or affection ... or a way to get things they wanted. And sometimes it was a weapon, giving them the only sense of control they might have in a relationship. But she didn't want to get too personal. After all, he was a stranger.

141

"Sometimes she got it without my help," he explained. Lindsay grimaced, finally understanding. "It took me a while to figure it out. And by the time I did..." He shrugged.

Lindsay was about to ask him about wife number three when she glanced in her mirror. The headlights that had been directly behind them since they'd left the hospital were still there. The white van remained close.

"What's wrong?" C.C. asked.

"I'm not positive, but I think we're ... being followed."

He sat bolt upright.

"Like I said, I'm not positive." His quick reaction had frightened her. So did the flakes of white appearing above his head. "Is there a reason someone would–"

He stared into the side mirror. "Turn there."

"Where?"

"Right there." He pointed at the 7-Eleven entrance less than twenty yards to their right.

"The 7-Eleven?"

"Yep. Do a quick ninety."

"Ninety?"

"*Degrees*, dammit. *Now!*"

The urgency in his voice jolted through her. Squealing tires, she made a sharp right, slammed on the brakes, then inched past a gas pump.

The white van whizzed past.

***

"Go around to the rear of the building." C.C. nervously watched the passing traffic. "Park near

142

the dumpsters."

"What's happening?" Lindsay asked uneasily.

"Just do as I say."

She stared at him in her usual unsettling way, then did as he asked. He could tell she was frightened. Her hands trembled gripping the wheel.

He waited patiently while she parked the Honda. It was time to do a quick check to see if the van had circled back. He had no idea who was driving. He didn't think it was the psycho who'd broken his finger. He pushed open the passenger door.

"What are you ... where are you going?" she asked. Her eyes were enormous in the darkness. Her hands gripped the wheel even after she'd put the car into park. He knew he had to do whatever it took to keep her from freaking out.

"I'll be right back," he said. "Want anything from the store?"

"The *store*?"

"That little brick building right behind us." If he could make light of all this, maybe she'd calm down. He'd done it before. It made everything go much smoother, staying calm. Panic and fear were contagious. "Potato chips? Ice cream? They sell beer too. What brand do you like? I'll–"

"Are you joking?"

He resisted the urge to glance around for the van. "I thought, since we're here–"

"Why'd we stop?"

"You said you thought a van was following us." He finally looked around casually, just to assure himself the van hadn't circled back.

143

"Yes, I did. And apparently you thought so too."

"But the van obviously wasn't following us, was it?"

She frowned. "What makes you say that?"

"It went right on by after we turned off." Those big brown eyes stayed on him as he asked, "You see him anywhere now?"

"No..."

He shrugged, still trying to downplay the situation. "Then I'd say we're safe in assuming he's gone. He probably wasn't even following us in the first place. Traffic's murder tonight. He was just going the same direction we were."

"C.C., what's going on?"

"Going *on*?"

"What's happening? Why are you acting like this?"

"Like what?"

She sighed, obviously exasperated. "You were angry before, at the hospital. You were angry when we left the hospital. When I told you about the van, you got nervous and told me to pull in here. You acted like you were in a panic. Now you're acting ... funny."

"Funny?"

She nodded. "And a little scary."

He shrugged again. "I haven't eaten since lunch. Aren't you hungry? It's eight o'clock."

Those eyes bored into him. He could tell she knew something was up. "You must think I'm a real ditz."

144

"I know you're not a ditz. I can tell you're smart, perceptive–"

"So why are you treating me like I just dropped off the turnip truck?"

"I didn't realize I was doing that."

"You're trying to make me feel stupid, but it's not working."

"Sorry."

"I accept your apology. Now ... tell me what's going on."

He sighed. "I guess I was trying to spare you."

"From what?"

"In case that van really *was* following us."

She gave him another probing stare, this one even deeper. "C.C., who *are* you?"

He closed the door. This was not only one bright girl, she was the kind a guy couldn't lie to. That David character she'd mentioned probably got tired of having his mind probed. But this wasn't the time to analyze stuff like that. He had to focus and find some way of smoothing this over, of making things right for her. And maybe that meant telling her the truth – at least some of it. "I'm a cop."

She sat back in her seat. She said nothing for a while. Then, finally, she nodded. "You really are, aren't you?"

"I just said I was."

"But you've been lying to me. It's hard to believe anything someone says after you've caught them in a lie."

"I've *had* to lie about a few things."

"Why?"

145

"Because of what you've done."

"What ... did I do?"

"That hit-and-run last Friday."

She stiffened. "What ... about it?"

"You shouldn't have reported it."

"Why not?"

"It can't be on the books."

"Why not?"

"Some important people want it to disappear."

"Important people?"

"People with money and connections. The car you IDed belongs to someone neither of us wants to mess with."

She sat in silence again, watching him – his eyes, his forehead.

"I'm serious," he said.

"I know."

"If you'd just stayed out of it..."

Her eyes flashed. "An innocent old woman was run over and left on the side of the road, like trash. Not one person in the world cared. Hundreds of cars passed, but no one stopped. It bothered me, you know? No one should die like that. And no one should die without someone caring. *No one*."

He didn't reply. The way she'd said it, with such intensity, told him that she would have done what she'd done no matter what, because that was the kind of person she was. It had been a long time since he'd met someone so honest. He had to protect her. He liked her, respected her. And he realized just how much better this world would be if there were more people like her.

146

"That's why I couldn't stay out of it." She sat back in her seat and closed her eyes.

He didn't reply.

"Well? Does that answer your question?" She turned to look at him.

He nodded.

"I suppose you think I'm weird. Well, I don't care. It's the way I am."

He made no comment. There was no need, because he felt the same way. He used to be like that too. It tore him apart, realizing what he'd become, what they'd turned him into.

"Do you still think I should've stayed out of it?" she asked in a little girl's voice.

"No. I don't think that at all."

Her huge eyes stayed on him. "So ... what do we do now?"

He shrugged. "You want some chips while we're here?"

Chapter 16

Sniffing heavily, Ernesto 'the Blade' Medina watched from the rear lot of the motel.

About fifty yards straight ahead, on the other side of the busy highway, the tan Honda sat beside a dumpster behind the 7-Eleven. The view was obscured by shrubbery, a chain link fence, and the passing traffic, but with the aid of the spotlight aimed at the area, the car was fairly visible.

Ernesto pulled a cigarette from his shirt pocket, lit it with his yellow Bic lighter, and sat back. He sniffed again. That last line of coke had fucked up his head real good, but he could still function. He'd been doing coke since high school. It took quite a bit to knock him on his ass.

Watching Cross was the important thing right now, anyway. The detective left the hospital with the skinny brown-haired babe about half an hour ago. Cross was a little fucked up. Looked like someone had done a serious number to his hand. No big surprise. Cross pulled shit only a psycho with a death-wish would do. Everyone knew it would only be a matter of time before Cross stepped on the wrong toes. He'd been snooping around the clubs for too long and made some badass enemies. Clubs belonged to Jo-Jo – strictly off-limits. Whoever pissed off Jo-Jo, that sucker's life wasn't worth a plug nickel.

Ernesto wondered what happened to Cross's hand. When the call came through to tail Cross from

Florida Hospital on Lake Underhill, they hadn't told him anything else. But they never did.

He reported to Solo these days. Solo did things for Jo-Jo and had connections in the DMV and OPD. Ernesto hoped that would work in his favor because of the shitload of moving traffic violations he hadn't paid for yet. He needed someone to take care of them for him, and Solo could easily do it. Solo said he'd do it, but Ernesto had to do a few errands for him first.

The first thing, of course, was to stop reporting to Cross. Cross had been making a nuisance of himself and was headed for a fall. It finally came just a few months ago, some burn Solo and some other big shots cooked up. After giving Cross a few bad tips, Ernesto dropped out of sight.

Cross went down hard. Once he no longer had any clout or credibility, Ernesto showed up again, telling Cross he'd been laying low because of all the shit flying around. Cross bought it, of course. He had to. With no friends left, he had to stay on good terms with whoever was still around. He kept giving Ernesto the same odd jobs, unaware that Ernesto was reporting to Solo. Ernesto's job was simple – tell them everything Cross did and said. And that sure as hell beat sitting at the bottom of Lake Underhill, feet caked in concrete. Besides, Solo paid more than Cross.

His cell buzzed, making him jump. The display made him shake so badly, he nearly dropped the phone in his lap. With a trembling hand, he answered the call. "Yeah?"

149

"Where the hell are you?" demanded Solo.

Solo didn't need to know where he was. Ernesto wasn't in the mood to be tailed as well. "I'm a few streets down from Colonial–"

"What the hell you doing? Whacking off?"

"I'm keeping an eye out. That's what you told me to do."

"You know damn well what you're supposed to be doing. Cross around? Or did you lose the son of a bitch?"

"I know where he is." Damn, he hated when they treated him like a moron.

"Where, *exactly*? And make this good."

"I'm looking at him right now."

"He see *you*?"

"I kept far enough behind. Lotsa traffic tonight." Cross *had* spotted him. Ernesto knew that when the chick had suddenly pulled off. He'd been much too close, but the asshole behind him made it impossible to put on his brakes and fall back in time. Zipping past was the safest thing to do. That was something else they didn't have to know.

"What's he doing right now?"

"Sitting in a car with a chick."

"What chick?"

"Never seen her before."

"Then how do you know he's with a chick?"

"Saw him with her earlier, coming out of the hospital."

"Describe her."

"Tall and skinny."

A pause. "Go on..."

150

"That's it."

"You know how many chicks fit that description in this town?"

"Want me to get closer? I'll let you know if I spot a mole on her tit."

"You're asking for it, moron."

Ernesto sucked on his smoke so he wouldn't slip and say anything that might get his throat cut. Solo was way smaller than Ernesto, but Solo's big-shot friends made him bigger and more dangerous. Let the asshole rant.

"Keep your distance. Let us know when he does something. Got it?"

"Yeah."

"We'll let you know when we want him to see you. *Capito*?"

Ernesto didn't reply. He hoped that day would never come. He wasn't comfortable getting chummy with someone he'd been ratting on. "Yeah. Whatever."

"All right, then," Solo said. "Do your job right and maybe you won't wake up dead in the morning." *Click.*

Ernesto stuffed the phone into the back pocket of his frayed denims, crushed his half-spent smoke in the dash ashtray, and took out another line of high-quality snort. Tonight definitely called for a double-liner.

***

Protective of his injured hand, C.C. stepped out of the car.

Lindsay got out on the driver's side and was

151

immediately enveloped in the muggy, exhaust-laden air. A hundred feet to their right, streams of passing headlights continuously lit up Semoran Boulevard like a fireworks display. Straight ahead, Sarah's Shirts 'N Stuff showed dark except for the yellow nightlight Sarah always left on in the window, as well as the spotlight aimed at the canopied entrance. Sarah's car was gone. With the exception of the pizza parlor at the end of the lot, the stores were closed. Three cars and a delivery vehicle dozed in front of the eatery.

"Are you sure you'll be okay driving?" Lindsay asked. "I mean ... with your finger..."

He laughed. "I've been banged up worse. This is nothing."

The patchy red haze touching his hair told her otherwise. But there were other things on her mind, as well. Half an hour earlier, when C.C. came back out of the 7-Eleven, carrying a tiny container of sour-cream-flavored Pringles and two cans of Busch Beer, she asked him how much trouble she was really in. He took considerable time with his reply, cracking open his beer while staring at the darkness straight ahead. He drank some beer and then said, "A lot." The black haziness hanging over him told her the worst.

Now, as he slid behind the wheel of his own car, she asked, "What's going to happen next?"

He sat back, his keys in his good hand, studying them as if they alone held the answer to her question. "They've given me twenty-four hours to make this right. Till around six o'clock tomorrow."

She was afraid to ask, but forced herself to. The inside of her mouth had gone dry, but she shoved the words out anyway. "What will they do if ... if you don't?"

He smiled, but his smile was forced. His colors immediately changed to red. "I'll figure something out."

"You really think you can?"

"I've been in tight spots before. Get some sleep. And don't worry." Using his good hand, he pulled his door closed and started up the engine.

She could no longer see him, but suspected his colors remained red as he backed up and drove away.

***

Although the drive home was just a couple of blocks, Lindsay feared someone was following her. Each time she glanced in her mirror, someone was creeping up on her. The first time was a pickup. Then, a utility vehicle. *Traffic,* she told herself. *The vehicle tailing you and C.C. was a white van. You don't see a white van now, do you?*

It was her imagination. Her paranoia. She was scared and had convinced herself someone was out to get her because she'd turned him in. The cops told him about her, so he wasted no time sending someone after her.

That didn't make sense, did it? Cops telling a bad guy about her because she'd reported a crime? Cops were no different from other people. They had families and friends, marriage problems and health problems. They suffered the same vulnerabilities as

153

everyone else. They got drunk at parties and probably talked to their friends about things that should be kept quiet.

C.C. said she'd angered important people. Once the word was out, these people would find out who she was and where she lived. Important people knew cops, right? She'd seen shows where cops were bought and sold—

You're being ridiculous. If the cops let information leak out, no one would come forward. Cases would never be solved. No one would volunteer for anything, or want to serve on jury duty. Crimes would no longer be reported. Cops needed the public on their side. They were the good guys and did their job to keep people safe.

She suddenly remembered what C.C. had told her. *"The car you IDed belongs to someone neither of us wants to mess with."* The thought made her tremble as she gripped the wheel.

***

Lindsay found Momma staring at the wall clock when she opened the apartment door.

"Nine-thirty? I called you at seven." Momma wore her red terrycloth bathrobe and tan slippers, a mixed drink in her hand. Her bloodshot eyes conveyed the message that her drink was probably not her first. "You told me you were coming home shortly."

"Sorry, Momma, I ... lost track of time." Lindsay went over to feed Marvin. She dropped the pellets onto the surface of the water, hung up her jacket, and went to get a drink of water. The

Pringles had made her thirsty. She'd only had a sip of the beer C.C. had given her. She didn't want to be stopped with beer on her breath.

Momma sat down at the kitchen table while Lindsay poured water. "Tell me about this guy."

"Who, Momma?" Lindsay decided to be vague. Sometimes Momma got the hint and just gave up. Besides, she didn't want Momma to know what was going on. Momma hadn't wanted her involved in the first place.

"The man you took to the hospital."

"He's an okay guy, I guess."

"What's his name?"

"He likes to be called C.C."

"What's he look like? How old is he? Is he married?"

Lindsay wasn't in the mood for this. Momma always made things a big deal. Lindsay didn't want to supply her with an endless string of lies just to keep her from finding something out. "He's okay-looking," she said. "I guess he's about thirty or so. I think he said he was divorced." There was no point telling her how many times C.C. had been divorced.

"Is there something you don't want to tell me?"

"No..."

"I'm getting this feeling you don't want to open up."

She shrugged. "Just tired, I guess. We really didn't talk about anything."

"You must have talked about *something* if you're only now just getting home two hours after you took him to the hospital."

"We were at the hospital for over an hour," Lindsay said. "Then he bought me a beer in gratitude."

"What does he do?"

"*Do*?"

Momma finished her drink. "He works, doesn't he?"

Lindsay drank the rest of her water and put the glass in the drainer. "He told me he's a cop."

"Uniformed cop?"

"He was wearing jeans and a tee-shirt. He might have been off-duty."

"He didn't tell you what kind of cop he was?"

"Like I said, we didn't get into personal stuff. I just took him to the hospital, then brought him back to his car."

Momma got up. "You don't have to tell me anything about him, baby. I understand." Momma rinsed off her glass. "You obviously found someone interesting and don't want to jinx it by talking about it. Isn't that about the gist of it?"

Lindsay sighed. Once again, Momma had reached her own conclusions. Lindsay knew better than object. "That's about it."

***

While Lindsay slept, Maisie's image appeared within a large gray cloud swarming with bright colors.

A black shape sat off in the distance, roaring loudly. Maisie began laughing. The shape crept closer, like a stalking cat. Growing in size, it penetrated the cloud. Maisie's image disappeared, her laughter diminishing as the roaring grew louder.

A mysterious figure shrouded in a reddish haze emerged from the shape. The darkness dimmed into heavy swirls of gray, rapidly vanishing into drab strings floating off into the blackness. The red swirls hovering around the man's face disappeared. He was grinning, his small dark eyes staring directly at her.

Gasping and covered in sweat, Lindsay sat up in bed. Shivering and moaning, she looked around and tried to penetrate the darkness. The familiar shapes gradually told her where she was and what had just happened. She was in her own room, and had just awakened from a horrible dream. In it, she'd seen the face of the man driving the Charger.

PART VI – WEDNESDAY
On the Payroll

Chapter 17

His head throbbing from the three strong drinks he'd sucked down the night before, C.C. drifted back to consciousness at around eight-thirty.

It took him a few minutes to realize where he was. Once that was accomplished, he rolled onto his left side, pinning his injured hand. A flurry of hot jagged pain scurried up his arm. Wincing, he grunted into a sitting position and remained totally still until the pain settled down, finally ebbing into a distant hum. He was definitely going to need the Vicodin.

After dry-swallowing a tablet from the vial on his night stand, he found a plastic baggy from the kitchen cabinet large enough to encase his hand. Using a thick rubber band, he looped it around his wrist, went back to the bathroom, and stood in the shower for ten minutes, letting the warm spray massage his body.

Drying off was a little awkward, but he managed, then shaved, splashed on cologne, and went back to the bedroom to dress. Since his first stop would be OPD, he put on his undercover uniform – frayed jeans, dark-blue oversized tee-shirt, and tennies. Uniform Drugs wouldn't question his presence in the building. He'd been following two

158

possible leads in an ongoing case involving a crystal meth connection – something else Uniform Drugs was aware of.

But that was before he'd found out about Lindsay. No one knew anything about that, just as no one knew what the man squeezing his balls had ordered him to do. C.C.'s sergeant, Murray Wills, was attending a seminar in Miami on the latest drug enforcement techniques. Captain Roberto Ruiz, Commander of the Drug Enforcement Division of OPD, usually gave the Undercover Drug Unit free reign, letting Murray and his small squad do what was necessary to accomplish their job. Since they had a stellar record of arrests, Ruiz didn't interfere. But if Murray was around, he'd surely ask questions. And Murray was due back in three days.

C.C. made sure he'd selected an oversized shirt. He needed the extra bulk. Ever since his painful encounter with The Cheerful Psycho the day before, he wanted a gun within easy reach.

He stepped into his bedroom closet to select his weaponry for the day. His small Wells Fargo safe, bolted into the wall, was concealed by his hanging clothes. He pushed them aside and unlocked it. He owned two Beretta PX4 Commercial Model 9-millimeter pistols, both of which rested in the consoles of his vehicles. Yesterday, as he sat helplessly with a gun pressed against his neck, the Beretta sat less than a foot away, totally inaccessible.

He promised himself he would never again permit anyone to sneak up on him. To ensure his safety, he needed a small model he could grab at any given moment.

He chose the Beretta Bobcat .22 and the tiny pancake holster that would fit in the small of his back. It was good for close work, although for distances of more than fifteen feet, he'd need to empty the clip and pray at least one of the slugs hit something.

He selected his trusty Bersa .380 for his hip holster. The .380 was slightly larger and heavier than the .22 and would also be concealed by the shirt. The Bersa was accurate up to twenty yards or so, and was small and easy to handle. It was also cheap enough to replace if lost or stolen. It had served him well before. He had as much confidence in it as in the larger, bulkier PX4. He owned three Bersa's and kept them all loaded and chambered.

While the coffee brewed, he sat on the sofa in the living room, eating a toasted raisin bagel while the Vicodin did its magic to his head as well as his hand. The local news came on. He watched closely to see if anything was said about the hit-and-run. If the media knew about it, it would mean Active Files had jumped right on it and the investigation was already in the works.

He had to put a cap on this quickly. In a perfect world, a girl like Lindsay Foreman would have nothing to worry about. But in a perfect world, an old woman would never have been run over and left for dead in the first place. The more he thought about it, the angrier he got. Why should anyone be allowed to get away with murder? Why should some jerk be able to kill an old woman just because

160

his daddy owned a corporation, a theme park, and a golf course? It was bad enough that C.C., who dealt with bad guys all the time, was forced to tangle with these jerks. But it was a totally different ballgame for someone like Lindsay to face the same horrible fate.

He had to face facts. Money ruled the world. It manufactured the TV he was watching, the coffeemaker brewing his morning java, the clothes he wore, the guns and bullets he carried, and the cars he owned. Money built the corporations that manufactured everything, and the corporations were run by men. The same men who were allowed to do as they pleased because of the immense wealth they'd amassed. And these big, powerful men didn't care about some old lady who couldn't cross the busy highway fast enough. Or the honest gal who happened to be walking by when the big man's idiot son slammed into the old lady.

From the TV, the local news reported the usual rapes, murders and arrests. A six-vehicle pileup on the Florida Turnpike. A new strip mall being built in an area in east Orlando, where a street of old homes were condemned and torn down. The weather, as usual, promised clear skies, a high of 89 and a low of 72, with 10 percent chance of rain. No disturbances in the tropics. It was too early in the season for anything developing in the Caribbean or coming off Cape Verde. The hit-and-run wasn't mentioned.

C.C. was relieved, hoping the investigation hadn't begun yet. He wondered if they'd been told

161

to delay it or were waiting for another tip to pop up before assigning someone to it. The fact that the victim was a transient helped. With no one else involved, and no angry relatives to deal with, such a case was often placed on a lower priority. There still might be time to sneak on over there and fudge the file a bit.

The coffee was ready. C.C. finished his bagel, got up, poured a cup, then went back into the living room to plan his day.

McGuire in Active Files would be his first logical contact. McGuire was an okay guy, and had been known to do a favor or two, such as being somewhat creative with the caseload, giving preferential treatment to some while letting others sit. McGuire drove a new Lexus, selected his clothing from high-priced stores, and wore jewelry – on a senior clerk's salary. All definite signs that the boy might be reporting to someone other than his supervisor.

C.C. decided to stop by Rossen's desk first. Rossen saw and heard everything, and might have come across useful information. If C.C. could get the big boy talking, he might find out a few things. But time was of the essence. He had just hours to do something about this, and had to use whatever resources were available to sabotage the case without anyone suspecting. Lindsay's life depended on it.

***

Slightly nervous, C.C. pushed past the glass doors of the police station just before ten o'clock.

Harried men and women rushed from one cubicle to the next, shuffling papers. Two young male exec types wandered up and down the halls, mumbling into cell phones. Grim-faced detectives escorted handcuffed youths and hookers down the hall to the interview rooms.

Rossen sat at his desk, handling a call. C.C. passed on his way over to the coffee station. "You need a refill?" he asked.

Rossen nodded. A moment later, he hung up and keyed something into the system. "Morning's been a kicker," he said.

C.C. poured two cups and brought them over. "I saw it on the morning news. Six-car pileup on the Turnpike." He handed Rossen his coffee. Rossen grabbed a mug crammed with sugar packets and held it out. C.C. took two. Rossen put the mug back down, squeezed out three packets, tore them open, and held them over his steaming cup.

"How many in the pileup were out-of-state?" C.C. asked.

Rossen chuckled.

"*All* of them?"

"Did you have to ask?"

C.C. sat. "I guess that would be pushing it, asking them to take a driving test before they reached the state line."

"They should have already taken care of all that." Rossen used a swizzle stick to stir his coffee, then slurped. He grimaced and put the cup down on his blotter. "How'd you fuck up your hand?"

"Caught it in the car door."

Rossen grinned.

"I know. I'm stupid."

"That's as bad as getting it smashed changing a damn tire." Rossen held up his right hand. His swollen index finger displayed an angry purplish-blue nail.

"Ouch. But at least you didn't break it."

"It still hurt like a scalded bastard."

"Don't you have a son for that?"

"Making the tire go flat? Or breaking my finger?"

"Point taken. How many fatalities in that pileup?"

"Three this time."

"Could've been worse."

"Yeah. There were nearly twenty involved."

"Something that intense on a busy, high-speed highway like the Turnpike should've claimed at least ten of them. Everyone hitting ninety or better, gawking at the flat landscape, the pretty trimmed grass, and the road signs."

"Burns my ass," Rossen said. "They come here from other states, expecting the rules to be different."

C.C. sipped his coffee and frowned. It was horrible. Obviously someone in a hurry had brewed it. "Yeah, they come here expecting Fantasyland."

"And turn the whole place into La-La Land."

"And everyone lies." C.C. saw his chance and jumped right in with it, hoping to steer the conversation his way. "They'll tell you they were just minding their own business, observing the rules

164

of the road, when a tree jumped out of the woods and lay down in front of their car."

"Or a deer."

"Or rabbit."

"Or snake." Rossen shook his head. "You'd think these clowns never saw a damn *snake* before."

"Tourists come down here for a vacation," C.C. said. "They don't want to have to deal with reality."

"So they see a deer, and since it's coming from Fantasyland, it's not real?"

"Basically."

"Even if it *did* happen like that, we still wouldn't get the real story. Everyone lies to us – especially tourists."

C.C. sighed. "Got to be *some* honest citizens out there."

"*I* haven't seen too damned many."

C.C. drank a little more bad coffee. He wanted to slap Rossen on the side of the head with a two-by-four. C.C. had to make some headway without spending the entire morning here. Bad enough he was forced to drink their shitty coffee less than half an hour after he'd made some really good stuff back at his apartment. "I was always taught to tell the truth," he said. "You were, too. You're only one generation ahead of me. Seems–"

"I got caught lying? I got the damn switch. Grew up in the sixties. People acted more like people then."

"I keep hearing that was a pretty good generation," C.C. said. "I'm really disappointed with mine. I grew up with shallow, spoiled people.

And it keeps getting worse. Kids today don't know anything about doing the right thing."

"Don't care, either." Rossen put down his coffee and went back to his computer.

Frustrated, C.C. decided to go down the hall to see if he could accomplish anything with McGuire in Active Files. Nothing but a dead end here. Rossen was a Neanderthal. You couldn't wind him up and point him. He was just one of those individuals you couldn't waste subtlety on.

He decided to give it one last try. "I'd like to know if anyone younger than thirty even *knows* what the right thing is."

"That Foreman girl," Rossen said, typing away.

C.C. sat up. "Who?"

"Skinny young thing, witnessed that hit-and-run last Friday. Came in Saturday morning to report it. You were here. You even asked about her."

"Ah. That tall, cute girl. What about her?"

"Kid worries me. That damn subconscious of hers. It's gonna get her in hot water."

"Just for IDing a hit-and-run vehicle?"

"Called yesterday, told me she suddenly remembered the plate."

"*That* should come in handy."

"It should..." Rossen's square, slablike forehead wrinkled up.

"Something else happen?"

Rossen frowned. "Just got another call from her, not fifteen minutes ago. Said she can identify the driver."

***

166

Gazing out the store window, Lindsay wondered if the figure in the chocolate-brown utility vehicle was watching her.

It had been parked in the center of the lot for a while, although she didn't exactly know how long. The stores were pretty busy all morning – mostly bank traffic, although the electronics store offered portable DVD players and MP3 players at half price for their early summer sale. The pizza place didn't open until eleven, but always had several customer vehicles parked out front, waiting anxiously for the place to open.

She'd noticed the vehicle in question about an hour after her phone call to the police department. She didn't see it come in, only that its driver remained behind the wheel, staring at the store window. She chastised herself for being paranoid. He was probably just waiting to pick up someone.

A few minutes later, as Lindsay rang up a customer, she caught a glint in front of the driver's face. Sunglasses? Binoculars? Or just a reflection of the sun hitting the windshield? She felt jittery and nervous with fear. Her talk with C.C. the night before had made her edgy. But what made her even edgier was her dream. Was Maisie actually trying to communicate with her? Or was all this just her imagination again? The colors she'd seen since Maisie's death, as well as the feelings she'd picked up when the 7-Eleven was about to be robbed, were one issue. She'd expected strange things to result from the traumatic events she'd been through in the last several days. But hearing Maisie's laughter and seeing the old woman's face in her dream was something else entirely. It was a dream, but still it had unnerved her.

And what about the man's face she'd seen? Was it actually the face of the man who'd killed Maisie? Or just someone she'd seen in a movie? Maybe even a customer in the shop she remembered from weeks past? She strongly suspected the face belonged to the man driving the Charger. But what if she was wrong? Could she live with the embarrassment?

Yes, she could. And the embarrassment would only be temporary. It would be a very small price to pay – especially if she was proven right. If there was even the slightest chance she could identify Maisie's killer, she had to take it. This was why she'd made the call to Sergeant Rossen.

"You actually *did* see the driver?" he'd asked.

"I must have," she'd replied, knowing better than to tell Rossen about her dream. If she told him where her source was coming from, he probably wouldn't believe anything else.

"How could you possibly see anyone?" Rossen had asked. "Did he stick his head out the window?"

"No..."

"He'd just hit someone. He wouldn't stick around to show his face, would he? Not unless he was an idiot. Or drunk. Or doped-up."

She could tell Rossen was having trouble trying to understand, yet forced herself to stay calm and rational. "I ... saw his reflection."

"At *night*?"

"Like I told you before, the headlights—"

"The lights behind him lit up everything. Yeah. I got that the first time around."

"It's possible, isn't it?"

He sighed. "How far away from the vehicle were you?"

She knew where this was going. "Close enough to make out the model and plate, apparently."

"Then I'd say yeah, anything's possible. Unlikely, but possible."

"What should I do now?"

"Do?"

"About IDing this guy."

"Want to come in and work with one of our sketch artists?"

"Is that how you do things?"

"You've already given us the make of the vehicle, as well as the plate number. That should be enough under most circumstances. But since this happened at night, with heavy Friday night traffic, a positive ID would seal the deal."

"Do you have a driver's license of the person who owns the vehicle?"

"Sure do."

"And a picture?"

"Of course. We'll interview him just as soon as the boys start up their investigation. But if you can come in and do the sketch, and if there *is* a match, the case would automatically be closed without us having to put in countless hours of wasted manpower."

"I can come in around lunchtime," she'd

offered, "if that's all right."

Lunchtime ... a little more than an hour from now. Her limbs shuddered each time she thought about it. After talking with C.C., she knew that people with money and power and connections stood to lose in this scenario if she continued pursuing justice for Maisie. People with lots of money and power and connections ... people that made a tough guy like C.C. very nervous.

Should she risk her life to do this, or call Rossen back and tell him she wasn't sure about what she'd seen? She might have *imagined* the face from a dream and hadn't actually seen *anyone* that night.

No. Each time she thought about keeping silent, the image of Maisie's broken body lying alongside the road flashed in her head. How could she live with herself if she didn't do what was right?

Instinctively she glanced outside. The figure in the SUV had disappeared. The cowbell above the shop door clanged as the door opened.

***

Art Radner quickly scanned the store.

Tee-shirts, shorts, fancy jeans, and metal hat trees stacked with baseball caps and colored visors filled the narrow room. Posters crammed in bins lined the far wall. No one in the store but the skinny brunette. Off to the right, a door marked *Manager* was shut. He guessed the room was empty, and the brunette was alone in the store. He'd seen only a tan Honda Civic sitting out front.

His instructions were simple: change the

brunette's mind about making another trip to OPD and get her to forget the whole thing. His plan would be wrecked if someone else came in. But since he'd lucked out for right now, he didn't have to worry about anyone else getting in the way. But he had to work fast. *No problem.* He was good at what he did, and the money he was being paid provided excellent motivation. Although he excelled at scare tactics, he preferred adding physical discomfort to the situation for effect. It made things much more enjoyable. It was one thing to scare someone, but hurting him a little tended to help him remember things better.

Art realized he had to be extra careful with a woman. Women bruised easier than men and often fainted or went apeshit. He couldn't use the same tactics here as he had with Cross. Cross was a cop. Pain and discomfort weren't exactly foreign to him. This girl would most likely freak if he broke something.

Quiet was the name of this game – which was why he'd been chosen to step into the picture. The girl was causing problems. His employers hated problems.

He strolled over to the poster bins, just to give her the illusion he was a potential paying customer. It would put her more at ease and might even lower her guard. In another minute or so, he'd call her over for assistance and whisper something threatening.

He riffled through a stack of posters, skimming past half-naked male rock stars, nearly naked female movie stars, flower arrangements, dogs, cats, birds – even a decent silhouette of a nude woman with her arms spread overhead. He settled on a black and white photo of Monument Valley. *Not bad.* He liked the mountains. He'd always wanted to build a cabin somewhere out west when he'd accumulated enough money to retire. He placed it in front of the stack and studied it. His eyes shifted to the right, toward the window in the front door. Still no one in sight.

***

Lindsay had wanted Sarah to come through the door.

Instead, it was a big guy with broad shoulders and large sinewy arms. He wore jeans and a white V-necked tee-shirt with *Gold's Gym* stamped across the back. On the front, a muscle-bound gorilla lifted a barbell so loaded up with weight that the bar had bowed. The shirt was tight – probably specifically chosen a size too small to show off his definition. He also wore wraparound sunglasses and a Gators baseball cap low on his forehead.

He went over to the poster display facing the far wall. She gave him a cheery, "Good morning," as was Sarah's store policy, but he didn't acknowledge her. His interest seemed to be reserved for the posters. She wondered if he was the man watching her from the utility vehicle. She snuck a quick glance at the parking lot. The vehicle remained where it had been, and the driver was gone. Of course she knew the driver could be in any one of the other stores in the strip mall. But she couldn't ignore the dark vibes she was getting from this man's presence.

She couldn't see his face – his Gators cap and the wraparounds hid most of his features. It was impossible to guess his age. He moved like a cat, but all she noticed was his muscularity. The reddish-blond stubble protruding from the bottom of his cap told her he was fair-haired. His skin was tanned, which told her he was probably local.

Uneasiness gripped her. His broad back faced her while he checked out the posters, but she could see him sneaking glances at the front door. Was he waiting for an accomplice, or keeping a watchful eye for a hasty exit? Sarah's wasn't a profitable store to rob. Unless the thief was interested in the contents of the register, tee-shirts weren't a key item on the common theft list. And the posters were simply too big and awkward to make off with undetected. But it was still wise not to take chances. There were far too many other frightening concerns a girl faced these days. She kept her foot close to the floor buzzer under the counter, just in case. She'd be safe as long as she stayed right there. And unless he called her over, she wouldn't have anything to–

"Miss? Can you come here?" he said without turning around.

Her heart skipped a beat. She took a deep breath. After all, he might very well be a legitimate customer. Looks often were very deceiving. He could be a nice, quiet guy with money to spend. Just because he could probably pick up her Honda and toss it didn't mean he wanted to rob the store. She needed to put a cap on her overactive imagination. Her nerves hadn't been very stable lately.

She gave the floor buzzer one last glance, then pulled herself away and moved rather stiffly over to that section of the store. He was staring at a classic Ansel Adams photo of Monument Valley. At least he had good taste. She stopped about five feet away. "Yes?"

Still studying the poster, he gestured her closer. She moved cautiously. The negative vibes had come back. They were dark and cold. She couldn't shake the growing fear that this guy wasn't nice at all. When she was about two feet away, he said, "Been working here long?"

A hot bubble encircled her head, making it difficult to breathe. His question suggested he had things in mind other than Ansel Adams. Her best bet was to get rid of him as quickly as possible. "Did you ... want to buy that poster?"

"I'm not exactly sure yet..." Deep-red swarms mixed with black tendrils encircled his cap.

He didn't come here to buy anything. Her pulse hastened. She slid her right foot backward. If only she wasn't so far away from the buzzer...

The cowbell clanged, announcing another visitor. He cringed. Her head hot, Lindsay jerked her face toward the sound. It was Sarah, thank God. She stormed past, carrying a white paper bag that probably contained her typical late breakfast Egg McMuffin. The two parallel crevices etched between her dark brows were deeper than usual. She

174

crossed the room, stomped over to her office, pushed open the door, and disappeared inside.

"Excuse me." Lindsay slipped past the hanging racks. Growing more at ease with each step, she began breathing easily again. When she was a safe twenty feet away, the smothering hot bubble vanished. The air smelled fresher, sweeter.

She peeked in the office doorway. "You okay?"

"Just fine," Sarah said tensely. She'd tossed her jacket on the cluttered table, sat down, and logged into her computer. "Fine, fine, fine. Everything's just fucking *fine*." The colors swarming around Sarah's thick mane glowed a fiery red.

"Why do I have this strange feeling you're not telling me the truth?"

Sarah stopped typing and looked up at her. "Does it show?"

Lindsay smiled. "The flames coming out of your ears are a dead giveaway. Edward?"

"Who else?"

Behind her, the cowbell clanged, making her jump.

"Too much coffee today?" Sarah asked.

Her body tense, Lindsay turned around slowly. The store was empty. She crossed the room and went over to the front window. The big, scary guy was getting into the chocolate-brown utility vehicle.

Chapter 18

After scarfing down a tasty sausage-and-cheese omelet, rye toast, and chicory coffee, Lenny 'the Touch' Alfredo left the Orange Avenue Breakfast Shoppe with a smile of satisfaction on his handsome, tanned face.

While strolling casually to the end of the block, he pulled the thick black cowhide wallet from his lightweight jacket pocket and opened it to see what goodies he could find. Credit cards, of course. Visa. MasterCard. Discover. American Express. Platinum. Gold. Silver. Eight of the bastards.

Lenny shifted the toothpick from one corner of his mouth and sighed. Didn't anyone actually use their heads anymore? This was *Florida*, for Chrissakes. The Tourist Capital of the United States. Also, the Tourist *Scam* Capital. There were pickpockets out there. Muggers. Carjackers. Every kind of scam artist imaginable. Just like every other town in the country, only worse. And it wouldn't exactly make a tourist's vacation more enjoyable if he were stupid enough to let his wallet slide out of his pants pocket while he was stuffing his pie-hole with pancakes, eggs, grits, bacon, and sausage, would it? Some people were just too stupid to understand how stupid they actually were. This was a rough world. All sorts of assholes running around out there, finding endless ways to set people up. Folks had to be careful nowadays.

Lenny opened the flap. Wisconsin driver's

license. Appleton address. Samuel T. Potts. Age 58. Height: 5 feet, 8 inches. Weight: 200 pounds. Lenny chuckled. That boy was dreaming if he thought he weighed 200. 250, easy, but probably closer to 275, once he put away that breakfast bonanza back there.

Eighty bucks in twenties and tens lined the back of the wallet. *Better than nothing.* What good were credit cards? He'd have to find a fence he could trust – and everyone knew 'fence' and 'trust' were two words that didn't belong in the same sentence. When all was said and done, what he'd get out of it amounted to roughly a hundred bucks. A royal pain in the ass. It didn't even pay for his time and the aggravation of risking his health and safety.

He pocketed the bills. Before going back inside, he took in the scene through the window. Potts hadn't budged from the table in the center of the long dark room, still stuffing his fat face with a soggy forkful of syrup-laden pancakes while his plump wife did her best to keep up with him. Lenny slipped in through the door. He tossed the wallet on the desk near the skinny elbow of the cute cashier standing there, counting the tiles on the ceiling. "Found this outside."

She pushed her long, streaked brown-and-gold hair away from her face and snapped her gum. "Saw ya pick it up before ya walked out."

Wow. Strange chick. He could've sworn she was only half-awake when he'd paid for his breakfast. "You see a lot for a chick that looks bored half to death."

177

"I ain't bored." She snapped her gum again and lowered her eyes the way all females do when they want to aggravate a guy by making him think they're interested in the real estate down there. "Just don't care."

She was maybe twenty, probably quit school, did the party scene and ended up pregnant. There was probably no man. She might've shown the guy how bored she was when she was getting laid. That was a big-time turnoff. Dudes didn't care much for chicks that popped gum and acted bored when they were fucking them. It was like playing tennis alone.

"So tragic and damaged for one so young," he said.

"He's gonna ask where his stuff is."

"I left the cards."

"What for?"

Lenny shrugged. "Aggravation."

She nodded as if she actually understood.

He went over to the entrance door. "You're not gonna ask me to have a nice day?"

She squinted. "What for?"

Yep. Strange chick.

Orange Avenue bustled with tourists. Lenny could spot them at a glance. No tan? Definitely a tourist. A quick scan made the clothes. Chances were good that they'd be brand-new. The third and last clue was how they walked around, eyeballing everything – skyscrapers, street signs. Orlando must be the only place on earth with skyscrapers and street signs. Someone with no tan, fresh clothes, and the look of total cluelessness definitely had his

178

pockets up for grabs.

A gaggle of blue hairs congregated near a tour bus parked at the curb at Church Street Station. Six of them in shorts, orthopedic shoes and straw hats, chattering away behind an opened map.

Lenny's grandmother wouldn't like him picking on old farts. Not that Granna was Mother Teresa, but Lenny saw no sport in fleecing someone her age – especially when they were probably all here on some sort of group plan and didn't have much spare change. Potts was different. A slob carrying around eight credit cards, scarfing down half the food in the restaurant, and too sloppy to notice his wallet had fallen out of his pocket? That boy deserved to have a bad day.

Lenny picked pockets and had a special knack for sniffing out valuables from rental cars, but that didn't mean he lacked principles. He considered himself cool, dignified. He figured it was the Italian in him. He opened doors for ladies, even called them *ma'am*. Hell, he'd even helped an old man with a walker cross the street a while ago. Didn't take anything from him, either. Stealing from oldsters just didn't appeal to his sense of fair play. In Lenny Alfredo's world, there was no such thing as a Blue Hair Special. Anyway, he didn't need to pick on the elderly for his pissing-around money. Florida literally *oozed* with suckers.

This was gonna be a good day. Five hundred bucks, easy. He'd spend a couple of hours here, then check out the rental agencies. The marks usually came out of the place with their keys glittering in their hot little paws and didn't have a clue where to pick up their vehicle. A pro like Lenny could bilk twenty or thirty bucks from them, easy, just with a line or two. Or a couple hundred by accidentally bumping into them, switching keys, and taking their car to one of the local chop-shops on Orange Blossom Trail.

Lenny reached the end of the block. A blur of movement beside him came with the smell of cheap aftershave. A rough hand grabbed him by the collar.

***

C.C. Cross dragged Lenny into the alley, behind a dumpster piled high with garbage.

Using his good hand, he let go of Lenny's collar, pressed his palm against the boy's scrawny chest, and shoved him roughly against the brick wall. Skinny arms flailing, Lenny squirmed like a fish on a line. C.C. turned to his left, keeping his injured hand out of harm's way. Lenny eventually settled down and waited nervously for C.C. to pull his hand away. C.C. made sure at least three feet separated them. Lenny Alfredo had the fastest hands C.C. had ever seen. The boy could easily pull the wings from flies in flight.

"You trying to break something, man?" Lenny made a show of fixing his collar and smoothing out his long, wavy black locks.

C.C. had to treat him this way. If anyone saw them working a deal, they'd ask questions. Lenny wasn't a known snitch, so it was necessary to bat him around a little. "I have to make it look good, don't I?"

"My poor, battered body says you're doing a fucking bang-up job – please forgive the pun." Lenny gingerly turned his head to the right, then to the left. "You can drop the psycho cop act. Nobody can see us back here."

"Don't be a baby. I just nudged you a little."

"Yeah, by slamming me into a brick wall. Do me a favor and don't ever actually *hit* me, okay?"

"Behave yourself and maybe I won't. You got a minute?"

He checked his watch. It looked pricey. Possibly lifted it from some unsuspecting tourist. "Make it quick. I've got a heavy appointment with a Magic cheerleader who just made it known on *Good Morning, O-Town* that she'd love to see Lenny's famous hands in action."

"Yeah, and I've got a bridge in Phoenix I need to sell."

Lenny noticed his bandaged finger. "How'd you fuck up your hand?"

Damn. Here we go again. "Got bit by an alligator."

Lenny gave a little nod as he eyed the hand. "That alligator crawl on his belly or walk upright and drive?"

C.C. frowned. He didn't want to get into explanations, made up or real. "I need a favor."

"What's in it for me?"

"A little walking-around money."

"How much?"

"Depends."

"On what?"

181

"How many more questions you ask. A hundred now, ten less every time you keep opening your mouth."

Lenny made a zipping motion with his hand across his lips, then stared expectantly, waiting for the details.

C.C. sighed. He didn't want to come right out and say it, but he had no choice. Time was running out. "It involves OPD."

"The *police station*?" Lenny ran both hands through his hair.

"It's important, Lenny."

"C'mon, man. Get real. The *police station*?"

"It's for a good cause."

"Why should I care about a good cause if I land my ass in jail again?"

"You won't."

"Every damn one of those cops knows me by sight. How can anyone forget such classic beauty?"

"You won't land in jail. I give you my word."

Lenny went silent. C.C. knew Lenny believed him. The boy just didn't want to be tossed in a cell with a bunch of jerks that went for pretty faces. Besides, Lenny was pulling in serious cash scamming tourists – mostly petty shit that no one even bothered to report.

"A hundred bucks," C.C. repeated, trying to make it sound tempting.

"Man, the *police station*..."

"*Two* hundred."

"They'll spot me as soon as I show this handsome face in the lobby."

"The area you're going to won't put your handsome face into contact with them at all. It'll be lunchtime, and most of them will be gone. You'll be in and out in thirty seconds, tops."

"I dunno, man..."

"Two-fifty."

Lenny looked aside. C.C. could almost see him mentally counting the money as he said, "Which area?"

"Active Files."

"That new wing?" Lenny thought it over some more, stroking the black stubble peppering his chin.

"There's a back door. It's even got a push-bar for quick exits. You won't be anywhere near the front entrance."

Lenny continued stroking his chin.

"Starting to sound better?"

"If only this face didn't attract so much attention..."

"Wear a cap. Sunglasses. Put on a fake goatee."

"And *hide* these gorgeous locks and this movie-star face?"

C.C. sighed. "As soon as you leave, you can trash your disguise and show everyone just how beautiful and sexy you are."

Lenny squinted. "You think I'm sexy?"

"No, but *you* sure as hell do."

"For a second I thought you were going funny on me."

"Don't be a dickhead. Do we deal or what?"

Lenny frowned and went silent again.

"Three hundred's my last offer."

Lenny's face beamed. "*There* ya go. For that kind of jack, I'll march right in there and personally hump the commissioner."

C.C. turned to leave. "By the way ... you haven't lost your touch, have you?"

Lenny held out his hand. C.C.'s brown cowhide wallet rested comfortably in his palm. "What do you think?"

***

Steve McGuire couldn't wait to leave the office for a well-deserved break.

The workload had been unusually hectic. More than a dozen cases since nine o'clock. European visitors, unable to read English road signs, causing havoc on the highways. A teen gang running wild at one of the theme parks. A tourist scam outside a ticket booth at another park.

The most important, of course, was the stink caused by the hit-and-run fatality last Friday night. From what Lou Rossen had told him earlier, the only eyewitness to the crime, Lindsay Foreman, had called in with a clear description of the driver. Foreman was due to come in around noon for a workup with a sketch artist. This case was turning seriously haywire. If someone didn't put a lid on it, it would literally blow up.

Steve left the building right after the call from Rossen, made his call, and received his instructions. The message was clear: *dump the file*.

His initial reaction was, *Shit I can't do that*. If anyone found out, the whole Department would fall under immediate investigation. But since only a small handful of people were even aware of what was going on, deleting the case wouldn't be that big of a deal. Steve was just glad his boss hadn't been privy about it beforehand. When the captain knew about a case, especially one involving a homicide, dumping crucial file information was not exactly a good career move.

If the Foreman girl was smart, she'd realize what she was doing and suddenly develop a memory blip. But that seemed unlikely. She'd been volunteering information since Saturday morning and didn't appear to be the type to just let it be. This wasn't Steve's concern. He did what was asked of him and let the process take care of itself. The less he knew, the better. That way, if something blew up and questions were asked, he wouldn't incriminate himself. The big guys knew what they were doing. As long as he did as they said, the only thing he had to worry about was how to spend all that extra money they dumped into his bank account.

Time to concentrate on more important matters. Laurie 'Luscious Bod' Todd from Accounting had arranged to meet him at the Steakhouse Grill on Jefferson at twelve sharp. He couldn't think of anything better than sharing a charbroiled T-bone and a pitcher of dark beer with the stacked redhead. He'd already shared a drink with Todd a few weeks before at a department benefit, but they hadn't gotten the chance to talk to one another. He'd soon remedy that.

Someone came through the doorway, and he glanced up from his computer screen. C.C. Cross approached, his expression showing something was on his mind. The last two fingers of his left hand were wrapped in white bandages. "How goes it?" he asked Cross.

"Can't complain. How 'bout you?"

"Never better. What happened to the hand?"

"Cut it shaving," Cross said, somewhat abruptly.

Cross looked dead-serious, but Steve knew better. Cross dealt with street scum and couldn't afford to let anyone know what he was thinking or what was going on in his life. He'd necessarily developed an invisible coat of armor and didn't let anyone penetrate it. Cross was a good cop, despite the rumor floating around that he'd been recently burned. Steve guessed it to be true. Cross wasn't giving off his usual gung-ho persona.

"You serious?" he asked Cross. "You actually cut your hand *shaving*?"

"Don't I look serious?"

"Yeah. You do."

"Glad to see the unflinching stare still works. You busy right now?"

"Just getting ready for lunch."

"This should only take a second. I need you to look up something."

Steve cleared the screen. "Case you're working on?"

"This involves the West Orlando meth dealer charged with that child kidnapping a couple of weeks ago."

"Sounds familiar." As Steve went into the

186

database, he thought about the Luscious Bod again. No problem. He'd be swapping brewskies with her in no time. "What's the perp's name?"

"Goes by Johnny O."

"Stands for O'Brien, I take it?"

"All we care about is the kid. O was involved in some messy custody battle last year that started bad and went south real fast. The woman either made tracks or went swimming wearing a pair of seriously heavy shoes."

"His wife?"

Cross shrugged. "Common Law, maybe. O was never very family-oriented. Too busy mixing up drain cleaner. We figure he took the kid just for leverage."

"Or a shield."

"Stick the kid in a high chair in the kitchen, where you're cooking your meth. Cops'll always back off."

"We've got no choice." Steve logged into Active Files and punched in the name.

Cross reached into his pocket and pulled out a slim wad of bills. "You have change for a hundred?"

Steve stopped typing. "What's going on?"

Cross riffled through his bills. "I just got hold of a pair of one-day base tickets for Disney, and I'm trying to unload them. I need smaller bills in case someone wants to buy them and I have to make change."

"You've got to be kidding." Disney tickets were ridiculously easy to sell. Steve had been there a dozen times in the last couple of years. It was a great place to take a chick. Maybe he could persuade the Luscious Bod to go with him if lunch turned out okay. "Single park admission?"

"For any of the parks. Got them from one of my contacts as a token of gratitude."

"You don't want them?"

Cross shrugged. "Don't have the time. Interested?"

"Depends. How much?"

"Forty apiece."

Steve gave a low whistle. "That's less than half price. You've got yourself a deal." This was too good to pass up.

Cross frowned. "They're in my glove box. Let's go get them. Unless you want to wait until lunch..."

Steve chuckled. He could easily imagine Todd all decked out in shorts and a tight-fitting halter top, eager to spend the afternoon having serious fun. "Don't want to wait for *those* boys. I'd better log out." Pulse racing, he sat back down. "They've been kicking our asses about proprietary stuff lately. We even had a seminar on it last week."

"Stay logged on." Cross turned toward the doorway. "I'll go get them and be back in a minute."

"I'll be right here."

Cross rushed out of the room. A moment later, he yelled something from out in the hall.

"*What* was that?" Steve yelled back.

Cross's voice came back. "I just said if you

want those tickets, I might be–" The rest of Cross's statement dropped off when something that sounded like a ring of keys clinked loudly on the tile floor, echoing down the hall.

Steve got up and hurried through the doorway. Someone raced by, bumping lightly into him. "Uh, sorry about that," Steve said.

The tall, lanky figure didn't miss a step. He rushed past Cross, who was bent over, picking up his keys, nearly clipping him as well on his way outside.

"What'd you say?" Steve asked, smoothing out his shirt sleeve, where the clumsy moron had touched him.

Cross twirled the keys in his hand. "I might be able to get you two more tickets if you can come up with another fifty."

Steve reached for his wallet. It wasn't where it should be. His face flushed. The desk – he'd left it there. Hadn't he? Of course he had. He didn't remember taking it out. He *must* have. So ... why didn't he remember exactly? *The tickets*. His mind had gone blank. "One second." He went back to his desk. *No wallet*. Fighting blind panic, he checked underneath his chair, his desk, then ran back out into the hall. He patted his pockets again.

"What's wrong?" Cross asked.

"My wallet ... it's ... *gone!*"

"You're kidding, right?"

He glared at Cross. How could anyone joke about something like that? His head was swimming. The panic fought its way back. His cash, his credit

189

cards. *Gone*. That guy he'd bumped into... "That *guy*. Did you ... happen to see him?" he asked weakly.

"What guy?"

"Tall and skinny, and wore a Gators cap and dark clothes. Asshole bumped into me."

"You think *he* took your wallet?"

"I ... don't *know*!" He rushed back into the office. It was truly gone. His pulse thumping erratically, he ran back out into the hall. "Did you see what direction he went?"

"Who?"

Damn, he hated when people acted stupid. "The jerk that bumped into me, dammit."

Cross glanced at the glass doors. "I think he turned right."

His head hot, Steve shot past him, shoving open the door and running down the concrete steps as fast as his legs would carry him.

***

Good thing McGuire's cube was the first one inside the big room and separated by a maze of partitions. Also a good thing it was lunchtime – a lot less people here. C.C. could hear someone typing away down the hall behind him, but it sounded a safe distance away.

He quickly scanned the case list. There it was, bigger than shit. He clicked on it. When it came up, the hairs on the back on his neck bristled. Foreman, Lindsay. Age 23. Height: 5'11. Weight: 115. Hair: Brown. Eyes: Brown. Blood type: O Negative. His eyes skimmed her East Orlando Address, her

190

graduation records from Winter Park High School five years earlier, with a high B average. One semester at Rollins College. The file listed her place of current employment, the name and home address of her employer, and her mother's name and age, and maiden name. Her address indicated Lindsay lived with her mother. Her mother's employment and details of her mother's divorce were also included, as well as information about the car she drove. The one thing conspicuously missing was any mention of the hit-and-run fatality. Something was definitely wrong here.

It took some seriously high-powered clout to scrub an open case resulting in a fatality. C.C. knew it had to be someone with even more clout than the folks pulling his strings. *But who?* That didn't matter right now. He didn't have much time. He quickly pressed the DELETE FILE button. The FILE-DELETE red flag came up: AUTHORIZATION REQUIRED. *Damn.* He needed McGuire's ID and password. He quickly searched the blotter and found yellow sticky notes everywhere. One taped to the bottom of his screen said: *STEVE-O, manoman1*. He tried it, and the FILE-DELETE immediately displayed, along with the time bar. In ten seconds, Lindsay's data vanished quietly into cyberspace. C.C. went right back to the ACTIVE FILES homepage, then hurried out through the open doorway.

McGuire was less than ten feet from the doorway, checking his wallet.

"You found it? Good deal."

"That jerk *lifted* it from me." McGuire's eyes were as huge as silver dollars. His face was flushed. "Would you *believe* it? A pickpocket? In a fucking *police station*?"

"Can't trust anyone these days," C.C. said. "But at least you got it back. Everything there?"

"Basically."

"Asshole probably didn't have time to clean it out, cops wandering around out there. He might've just tossed it and ran."

McGuire's face was grim. "He had enough time to clean out all my cash, though."

C.C. shook his head. That damned Lenny and his obsession for cash. But at least he'd done his job. "Cards still in there? ID? Driver's license?"

"Yeah, everything else is there. But now I don't have the money for those tickets!"

"How about the ATM down the hall?"

McGuire looked even more pitiful. "Can't do it until payday. You wouldn't take a post-dated check, would you?"

"Sorry."

"Damn. That's not fair."

"Sucks, big-time."

"C'mon, C.C. Do me a favor."

C.C. couldn't stand watching a man who looked like he was ready to get down on his knees and beg. "I'll send them over the next time I'm in the building."

"Thanks. And don't worry. I'll see that you get your money."

C.C. hurried down the hall, wondering once

again who had enough clout to scrub an active file.

Chapter 19

Lindsay sat in her car, staring at the OPD building as if some monster waited for her inside.

Despite her fears, she knew she was being silly. Inside, cops and other individuals diligently tended to their daily job functions. She'd been here just days ago. What was different now?

The colors had changed everything. Lindsay could read people – their moods, their emotions. She could see their lies, their truths, their sadness, happiness, fear. All sorts of things most other people couldn't even begin to comprehend. And since she could now read people, she realized how much more frightening they were.

Her new ability had made everything dark and mysterious. And dangerous. It had somehow changed her, and this new perspective made her feel like a stranger in her own body.

Just days ago she'd gotten out of the Honda and walked right into the police station, told them what she knew, then left. Now she sat here, wondering if she was doing the right thing. She knew she was, but the fact that she was fighting with herself about it told her something was definitely wrong.

When she was five years old, she told Dad she'd just seen a local boy shoot a cat with a BB gun. She wanted to go to the police and tell them about it, but instead of putting her in the car and driving her there, Dad had sat her down and told her about life. He'd said the world was often dark and frightening, filled with bad people who did bad things. She had to be brave if she wanted to stand against them. He'd told her she didn't have to be brave to do the wrong thing. That was easy. Doing the right thing was much more difficult. It often required a person to think carefully before acting – which was why so few people chose to do it. But if she wanted to be different and show good moral fiber, she had to be brave.

In grade school, when she saw someone doing something wrong, she reported it and was instantly ostracized by the other kids. It was painful and humiliating, but she stood her ground. The kids ostracizing her were cowardly, approaching her in packs, like wild dogs. They screamed at her, yelling cruel things. She ran home many times, bruised and bleeding from being slapped, shoved to the pavement, and kicked. She lay in her bed on weekends, staring at the ceiling, wanting to grow up quickly, to magically become an adult. But what would that accomplish? Adults grew up doing the same mindless things they'd done as children. Adults were just big kids. They were no smarter, and no more mature or honest than they were as kids. Instead of maturing as they grew older, they only grew physically. As adults, they not only called others names, slapped them, and shoved and kicked them, they ran over old ladies and robbed stores. They did terrible things to their wives, their girlfriends, their children, their pets. Repulsive acts baffling the imagination. And anyone who tried to fix the situation set himself up for trouble.

Lindsay was convinced the man who'd come into the store hadn't wanted to buy anything. His colors suggested something dark and sinister going on inside him. And maybe that was why she was terrified about going inside. Because of him, the white van, and what C.C. had told her at the 7-Eleven. But it didn't matter, did it? Maisie deserved to have someone on her side. It didn't matter that she was dead. She shouldn't be forgotten. The man responsible should pay for ending her life.

Her pulse racing, she opened her car door and felt the flow of warm air hit her. Just as she was about to step out, her front passenger door swung open.

***

For the last ten minutes, the girl had been sitting in her tan Honda parked in one of the visitor spaces adjacent to the front entrance of the OPD building.

Standing behind his SUV in the parking lot across the street, Art Radner suspected she was probably gathering the courage to go inside. She *should* be scared. She was going up against the wrong people. He was told that the case was scrubbed, that all he had to do was convince her to forget about it.

His failure at the tee-shirt shop had irritated him. If the woman who ran the place hadn't come in, he would have delivered his message, and the issue would now be closed. He'd be back at the apartment, surrendering himself to Jenna's expert hands, or having her surrender her perfect body to him.

Art considered himself a perfectionist. It was his personal credo to finish what he set out to do. A professional, especially in his line of work, did his job well and made sure he finished it. Usually there were no second chances, but if another opportunity was offered to get the job done, it better *get* done. This profession didn't tolerate mistakes.

He circled around the SUV and headed for the street. This time, he'd deliver his message. Just a few choice words would be all that was needed. He'd only hurt her if necessary – but after his first failure, it was going to be difficult to operate with cold reserve and not indulge in a little extra roughness. If she even let out a gasp, he'd treat himself to some added entertainment. He could do it at his leisure in her car. One hand clasped over her mouth while the other did a little damage.

His only regret was that the damage would come much too quickly. She was tall and slender, so her bones would be delicate. He could imagine her heart fluttering against him in her struggles. The idea excited him – and also irritated him. *You're a professional. Think of the job.*

His thoughts went back to the task at hand as he stepped off the curb to cross the street.

***

Startled, Lindsay gawked, and her heart hammered as C.C. got in the passenger seat and quickly slammed the door shut. He looked upset and angry. Short white tendrils touched the top of his head. "Close the door," he said.

"But ... I've come to give them a description of

197

the driver..."

"Do as I say, all right? Back out and drive away."

The white tendrils swirling around him thickened. Some darkened, turning gray, then black. His eyes, clear and bright the last time she saw him, were now cloudy and bloodshot. His brow was creased. Something was horribly wrong.

Without another word, she closed her door.

***

When Cross came out of the building, Art dashed back to the other side of the SUV.

Cross rushed right over to the Honda and got in. About twenty seconds later, the girl started up the Honda and backed out.

Interesting. Apparently Cross decided to play interference. *Good deal.* Breaking the boy's little finger had done some good after all. It wouldn't be necessary for Art to deliver his message. *A shame, though.* He'd really wanted to administer a little S&M on the girl.

With a deep sigh, he went back to the SUV, climbed in, and pulled out his cell. After the usual series of clicks, the familiar voice came on. "Has the girl contacted the police?"

"Cross met her and apparently changed her plans. She pulled right out and drove away."

"Excellent. It seems that our volatile situation has resolved itself."

He saw no reason to tell them about his failure. It was prudent to tell these people only the minimum information necessary. "It does look that

198

way," he said.

"To make sure things don't unexpectedly revert back, it might be necessary to visit their home and see if there's some sure way to discourage her from having a change of heart."

"*Their* home?"

"She lives with her mother in an apartment one block west of Semoran Boulevard, south of East Colonial Drive. The mother is working. She won't be home."

"You want her to know about this?"

"She should be involved. At least indirectly."

"You're not saying you want me to *talk* to her, are you?"

"Do what is necessary to make them nervous. It might make the daughter see things more clearly. She should understand the consequences she could face by talking to the authorities." *Click.*

***

Her hands gripping the wheel, Lindsay pulled into heavy traffic. "Where are we going?" she whispered.

C.C. forced himself to maintain an air of calm. He didn't want to frighten Lindsay any more than she already was. Couldn't have that – especially since she was driving. He could tell she was already halfway to the panic mode by the way she kept a vise grip on the wheel. As subtly as he could, he risked a glance in the side mirror to scan the hectic scene behind them for signs of a tail. "Just drive. We need to talk."

He saw no sign of anyone staying close among

the three lanes of vehicles following them. But that didn't mean anything. These guys were good at shadowing. It was nearly impossible to know where they were.

Just a few minutes earlier, just as he was about to leave the OPD building, he'd noticed someone approaching the parking lot while Lindsay sat in the Honda. The figure was fifty yards away and partially hidden behind parked cars. He could have been on his way into the building on personal business, but his baseball cap and sunglasses had raised flags, even though it was a standard method of sun protection for Florida residents. The man who'd accosted him at gunpoint the day before wore the same attire. This figure also sported a pair of massive shoulders and arms, which could indicate the strength and power required to snap a man's finger. C.C. had fought down the urge to confront him. If he was the man the League had sent, he'd probably still be armed. Anyway, it was more important to get Lindsay away than risk death or severe injury to himself or both of them.

Lindsay's latest call to Rossen and her appearance at OPD had obviously upped the stakes, prompting the League to cancel their original twenty-four-hour deadline. He had to find a way to help her. She had no idea what she was getting into. Putting her into this was like dropping a toy poodle into a pit of hungry crocodiles. He realized what this meant but didn't care. He'd lost his self-respect when they'd burned him. Along with his self-respect, he'd also lost his drive and his desire to do what he was trained to do. For months he'd backed off when he should have jumped in, turning his back when he should have made an arrest. His loyalty to his job and his career had taken a backseat to his fears. Now he did only what he could without threatening the interests of those who'd framed him. He'd sunk to the lowest levels possible and had numbed himself into thinking he could survive this way. And he had, for a while.

However, meeting this sweet kid had made him realize just how low he'd actually fallen. Her honesty and her straightforwardness had shocked him back to reality. Her innocence made him take a good long look at himself. And when he did, he felt worse, because he didn't like what he'd become. But it also made him realize that no matter how much he'd lost, he might be able to get it back.

"I really have to get back and tell them what I know," she said. "I said I'd come in at lunchtime."

Once again her innocence stabbed at him, making him feel even dirtier. *Fight it. You can redeem yourself. It won't be easy, but you can do it. If you don't, this genuinely good soul will die*. To help her, he had to stop feeling sorry for her and make her aware of what she – what *they* – were up against. "That wouldn't be a good idea right now," he said, forcing the words out of his throat.

"Why not?" She was staring at his hair again.

"You'll be in serious trouble if you go back there."

"With who? The man who ran over Maisie? I'm not afraid of him."

201

"I realize that."

"He killed her."

"I know."

"Even though she was homeless and had no one, that didn't make her less of a person. A lot of people think the homeless are nothing but trash. They're invisible. People walk past them and ignore them and look through them all the time. Maybe *that's* why Maisie was run over. But it's still wrong. Maisie was a person. The homeless are people just like anyone else."

"I totally agree."

"Then what's the problem?"

"There's a lot more to this than you think."

"Someone doesn't want me doing this, right?"

He nodded.

"Someone other than the jerk who killed Maisie?"

"Exactly."

"It's not ... the *police*, is it?"

"I wish it were that simple."

"Who, then?"

"A small group of powerful people."

"Do the police know about them?"

He nodded again.

"You mean ... the police *know* and ... and *let* them do what they want?"

"No one lets them do anything. They just do it."

She stopped at a red light and stared at him. "And the police don't *care*?"

He had to remind himself that she'd graduated from high school only a handful of years earlier.

When he was her age, he'd already graduated from the Police Academy and was just as naïve as she was. Just as inexperienced. Back then he thought he could make a difference. He was one of the good guys, and everyone knew the good guys had justice on their side. Justice would triumph. It was the American way.

It didn't take him long to discover just how naïve he actually was. Didn't take him long at all to see the corruption. The deals. The hypocrisy. The games the judicial system played. The more expensive the defense attorney, the more a high-level criminal could get away with. Some creep could murder someone in plain sight, hire the best defense money could buy, and be back on the streets, his slate wiped clean. The smoking gun theory just didn't matter. Neither did eyewitnesses. Or evidence. The only thing that actually mattered was money. Bargains were sought after like items in a sale bin. Deals were made over lunch or golf. Once the high-priced haggling was finished and the right palms were greased, the bad guy was back in his comfortable limo, his chauffer taking him safely back to his twenty-seven-room mansion. The legal system was in shambles, and no one cared anymore. As long as greed prevailed, as long as people could buy and sell other people, the status quo would never change, and God help anyone who tried making waves.

But Lindsay didn't know this. She'd seen an old woman mowed down by someone in a high-performance muscle car. It was a crime, a felony.

And, like most others who didn't know how the system worked, she thought it was cut and dried. But what she hadn't seen was much worse. What powerful, corrupt men could actually do was infinitely worse than running down an old woman. He didn't want her to know about the real world. He didn't want anyone with a good heart to know. And it grieved him to be the one to tell her. "It's like this," he said, his voice unsteady as the light changed and they started moving with traffic again. "Things run a certain way, but not in any way you might be aware of."

"The police department?"

"The judicial system, the entire legal system itself, whatever you want to call it. In this case, I'm talking about Orlando. A lot more rich, powerful, corrupt people live here than in other big cities, and they've made a whole new set of rules. And these rules affect everyone."

"Why?"

"Because of the theme parks, the tourists, the pricey land, international visitors. The crooks have moved right in and taken over."

"Taken *over*?"

"Who do you think owns the land the theme parks are sitting on? The strip clubs? The malls? The condos? The golf courses?"

"*Everything's* crooked?"

"It's been turning this way for years. Look at the drug industry, for example. For years, this state has been the main pipeline to the rest of the country. There are more drugs coming in through Florida than all the states bordering Mexico, combined."

Another light changed. Her hands shaking, Lindsay managed to keep with the rest of the traffic flow as she asked, "Because of Miami?"

"Because of the shape of the state. Its location. Florida has more than eight thousand miles of coastline providing unlimited access and opportunities for drug trafficking organizations that use maritime conveyances. The short distance between Florida and the Bahamas also serves as a smuggling corridor along the southeast coastline. Mexican organizations have been smuggling and distributing cocaine, crystal meth and marijuana from the panhandle to Palm Beach County."

"But what does this have to do with me?"

"The man you're trying to nail, quite bluntly, is hands-off."

"What ... does *that* mean?"

"He's directly involved with the most powerful people in this city. That means he's someone you need to stay away from."

"So the police know what he did?"

"They probably know by now."

"And they don't care?"

"It's in their best interests to look the other way."

Her eyes glistened. "That's ... not right. It's ... *awful*."

"It's the way things are."

"So the police ... are actually *involved* in this?"

"OPD is generally honest. But a small part of it is secret, even to itself, a part even the highest heads aren't aware of. It involves a few individuals in key positions who've sold themselves to the highest bidder."

"Like who?"

"All we know is that it goes pretty high up. It involves politicians, of course, because wherever there's corruption, politicians will always be directly involved."

"How do *you* know about all this?" she asked after a short silence.

He didn't want to tell her. She was already frightened. Her skin was very pale.

"C.C.? *Please* tell me..."

Now it came down to the truth. He didn't want to tell her, but she had to know. He just hoped she wouldn't hate him or tell him to get out of the car. He slouched in his seat. His broken finger had started throbbing again. He needed a Vicodin but didn't want anything to cloud his brain. Anyone could be out there, looking for them right now. "I'm ... one of them," he said, his throat constricting.

Chapter 20

Hidden behind the SUV's tinted windows and lowered visor, Art Radner scanned the half-vacant apartment complex parking lot one last time. Just a few vehicles, most of them older model pickups and economy cars. A couple of old Camaros, their paint peeling, sat beside one another at the end of the lot, near a small storage shed. It was 1:55. Everyone was probably at work. A nifty time for a visit.

He opened his small black leather pack and selected the appropriate tools. The building, undoubtedly built prior to the seventies, probably used old locks and hardware. There should be no problem with the door.

He'd been told the Foreman women usually got home between six and six-thirty. Cross was probably still with the daughter somewhere. Hopefully she'd forget about making another trip to the police station. If she returned to her tee-shirt shop like a good girl, everything would turn out just fine.

Since his instructions were to use the mother for leverage, he decided to give the apartment a thorough check before driving out to Industrial Park. He was told that the mother drove a black BMW. Nice set of wheels. A couple of flat tires and a keyed driver's door, with a note stuck to her windshield explaining the reason for the deed, would be all the woman needed to understand what she and her daughter should do to stay out of trouble.

The front door of the apartment, standard for older buildings, presented no problem. He was able to slip the lock and gain entrance very quickly. The apartment, comfortable and well-furnished, appealed to the eyes. The light-blue living room walls provided a relaxed atmosphere. Lace curtains, valances, and other subtle feminine touches softened the room. Women's magazines, art books, and a couple of the latest tabloids cluttered the round cocktail table. A foot-tall shining glass pelican stood just off-center. A flashy Betta fish swam around by itself in a small tank on a shelf in the corner. Probably the girl's. Young girls usually kept pets.

He watched it for a little while. He'd always enjoyed watching fish. They fascinated him, made him relax better and quicker than the world's finest massage. This one was particularly cool to watch. *Should I?* He shook his head. It would take too long to find a suitable glass, and the little guy would probably die before he could take it back to his apartment. Fish were funny about their surroundings. He made a mental note to buy one for himself at his earliest convenience.

The first bedroom was done in light-sage, with white lacy curtains and a lush gold rug. The bed was made hastily. Art hated a messy bed. It made him nauseous. As a boy, he never left a room – any room – without making sure it was neat and spotless. It was a fine policy to live by, one that made him a much better person. He pulled the blanket tighter, fluffed the pillows, then centered them. No excuse for not making one's bed properly, was there? A nicely-made bed made the room classier, his mom always said.

Dresses, skirts, blouses, and dozens of tee-shirts filled the racks in the closet. They were obviously for someone tall and slender. He couldn't see a woman in her mid-forties wearing tee-shirts with *Sarah's Shirts 'N Stuff* stamped on the front, or Snoopy or Woodstock printed on the back.

He scanned the rest of the bedroom and opened drawers. Everyone had secrets; he didn't think he'd have a problem finding something interesting. He was quickly proven wrong. The girl was either the most boring person in existence or just didn't keep anything cool in the apartment. No sexy panties or bras anywhere in her drawers. Her jewelry case also lacked imagination. Several pairs of tiny pearl ear studs, three plain necklaces, a couple of silver bracelets, a class ring, and a promise ring filled the tiny drawers.

Her computer was locked. No sign of a username or password anywhere on her blotter or screen. No matter. Her desk drawers revealed nothing but pens, pencils, and notepads. A box contained instructions and several programs for the computer.

He went into the bedroom on the opposite side of the apartment's central living area. The mother's bed was even messier than the daughter's. It looked like whoever was sleeping there had pushed the sheets aside, got up, and left. *Disgusting.* Art couldn't possibly tolerate a bed looking like that. He knew he'd feel much better once he made it. He always received a genuine rush when he repaired someone else's shoddiness. He hoped it would do a number on the mother's mind. Art liked playing with people's minds. He decided to mention something about that in the note he stuck on her windshield. Something like, *You really need to start making your bed*. Or, *Your sloppiness sets a poor example for your daughter*.

He pulled the sheets taut, tucked in the corners, and fluffed the pillows. *There. Good as new.*

He went into the mother's bathroom and nearly choked. The room badly needed an air freshener. And the toilet lid was up. *Gross.* An open toilet irritated him worse than a messy bed. Holding his breath, he closed it, then quickly went back into the bedroom.

He found some nifty unmentionables in the mother's dresser. Three transparent brassieres and pairs of matching panties, all courtesy of *Frederick's* of Hollywood. Some bondage and S&M DVDs lay hidden beneath a dozen colorful scarves and panties in the top dresser drawer. Also a vibrator. *So ... Mumsy likes being tied up with scarves.* Too bad he couldn't oblige her.

He left the room, went down the hall, and checked the kitchen. Nothing interesting in their fridge, just the usual staples – eggs, butter, bread, cream cheese, strawberry jelly, and two six-packs of Budweiser, plus a few cans of Dr. Pepper and Sprite. A small bottle of port wine stood in the door shelving among the salad dressings, ketchup, pickles, mustard, and salad olives. Disappointed, he went back out into the living room.

All he'd found out was that the girl led a boring life and that her mother liked rough, kinky sex. That wasn't much to help him gain leverage with the daughter. Half the women he'd known liked rough sex or kink. And nearly three-fourths of the older women he'd known were into it as well.

The sound of the lock clicking open made him jump. His lightning quick reflexes slamming into overload, he spun around. His Beretta .25 materialized in his palm just as the door opened.

***

Fighting the heavy queasiness in her gut, Lindsay swerved into a busy strip mall not far from Red Bug Road.

Middle-aged women and men came out of the supermarket, pushing shopping carts. Two younger men in tee-shirts and jeans left the liquor store, carrying brown paper bags. A plethora of activity could be seen in the Duds-N-Suds laundry window in the center of the mall. A line of cars waited at the Chinese restaurant takeout window at the other end.

Lindsay parked in one of the few vacant spaces facing the highway and turned off the engine. She sat in silence, taking deep breaths to calm down. The back of her neck had become searing-hot. Her hands shook. She forced a hot gooey lump back down her throat. She had to keep herself together, somehow. She couldn't lose her temper – that never solved anything. Most things could be solved by

211

staying calm and asking questions to find out what was really going on. But she was having a hard time remaining calm.

C.C. couldn't *possibly* be a bad guy. He'd helped her outside the Corral. That drunk could've been armed, for all she knew. Not many people would have even bothered to do what C.C. had done. And, on the way back from the hospital, he'd warned her about what was happening. He'd also said he was going to fix it, make it right. No, C.C. *couldn't* be one of them. But the light-blue and green colors floating around him said he was telling the truth. So did the look of defeat in his tired blue eyes.

"You told me you're a cop, didn't you?"

A nod. The blue and green fluttering around him didn't change.

"You also said the police were good – at least, the ones you know about."

"They are."

"You also told me you were going to make this right."

"I tried."

"What happened, then?"

He shrugged. "I ran out of time."

"I'm confused."

"I don't blame you."

"I'm serious, C.C. None of this makes sense. It stopped making sense when I went into the police station Saturday morning."

"That was when you stirred the pot."

"I saw someone run down an old woman. All I

did was report what I saw."

"But when you did that, you put yourself in their ballpark."

"Ballpark? This is a *game*?"

"To them, it is."

He couldn't possibly be serious. "A woman was killed, and they're calling this a *game*?"

"To them, the whole thing is a game. They make the rules, and we all have to go by what they say."

"*Rules*?"

"And Rule Number One says that no one can touch them, hurt them, or interfere with their lifestyle – no matter *what* they do."

"I've never heard of such a thing."

"It's how they work, and we have to go by it. This was why I stepped into the picture in the first place."

Something felt odd. His blue-green haze suddenly turned cloudy with white swirls. "You saved my life yesterday."

He turned away. The white swirls remained, but the blue and green faded, turning into splotches of red. "You did, didn't you?"

He didn't respond, and the white swirls grew in size. The red remained floating in their midst. Why was he lying? And why was he afraid? "C.C.? Please look at me." He could hardly meet her eyes as she prodded, "Didn't you save my life?"

He stared at his lap. "That was all ... staged."

"You mean rehearsed? Planned?"

"I ... needed you to trust me."

"*Trust* you?"

"So I could get to know you better."

Her temples fluttered. Her skin flushed. She could feel the heat of anger returning. "How *much* better?"

"I had to get you to confide in me. The people I'm working for ... they don't like to be kept in the dark. They have to know what's happening all the time. They–"

"I thought you were a cop!"

"I am."

She didn't want to ask him, but knew she had to. It was important that she find out. "Who else are you working for?"

He slumped forward and rubbed his eyes. He looked pitiful, like a recovering addict on one of those reality shows. She actually felt sorry for him. In spite of what he'd just said, he was a nice guy with a good heart. She had no idea what was going on with him, but knew there had to be extenuating circumstances. Nothing would convince her otherwise. "Tell me, C.C. I deserve to know."

"I was burned for something I didn't do."

"By who?"

"I was working undercover on a drug case. I was just about to find enough dirt on one of the big guys operating a pipeline. I was only days shy of putting him away."

"Who?"

"The less you know, the better. I got too close, and a burn order was put out on me. The burn was really effective. It put me right where they wanted

214

me. I immediately backed off. I told my boss I couldn't proceed due to false leads and insufficient evidence. Now I'm on the payroll of the very people I was trying to bring down. I've been giving them information for the last few months. I report to them as well as to Drug Enforcement."

"What happens if you just tell them to–"

"If I don't do as they say, they'll send some incriminating evidence to OPD and I'll be tossed out of the Force and face criminal charges. I'll lose my pension, my career – everything."

"Incriminating evidence?"

"Stuff they planted."

"Can't you fight this?"

"Too many people are involved. I made too many enemies. Some really bad people want my blood."

"But you're a good cop. You don't deserve–"

"What I deserve has nothing to do with this. I'm in this much too deep. And now you are, as well. They know about you and want to know what you plan to do."

"So *that* was why you staged that thing outside the Corral?"

He nodded. His colors turned blue and green again. The slivers of white remained but had grown dimmer.

"Who *was* that jerk? Someone you know?"

"His name is Pockets Sheldon. He's a petty criminal. He works the tourists and does harmless scams. He does odd jobs for me once in a while."

"*Pockets*?"

"His real name is Hiram. He doesn't care for it."

"He likes *Pockets* better?"

He shrugged.

"At the Corral, he said everyone called him Hi."

"He uses his real name when he's trying to score."

This was amazing. The man who'd helped her hadn't actually helped her at all. He *was* one of them. But for some strange reason, she didn't fear him. Nor did she hate him for what he'd done. She'd seen cop shows and read crime stories about burned cops and incriminating evidence. She'd also seen how dirty the bad guys were, how they'd stop at nothing to nail a good cop. She'd never known anyone personally who'd been burned. She could only imagine how difficult it would be to turn a good man like C.C. into a criminal.

"You want me to get out of your car?" he asked.

"You think that since I now know about you, I won't want you around anymore."

He nodded.

"Tell me one thing. What were you going to do when you found out what my plans were?"

"I didn't get that far."

"Why not?"

"The game plan ... sort of changed."

"What changed it?"

He held up his bandaged hand.

Things were beginning to make sense. He *had* lied about his injury. "You didn't get your hand

216

stuck in the car door, did you?"

"One of their persuaders found me in the parking lot outside your store."

"Persuaders?"

"They do errands for the big boys, making sure certain things don't upset the situation. They warn people about opening their mouths. They threaten, break bones, and kill people. Whatever it takes to keep the big boys happy and content."

No wonder he was so angry on the way back from the hospital. Her pulse hastened when the image flashed before her eyes. "What does this ... *persuader* look like?"

"I didn't see him."

"How could he ... break your finger ... without your seeing him?"

"He caught me from behind. I saw sunglasses and a baseball cap in my rearview mirror. I also saw someone approaching you when you were sitting in your car at the police station. It might have been him. He looked big and strong, and very capable."

Sunglasses and a baseball cap. Big and strong. Very capable. It *was* him. It had to be. "About six-two? Two hundred pounds? Light complexion?"

His eyes grew. "How ... do you–"

"He came into the store this morning, before I drove to the police station."

"He ... came *in*?"

"Sarah showed up, and he left. I had a strange feeling about him. He didn't *feel* like a customer. He called me over when he was checking out the posters. He asked me how long I'd been working there. Do you think maybe he came to scare me or something?"

"He broke my finger without exerting himself too much."

"Why'd he *do* that?"

"I was taking too long with you. They sent him to remind me what my job was."

"By breaking your finger?"

"I guess he figured I'd take him more seriously."

"That's something right out of the *Godfather*."

"These guys are psychos. And they all have their own different methods. This character's scary in all the wrong ways. He seemed cheerful, which tells me he was actually having fun. He obviously enjoys his work."

Something occurred to her. Somehow it seemed more important than anything else. "Why *were* you taking so long?"

He didn't reply. He looked down at his lap and sighed. "I ... didn't want to do any of this."

"Why not?"

He turned away. The blue and the green vanished, but not the white. "What are you afraid of?"

He gawked at her. "Afraid?"

"You're afraid to answer my question."

He sat back and his head fell back onto the neck rest.

"What's changed?"

"Meeting you."

"Why should that change anything?"

"You made me realize how low I'd sunk. What I'd become. What they'd turned me into."

"How'd I do all that?"

"Your honesty. It's been a long time since I've met anyone like you."

Her skin tingled. She could only imagine what colors were floating above her head. "I just saw something horrible and knew what had to be done. It was plain and simple to me."

"Life ceases to be plain and simple when you're a cop and have to deal with people in hopeless situations. And when I met you, I didn't like what I saw the next time I looked in the mirror. I also didn't like what they wanted me to do."

A sliver of ice slid down her spine, and she trembled. "What ... do they want, C.C.?"

"You don't want to know." The white wisps around his head thickened.

She knew she shouldn't question him any further. "You know what's really funny about all this?" she said, trying to change the subject.

"There's something *funny* here?"

"You staged that thing at the Corral to get me to trust you."

"And?"

She shrugged. "Well, it worked. Because–"

A white van creeping past showed in her rearview mirror. "It's that white van again. Behind us."

He jerked in his seat. "The same one you saw yesterday?"

"I ... think so."

He kicked open the door and jumped out. By the time he'd circled the Honda, the van had already reached the end of the lot. It pulled out into traffic and hurriedly crossed the busy highway, heading south.

***

The Foreman woman and Derek Tanner looked like they'd been engaged in a little good-natured wrestling – probably just before deciding to unlock the door.

The woman's thick dark-brown hair was slightly mashed on one side. Her light-gray jacket had fallen open. The top four buttons of her green blouse were undone, revealing her black lace bra. Splotches of her lipstick marked Tanner's lips, left cheek, and forehead. His hair was also mussed. The knot of his red cotton tie had been pulled down, exposing his tanned flesh. But right now, their focus was solely on Art.

"Who the hell are *you*?" she demanded in a choked voice. "And what the fuck are you doing in my apartment?"

"Easy, lady," Art said. "And watch the language."

She was obviously so upset that she didn't realize her bra showed. She probably hadn't even noticed his gun. "Listen, you–"

"Dorothy." Tanner's eyes were fixed on the Beretta in Art's palm. Men seemed more apt to notice guns faster than women. He grabbed her upper arm. "He's got a *gun*."

The mother's eyes lowered, then grew. "Oh,

220

shit..."

Time to organize this little party. "You. Tanner." Art gestured to the door. "Close it. And nothing funny."

He stiffened. "You ... *know* me?"

"I know who you are. Now close the door."

She jerked her face toward Tanner. Her cheeks reddened. "Derek? What the hell is going on? There's a man in my apartment with a gun, and he seems to know you!"

"Well, I don't know *him*!"

"Shut up, both of you." Art didn't want this to get out of hand. The woman shouldn't be acting up with a gun pointed toward her. Most people instinctively behaved with a gun barrel aimed at them.

Tanner closed the door – a little shakily, but he managed. *Good thing.* Firing a gun in an apartment complex wasn't wise. The Beretta, small as it was, made an impressive bang. "Now come over here and sit down."

"Wh-What ... do you *want*?" The woman's eyes strained the sockets, and she trembled. Her hands had closed into white fists. She was dangerously close to coming apart.

He was going to have to work fast. "Are you deaf? I *want* you to sit *down*."

"I mean ... that g-gun..." She pointed to it. "What do you–"

"Just shut up and sit down."

Tanner nudged her, and they both sat close to one another on the couch. The mother continued trembling. Her jaw slowly dropped. Art could sense a scream building in her lungs. "Tanner, do me a big favor. Take that hankie out of your jacket pocket."

Tanner did as ordered.

"Good. Now roll it into a nice tight ball."

Once again, Tanner complied.

"Good, professional job. I'm pleased and impressed. Now ... stuff it in your girlfriend's mouth."

"Huh?"

"Do it."

She pulled back and glared, but Art took one step closer, and she reluctantly let Tanner do the deed.

"Good. Now ... put your left arm around her shoulders and clamp your hand firmly over her mouth, and we'll all be happy."

Tanner carefully did as he was told. The mother's eyes grew even larger as Art pulled out his cell. "Who ... what ... are you doing?" Tanner asked.

"I have to find out a few things."

The mother whimpered softly. "Who ... are you working for?" Tanner asked uneasily.

"You're going to look awfully silly with your other hand slapped over your own mouth," Art warned. Tanner took the hint and shut up.

Art made the call and listened for the familiar clicks. When the line opened, he spoke softly. "I'm at the Foremans'. The mother came in with Derek Tanner."

"That is most unfortunate. We haven't heard

222

from Cross, so we must assume he's working against us. We can no longer count on the girl to listen to reason."

"What shall I do?"

"Are you sure the boyfriend is Tanner?"

"Reasonably."

"Describe him."

"Looks like the guy who played James Bond, only skinnier."

"Which Bond? There are five or six of them."

"Not the new guy. The one before him."

"That's Tanner." A pause. "This might not be as tricky as we think. Tanner SoftSystems has several government contracts pending. Our contacts can cancel them at any time. Get him out of there."

"He might not want to leave without the woman."

"With a hundred million in contracts, we think he will."

"What about her?"

"She's seen you. She's now a problem. The daughter's enough of a nuisance."

"Understood."

"Excellent. Just make sure Tanner doesn't see anything." *Click.*

Art pocketed the phone. "Tanner, get up."

Tanner pulled his hand away from the mother's mouth and stood.

"How'd you get here?"

Tanner shrugged. "I drove."

"You drove her?"

"I followed her here in my Vette."

"Two cars?"

"I've got to be at the airport in an hour. She has to be back in the office. We were just going to–"

She angrily spat out the hankie and wiped her mouth. "Shut up, Derek!"

"I was just telling him–"

"*Both* of you, shut up."

Silence. To Tanner he said, "Get out."

"What?"

"You heard me."

"But what about–"

"You've got a slew of government contracts pending, correct?"

He nodded proudly. "Big ones."

"You don't want them to go bye-bye, do you?"

He gasped. "They're worth–"

"I know what they're worth. Remember that, if you decide to mention anything about me or this incident to anyone. Got it?"

Tanner glanced at the woman, then at Art. After a deep sigh, he hurried for the door.

"Derek?" The mother's voice sounded like a squeal.

Art picked up the soaked hankie by a dry corner. "You forgot this." He tossed it.

Tanner caught it and stared at it, as if he had no idea what to do with it. Then he shook it, carefully refolded it and put it back in his jacket pocket. He opened the door, slipped through, and closed it quietly behind him.

"*Derek!*" she shouted, watching the door close.

Art slammed the edge of his right hand into the

back of her neck.

***

C.C. frantically punched buttons on his cell phone as he got back in the Honda.

"Who are you calling?" Lindsay asked, her face pale.

"I've got this friend at DMV."

"You saw the plate?" When he nodded, she objected, "But we can't even be sure it's the same van that was following us from the hospital."

"If that van's really after us, the plate's probably stolen. Calling it in won't do us much good, except to tell us whether it's stolen or legit."

Briggs answered on the second ring. "What's up?"

"I need the make on a plate. It could be stolen."

"You sound like you've been running. Got an angry husband after you? Or just old age settling in?"

"Actually, a herd of Magic cheerleaders went by in a red convertible."

"Uh-huh. How fast do you need this?"

"Now."

"Let her rip. I'll run her through, see what we come up with." C.C. gave Briggs the number, and he said, "Give me a couple minutes," then hung up.

C.C. sat back. "This could take a little while."

"What was that thing you said about the cheerleaders?"

"My friend thinks he's a comedian."

Lindsay went back to staring at the traffic. "What's going to happen?"

225

"This'll be sort of a Catch-22 thing. Like I said before, if the tag's stolen, that's a pretty clear indication someone's following us. If it was just an innocent guy, the scan will give us his name and address. That won't give us anything useful, but either way, we'll know whether we're being followed, so at least we won't get caught off-guard."

"I've been ... caught off-guard before," she said, still staring straight ahead.

He could tell something was on her mind. "When was that?"

"Finding out my ex-boyfriend was cheating on me. And ... meeting you."

Her confession sent a jolt through him. Lumping him in with her cheating ex didn't sound so good at first, but he quickly suspected she wasn't making a direct comparison, just saying she'd been blown away, completely surprised. Maybe she was hinting at something more, where he was concerned – and maybe he was just reading things into what she said. He felt blown away by her too – her simple honesty, her undeniable admirableness ... and something else he wasn't quite ready to deal with. But knew better than tell her any of that. Too many things were happening right now, and he didn't want to complicate the issue. The main concern now was to keep her safe. He knew he was being hopelessly optimistic, but at least he had a contact or two who could help them if they were forced to go underground. He hoped that wouldn't be necessary. Going underground meant they'd run into the scum of the earth.

His cell buzzed. It was Briggs. "Plate was reported stolen three days ago."

"I was afraid of that. Thanks anyway." He pocketed the cell.

"So there *is* someone after us, then?"

"Looks that way."

"What do we do?"

"I'm not sure yet." They had to drive back to the police station so he could retrieve his car. Then he could follow her back to the tee-shirt shop. He didn't think anything would happen there – not with potential witnesses wandering around. But he had no idea what to do after that. He couldn't very well act as her bodyguard. If they wanted her, they were going to get her. There were just too many of them, and they had the money and the resources to bring in as many troops as necessary.

"These people you keep talking about," she said. "Who are they?"

"I've already told you."

"If they're after me, I'd like to know more." Her eyes stayed on him. "I deserve to."

She was absolutely right. If these jerks were bent on eliminating her, she certainly deserved to know who they were. "Not too many people know about them, but since I tend to operate close to their circle, I've heard about them. They refer to themselves as the League."

Lindsay groaned.

"What's wrong?"

"You've already told me they view everything

as a game. They even call themselves the *League*. Like baseball."

"I never thought of it like that."

"So who *are* they? I mean, *what* are they?"

"A small group of businessmen. I have no idea how many they are, but my guess would be less than a dozen."

"And they run the entire city?"

"They've been doing it nearly forty years."

"And they're all businessmen?"

"Most of them own huge parcels of land. Others own banks, shopping malls, golf courses and casinos. There's even a politician or two wandering around in there. Together, they form one formidable group."

"And they don't seem to care when a helpless old woman is run over and left for dead."

He didn't reply. There was no need to.

"I don't care. I still want to go back and make that ID."

"Lindsay." This was incredible. After all that was happening, she was still bent on following through with her plan. "Don't you realize the position you've put yourself into?"

"I *have* to do this. Whoever killed Maisie should go to prison. I don't *care* who he is."

"Is it worth your life to pursue this?"

"What good is my life if I don't?"

He'd never encountered anyone like her before. But as honest as she was, he suspected there might be something more to this. No one would risk so much to help a stranger. He tried a gamble. "Did you talk to the woman before she died?"

"Just a few words. Why?"

He shrugged. "I'm just curious why you're so obsessed with this."

"She had no one else."

That said it all, didn't it? It was something learned in grade school, yet forgotten – or ignored – once the distractions of maturity set in. It certainly was a sad state of affairs. People sat in front of the TV at night, sucking down beer and potato chips while the local news informed them of countless atrocities. Murders. Rapes. Child abuse. Animal abuse. Acts of terrorism. Stock manipulation. Political corruption. The manufacturing of weapons of mass destruction in other countries. Yet nothing fazed anyone anymore.

"When someone opens my file," Lindsay said, as if to herself, "they'll see that I tried to do something about this. Maybe they'll get curious and look into it for themselves."

C.C. shifted uncomfortably in his seat. It felt like a bucket of ice had slammed him between his shoulder blades. "That ... won't happen," he said with difficulty.

"Why not?"

"I ... deleted your file."

She cringed. "You *what*?"

Another jolt of ice swept through him. He sat in silence, his pulse racing.

"C.C.?"

He'd done it to help her, but her reaction unnerved him, made him feel dirty all over again. "I snuck into Active Files and used one of my contacts to get the manager out of his office. Then I deleted your file."

"*Why?*"

"Everything about you was in there. You. Your mother. Her divorce. Everything. They obviously got into the FBI database and put it together. But nothing was in there about the hit-and-run. Nothing mentioned at all. I figured if you weren't in there, no one else would know about you."

She sighed. "You did it to ... to save my *life?*"

He shrugged.

"Thank you."

"Don't thank me yet. I'm not even sure it worked. They keep most of their stuff on backup files. All I did was delete it from McGuire's computer."

"McGuire?"

"He directs all the cases when they come in. I think he's on the take. He drives a Lexus, wears designer clothes, and collects jewelry. He seems to have more money than he should. Anyway, the case should have been in there, with a lot less stuff about you personally."

She sat back and shook her head.

"So you really want to go back to the station?"

"Yes."

"You realize what will probably happen after your visual goes into the system?"

"I don't care. I have to do this."

"All right, then." She was being stubborn, but he understood. He admired her even more. "Let's go back."

Lindsay reached for the ignition, then stopped and sat back. The strangest look covered her face.

"Lindsay?"

No reply. Her face had turned deathly pale.

"You okay?"

She slowly turned to face him. Her eyes were wet.

"Lindsay, what's wrong?"

"It's ... Momma," she whispered.

"What about her?"

"Something's happened ... at the apartment."

"How do you ... I mean–"

"C.C. ... I think Momma ... might be... Something's *happened*."

Chapter 21

Lindsay stared dumbly at the cell phone in her trembling hand, no longer feeling it, yet knowing it was there. Wanting to curse it, to hurt it for what it was doing to her. Wanting to scream at it and plead with it at the same time. There was no answer, just Momma's cheerful voice asking her to please leave a message.

That didn't mean anything, did it? Nothing bad, anyway. *Yes. It did.* Right now, it meant the difference between life and death.

You're being silly and way overly-dramatic. You need to settle down and take deep breaths. Just relax and tell yourself you're imagining things. Nothing terrible has happened.

The passing traffic had become wavy streams of blurred shapes moving in front of her eyes like the colors she'd seen since Maisie died. All sorts of colors meaning all sorts of different things. But just because she could see colors, sense things, and have strange dreams ... that didn't mean she could *predict* things, did it?

Momma was busy. She was at work. Right now she was probably with Derek Tanner and couldn't take time off to return her call. They were having one of their afternoon meetings. That made sense. Derek had meetings all the time. And when he called a meeting, Momma was right there at his side. And they didn't like to be disturbed.

C.C. was walking around in the parking lot,

talking to someone on his cell. If something happened, they'd know. They'd tell him. And he'd tell her.

Nothing had happened. She was sure of it. Momma was just fine, never better. She just couldn't talk right now. But what was that bright flash just a few minutes ago? That overwhelming coldness seeping down her back like icy molasses? That image of Momma slumped on the sofa with a large dark figure standing over her? Was Maisie communicating with her again? Was it another dream? Or just a sense of dread brought on by her fears?

Momma's fine. In a few minutes I'll call again, and she'll answer this time. C.C.'s coming back any time now to say there was no report of an accident involving anyone answering Momma's description–

The door opened, driving a gasp harshly from her throat. C.C. situated himself in the seat beside her. His face was drawn, the crow's feet framing his eyes deeper than usual. She forced herself to turn away. *Don't look. Not now. Stare at his hands, his jeans. The bandage over his broken finger that obviously needed changing. Don't look at his head. You don't need to right now. Don't–*

Despite her efforts, her gaze drifted up ... up ... until she saw the smoky monster hovering around his head. The glistening white storm moved restlessly around him. *Fear. Horrible fear.* "No." She didn't want to hear it. She couldn't. She refused to believe it.

"Lindsay..."

233

"No!" She twisted around. She couldn't look at him. The fear had become too real, too stifling. The coldness, a heavy, suffocating cloak covering her, had turned everything into a sea of eternal blackness.

He placed a hand on her shoulder. She cringed at his touch, the heat in his hand, and pulled away.

"Lindsay, they just told me–"

"No. No. It's not true. *Not true*."

The heavy cloak settled around her neck, choking her. *Stifling. No air. I'm smothering.* She had to get out of the car. The door handle wasn't where it was supposed to be. Someone had switched things around when she wasn't looking. It had become a solid, impenetrable wall, imprisoning her. This wasn't right. It *couldn't* be right. It was the same door she'd used not very long ago. It had a handle, a lock – even a button for the window. She got in, didn't she? If she could get *in*, she could get *out*. She snatched at it with both hands, the pain in her fingers and knuckles shooting up her arms like hot electrical currents. She soon realized she was punching the door and crying and could no longer see through her tears.

C.C. tried touching her again, his hands just as warm as moments before. This time she didn't resist. She didn't want to fight him anymore. She didn't want to fight anyone anymore. She wanted to close her eyes and make everything go away ... and turn back time before she'd made the call to Momma ... and maybe even before that. Before Maisie, when things made more sense.

C.C. cradled her in his arms. Even in her

darkness she remembered to be careful. She might accidentally bump his broken finger. But that was no problem because she had no intention of doing anything right now. She just melted into his sphere and let him hold her. The blackness grew more comforting as she sobbed softly into the warmth of his chest.

***

Lindsay took the glass C.C. handed her and put it in her lap.

It was cold, with an ice cube floating around in it. It looked so lonely, all by itself. She thought of Marvin, her mighty Betta, and wondered how lonely he was. Then she remembered what had happened when she'd given him a companion. Such a long time ago. Marvin. The apartment. Momma. Their life together. A lifetime had passed in just a few hours.

The couch was comfortable, soft. She'd never seen it before. She hadn't seen the apartment before, either. It was large, done in blues and golds. A TV sat on a corner unit to her left, near the entrance hall. A fireplace dominated the wall to her right. She didn't think it was real – just one of those units people bought to make the room warmer. You didn't really need a fireplace in Florida, but it sure looked nice.

She didn't remember how she'd gotten here. Everything had become a blank, a heavy blackness covering her like a shroud.

C.C. squatted in front of her, anxious for her to sip the drink. She didn't want to, but figured she should. He seemed so worried right now, his eyes bloodshot, his cheeks drawn. She knew he was trying to be a good host. She surely didn't want to hurt his feelings.

She sipped and shivered at its bitterness. She should've known. She hated the taste of whiskey – hated it since she was a kid and snuck a sip of Dad's drink one evening when they were entertaining and everyone had gone outside to look at Dad's new car. It was a Lincoln, right out of the showroom. Light-blue, with a white interior and leather seats. *"My sweet lady,"* Dad called it. He was so proud, he showed it to everyone. Even the mailman. And while the house was empty, she took a tiny sip of a drink and immediately wanted to put it back in the glass. But that was something a lady wouldn't do, so she ran into the kitchen. To kill the foul taste in her mouth, she scarfed down handfuls of pretzels and chips from the large bowls on the kitchen table Momma had fixed for later, when everyone played canasta.

Momma wasn't too wild about whiskey either, drinking only a rum and coke whenever she made Derek his Scotch and soda. Momma usually liked light beer and only had something stronger because she didn't want Derek to drink alone...

Momma. The fog surrounding her suddenly lifted. "What ... happened?" Her voice sounded like it was coming from someplace far away. She remained gazing at her drink. She didn't want to look at C.C. She feared that if she was looking at him while he said something terrible, she'd hate him forever. She didn't want to *watch* him saying something that would destroy her. Maybe she could imagine some other voice saying it. Or maybe just ignore what he said.

He sat down heavily in the squishy leather armchair facing her. She knew it was leather because it made that belching noise leather made when the cushions were mashed down. "I thought it best if I brought you here," he said softly.

"Where ... am I?"

"This is my place. I thought maybe you'd be more comfortable–"

"Tell me ... what happened," she said. Her voice had automatically dropped to a whisper at that last word. She didn't want to know, not really. But she needed to know. Not knowing was making her crazy. *I'm really messed up. And I've only had one tiny swallow of whiskey.*

"You'd better drink some more of that–"

"What *happened*, C.C.?" The rage within her had become a giant surge, encircling her like flypaper dipped in hot wax. "Why are you giving me whiskey? I *hate* whiskey."

He sat all hunched over, wringing his hands. He appeared older, more tired. His face was pale, his features taut. She felt bad for him. He picked up his glass. It clinked like hers, only much more, even though there was only one cube in it as well. She suspected his hand was shaking. This frightened her. Men were supposed to be strong. It frightened her to see a man trembling.

"No one actually saw what happened," he said.

"Your mother ... apparently tripped on the curb ... in front of your apartment."

That wasn't so bad, was it? Everyone tripped. No big thing, right? Momma would be fine. Then why was C.C. so pale? "Is she ... all right, then?"

He had more of his drink. "She tripped on her heel. It broke, and she went down hard."

Hard. That single word ripped through her. The way he'd said it sounded final. Lindsay took a deep breath. "*How* hard?"

"Her head smacked the bumper of her car."

Mellow. Have another swallow of that awful stuff. It won't hurt you and might even help. You need it. She sipped, gagging as it went down. It landed heavily in her stomach, turning everything warm. She lowered the glass back in her lap and tried to accept what C.C. had just told her. *Tripped. Broke her heel. Smacked her head on the bumper of the BMW.* Somehow she couldn't shake that image of Momma slumped on their sofa.

The sadness in C.C.'s eyes told her how hard this must be for him. His colors were very dark, with white wisps trapped within them like strands of twine holding everything in ... everything such as fear and sadness and other things she didn't want to know about. He suddenly grew blurry through the warm tears filling her eyes.

***

Before leaving his apartment, C.C. had made a few more calls to the station. Then, according to Lindsay's instructions, he made the necessary arrangements to have her mother's body sent to the

238

local crematorium. Luckily, Lindsay didn't want to rush right over and ID the body. That made things a little easier. She'd only wanted to return to her apartment – which didn't make things easier.

C.C. eased to a stop at a busy intersection on Semoran Boulevard, just a few miles north of Colonial Drive. They were in the Audi he never drove because he hated what it represented. But he'd left his Mustang parked at the police station when he'd jumped into Lindsay's Honda, and he didn't want to drive her car again, in case they might be followed and needed to ditch the tail. Of course the pale blue Audi wouldn't be hard to spot. Still, it was the Audi or the Honda. Under the circumstances, he figured he'd let the League's little 'gift' earn its keep.

Lindsay had been quiet during the ride, alternating between silence and quiet sobbing. He'd wanted to comfort her but thought it best to leave her alone. Everyone grieved in his own way. He'd learned that a long time ago. Besides, it wasn't practical or honest to tell her everything would be okay. He had no idea what the future held for either of them. The best he could do was to be there for her.

He hadn't wanted to take her, but when she said she'd drive there herself if she had to, he decided to let her have her way. His friends at the department said her mother's death didn't look suspicious, but he knew how the League operated. They employed only the best stagers. To the casual observer, Dorothy Foreman had succumbed to a freakish accident, hit her head, and died. But to C.C., who knew what was at stake, it just didn't seem reasonable that the woman would suffer such a strange accident at this time. But he knew better than voice his thoughts. Bad enough Lindsay had to accept the fact that her mother was gone. He didn't want her to know that the woman had most likely been murdered because of something Lindsay had done.

The light turned green. C.C. proceeded with the rest of the heavy evening traffic. "We don't have to do this, you know," he said, hoping she'd reconsider.

She sighed, looking straight ahead. "I need to."

Closure, no doubt. She wanted to spend time in familiar surroundings, possibly going through her mother's things. Or maybe checking her mother's papers to make sure the will and the insurance policies were within reach.

Once again he tried figuring out how she'd picked up on the accident. He'd read a little about intuition and even ESP, but this seemed much deeper than that. This mirrored those times she knew when he was lying and when he was telling the truth. This was right out of the *Twilight Zone*, and if anything spooked him, it was stuff like this. "You still haven't told me how you knew something happened."

"I had a feeling."

"That's all it was?"

"With an image as well."

"An *image*?"

"I saw Momma ... slumped on the sofa," she

240

said, her voice a whisper.

This was even weirder than he'd thought. Lindsay's strange abilities actually made his flesh crawl. And what Rossen had said earlier – "*That damn subconscious of hers*" – certainly didn't make him feel any better. He couldn't shake those weird vibes whenever he caught her staring at his hair or his forehead. And those times she'd accused him of lying to her, when only someone with superior mental powers would know, truly baffled him. That is, unless she was actually *involved* in some way.

He dismissed that idea immediately. Lindsay couldn't be involved with someone like Big John Santella or his kid Jack. The kid liked strippers. Big tits turned him on – the bigger, the better. He went apeshit for silicone, collagen, and tattoos. A girl like Lindsay wouldn't even turn his head. Big John went for blondes, big tits, long legs, and revealing outfits. He liked them tall, flashy and expensive. And he also wanted them to jump at his every command. Lindsay was a quiet girl who kept to herself, dressed modestly, and drove a Honda Civic. So where was the connection?

Something definitely didn't feel right, and he had to find out about it while there was still time. He had to work fast. She'd irritated someone in the League – possibly the younger Santella, since he was undoubtedly the one who ran down the old woman. They'd retaliated by offing her mother, which was a little harsh, even by their standards, but he saw no reason to consider the mother's death as just an unfortunate accident. It happened at the wrong time. He just wasn't sure why they'd done it. "The image you saw." He hated grilling her about this, but he had to know for sure. "You're *sure* it was your mom?"

"Positive."

He rubbed the back of his neck.

"What's wrong?"

"Something just isn't working for me."

"I told you, it was an image. I saw it. It was as clear as day."

"Lindsay, your mom broke her heel, tripped, and hit her head."

"Maybe that's how it looked..."

"One of your neighbors saw her lying there and called nine-one-one."

"I'm positive she didn't die that way."

This made less and less sense. "But they found her–"

"C.C., *it didn't happen that way*."

Her wet eyes and fierce expression convinced him she actually knew what she was talking about. Or at least *thought* she did. But how? Was it her subconscious? Or was she some sort of clairvoyant? "You're absolutely sure about this?"

Her wet, bloodshot eyes remained dead steady on him. She suddenly seemed quite calm. "Momma died in our apartment. And it wasn't an accident."

***

It was nearly eight o'clock when C.C. eased into the softly-lit parking lot and pulled into Lindsay's space in front of the apartment complex.

He flicked off the lights and the ignition and sat

242

in silence, hoping she wouldn't notice her mother's BMW and freak. She sat beside him, staring at the building. Even in the darkness of the car, he could see the terror on her face ... the grief, the hurt, the anger. Her whole life had changed in just a few hours. Reclaiming it would become a long, agonizing process.

C.C. had experienced this same thing years ago, when he'd returned home after his father's funeral. The family photos on the walls seemed like pictures of old friends he hadn't seen in years; the knickknacks on the shelves no longer familiar, but items belonging to a family he once knew. The house actually had a strange smell. He'd grown up in it, yet it felt as if he'd just entered it for the first time.

Lindsay was probably remembering both good times and bad, recalling things she hadn't thought about in years. Family picnics, school functions ... remembering her mother as a younger, more vibrant woman, content with what life had dealt her before age, disappointments, and life's tragedies had knocked her down. Before it had all ended so quickly.

She was forced to come to terms with the realization that for the first time in her life, she was truly alone. Her mother could no longer be counted on for comfort or support. The only thing left was her mother's worldly possessions. There would be family photos of good times and treasured memories frozen forever within four-by-four glossies that couldn't talk, cry, laugh, or listen. Her mother's presence would remain in her memory with the aid of those visual reminders, but her spirit would forever be gone.

She kept staring straight ahead at the front entrance. To their left, the BMW snoozed in the hazy darkness, heedless of the innocent life it had recently claimed, sleeping soundly in the visitor's space–

Visitor's space. Something odd picked at his senses. It was the detective in him, his sixth sense automatically analyzing the situation, sifting through the scene for elements that didn't belong there. When he suspected a *wrongness* staring him in the face, he knew there was always a good reason for it. "Why did your mom park there?"

Lindsay turned slightly toward her left, an inch at a time. He could feel her shaking in her seat. When she saw the car, she turned away quickly.

"You okay?"

A nod.

"You sure?"

Another nod. "Momma parked there whenever she came home for lunch with Derek."

"Derek?"

"Derek Tanner. Her boss and boyfriend. She always let him park in her space."

Something seriously foul was going on. He was even more determined to keep her from going inside. "We don't have to go in there if you don't want to. Maybe later, when you feel like it."

"I have to." She took a deep breath, two deep breaths, and finally gathered the courage to pull out

244

of her tense pose and push open her door.

C.C. pulled the tiny Beretta from its pancake holster in the small of his back and kept it buried in his fist, out of Lindsay's sight. He led the way to the building, stepping aside as she neared the front door. She froze about three feet away, her hand out, the key shaking in her fingers. Her wet eyes glistened.

"Want some help?"

Still gawking at the door, she handed over the key.

He took it with the thumb and index finger of his bad hand. While Lindsay stared uneasily at the door, he slipped the automatic in his left armpit and transferred the key to his good hand. Then he opened the door and stared into the darkness of the foyer. "Stay right here," he whispered. "I'll only be a second." He retrieved the Beretta and held it out, then slipped silently inside, found the light switch, and flicked it on. Two lamps in the living room and the overhead hall light brightened up the area. He didn't know what he'd expected. The professional in him told him that if Lindsay was right about the image she'd seen, something bad had happened in here.

Leaving the door open, he tiptoed inside and flicked on more lights. The living room closet took one second to check. Some coats, a sweeper, and a couple of brooms and dust pans. Nothing suspicious in the kitchen. The hall closet held nothing but towels, packages of toilet paper, and rolls of paper towels. The hall bathroom was also clear, as was the first bedroom. He checked under the bed, then the closet. He used the same procedure for the second bedroom, closet, and master bath.

He holstered the Beretta, went back out into the living room, and gestured for Lindsay to come in. She shuffled in awkwardly and stopped less than two feet inside the doorway, standing stiffly, hugging herself, her frightened eyes fixed on the sofa.

"You still want to do this?"

She nodded.

He closed the door behind her. The sofa was neat – the pillows fluffed and positioned, the plaid afghan draped neatly over the back. No blood. No sign of a struggle.

Lindsay still didn't move. "The sofa. It's ... wrong."

"What's wrong about it?"

"We practically live on that sofa. We usually eat supper on it while we watch TV. I haven't seen it this neat since they carried it in from the furniture store."

Yep. Foul, all right.

Lindsay went over to the corner hutch near the picture window. A small fish tank occupied a shelf, with a shiny turquoise-blue Betta swimming around in it. Lindsay picked up an orange fish-shaped container from the shelf above it and sprinkled some food into the tank. The Betta immediately swam to the surface, gobbling its dinner in seconds. Lindsay put down the container and watched the fish even after it disappeared behind a plastic blue structure and some tiny trees at the bottom of the tank.

He gently touched her shoulder. She flinched. "Do you want to check things out?" he asked.

"I'm ... not thinking very well right now. I'm ... zoning out."

"It happens." He turned and went down the hall, then turned around to make sure she was still behind him. She'd stopped in the hall entranceway and was staring at the sofa again. "We can go back to that later, if you like."

She pulled herself away and followed him into her bedroom, then gasped.

"Lindsay?"

She stood deathly still, gawking at the bed as if it held some horror only she could see.

"What's wrong?"

"I *never* make my bed."

"Well, it's made now."

"I ... didn't do it."

This was getting weirder by the minute. First, the sofa. Now this. "Maybe she came in this morning when you were in the shower–"

"Momma *never* comes – came – into my room."

"Never?"

"Not since I asked her not to." Her eyes welled up again, and she dabbed at them with a wad of tissues clenched in her hand. "We had a row one time. She barged in on me when I was working on the computer, and I told her I'd appreciate it if she knocked the next time she wanted to come in."

"Didn't go over very well, huh?"

247

Lindsay chuckled softly, almost breathlessly. "Momma was one stubborn lady. She said, 'Sure, no problem, I'll call you on your cell and make an appointment a week in advance. Maybe you can fit me into your schedule.' That was the last time she ever came in here."

"And that was when?"

"Probably six or seven months ago."

He stared at the bed. Very neat and meticulous, but the girl said she didn't do it. And if the mother never came in, she didn't do this, either. So who did? And what about the sofa?

"Even if Momma did come in, she wouldn't have touched the bed. Momma didn't like making her own bed, either. We're both slobs."

He went into the other bedroom and stared at the bed. He'd barely noticed it before because he was looking specifically for other signs of activity. But since Lindsay had just explained their neatness issues, its appearance stood out like blazing neon. The same straight, sharp corners as with Lindsay's bed, the same pattern with the pillows. Everything smooth, folded carefully and pulled tight.

Lindsay stood beside him, her eyes wide. "This is really *weird*."

"I was about to say the same thing."

She walked right over, glanced at the open bathroom doorway, and flinched. "The toilet lid."

"What about it?"

"It's ... *closed*."

"What's so odd about that?"

"Momma *always* left the lid up."

"Always?"

Lindsay shrugged. "I hated that, too. It didn't matter in here because I never came in and didn't have to look at it. But Momma also left it up in the one down the hall – which did bug me. I knew better than say anything. With Momma, you just let things go and kept out of her way. If something ticked her off, she told you about it." She went over to the bed, bent and gently touched one of the pillows. She pulled away and backed up.

"*Now* what's wrong?"

She stared at the bed, then her hand. She rubbed her fingers together and shivered.

"Lindsay?"

Her face had turned pale. "Someone was here. In this room. A man."

"You mean Tanner?"

"I don't think so." She closed her eyes. When she opened them again, they were wet. "The man who murdered Momma ... was in this room."

The same eerie feeling he'd experienced before when she'd picked up on her mother's death had returned, but this time it felt frighteningly tangible. He strongly suspected Lindsay could actually sense what had happened. "You're sure?"

A nod.

"Did you get another flash?"

"This time it was a strong, creepy feeling."

"How do you know it wasn't Tanner?"

"I just do. I have no idea how. And ... I think I've met him before."

A wave of shock washed over C.C. "Anything

else you're picking up?"

"Not yet. But I think I'll know who he is before long."

"You're ... gonna have to tell me how you do this," he said uneasily.

"I have no idea how I'm doing it."

"Is this something you've been able to do all your life?"

She shook her head. "I've only been doing it since last Friday."

"Friday?"

"When I helped Maisie."

250

Chapter 22

From his SUV parked at the other end of the lot, Art Radner watched the two figures entering the apartment. His employer called less than an hour ago and told him Cross had called OPD to ask about the girl's mother. *Strange.* Cross was probably calling to check in and accidentally got hold of someone who'd heard about the mother's unfortunate 'accident.' Since it wouldn't make the local news until next of kin was notified, Cross couldn't have learned about it any other way.

The girl was obviously traumatized. She moved stiffly, barely bending her legs. Even in the dim light of the street lamps, her trembling was plainly visible. Cross stayed close, acting the part of a true Lancelot. The girl would need time to mend. She most likely wanted to come right home and comfort herself in familiar surroundings. This could turn out very well. Her life would be put on hold. If her grieving period mirrored that of most other young females faced with the sudden death of a parent, it would be months before her life got back on track.

He wondered if the girl had any suspicions about her mother's death. *How could she?* It was a well-staged accident. The mother's ankle twisted the wrong way, causing the heel to break off. Females broke their heels or fell off them all the time. And when they did, they went down hard. Many were lucky to grab onto something to break their fall. The Foreman woman wasn't so lucky.

Art reminded himself that Cross was now the main issue. Since the girl was at least temporarily out of the picture, Cross presented their only threat. Eliminating the girl right now would be stupid. Her untimely demise would cause attention, resulting in an unwanted investigation. But now Cross would have to be taken out of the picture. He hadn't called to tell them about his progress with the girl. Instead, he'd decided to help the girl – clear evidence that he'd sided against them. Cross had just signed his own death warrant.

This had to be handled correctly. It had to look like Cross had gone crazy and killed himself. A dishonest cop rumored to be on the Mob's payroll suddenly going berserk and eating a bullet would make terrific headlines. It would also take the public's attention away from other issues.

Art had done this same sort of job a dozen times before. The easiest and simplest method was to chloroform him, then take him to a convenient location – probably his Winter Park apartment – and pump half a bottle of booze into his system, then feed him one of his own bullets. Cross had more than a dozen firearms registered in his name. Picking the appropriate one should only take a few minutes.

The only problem would be collecting Cross without the girl being aware of anything. Art couldn't very well sneak inside. Cross's superior senses would easily pick up on a door being unlocked. He had to find some way of luring Cross outside. Once Cross was unconscious, Art could pull him into the back of the utility vehicle. It would take less than half an hour to transport him to the apartment, and no more than another hour to fill him with booze and feed him the bullet.

Art pulled his trusty leather sap from his toolkit and checked his jacket pocket for the chloroform packet. Another pocket held a small roll of duct tape. He fitted the key into the ignition and put the SUV in gear. A smile of contentment overtook his face.

***

After assessing the situation, C.C. feared Lindsay's connection with the old woman might be responsible for her strange sensations, but probably not in the way Lindsay thought.

She'd seen an old woman run over and left for dead. The experience was definitely both heart-wrenching and disturbing. Something like that would mess up anyone's head. The woman's death could have affected Lindsay's subconscious, shifting things around and, in doing so, uncovering untapped treasures that would have otherwise remained unnoticed. If the dead woman had possessed strange powers, their substance and origin had died right along with her. Nothing was known about her. The old woman was apparently homeless, and the homeless liked to be left alone, to remain invisible. For them, life was much more tolerable that way.

Despite his skepticism, C.C. knew about strange happenings. He'd seen things in his years on the force he wouldn't have even considered before entering the academy. People pronounced dead abruptly sitting up and walking out of the hospital. A homeless man hit over the head in a robbery suddenly able to quote complete lines from Shakespeare, Dostoyevsky, and Tolstoy. A dog trotting across I-4 during evening rush hour without being struck or killed. A vagrant picking up a discarded Lotto ticket in a 7-Eleven parking lot and discovering it was worth ten million bucks. Strange, to be sure. But all true.

Lindsay could tell when he was lying and when he was telling the truth. She sensed things, saw images. Just hours ago, she knew her mother was dead. They were miles away when it happened, but she *knew*.

Her hands clasped together, Lindsay fearfully approached the sofa. She looked like a little girl reporting to the principal's office for doing something naughty. She stopped near the coffee table and stared at the sofa. Her body trembled. Then, taking a deep breath, she gently touched the cushion with her fingertips – and pulled back, as if scorched by flame. Her eyes filled. "Momma ... she was ... *here*."

"When?"

"Not long ago."

"Anything else?"

"Pain. Horrible pain." She held her fingertips in front of her ashen face, studying them. They were flushed.

"Do they hurt?" he asked.

"They're warm. Tingly."

Strange. But he believed her.

She lowered her arm. "Derek was here, too. They were both sitting here."

"Aren't they – weren't they working today?"

Lindsay reddened. "They'd come home for..."

"I get it."

"Momma really liked Derek. He seemed to like her, too."

He wasn't thinking about Lindsay's mom. He was thinking about Derek Tanner. *Tanner comes home with Lindsay's mother for an afternoon quickie. That part makes sense. Nothing odd about it at all. Stuff like that goes on every single day in every town and city in the country.* But what didn't make sense was the expensive car sitting outside in front of the building. "Did they always use two vehicles?"

"Derek usually had appointments after lunch. He made a lot of trips to Tampa and Miami. Sometimes he picked up a business associate from the airport or one of the hotels. Momma always had to go back to the office."

He played it again in his head. *The mother and Tanner drive here for their quickie. Then the mother says something to press Tanner's buttons. He gets physical, and she hits her head on the coffee table. He panics and stages it outside to look like an accident.* That made no sense. Why take her outside? Why not call 911 and try to save her? If Tanner *had* done her in, would he have straightened the sofa and made the bed? Maybe ... if he was trying to cover up evidence of his being there. "Lindsay, tell me about Tanner. Is he the physical type?"

"You mean, would he..." Her eyes widened. "Derek wouldn't hurt Momma."

"You're sure?"

"Everyone at Tanner SoftSystems knew about them. Everyone knew they always had lunch together. Derek wouldn't do anything that would hurt his company. And Momma was valuable to him. He wouldn't–"

"Does he have a temper?"

"Derek's arrogant and snobbish. He's also a jerk, but he'd never–"

"Lindsay, I'm sure you know that when a woman pushes a man's buttons, he ends up doing things he wouldn't normally do."

"I *never* saw them fight."

"If Tanner came home with your mother, what happened? The way this looks, they did their thing, then he left. But your mother stayed here and was found outside, near her car."

"Someone broke in. Someone broke in and–"

"Lindsay, what does Tanner's company do?"

"It's some kind of software brokerage. I don't know exactly, but Momma says they always win big government contracts."

The government. Big money. Tanner was probably a hands-off. That might explain his quick exit. He might have been warned. In fact–

The living room suddenly blazed with a searing white light.

***

C.C. pushed Lindsay into the hall, nearly knocking her down.

256

Shocked by his strange reaction, she instinctively grabbed his left arm for balance and immediately discovered how strong he was. It didn't tax him at all to support her weight with only one arm. But she couldn't help wondering why he'd reacted this way. She tried looking into his eyes, but he'd turned sharply and peered around the corner.

"I hope I didn't hurt you." His eyes finally settled on her. His colors were blue and green, with white tendrils. He was sincere, and a little scared. "I had to move fast."

"I'm fine." His arm rested against the small of her back. It felt like it belonged there. She leaned into it even before realizing what she was doing, but he pulled away. In one smooth movement, he spun around to face the front door.

A gun had appeared in his hand almost as if by magic. "Stay here," he whispered. "I'll be right back."

"Where are you going?"

"I have to see what's happening out there."

She wanted him to stay with her. She didn't know what the fuss was about. "Probably someone parked out front left his lights on. That's happened once or twice before."

"Maybe." His eyes had gone cold. His blue and green had turned into black and white strands.

Her neck and arms grew warm while her brain worked busily. C.C. was a cop – a good one. He most likely had a sixth sense about things like this. When something didn't seem right or feel right, he knew instantly. Speaking of not feeling right...

Momma. The sofa. The white van. The man who'd come into the store this morning. What C.C. said about the man driving the Charger. The people they'd gone up against. *Momma's dead. Someone ... killed her. And here I am, thinking the bright headlights are the result of someone's carelessness. I'm so stupid...* "You actually think someone ... might have shined their lights in here on purpose?"

"I don't hear anyone's engine running out there. Do you?"

Shards of ice plunged down her limbs.

C.C. squatted and duck-walked over to the sofa, then to the entrance. He reached up with his good hand and turned off the living room light as well as the front porch light. He turned the doorknob, eased the door open about a foot, and slipped outside. The door closed softly.

An invisible cloak of ice encircled her. C.C. was gone. So was Momma. And whoever killed Momma might be the same person who'd left his high beams pointed at the living room window. But why would he do that? Why would anyone–

Oh my God. The cloak of ice tightened around her. Someone had just *lured* C.C. out of the apartment. *The police.* She had to get them here fast, before something horrible happened. She'd left the cell in her purse. And her purse was in C.C.'s car outside. *Idiot. This is your home, remember? The phone in the kitchen.* She slipped through the doorway and scooped up the phone, then fumbled and dropped it. Picking it up again, she stared blankly. *What number? Nine-one-one. Punch it in!*

258

Her fingers wouldn't cooperate. Neither would her brain. She couldn't find the nine. Then she slipped and hit redial. *Good Lord. What's wrong with me?*

Don't lose it. Think rationally. C.C. might be in trouble. She could never forgive herself if he was in danger and she didn't do something to help – especially since all this was happening because of something she'd done. She dropped the phone and crossed the living room. Her heart thrashing, she pulled open the door. On impulse, she flicked on the porch light. A large man stood over C.C., who lay sprawled on the concrete. He took a step back and held up an arm to shield his face. A moment later, he lowered his arm. It was the man who'd come into Sarah's shop.

"*Now* you've gone and done it, silly girl," he warned.

She fought to find her voice. "Wh-What have you ... why ... is he–"

"You really have a nasty habit of showing up at the wrong time. You need to work on that, girl. Your timing *sucks*."

"What have you *done*?"

"Back inside."

Obediently she backed up. He picked up C.C. easily and draped him over his left shoulder, wrapping his massive left arm over the back of C.C.'s thighs to keep him from sliding off. Then he followed her inside.

Lindsay tried speaking again but stopped when something appeared in the man's right hand. A tiny black gun with a short, skinny barrel peeked over his index finger like the single eye of a curious little creature. It was aimed directly at her.

Now that he wasn't wearing sunglasses or his Gator's cap, she could see his features. He was actually good-looking, but the gun in his hand and C.C.'s body draped across his shoulder made him scary and despicable. He took another step into the apartment. Without taking his eyes from her, he kicked the door shut.

Lindsay cringed at the harsh sound.

"Please don't be one of those girly-girls and scream," he said. "Otherwise, I'll have to use this." The gun twitched in his hand.

"You're the man who ... you came into the store today..."

"Good memory." The man's face relaxed. "We didn't get to talk much, though. Your boss came in and ruined our moment. Her timing sucks, too." He kept the gun trained on her. He didn't even shift his gaze as he switched the firearm to his other hand. Then he reached behind him. The clicking of the lock made her jump.

He put the gun back in his right hand, walked over to the sofa, and dropped C.C. onto its cushions. C.C. fell like a rag doll and did not move.

"He's not ... *dead* ... is he?" It was getting harder and harder to deal with all this. First, Momma. Now C.C.?

"Not yet, but you walked in on us just as I was getting ready to do my thing." His attitude made it sound like he was actually having fun. His free hand slid inside his black lightweight jacket. A small roll of silver duct tape appeared. He spun it around his index finger. "You wouldn't mind wrapping some of this stuff around the cop's ankles and wrists, would you?"

"Why ... why are you *doing* this?"

"I don't want him going anywhere. It's not that I don't trust him – I just don't trust him. Know what I mean?"

"Why ... why are you here? What do you want?"

"You really don't need to know."

"But what have I *done*?"

"You've been pushing too many buttons, sister. I came to warn you to shut up, but since you went outside and saw something you weren't supposed to, you've upped the ante. It's nothing personal. You're just a naughty little girl who needs to be punished." He held the tape out.

She gaped numbly at it. *Tape. Wrap it around C.C.'s wrists and ankles.*

"C'mon, girl. I don't have all day."

"What are you going to ... do with us?"

"It's a surprise." The blues and greens hovering above his massive shoulders were tinged with black strands. Death, as well as truth and happiness. She remembered something C.C. had said about the League and how they operated. This man was one of their 'persuaders.' He'd just handled C.C. as though he was a bag of groceries.

"You're the one who broke his finger."

"That's one of my many specialties." His grin dazzled in the living room lighting.

"*Specialties*?" Breaking someone's finger is a *specialty*?

"You sure talk a lot. Here." He peeled off a six-inch length, tore it off with his teeth, and held it out. "Slip this over your own pie hole and turn around. I'll deal with your boyfriend after I fix you up. Like I said, I don't have all day."

Her hands shook terribly, but she was able to grasp a corner of the tape from him. The brief contact caused a hot surge flowing into her arm that made her jerk. She almost dropped the tape. Another realization hit her. This one slammed into her with the force of a sledgehammer. *This animal ... was here before. On the sofa.* "You're the one ... you ... I *know* you ... you were ... you were the one..." Her throat could no longer function. The cold lump had come back. Her body shook violently. The tape dropped to the carpet and folded over, sticking to itself.

"Oh, now look what you've done." He shook his head and clucked.

She remained shaking, gaping at him, imagining Momma on the sofa, this monster pushing her down, Momma trying to scream, this monster saying something he thought was funny, all the while planning to kill her.

"You're being *such* a problem child." He tried peeling off a corner from the roll in his free hand but had to take his eyes off her briefly.

Momma's glass pelican stood on the end table just a couple of feet behind her. She reached behind while the madman fought with the tape, but her hand didn't make contact with anything solid. *Let it come to me. Let Momma come back and help me...* She flinched when something smooth and cold filled her palm. *My God ... I must've been closer to it than I thought.* Her heart pounded wildly as she wrapped her fingers around its long, smooth neck and pulled it against her. She stood deathly still, her left hand closed in a tight fist, her right keeping the solid glass knickknack firmly against her right buttock.

He tried to tear off a strip from the roll. He started a new tear, then handed her the roll. "Rip that off and let's get this show on the road."

She had trouble opening her left hand. She wanted to slap him in the face but knew that, even in her fury, she probably wouldn't be able to hurt him. When she finally managed to take the roll in her shaking hand, it fell from her grasp.

His eyes left her, following the tape as it rolled toward him on the carpet. "This really isn't your day, is it?" The tape stopped near his tennis shoe. "You sure are doing your best to chafe my short curlies, girl." He bent to pick it up.

Her right arm whipped around in a wide arc and came down viciously toward his head. But her inner self instantly stepped in, redirecting her efforts. Despite her fury, her hatred, and her desire to destroy this animal, she jerked her body slightly toward her left. The pelican swished by, missing him by less than an inch and knocking her off-balance.

She'd *wanted* to hit him but *didn't* want to. She

wasn't a killer. Never was, never would be. She disliked hurting people's *feelings* – how could she even *think* of *killing* someone? *But he killed Momma. How could you hesitate? Even for a moment?*

He straightened and moved the gun toward her. "*That* certainly was a seriously naughty thing to do, little girl. Now I'm afraid you've *really* got to be punished."

She closed her eyes and waited for the end to come. *Soon I'll be with Momma.*

The gun went off, shattering something dangerously close to Marvin's tank. She opened her eyes. C.C. had leaped from the sofa and, spinning the big man around, struggled for the gun. C.C. was smaller, lighter, and had only one good hand. The gunman had no problem pushing him away. The gun came up again, aimed at C.C.'s face.

Lindsay suddenly realized she still gripped the pelican. Its coolness had strangely become so hot, and it was like gripping a poker taken directly from a fire. But instead of dropping it, her fist refused to let go. The smooth solid object had become an extension of her own hand. *You have no choice. It's either this monster or C.C.* Without a moment's hesitation, she hauled off and swung again. The pelican's feet caught him squarely on the back of the head, forcing a surprised grunt from him. He went down hard, smacking his face on the coffee table before landing with a thud on the carpet. One of Momma's fashion magazines jarred loose from the pile, fluttering to the carpet beneath the table.

The killer's gun hopped five feet across the carpet and lay at her feet. She backed away as if it was a poisonous snake.

C.C. sat up and rubbed his forehead. He stared at the man on the floor, then at the gun, then at her. He crawled over and felt for a pulse.

"Is he ... dead?" she asked in a harsh whisper.

He didn't reply.

"C.C.?"

Lindsay saw C.C. barely nod. Still gripping the pelican, she stumbled to the bathroom.

***

The evening had slipped a dark-gray curtain over the apartment complex, making everything filmy and bleak.

Huddled in the passenger seat of C.C.'s Audi, Lindsay prayed that the cold numbness enveloping her would shield her from the horrors of the real world. A hundred yards to her right, C.C. talked to the police and the ambulance people. He'd been thoughtful enough to help her into the car, then move it to a visitor's spot far enough away from the commotion. As an added precaution, he stayed close to the apartment entrance and directed the activity. Two policemen came back out and walked over to him. They talked again very briefly before going back inside. Two others wandered off, talking to their cell phones.

The scattered groups of residents emerging from the complex made her tremble. Some stood behind shrubbery, others on front stoops, chattering away. She'd never seen most of them before but knew a few by sight. She'd talked to others briefly on laundry day. They were people she lived near, yet none knew her or what just happened.

The EMT people eventually wheeled out the covered gurney and slid it into the rear of the ambulance.

Lindsay turned sharply away. Despite her efforts, she couldn't ignore what she'd done. He was probably the same age as C.C. He was a big, strong, handsome man. He was a killer, but nevertheless a man. She'd bashed in the back of his head with Momma's glass pelican. A hot, unbridled rage had taken over. She'd *wanted* to do it. She'd *intentionally* murdered a human being.

The cold numbness grew heavier. She closed her eyes and let it wrap its thick, icy tentacles around her. If only she could will herself to drift away to some other place, where people didn't play deadly games...

How could she show her face in the complex again? How could she face Sarah at the shop? The customers? How could she face *anyone*? Even if she did manage to dodge a prison sentence, how could she possibly live a normal life?

Had this same sort of thing happened to Maisie? Had the colors, the feelings, and the strange powers taken their toll? Had this weirdness corrupted her life? Was this the reason she'd ended up homeless? Why she'd died all alone?

The door opened, making her jump. C.C. held out a Styrofoam cup. The last thing she wanted was to put something into her empty stomach. After

266

she'd thrown up in the bathroom and forced herself to turn away from the pale, drawn face staring back at her in the mirror, she didn't think she could eat or drink anything ever again. "I don't want any coffee, thank you."

"It ain't exactly coffee."

Sighing tiredly, she took it. It smelled faintly of whiskey. This was the second time today he'd given her booze. She tried to remember why he'd done it the first time. Her mind was a mess. All she could think of was how bad the first drink tasted. "I really don't think I should..."

"Drink it. That's an order."

She took a tiny sip. The warm liqueur burned once it hit her stomach. The throbbing eased up, warming her. "What *is* it?"

"Just drink it. It'll help you relax."

She drank a little more. Then, smarting at the sudden dizziness, she handed it back to him.

"Finish it. I'll be right back."

"Where are you going?"

"I have to answer a few more questions, then we're out of here."

"Where are we going?"

"My place again, I'm afraid. Until we figure something out."

"C.C., I don't think..." This just wasn't right. She couldn't stay with him. She couldn't just kill someone, then quietly leave town, could she?

"Trust me, okay?"

"Don't they want me ... to answer some questions?"

267

"I handled it."

She studied his face. His colors were blue and green, with some reddish tendrils mixed in among them. He was lying about something. "What aren't you telling me?"

His face flushed. "We'll talk later, all right?"

"Will you tell me the truth then?"

"I promise." The red tendrils vanished.

Somewhat relieved, she closed her eyes and let herself drift off.

***

A gentle tapping on her left arm woke Lindsay, and she opened her eyes.

The glare of a streetlamp shining into the car made her turn away. She glanced at trees, bushes, a cobblestone walk, and spotted Spanish tile roofing. The setting seemed vaguely familiar, but she wasn't quite sure where she was. "What time is it?" Her voice, weak and raspy, crawled sluggishly out of her throat.

"It's almost midnight. C'mon. You need sleep."

The beginnings of a headache stirred distantly – no doubt from that drink he'd given her. Maybe if she dozed off for a little while, it would go away. She closed her eyes and laid her head back.

"Get up." He nudged her elbow.

Instinctively she pulled back. *Easy, now*. This was C.C. It was just a nudge. She wasn't ... she wasn't *back there*. She pushed the door open. Grabbing the door frame, she pulled herself out of the car. A wave of warm dizziness swept through her.

C.C. circled the car. He was carrying her tan leather suitcase. "I packed some things for you."

He'd obviously gone through her dresser drawers, probably after the police had finished their investigation. She wondered if she should be embarrassed. It took her only a moment to realize he'd done her a huge favor.

Another swell of dizziness washed through her. The urge to lie down grew much stronger. She was much too exhausted to argue or even talk. It had become more difficult to stand. The only thing she wanted right now was a warm bath and sleep. She could burn her clothes afterward. They were damp. They smelled. It wasn't B.O., it was something else. The man she'd killed ... his smell had slithered onto her clothes like a vile serpent. She'd never be able to wear them again.

C.C. took her arm, and together they went down the bush-lined cobblestone walk.

PART VII – THURSDAY
Upping the Ante

Chapter 23

The elite Gold Crest Country Club fronted a section of undeveloped Orlando woodlands just a few miles southwest of Central Florida's biggest theme parks.

Giuseppe 'Jo-Jo' Lanza and 'Big John' Santella owned Gold Crest as well as the land it occupied, and the shopping mall and condominium complex two miles down the road, where many tourists stayed while spending most of their time at the theme parks. The eighteenth hole of Gold Crest ended just twenty yards from the path leading to the rear entrance of the Country Club. The immense two-story glass-and-brick structure glittered among the professionally-trimmed greenery as spectacularly as a diamond embellished green velvet. A two-hundred-acre tract of woods earmarked for the future development of luxury condominiums sprawled behind the complex.

Pleased with his game, Jo-Jo Lanza handed over his monogrammed custom-made putter to his fresh-faced caddy. Jo-Jo adjusted his visor over his tanned bald head and nudged the red-tinted wraparound sunglasses a fraction of an inch up his bulbous nose.

The sky was beautiful, marred only by a jet

stream forming a puffy white scratch piercing the seamless light-blue. Typical Florida morning. A state famous for its blinding sun, heat, electrical storms, humidity, and hurricanes. But the bikinis and the fact that you never had to endure extreme cold made it all worthwhile.

Big John was not having a good morning. Jo-Jo couldn't blame his *compadre* one bit. Raising a punk kid would grate on anyone's nerves. The new generation could drive anyone crazy. These kids wanted it all – money, fast cars, and sex – but they didn't want the responsibilities that came with it. Jo-Jo knew all about the new generation. His two daughters, both now in their forties and living with their families in Boca, raised spoiled kids as well.

Jo-Jo had finished the hole with a four, Big John a six. Santella was gonna be a bear the rest of the afternoon. The big boy hated losing – especially at a hundred bucks a stroke. Jo-Jo recorded the final tallies into the scorecard and chuckled softly. Best not gloat *too* much. Santella might go apeshit and toss his putter again. That last time nearly shattered a dining room window. Expensive glass, ran two grand for a single sheet.

"Three strokes, *paisano*," he told his friend. "At a hundred a stroke, that means you owe me–"

"I went to school too, old man." Big John pulled out a thick wad from his pants pocket, peeled off three bills and handed them over.

"Ah." Jo-Jo grinned. "Now I can treat us to lunch." He handed over one bill to their caddies, told them to split it, then started up the path. "You

271

know what your trouble is, *paisano*?"

Santella pulled a slender, custom-rolled Italian cigar from the pocket of his imported silk shirt. He found his gold lighter in the side pocket of his custom-tailored Bermuda shorts and lit up. He said nothing.

"Your mind ain't on your game."

Santella pushed out a plume of gray smoke, which immediately broke up into lazy tendrils drifting away in the warm breeze. "No shit."

"Matter fact, I'd say your mind's *so* fucking far away, you don't even remember what we been doing this morning."

"We've been playing golf. Nothing wrong with my memory."

Jo-Jo took one of Santella's offered cigars and lit it. "You're half right. *I* been playing golf."

"And what the fuck have *I* been doing? Jacking off? I'm out here too, old man – same as you. Instead of whipping off a piece from my blonde babe, I drive out here for a quick nine and spend the next couple hours listening to an old man's bullshit."

Jo-Jo puffed away on his cigar. "You're out here, all right. Physically, anyway ... going through the motions. And don't forget, *you* were the one who called to hook up for the game. But, like I said, your head's somewhere else."

Santella shrugged.

"You worried about that business with your boy?"

"Don't fucking remind me."

272

They walked through the wide sculpted archway. The waiters and hostesses all bowed politely as Jo-Jo and Santella passed through the French doors, entering the ornate dining room.

Jo-Jo liked polite, friendly people. It showed respect, made him feel good about himself. Respect was important. The world would be a much happier place if everyone showed one another a little respect. *I should run for President. The country wouldn't have so many problems if these arrogant assholes spitting out babies and sponging off the government showed some responsibility.*

They took their usual corner table overlooking the tennis courts. Two slender, long-haired babes battled it out in the court nearest their window. The tall, skinny blonde had long legs and nice titties. The brunette wasn't as tall but filled her white blouse and shorts really well. She also had great legs. Both looked around twenty-five or so.

"Nice," Jo-Jo said. Babes were one thing he could never get enough of. Funny how a man grew older but his taste for women never changed. Here he was, pushing seventy, and the sight of a slim, big-breasted young thing still put his *cojones* in an uproar. "Good scenery this morning."

"I'll take *both* babes," Santella said.

Jo-Jo chuckled. Put Santella in a room with twenty babes and he'd end up trying to nail them all.

The waiter stood beside them, waiting patiently.

"So whatcha want this morning, *paisano*? Breakfast? Or just some Espresso?"

Santella's gaze didn't stray from the two babes.

"I'm too fucking pissed to bother with food this morning."

"Two Espressos," Jo-Jo said. "I'll have some buttered toast. Rye. No seeds. Bring plenty of strawberry jelly."

The waiter hurried away.

"Your boy can be a dickhead, but he shows good business sense, *paisano*."

Santella dropped ash into the glass ashtray at his elbow. "Shame he's such a *sfachim* in other areas."

"We *all* fucked up at his age. What is he now? Twenty-five?"

"Twenty-six. Almost half my age and he's still a fucking kid."

"You spoiled him. You and that woman you were married to."

"*I* wanted him to be a man. *She* wanted him to keep being a boy. It's been over fifteen years since we split up, and he's *still* a boy. Bitch fucked him up good."

Jo-Jo shrugged. "Give him more responsibility. He'll learn."

"Boy's got a good head. Went to Rollins and made A's and B's when he wasn't chasing skirts."

"Like his old man."

Santella shrugged.

Jo-Jo figured Santella should be reminded of how well his son was doing. Running coke from Orlando to Biloxi was no minor chore. The guy in charge had to find the right drivers and the right vehicles, and make sure the stuff was packed

274

correctly, then delegate the work to the right men. And he had to be tough. Someone stiffed him or lifted a sample, he had to find out quick.

Jo-Jo lowered his voice. "He's done good with his route."

"He still fucks up."

"Not with his route. He knows how to handle things. He delegates well, knows how to pick his men–"

"He's a moron when he gets with his friends."

"You talking about that small matter the other day? Alvarez's kid?"

Santella's dark, fleshy features flushed instantly. "What the hell else? He got the cops into this. It almost made the fucking *Sentinel*, for Chrissakes."

The waiter brought their Espressos and Jo-Jo's toast and jam. Jo-Jo shooed him away quickly and checked to see that no one was within earshot, just a couple of tourists at the other end of the huge room. This was serious. It could delay a shipment, and anything that delayed a shipment cost money and agitated a lot of people. Julio Alvarez was in the same pickle as Santella. He also had a kid who frequently turned into a dickhead and had no idea how to put his dick back in his pants. But Alvarez had helluva lot more to lose. He was being groomed for the state senate. Any scandal would kill his chances.

Jo-Jo didn't want to see that happen. Alvarez had connections in Miami with the Colombian cartel. Alvarez's political success would ensure Jo-Jo's sale of two hundred acres of his woodlands to several prime Miami people who needed to branch out with their South American and Mexican connections.

"*Paisano*, at his age, I was naïve, too. But I learned what was what, and—"

"That moron son of mine." Santella mashed his cigar in the ashtray. "He let Alvarez's kid use his muscle car."

Jo-Jo didn't want to think Jackie Santella was stupid enough to jeopardize a shipment, but Big John was acting more uptight than usual. Something else had obviously happened. "Not a problem. A homeless woman. Who the hell cares?"

"That goody-two-shoes bitch that saw it, evidently."

"I thought that was taken care of."

"A lot of shit's gonna fly right into our laps if we can't keep a lid on this. This is why I'm gonna need your help."

"Then I'm gonna have to know everything about this. What else is so fucking important, *paisano*?"

Santella dragged his chair closer. His tanned face had gone pale. "Jo-Jo ... there was *stuff* in my kid's car."

"Stuff?"

"Coke. As well as payoff money."

Jo-Jo felt the blood draining from his body. "Go on," he said softly.

"When Alvarez's kid ran down that old woman, the smartest thing he coulda done was get the fuck out of there."

276

"Keep going."

"My son had over half a mill in hundred-dollar notes in the back seat. The usual stuff we use for greasing our Biloxi friends."

"What else?"

"Half the damned shipment was in the back seat. He was bringing it in for transport when he got a call from one of his old college friends. The gang was at the local hangout. That dump on Goldenrod. He went there and got shitfaced. Alvarez's kid was there, too. And when he asked Jackie to borrow the Charger for a spin..."

Jo-Jo took a deep breath. *Focus. Calm.* Keeping cool when the morons all around were fucking up deserved both admiration and a ton of respect. But this was big – *real* big. It was the kind of thing that brought down ordinary men. *Calm. You're the boss. Act like one.* He took another deep breath and immediately felt the calm taking over, helping him recover, see things more clearly. "How much blow was in the car, *paisano*?" he asked softly.

"Around two million, street value."

Jo-Jo sat back in his seat and rubbed his eyes. *Shit.* This was all they needed. One lost or fucked-up shipment, and Biloxi would be down on them like a pack of wild dogs. "But it's safe now, isn't it? Your kid got his car back. Maybe a couple dents, a little blood on the paint. Wash the stuff off, take the car in and have it cleaned up, the dents pounded out. A thousand bucks, tops. It isn't like this fucked up the Biloxi run ... is it?"

Santella just sighed.

Jo-Jo's cheeks turned hot and tingly. Another deep breath was definitely required now. He took it and thought, *Calm. mellow.* "I don't like no sigh, *paisano.* I ask a question, a sigh ain't what I want to hear. I want an answer. So tell me what your fucking *sigh* means."

Santella leaned forward. His voice was just a whisper. "It's gone, old man."

Jo-Jo's heart skipped a beat. Santella surely didn't mean what that sounded like. He couldn't. No. Things couldn't *possibly* be that fucked up.

"*What's* gone?"

"The shipment. It walked."

***

Lindsay awoke to find herself in a strange room.

It was small, its walls fairly dark. A bronze lamp stood on top of a small nightstand in the corner. A stained wooden dresser sat against one wall. Straight ahead, slender beams of glittering sunlight peeked in through the blinds. She didn't remember sleeping or even falling asleep. She vaguely remembered C.C. bringing her in here. He'd put down her suitcase, then quietly left the room. Everything else turned dark and sketchy, then ceased to exist.

She wore her bra and panties. She must have taken off her clothes herself. She probably lay down, covered herself and just closed her eyes. The nightmares came back in filmy waves. Images of Momma lying beside her BMW. The man with the gun dropping C.C. on the sofa. C.C. struggling with the other man. Momma's glass pelican jumping into her hand. Then...

She rubbed her wet eyes. *Stop the self-pity. Life goes on. You've heard that many times before. You just didn't have any conception of what it really meant. Until now.*

She swung her legs over the edge of the bed. A heavy wave of dizziness made the room sway like a ship during a storm at sea. She closed her eyes and waited for everything to settle down.

Her clothes sat next to the door, wadded up in a ball. The outfit she wore last night, when she killed a man. She jerked her head away. More tears filled her eyes.

Life goes on. In spite of everything, life didn't stop – or even slow down – for anyone. In spite of the fact that Momma was dead – and the man who'd killed her. Life had no choice. And neither did she.

She got out of bed. Her suitcase sat on the floor in front of the dresser. She bent and opened it. C.C. had collected some of her clothes and brought them here. That was *so* nice of him. So thoughtful.

She put on her gray sweatshirt and jeans and opened her overnight bag. Her brush, comb and pocket mirror sat in there with her other stuff. She ran a hand through her hair. It could stand a wash, rinse, and major overhaul. Should she brave a trip to the bathroom? Could she stand to look at the face staring back at her in the mirror? Would she *ever* be able to look at herself again?

She picked up her comb and forced it through her knotted hair, then put it back and went over to the door. Ignoring the mess on the floor, she pulled open the door. The smell of crispy bacon perked her right up. How could she be hungry after last night? Maybe it was because she'd purged her guts the previous night and hadn't put anything in there since. The fresh, delicious smells made her stomach moan. She went down the hall and stopped in the kitchen doorway.

C.C., in red tee-shirt and denim shorts, flipped eggs at the stove. He wore an apron. A macho guy like him wearing an apron? Despite her dark mood, she wanted to smile. "Good morning."

He spun around. "I didn't think you'd be up so early."

She suddenly felt guilty for sneaking up on him. Maybe he'd wanted breakfast by himself. A guy like him certainly wouldn't want anyone to see his apron. It said *KISS THE CHEF AND PASS THE BEANS!*

Maybe it wasn't too late to just slip quietly away. "I'm sorry. I guess I can go back and try to–"

"Sit down and have breakfast with me. You're probably famished."

"I don't know if I can eat anything..."

"Just some coffee, then."

Despite her initial reluctance, coffee sounded good. She climbed onto the barstool.

He brought over a cup and went to fetch the pot. "You do drink coffee, don't you?"

"I love it."

He poured her a cup and slid over the sugar and cream. She put in some cream and sugar and stared at it, trying to remember the last time she and

280

Momma had had coffee together. The memories wouldn't come. So much had happened. The last few days had metamorphosed into an avalanche of painful images.

"Is it all right?" C.C. slid over a plate of eggs, bacon and toast, and sat on the stool beside her. His colors, blue and green, had some white mixed in there. Fear again. He was probably afraid she might do something stupid.

She drank some coffee. Its aroma and its warmth instantly calmed her. "It's fine."

He picked up a piece of buttered toast. It smelled good, but she didn't want to try eating anything just yet. She couldn't just jump right back to her normal self, could she? She'd just killed a man. All those legal things hadn't started happening yet. C.C. had obviously coaxed the police to hold off taking her in. But she knew better. Nobody that didn't have some important clout could kill someone and walk away. And she had no clout whatsoever, no money to bribe her way out of trouble, and no stomach for being on the run. For people like her, murder was something the police didn't take lightly. Nor did the Judicial System. *Nor do I*, she thought, and forced back more tears.

"Have some toast."

Maybe *that* was why C.C. was afraid. They were coming for her, and he had to baby-sit her and make sure she didn't run away or do something stupid. She could *never* run away. She'd killed a man and deserved everything that came with that violent, disgusting act. She realized she no longer

281

cared. She wasn't the same person anymore. They could take her away because she was alone and had no one. Just like Maisie, except that Lindsay was younger and had killed someone.

She'd never set foot in that apartment again. The blood and the smell of the man she'd killed would linger on that living room carpet forever, and there was no way she'd ever go back there for *any* reason...

...except Marvin. She hadn't fed Marvin. She *couldn't* stay away. Marvin would die. He shouldn't have to suffer or die because of her. "I have to go back to the apartment."

He stopped munching on his toast. "When?"

"Soon."

"I thought you said–"

"Marvin needs to have his dinner."

"Who?"

"My Betta."

C.C. didn't reply.

"Is it all right? I mean, they won't mind, will they? I'll let you have him so he doesn't have to–"

"They?"

The warm tears filled her eyes, distorting everything. "It'll just be ... until we get him in a glass or something ... and bring him back here. They surely won't mind *that*, will they? I don't want him to ... to starve. He doesn't eat much at all. You won't even know he's around. I'd be *so* grateful. That is, if you don't mind keeping him while I'm away ... after they put me–"

"Lindsay, what are you talking about?"

"The police. They're ... coming for me, aren't they?"

"Why would they want to do *that*?"

Was he playing with her? His colors hadn't changed, although the white strands had gone. That was a good thing, wasn't it? White was a no-no. White was bad. It meant fear. Or terror. Or both. But she was just guessing. Maisie hadn't told her anything about any of this. No matter what white meant, she couldn't understand why it had disappeared. "I ... *killed* that man. I'm a ... a murderer."

He raised his coffee cup to his lips. He didn't say anything, but his colors had turned darker.

She remembered something he'd said the night before, after he gave her that strong drink. He'd 'handled' the whole situation. He hadn't gone into detail, but she knew he wanted to tell her something else. "C.C., what aren't you telling me?"

He put down his coffee cup. "No one is coming for you."

"But ... I killed–"

"As far as they're concerned, *I* killed that asshole Arthur Radner."

"Who?"

"The man who tried to kill us."

"But ... why would they think ... how could they–"

"I told them I did it."

She sat in stunned silence. Was this all a dream? Was he lying to her? No. He couldn't be. There was no red floating around his head. No red, no black, and still no white – just blues and greens. He'd told her the truth. "But ... why didn't you tell them what really happened?"

"You'd been through enough. Anyway, it was self-defense. It went easier that way. They understood. The case closed pretty quickly."

"They already closed the case?"

"He had a gun. I had to use deadly force. Two lives were in jeopardy."

The tears gathered again, blurring him and his colors.

"You gonna be okay?"

She nodded.

"You're sure?"

More tears slid down her cheeks. She wanted so much to hug him.

"You wouldn't like something else? A hankie? Or maybe a towel?"

She shook her head and sniffed. He handed her a paper towel. She put it in her lap and stared at him through her tears, unable to keep her smile from going away. Her nose needed wiped, but that didn't matter right now. A lot of things didn't matter right now. She didn't even care how she looked. Or if her hair was a mess. "Why ... did you do that?" she finally asked.

He sighed. "When I first found out how you'd helped the old woman, that you didn't even care that some bad people were after you, I promised myself I'd help you any way I could."

"Why?"

"You were the most honest person I'd ever met.

I had to protect you. This world's seriously messed up. Even so, it would be even more messed up without people like you. That's scary. Okay?"

She nodded.

"Would you like to have a shower a little later? It might make you feel better."

Again, she nodded.

"Then we could just hang around here and relax. I could put on a movie. I've got a decent movie collection. Or music. You like jazz?"

Her heart fluttered. She couldn't believe that something like this could happen amidst such horrible circumstances. "I *love* jazz."

"Really?"

"You seem surprised."

"None of my ex-wives liked jazz."

"Well, I always have."

"Great." His eyes lit up. "I'll put on one of my big band CDs. Or Brubeck. But it's up to you. We can do whatever you want."

"I'd like to do *two* things, actually." She looked down at her lap and suddenly wished she'd spent more time combing her hair and maybe washing her face. Some makeup wouldn't hurt, either. "I'd ... really like to hug you right now."

White wisps surrounded his head. In spite of it, he reached toward her, and they embraced. She felt his heart thundering against hers, which was doing the same thing. His cheek pressed against hers, igniting a fire within her she hadn't felt in a long time. She wanted *so* much to kiss him, but knew it wasn't the right time.

He pulled away long before she wanted him to. "Now ... what's number two?" he asked.

She waited for her heart to settle down, then took a deep breath. "I have to feed Marvin."

286

Chapter 24

Since Madeline, his wife of forty-two years, died from a cerebral hemorrhage three years earlier, Jo-Jo Lanza lived alone.

However, he was far from lonely. His love of travel, golf, the frequent demands of his vast business interests, and monthly visits from his daughters and their families kept life interesting.

His twenty-room Spanish-style estate sat on twenty acres of prime Central Florida real estate presently going for more than a million dollars an acre. The estate included a servant's quarters annex adjacent to the main building, a kidney-shaped swimming pool, and a two-thousand-square-foot recreation building that included a pool table, ping pong, foosball, and half a dozen high-tech video games the grandkids played when they came to visit. The well-tended grounds included a tennis court, a huge gazebo, flower gardens, orange and grapefruit trees, fountains, and a two-hundred-yard driving range.

A shrine built into the corner of the rear patio could be seen from the French doors of Jo-Jo's master bedroom suite. A four-foot white porcelain statue of the Blessed Virgin posed serenely on a circular alabaster pedestal in front of the blue marble slab. The words, *Hail Mary, full of grace...* were etched in two-inch square letters on the marble. Assorted flowers surrounded the pedestal. A noted Sicilian sculptor had been brought over for the project. The statue was hand-sculpted, the five-foot slab of smooth Sicilian marble specifically fashioned for the display. Religion was very important to Jo-Jo. He credited his successes in life to his staunch belief that his God was righteous and forgiving, rewarding those who believed in Him.

Jo-Jo built the place nearly twenty years earlier, when he'd first moved to Central Florida. Since the giant flotilla of '79, the Cubans had taken over Miami. Jo-Jo had owned several casinos, bars, and high-rises in the Greater Miami area. He'd sold off the high-rises but kept the casinos and the bars, and let the Hispanics run them. Hispanics, like the Italians, were a proud people. But where big money was involved, neither the Italians nor the Hispanics cared *who* signed the checks.

Jo-Jo had done well in Central Florida. He'd built bars, strip clubs, golf courses, two high-rises, and a theme park. His connections were legendary. Life was far from perfect, but once minor irritations were taken care of, it would go right back to being as good as it could possibly get. Big John's kid had put a kink in the works, and unless something miraculous happened, it wouldn't be resolved so easily. The missing shipment was to supply Biloxi with its monthly cocaine and protection money, and Jo-Jo's connections weren't pleased that it was already days late. To pacify them, he'd told them just a few minutes ago that the shipment would be there in twenty-four hours. Jo-Jo hadn't liked lying to them, but he was confident he and Big John would be able to find the right people to retrieve that shipment.

He heard a knock on his study door. "C'mon in."

Face flushed, Big John bulled his way in. He picked up the bottle of Napoleon brandy from the silver tray on the polished oak credenza and poured a stiff belt, then collapsed in the padded leather chair. Jo-Jo didn't like what he saw. It usually took quite a bit to get to the big Sicilian. Right now Big John looked like he'd just crawled away from a train wreck.

Jo-Jo sat back down and picked up his cigar. "I talked to the police commissioner and tried the buddy-buddy bit. You know, how's everything? What's new?"

"He didn't tell you anything?"

"I can only go so far with him. I can't ask him to stick his neck out. He's got people to answer to."

"What about our OPD connections?"

"They told me they hadn't heard of anyone trying to peddle a load of fresh Colombian. I got hold of a couple local guys who fence stolen money and blow. You know them."

Big John drank some brandy and grimaced. "Catalano and Valdez are assholes. Can't trust 'em."

"But they know better than lie to me. *Paisano*, whoever took that shipment either knows what he's doing or has already taken it out of the state."

"If he knew what he was doing, he wouldn't have taken the stuff in the first place."

Jo-Jo sighed tiredly. "I also just got off the

phone with Biloxi."

"How's the Grand Palace taking this?"

"I told them the shipment would be up there in twenty-four hours."

"*Jesus...*" Big John shook his head. "You're crazy, old man."

"*Paisano*, I can't just break open my piggy bank and buy two million bucks' worth of high-grade, cut HCl in fifteen minutes. And the next shipment coming in from Miami isn't until the end of the month."

"What about the Bahamas? Bimini isn't far from here. We could call ahead, charter a fishing boat–"

"DEA Miami Field Division's been watching Bimini as well as the Bahamas archipelago. Nassau County checks every fucking boat coming in."

"This really sucks."

"That shipment's gotta be *some*where."

Big John rubbed his eyes. "We're talking about two large suitcases. They're heavy, too. But the suckers could be anywhere."

"Check everything on your end?"

"Everything and everyone."

"No one on your payroll has a beef with you?"

"Everyone's afraid of me," Big John said. "Every single asshole working for me won't fart unless I say it's okay."

Jo-Jo blew some cigar smoke toward the ceiling fan. "Even so, the shipment's gone. *Somebody* took it."

"This damned place is too fucking spread out to

find that stuff in twenty-four hours. It could be in St. Cloud, Kissimmee, Casselberry, Altamonte..." Big John took a cigar from the cherry box on the desk and lit up. "Too much area to check that quick."

"We have to trace this back. From the source."

"Which is where?"

"That fucking dive – where else?"

"Half a dozen hotshot punks sat with my boy, sucking up the booze and acting like idiots. Any one of 'em could–"

"Find every dickhead that was in that bar that night."

"How the fuck am I supposed to do something like that in such a short time?"

"*Paisano*, we both have friends in high places, but we have to be careful who we use. Our political connections wouldn't know anything about this. All they care about is where to get it and how much they have to pay. Same with the Chamber of Commerce, the City Council, our realtor friends, developers, and just about everyone we know at OPD. Anyone gets wind of this, we'll look like idiots."

"We own all kinds of people, but finding someone good is the problem."

"We need someone special for this, *paisano*. Someone who's dirty."

"And knows the streets."

"And has the same connections we do."

Big John sighed deeply. "Finding someone like that could take time. That shipment disappeared Friday night. It was supposed to go out Monday.

That was *days* ago."

"That's another thing that's been bugging me. Why'd I only find out about this at the Country Club this morning?"

"I only found out about it last night." Big John shrugged. "What can I say? My kid's a dickhead. He was afraid to tell me."

Jo-Jo shook his head. Good thing he had daughters. They presented other problems, yeah, but they never got in the way of business. "Hopefully, whoever took it knows what he did and is laying low."

"We need to check our list of enemies."

"That would take too much time, *paisano*."

"Our best bet is finding someone dirty, smart, and knows the streets."

"Wait a minute." Jo-Jo sat up. The idea popped up like a puff of white smoke. "We own somebody that can find that shipment. He's good, but he probably won't want to do this."

"What's the problem?"

"The man is our undercover cop. Cross."

"I don't see the problem."

"You don't understand. We ordered a hit on him. Remember?"

"So what? We tell him everything's square if he finds that shipment. He's already bad, right? He don't wanna *be* bad. He'll do anything if he thinks it'll buy his freedom."

Jo-Jo had a little brandy. It was a long shot, but it just might work. "Cross is no dummy."

"We don't want no dummy. Dummies are a

dime a dozen, and they always fuck up."

Jo-Jo put down his cigar. "He figures he's got nothing to lose, he might tell us to kiss his ass. But if he thinks we'll set him free, he'll jump at this."

"Last I heard, he's keeping close to that young chick. The one who saw Alvarez's kid run down the old woman. It wouldn't be hard to track him down. We can use that old friend of his."

"That's right. He's on our payroll. He ought to earn his money for a change."

"And since he fucked up his last job, he owes us."

Jo-Jo grinned. "This'll give him the chance to redeem himself."

Big John shoved a large hand through his thick black hair. "I still can't understand how Cross got the jump on Radner. Radner was good. Big, strong, tough, and smart. Sound like a fish story to you?"

"Dead is dead, *paisano*. All I care about is getting that shipment back. We have to get Cross for this."

"What if he don't *wanna* do it?"

"He's got to believe he'll be cut free."

"Fucker can be stubborn."

"He might readjust his thinking with more at stake."

"More than his life?"

Jo-Jo blew out a thick plume of cigar smoke and grinned.

***

Shivering, Ernesto Medina sat on the Foreman chick's sofa, watching an old rerun of *Gilligan's*

Island on the TV set.

Christ, he needed a smoke and a line. Maybe *two* lines. But lighting up in a strange chick's pad would be a serious boner. Wasn't even an ashtray in the room. Even a dork would smell the smoke and suspect something was up. Anyway, he'd left his smokes out in the van, just in case he couldn't stand the wait. He knew he'd get the shakes. He also knew lighting up in here would fuck up the job. If he fucked up, Solo would personally slit his throat.

So far, Gilligan was mellowing him right now. Actually, the Ginger babe was the one doing the job. God, would he ever like to tap *that*... Even so, the damned craving was getting worse. Best wait. She didn't show up soon, he'd rush out to the van and sneak a quick one.

She had to come back, Solo said. This was her home. Her stuff was here. Not much, though. He'd checked both bedrooms. Not even enough jewelry to bother with.

No problem. Watching the Ginger babe slinking around in her slip kept him occupied. Right now she was in her tent, brushing that thick red mane. He could watch her do that all night – even longer if she were in her bra and panties. No chance of *that*. Back then, TV babes *never* showed their bra and panties. Good thing, though. If that babe slinked around in her underwear, he'd surely forget himself and do something *really* stupid. Solo would be on his ass again.

Not a chance – especially for a job so simple, any dork could do it. Just bundle up the chick and take her to Solo's club. Babes Galore wasn't actually Solo's place, but Solo wouldn't say otherwise unless somebody important asked him. Everyone knew the club really belonged to Jo-Jo.

Anyway, the Foreman chick was causing problems with the big guys. Ernesto didn't know exactly what she did, but rumor was that Big John Santella wanted her out of the way. Bad news. Nobody with any smarts would want Big John after him. Big John was even nastier than Jo-Jo. And since Big John was on top of this one, Ernesto figured he'd better not fuck up. He didn't want Big John after his ass. Solo was bad enough.

Once he delivered her, he'd be home free. Solo said he'd fix those tickets for him, maybe even give him more pocket money than usual. Solo might even give him one of his girls for the night. Babes Galore had the best lap dancers in the city. Most were around twenty and could do bikini ads for *Victoria's Secret*. They weren't cheap, though. Only top-of-the-line worked there, and when a gal was top-of-the-line, she could demand top rates.

Ernesto would do this job right. Chicks usually did what they were told, once they saw Mr. Blade. Even the stubborn ones cooperated. Along with the lock-pick set, they'd given him a packet of knockout juice to work with. This wouldn't be tough at all.

The Ginger babe stopped brushing her hair when Gilligan came into her tent babbling away about the captain after his scrawny ass. Stupid shit. Ernesto couldn't get over some guys. *Hell with the fucking captain, just bend that babe over her dressing table and go to town.*

Ernesto fidgeted on the couch and looked at his watch, then ran his hands through his hair. *She better get here fast. Man, I need a smoke!*

***

Lindsay had followed C.C. to the police station so he could bring his Mustang back to his apartment.

She'd thought about it then – what she still needed to do. But she didn't want to push things so soon after everything that had happened. Right now, all she could think of was getting Marvin and getting away from the apartment. But to get him, she first had to go back to the apartment.

Riding in the passenger seat of C.C.'s Mustang, she looked over at him. Thick black bars with heavy white splotches touched his shoulders as he drove. Lindsay could tell he didn't want to go back to the apartment. That League, no doubt – the people who'd killed Momma, broken C.C.'s finger, then sent someone to kill both her and C.C. The same people who used their money to kill and hurt others. She couldn't let them frighten or intimidate her. She wouldn't let anyone change who she was or what she wanted to do. She'd been independent since she was a child. It always felt right to go off by herself when everyone else stuck together in pairs or small groups. She never liked being influenced by others, and the few times she found herself in a group, she felt as if she'd shed her free will as well as her identity. Alone, she could think better. Everything made more sense. There were no distractions.

There couldn't be distractions with this situation. It was cut and dried. Black and white. And if C.C. didn't understand, she couldn't help it. But he understood – she was certain of it. That was why he was so quiet. But his silence was disturbing. So were his colors. "You're angry," she said.

He just sighed. His colors did not change.

"I can tell. You're definitely angry."

"Lindsay, I told you before–"

"You told me it wouldn't be safe. Someone is probably watching the place."

"I'd be surprised if someone *isn't* watching."

It didn't matter. Life went on in spite of what people wanted or didn't want. "Marvin has to eat."

"I know."

"But it doesn't change how you feel, does it?"

"I've seen what they can do." He held up his bandaged hand. "I got off lucky."

The back of her neck bristled. "Momma didn't."

He shook his head. "I'm sorry, Lindsay. I didn't ... I shouldn't have said–"

"It's true, isn't it?"

He nodded. His colors softened, grew thinner.

Now it was more important than ever to do what she'd planned yesterday morning. "After we pick up Marvin, I have to go back to the police station and make this right."

He groaned. "Lindsay, you can't *mean* that."

"I *have* to do this. Otherwise, Momma died for nothing."

C.C. just sighed.

"Are you going to take me? Or should I call for a cab?"

"You know the answer to that."

Pale strands of red intermingled with the white. She didn't know if he was lying or if guilt had entered into this. "I don't want you to do anything you don't want to do."

"I *want* to do it." Patches of a deeper red appeared.

"You're lying."

"No I'm not."

"You most certainly are."

"Lindsay, how the hell do you know–"

His cell buzzed. He pulled it out, eyed the display and frowned.

"What's wrong?"

"Nothing." More red.

"You're lying again. Who *is* that?"

"Someone I don't want to talk to right now."

"It's ... one of *them*, isn't it?"

He didn't reply. The white quickly overpowered the red.

"You're scared."

He scowled. "One of these days you're gonna have to tell me how you do that."

"So why are you scared?"

He pocketed the cell. "Why do you think?"

"What do you suppose they're going to say?"

"They're going to tell me to get my affairs in order and to help you get yours in order. They probably ordered another hit. This time it'll be on both of us."

298

"Would they actually *tell* you stuff like that? Wouldn't it make it harder for them?"

"They've got their noses and their money in just about everything. There's nowhere we can go. And who'd want to go against them? Besides you."

"*You're* doing it."

"That's different."

"What do *you* stand to gain from all this?"

"I'm not gonna let them get to you. Not as long as I'm alive."

A cold clamminess covered her shoulders, making her shiver. "You *really* think they're going to pay someone to kill us?"

"They paid Radner. When one guy fails, they go to Number Two on their list."

"They have a *list*?"

"They probably have a book."

Her head grew cold as well. "This is incredible."

"I told you a couple of days ago that you're messing with the wrong people. They're not going to let you do anything that might cause trouble for them."

"I'm hoping the police will protect us."

"Lindsay you're *so* naïve."

"Maybe so, but I'm not going to let anyone dictate what I should do and who I should stay away from."

He pulled off Semoran, went down the two-lane street, and turned into her apartment complex. It was just before twelve. Mostly everyone was at work. The usual number of cars, trucks and SUVs sat in a neat row in front of the building. Most looked familiar; she didn't see anything suspicious.

C.C. eased the Mustang over to her front stoop and parked beside Momma's BMW. She still couldn't look at it, and shifted her gaze back to C.C., who was staring at the dark living room window as he flicked off the ignition.

"Now what's wrong?"

"Just a little jumpy."

"You think someone's inside?"

"Could be."

"Only one way to find out, right?"

***

Outside the living room window, Cross's Mustang pulled up and parked.

Ernesto snatched the remote and killed the TV. He rolled off the sofa, nearly hitting his head on the coffee table as he landed face-down on the carpet. What the hell was *Cross* doing out there? They hadn't said anything about Cross being with the chick. Maybe he was just dropping her off.

Ernesto crawled over to the window and peeked. Cross was *getting out*. This was bad. Cross could turn into a serious badass when somebody got on his wrong side. And Ernesto only had enough juice for the chick.

Pulse racing, he scrambled to his feet and ran over to the apartment door. Couldn't let Cross find him here. The chick was one thing, but Cross? *No way.* This wasn't right. Solo was fucking with him. *Jesus God. Gotta get out!*

Ernesto made it the front door, realizing he'd

never make it out without Cross spotting him. *The closet.* It was his only option. He rushed over. His hands shook wildly as he reached for the closet door, yanked it open, and jumped inside.

***

C.C. opened his door with his good hand, then turned back to her. "You'd better stay here. I'll put Marvin in a glass. Just tell me where everything is, okay?"

Her face grew warm. "Why are you treating me like a child?"

"I'm just being cautious – in case someone *is* waiting. Things could turn nasty, and you need to be forewarned–"

"C.C., I just killed a man." It actually came out easier than before. "Doesn't that entitle me to be treated like an adult?"

"You're right."

"Thank you."

"Don't thank me yet. This could be our last day on earth." The white bars above his head thickened. The fact that the red had vanished made the situation even worse. He pushed open the door.

She opened hers, slid out and straightened. The image of a dark figure flashed brightly before her eyes, and she froze.

C.C. came over. "What's wrong?"

"Someone ... there's someone ... in the apartment," she rasped.

Without turning his head, his eyes darted toward the window again. He moved closer to her. "How do you know?" he whispered.

301

"A feeling."

C.C. closed her door, put his left arm around her shoulder and nudged her forward in front of the car. "Any idea where he is?"

She liked having his arm over her shoulders but forced herself to stay focused. This was no time to get distracted. "I think he's hiding."

"How many are there?"

"Just one."

Her body had grown hot and stiff. She could barely feel her legs. Thank God his arm kept her from collapsing. "What ... do we ... do?" she whispered, the words coming out of her throat in short, tiny bursts.

"Just follow my lead."

She could feel his arm shifting, moving underneath his oversized sweatshirt as they approached the apartment entrance.

***

His heart thrashing, Ernesto pressed his ear to the closet door.

Cross's voice echoed out in the hall: "I'll be right back. I'm gonna see the apartment manager about that business we discussed. Okay with you?"

The skinny chick said, "You really don't have to, you know."

"No problem. But keep the door locked. Don't open it for anyone but me."

The door slammed shut.

Ernesto heard water running in the kitchen eased out the breath he was holding. *Now I can get the fuck out of here*. He cautiously opened the closet

302

door and stuck his head out. *Clear.* He slipped through the narrow opening and tiptoed across the carpeted floor. He reached out for the doorknob, and a hand quickly appeared behind him, slicing down onto his forearm. An angry jolt of red-hot pain danced up his arm. He doubled over and gritted his teeth. The same hand grabbed a fistful of his sweatshirt and spun him around.

Cross quickly released him. *"Medina?"*

"Man, you pack a punch." He massaged his throbbing forearm.

"I thought you were dead."

"I got better."

"I see that."

He might be able to squeeze through this without Cross beating the shit out of him. It might even be possible to figure out a way of getting *Cross* to take the chick to Solo's. "I ... had to lay low for a while," he said.

"Where?"

Get a good story going. It shouldn't be that *hard.* But his head just wasn't working right. His last fix was hours ago. He hadn't had a smoke in an hour. Christ, he needed one. "I heard you got burned. I had no choice."

The chick came out of the kitchen, stopped in the doorway, and stared at the floor at Ernesto's feet, near the coffee table. She was nervous. Even shook a little.

Chick liked his shoes. Hell, they went for a hundred bucks. Everyone appreciated a nice pair of high-class tennies.

She wasn't bad, though. No knockout, but her hair was long and thick and she had the biggest brown eyes he'd ever seen. Not much tittie, but some nice curves for a skinny chick. With makeup and a little silicone, she'd be seriously hot.

"Lindsay, this is an old friend. Blade Medina."

"Blade?"

He shrugged. "I ... carry a blade."

"A *blade*?"

"He's from the streets," Cross said.

The chick stared at his hair. He reached up with both hands and smoothed it back. All the chicks went for Blade's thick, coal-black hair. If Cross wasn't here, it would've been a snap, giving her the juice. She'd probably be staring at his hair and wouldn't even notice him pulling out the packet and sticking it in her face.

"You're ... a *friend* of C.C.'s?"

"I do odd jobs for him."

Cross continued to stare. Probably thinking this out. "So what are you doing *here*?"

His heart raced. Damn, he needed a smoke. His nerves were all fucked up – especially now, since he'd just figured out Solo had fucked him good. And Cross hadn't made things easier – not with that Bruce Lee number at the door. "I ... heard about what's been going down," he said, swallowing.

"What's been going down?"

"There's a hit out ... on you."

"I know."

"Her, too."

She went back to watching his hair. *Weird*

304

chick.

"We know," Cross said. "So ... why are you here?"

He forced his mind off his need for a fix. "Hell, I came to warn you."

"How'd you know I'd be here?"

"They told me you would."

"Solo?"

Ernesto nodded. Cross knew all about Solo. Cross almost nailed the asshole a couple times. "They're coming for you. I heard about it and decided to get to you first. Otherwise, it'd be too late."

"All right. You're here. Now what?"

"I figure I'd get you and the lady out. Then we could lay low."

"A hit's a hit. You know that. Only two things can happen. The hit goes through or the hitter is stopped."

"I ... didn't get that far in my thinking. I just wanted to get you out."

"Where?" Cross obviously wasn't buying any of this. His arms were crossed over his chest as he stared Ernesto down. And he had that look, said he smelled something rotten.

Ernesto's knees began to shake. "I ... have a place."

"Since when?"

"I found this lady. She's fine and classy."

"You found a *classy* lady?"

"You don't think I can find a classy lady?"

"I just don't think you can hold onto one."

Fucker knew how to hurt a guy. "Well, I found one anyway. She works at Babes. I've been shacking up with her."

"Where?"

"Not far from the club."

"That neighborhood's pretty thick with Lanza's men."

"I figure I'd get you out first and make a few calls, see if I can find a good place where you and the lady can hide."

"I don't know." Cross turned to the chick. "What do you think, Lindsay?"

She began staring at Ernesto's feet again. "I don't want to be here right now."

Cross uncrossed his arms. "This better be on the level."

"Why would I risk coming here to warn you about the hit if I wasn't on the level?"

"I haven't quite figured that out yet."

"C'mon. There isn't time."

Cross turned to the chick. "He's right. We'd better leave while we can."

She went into the kitchen and came back with a small round glass, then went over to the corner hutch beside the picture window.

Cross said, "Lindsay, we can't take Marvin right now."

"We can stop at Sarah's. She'll take care of Marvin for me."

"But–"

"It's on the way."

"Marvin?" Ernesto asked.

"Her Betta."

Yep. One seriously weird chick. But Ernesto hadn't met *any* chick who *wasn't* weird.

Chapter 25

Looking both tired and harried, Sarah handed over the credit card and the bag of purchases to the short, slender, tattooed girl who stuck the card back in her wallet and hurried out of the store.

"Where have *you* been all morning?" Sarah asked when Lindsay came in. Her eyes lowered to the small round glass Lindsay held in both hands. Marvin darted around inside, noticeably uneasy about his new surroundings. "You didn't even *call*. That's not like you, girl. I was just about to call the hospitals to see if–"

"I don't have time to talk." Lindsay hated herself for doing this. Sarah was her friend. They shared their secrets, their problems. Sarah needed to know about Momma, what had happened. It hurt, not being able to tell her. "I've ... got to go. Right now."

"You just got here..."

"I know this is awfully sudden..."

"We need to talk." Sarah led the way to her office.

Lindsay forced herself to keep from looking at her tiny fish. She'd had Marvin nearly two years. He'd been just what she needed when David left her. She couldn't bear losing him so soon after losing Momma. "Will you do me a very large–"

"Where have you *been*? You had me scared, Lindsay."

"Will you please feed Marvin while I'm

away?"

"What *is* this? Where are you going?"

"I ... can't tell you."

"What? What's going on?"

"Sarah, please. I need you to ... just ... help me out here."

Sarah was seriously disturbed, with a white fog enveloping her head. "How long ... will you be gone?"

Lindsay looked away. "I don't know."

"But can't you at least tell me what's going on?"

"If you'd just feed Marvin, I'll be really grateful." Lindsay placed the glass gently on the green blotter. Marvin spun around to gape at Sarah, then turned back to Lindsay as if to say, *What's going on? Where's my shelf? My castle? My shade?*

Sarah sat down. Thick white bars floated above her head. She wanted the truth but was afraid – possibly of what she saw in Lindsay's eyes. Lindsay was grateful she didn't have the time to tell her.

"Honey, *please* tell me what's going on..."

"I can't." A heavy wash of guilt plunged through her.

"But you just can't *leave* without–"

"Time to move." C.C. came in, out of breath. He'd probably decided she was taking too long. "Now."

Sarah smiled uncomfortably at C.C., then reached up to push some hair away from her face.

"You're Sarah?"

"Yes..."

"I'm C.C."

"Hello..."

"Lindsay says you're really a great lady. Wish we could stay longer, but we've got to go."

"Wait. *Please*. This doesn't make any sense."

"Marvin gets three tiny grains every day, all right?" Lindsay put the plastic fish food dispenser on the blotter beside the bowl. Marvin moved closer until his nose touched the glass. He stared at the giant fish longingly. "Just because he does that doesn't mean you have to feed him. He wants you to feel sorry for him. But if you give him more, you'll have to change his water."

"Lindsay. C'mon." C.C. had backed up to the door.

"But why can't you at least tell me–"

"Now." He grabbed Lindsay's arm and pulled her toward the doorway.

"Just give me a little hint and then I won't have to ask any more stupid questions. I promise."

"Can't," Lindsay said. The look on Sarah's face pulled at her heart. The myriad of colors spinning around her head made Lindsay want to cry.

"The less you know, the better," C.C. said.

"But do you have any idea when you'll be back?"

"I'm really sorry about–"

"It was really nice meeting you, Sarah. You have beautiful hair." C.C. pulled Lindsay out of the room.

***

"Sarah's a worrier," Lindsay said as she got

back into the Mustang. "She's going to make herself sick over this."

"Sorry." C.C. pulled out. "But we couldn't tell her anything."

"I feel so bad about this. Sarah's really sweet. The best boss I could ever hope for."

"She seemed really nice."

"What you told her was nice."

"She does have great hair." He inched up to the curb to turn onto Semoran. Traffic was heavy. "I thought since we were already scaring her half to death, I might as well toss in at least one good compliment."

A frightening thought occurred to her. "She won't ... get *hurt*, will she?"

"What do you mean?"

"They won't question her ... If they know we stopped here–"

"The League?"

She nodded.

"She doesn't know anything."

"But won't they ... I mean, won't they try and find out if she knows anything for sure?"

"You've been watching too many crime shows."

"I hope you're right."

"They'll know we didn't tell her anything."

"How do you know?"

"They know *me*." C.C. pulled out and they headed north, in the left lane. A block later, he switched to the turning lane that would take them onto Colonial and to downtown Orlando. The blue and green hovering about him made her feel much better. He wasn't lying. He meant what he said. Sarah would be safe. Nothing to worry about – at least, for now.

She turned around. Blade Medina followed them close behind in an older model maroon van. As soon as an opening presented itself, he passed on their right and pulled directly in front of them. "Why'd he do that?"

"He wants us to follow him."

She couldn't believe what they were doing. That man was full of bad vibes and carried around the darkest colors she'd ever seen. Blacks and grays swarming around his thick black hair in a sea of blood-red. "He's really your friend?"

"He was my snitch. More like an employee."

A snitch. She'd heard of that before. "You mean he told you things?"

"He's from the streets. He knows what's going on. For information I'd give him cigarette money and a little extra so he could buy a lap dance once in a while. It made him happy."

"He's an addict, isn't he?"

"Coke, meth sometimes – although he told me a while ago he kicked the meth. But he smokes like a fiend."

This wasn't making sense. "And he actually worked for you?"

"He spends a lot of time at the strip clubs. He hears things all the time. Has friends in the right places. Whenever something was going down, he let me know. It paid off several times."

312

Lindsay wanted to tell him about the colors, the lies, but didn't know how.

"When you're undercover," C.C. said, "you've got to use any means available to get the drugs off the street. Sometimes – hell, a *lot* of times – you have to deal with scum to find other scum. I didn't like it, but I had no other recourse but–"

"He lied, C.C." There was no other way of saying it. "He lied to us."

He shrugged. "Like I said, he's a street kid. They all lie to survive. When he was working for me, I had to watch him closely. The last couple of tips he gave me turned sour. I got burned not too long after. I don't know if he did it on purpose or if he just heard it wrong. That's one thing I intend to find out."

Lindsay's pulse fluttered. "He lied ... about everything."

"For instance?"

"He didn't show up in my apartment to warn you."

The light turned green. Still watching her, he eased forward, keeping close to the van directly ahead. "What else?"

"Like I said – everything. Coming here to warn us. Taking us somewhere safe."

"What about the part about his lady?"

"No lady."

He sighed. "What about ... that place he was talking about?"

"There *is* no place."

Traffic sat bottlenecked at the intersection of

313

Colonial and South Orange Blossom Trail. C.C. kept his eyes on the van directly in front of them.

Lindsay could tell something was about to happen. His colors had turned black and white and spun around quickly, like a tiny funnel cloud.

"You okay?" she asked.

He didn't reply.

"You're about to lose him, aren't you?"

"One of these days you're going to tell me how you keep doing that."

The light changed. The van eased forward. Medina went through the light and turned left, keeping close to the pickup directly in front of him. But instead of roaring through behind him, C.C. squeezed in behind the red Saturn in the next lane and went straight through the green, heading west on Colonial.

Lindsay jerked her head to her left. Medina's van had become part of the thick flow heading to town.

***

A sea of heavy traffic flowed to the next set of lights. C.C. kept weaving from lane to lane, trying to gain as much distance as possible.

"Where are we going?" Lindsay asked nervously.

C.C. glanced in his rear-view mirror. The white wisps above his head, as well as the black splotches intermixed with them, had grown thicker. "As far away as we can. The fact that they're using punks like Medina tells me they're getting desperate."

"He's not ... he doesn't *kill* people, does he?"

"Like I said before, he's just small potatoes. He does informant-type stuff."

"But he mentioned a knife."

"He's a street kid. They all carry knives. He doesn't have the stomach to kill people for money."

This didn't make any sense. "If they want us dead, why'd they send *him*?"

"To lure us closer. Since Radner failed, they're being more cautious. Radner was a professional. It's almost impossible to bring one of those guys down."

Lindsay sighed. *If only he hadn't killed Momma...* "But why Medina?" she asked.

"They probably hoped I'd trust him. I have a hunch he's been working for them all along. I also suspect the League used him to bait me when I was about to nail Solo. Medina was probably the one responsible for me getting burned in the first place."

"So what's our next move?"

"I have a few connections in town. We have to hide."

Her head grew warm. "For how long?"

"This could take a while. I won't lie to you – even if I could." His blue and green colors told her the obvious, but the whites framing them couldn't hide the fear.

"But what good will hiding do? They'll find us eventually, won't they?"

"Depends on how badly they want us. Judging by what's been happening, I'd say they want us real bad."

"All because of me." She sat back in her seat

315

and wished she'd never been born.

"Don't beat yourself up."

"Can't help it. If I hadn't been so pig-headed..."

"You have principles. I respect that."

"Even after all that's happened?"

"Especially after all that's happened. It makes this even more important."

That was one way of looking at it. But if she'd decided to just forget about Maisie, Momma would still be alive. It was difficult to keep thinking she'd done the right thing, especially now. "Can't we go to the police?" she asked. "Maybe they can give us protection, like ... Witness Protection or something."

"Witness Protection usually includes a trial. To qualify, you'd have to be scheduled to testify against organized crime or an individual accused of a federal crime. Then we'd have to get a federal marshal in on this and protect you for the duration of the trial. Any idea how difficult it would be, keeping you alive for that? Especially when we have no idea who's bad and who's working for whom?"

She didn't reply. The severity of all this numbed her.

"Like I said, don't beat yourself up. You did the right thing."

"I'm beginning to wonder."

"I'm not. And if there's a way out of this, I'll definitely–" He stopped talking and stared in the rear-view mirror.

Lindsay jerked her head around. Flashing red

lights drew down right behind them. The back of her neck tingled. "*Now* what do we do?"

C.C. coaxed the Mustang over to the shoulder, in front of a Toyota dealership. "Play it by ear, I guess."

"You weren't speeding, were you?"

"I wasn't paying attention. I must have been. But take it easy. I might know these guys." He stopped, put it in park, and opened the door. "I'll be as quick as I can."

Her heart racing, she watched as he approached the police car.

The driver got out. He was big – a good three inches taller than C.C. and broader in the shoulders. His partner also got out, flipped open his notepad, and took down C.C.'s license number. The driver spoke with C.C. for a few seconds, then pointed to the squad car. C.C. squeezed between the cars and slid into the passenger side. The driver also got in. The other cop approached her side. He wasn't smiling.

Her heart thrashed loudly as she rolled down the window. He bent toward her and tipped his hat. "Afternoon, miss."

"Hello."

"Could I see your driver's license?"

Why was he asking for her license when she wasn't even driving? "Why do you want to–"

"Please, miss."

"But I'm not even–"

"Miss, if you don't comply, I'll be forced to arrest you." Red and black swarmed around his

317

broad shoulders. A few wisps of white floated above his hat. Something was terribly wrong. This didn't feel right.

She turned around to see what C.C. was doing.

"Miss?"

Her hands shook as she opened her handbag. For some reason, she couldn't get her fingers to cooperate. They were just as useless as they were in her apartment, when she tried using the phone.

Just as she found her wallet, she caught movement to her right, where he stood, and a whiff of something minty. She jerked her face in his direction. A blur of something shot quickly toward her. A damp rag covered her face. The strong minty smell enveloped her, making her gag.

She tried pulling away, but the pressure on her face increased. She couldn't breathe. A choking fit tore through her. Her chest was on fire. A large hand closed around the back of her neck, preventing her from jerking free. Darkness came heavily, like the slamming of a coffin lid.

Chapter 26

The small, messy office displayed no outward sign that it was being used by a pathetic weasel. The cluttered metal desk, the expensive office chair, and the half-empty bookcase behind it all seemed quite normal and expected. But it was Solo's office, and Solo was an insufferable weasel.

His right hand squeezing the padded arm of the chair, C.C. sat facing the desk and wondered what would happen if he suddenly jumped up, spun around, and attacked the man standing behind him. It would be difficult, if not impossible, to effectively work from his present position. He didn't know if Landon had his Glock out, where the man's hands were, or how far away he was from the chair. Besides, C.C. had only one usable hand.

To test his theory, he turned his head. The barrel of the Glock pressed firmly against his right cheekbone. "Eyes front," Landon said.

C.C. settled back in the chair, going over the events that had brought him here to Solo's office. He'd cursed himself a dozen different times on the way over. He didn't have to remind himself how stupid his actions were. He'd vowed to *protect* Lindsay – not watch stupidly as a goon in a blue uniform drove off with her. The promise he'd made to himself, to her, had become nothing more than empty words.

A fake traffic stop, of all things. He should've known they'd pull something like this. A rookie would've seen through this. But he figured the stop was legit. He'd been speeding and swerving through traffic, which could be viewed as driving under the influence. It didn't take him long to realize it was a scam. When he saw Murphy chloroforming Lindsay right in front of him, he knew the League had finally gotten them. And when he groped for the door handle of the squad car and felt the square barrel of Landon's Glock pressing against the back of his neck, he knew they were in serious trouble.

"Just relax," Landon had said in a firm voice. "Hand it over." Knowing the procedure, C.C. pulled the Bersa, butt-first, slowly from its holster and relinquished it. When Landon ordered, "Now the other one," C.C. knew these jerks were too smart to mess with. He reached behind him, pulled the tiny Beretta from its pancake holster, and forced himself not to shoot Landon in the face with it. He'd meant to sound threatening as he warned nothing better happen to Lindsay, but all Landon had said as Murphy drove away with her in C.C.'s Mustang was that she'd be perfectly fine and was being taken somewhere for 'safekeeping.'

Now, as C.C. sat in 'Slick Al' Solo's office in the rear of Babes Galore on South Orange Blossom Trail, he tried weighing the facts. Lindsay was chloroformed and taken away, but they hadn't done anything to him. No chloroform, no rough stuff. They'd taken both his guns but hadn't handcuffed or blindfolded him. Not exactly SOP for a kidnapping. Or a mob hit. They wanted both of them and, as far as he knew, they wanted them both dead. So why did they split him and Lindsay up?

The door opened. Short and slender, his shiny, coal-black hair slicked back, Solo came in and closed the door quietly behind him. Around forty, Solo used makeup to cover the cracks and blemishes on his pockmarked face, and regularly plucked the thick triangular patch of stray black hairs between his thick brows. He dressed exclusively in dark Versace suits and spent a fortune on patent-leather Italian slip-ons with special high heels, making him four inches taller than his five-foot, four-inch frame. He had the small, blinking black eyes of a mouse, a hooked beak shaped like an ice pick, and razor-sharp cheekbones. His glossy manicured nails highlighted his small hands.

Solo had shortened his name from Solari, then moved from New York City to Central Florida around twenty years ago to hook up with Lanza when Lanza came up from Miami. Solo was small-time – bookmaking, strippers, cocaine – but didn't know how to keep his mouth shut, and on several occasions had nearly been shipped back to New York City in a packing case for irritating Lanza. To keep him out of his hair, Lanza let him run Babes Galore and a couple of other clubs.

Since he'd been a small-time hood all his life, Solo didn't quite know how to stay respectable. Lanza's connections kept him out of trouble, but Solo was his own worst enemy and was constantly looking for ways to branch out on his own. C.C. had nearly brought Solo's operation to a grinding halt six months ago, when he'd found a working meth lab on one of Solo's investment properties. C.C. would have been successful if he hadn't been burned. He didn't see any reason why Solo had brought him here other than to personally supervise the hit.

"You look shorter," C.C. said, tilting his head, as if carefully considering Solo's appearance. Best test the waters quickly and see what was going on. Solo had a hair-trigger temper. He was also sensitive about his height. "You need to buy higher heels. Or wear a stovepipe hat."

Solo's eyes stayed on C.C. "Get lost, Landon."

"You sure?"

"Get the fuck *out*."

Landon left the room. Solo sat down. He opened a silver case, pulled out a cigarette, and carefully lit it. His eyes didn't stray from C.C.. "Nice of you to come and see us."

"It was either scrape the dog shit off the bottom of my shoe or spend time with you. I guess I lost the toss."

"Funny. A real comedian."

"Where's the girl?"

"No need to worry." Solo exhaled cigarette smoke in C.C.'s direction. "Since you decided to lose your old friend Medina, I had no choice but intervene."

"Intervene. impressive. Learn a new word today?"

Solo blew more smoke at C.C. "You and Medina have a tiff?"

322

"Medina's a weasel. Just like you, only taller. Where's the girl?"

"Forget the girl. This meeting is about you."

"Meeting? Is that what this is?"

"What else would it be?"

"From where *I* sit, it feels suspiciously like a kidnapping."

"You're a tough, smart-ass cop. You deal with street people. How can a cop as tough as you let himself be kidnapped?"

"Hard not to be, when your handlers own so much of the city."

Solo winced at the word 'handlers.' "*Thought* you'd understand," he said.

"Sure do. But just in case *you* don't, I'll put it this way. If you don't tell me where the girl is, I just might decide to pull off one of your pumps and use it to knock a knot on that hard Italian skull."

"*That* oughta kill the girl," Solo said, a grin touching his rodent-like features.

C.C. sat back. His mind reeled.

"She's safe right now. But she's only safe as long as you play ball and stop acting so tough."

"I've been playing ball with you assholes for six months. Look what it's done for me."

"You done pretty well. You got money in the bank, new set of wheels–"

"And I'm dirty. Like you and the rest of your pack."

"Not like me, Cross. I know where I belong."

"*I* know where you belong, too."

"Don't pull that shit. We both know what's

what. You could've told us to fuck ourselves from the beginning."

"I would've found my ass in a federal pen."

"Each act comes with its own individual set of consequences."

C.C. found it difficult to ignore Solo's arrogance. "Sounds like you've been studying famous quotes as well as new words."

"Like I said, stop acting so tough."

"Only if *you* stop trying to sound like you just spent a minute or two at the public library."

"Dammit, Cross–"

"Tell me what's going on. The League wants me dead. There's got to be a reason why I'm still walking around."

"You've become useful for the time being."

"Keep going. I have this strange feeling you might actually be trying to tell me something."

Solo stubbed out his smoke. "In plain English, we're missing some merchandise."

Interesting. These idiots had somehow mislaid a shipment of cocaine. But he knew better than say anything else. With the Mob, you acted stupid whenever you had the chance. "What do you mean, *missing*?"

A shrug. "Missing. Gone. It was in the car your girlfriend saw the other day. One of Jack Santella's asshole college friends borrowed his car."

"What sort of merchandise was in it?"

"Jack was carrying payoff money for his dad."

"And now it's missing?"

"We want you to find it for us."

324

"And if I don't?"

Solo shrugged. "The girl dies."

***

Lindsay opened her eyes and immediately caught a strong whiff of mildew.

Darkness. *I'm lying down ... in a lumpy bed.* To her right, a tiny glint of brightness picked at the corner of her eye. *Blinds pulled almost shut. I've got to open them, see where I am.* When she tried to sit up, a heavy wave of dizziness and nausea forced her back down.

"Just relax," a woman's voice said on her left.

Lindsay waited for the nausea to subside. She wanted to turn her head and see who belonged to the soft voice.

"When you're ready," the voice said, "I'll help you to the bathroom."

Lindsay swallowed some warm sourness, then cleared her throat. "Who ... are you?" The words scraped her throat like shards of glass.

"I'm Ronnie. They told me to stay with you, make sure you're okay."

They. Reality stormed back. The traffic stop. C.C. The big cop. The damp, minty rag. Blackness. *My God. I've been kidnapped. But why?* She had no money, nothing of value. They were only interested in her because she knew about the man who'd run over Maisie. And because of that, they wanted her dead. *So why am I still alive?*

She tried sitting again. The nausea came back. She lay back down and gently turned on her left side. That went all right, so she took a breath and

325

opened her eyes. The room shifted a little, swayed, then settled down.

A woman around her own age sat in a chair a few feet from the bed. She had long blond hair, big blue eyes, high cheekbones, and a fine-featured face. She was slender and large-breasted, wore a red short-sleeved tee-shirt, and dark blue shorts. "What's your name?" she asked.

"Lindsay." It came out with difficulty. "Lindsay Foreman." She tried once again to sit up. The nausea forced her back down.

"Want some water?"

"Please..."

Ronnie picked up a glass from the nightstand and stood up. She seemed really tall. It took her forever to lower the glass. Lindsay tried propping herself up. Ronnie tilted the glass and coaxed a few drops onto Lindsay's tongue. Some slid down both sides of her lips, cooling her chin and neck. She swallowed. The nausea subsided a little.

"Thank you." Lindsay forced herself up and let her legs fall over the side. More dizziness. She fell back down onto the mattress.

Ronnie put the glass back on the nightstand. "You sure you wanna do that right now?"

She fought the overwhelming urge to throw up. Not here. Not on this bed. And certainly not in front of this stranger. "Please ... can you help me to the bathroom?"

Ronnie took her arm by the wrist and pulled it over her shoulders. Lindsay forced herself to her feet and fought back the nausea. Together, they

326

staggered across the carpeted floor, to the adjoining bathroom. Thankfully, it was dark.

Ronnie paused on her way out. "I'll be right outside." The door closed quietly.

Lindsay sank to her knees and raised the lid. She pushed her hair out of the way and, grimacing, lowered her face.

***

An eternity later, she rinsed out her mouth and washed her face with cold water.

It was easy to ignore the heavy throbbing in her stomach. Food was the last thing on her mind. She tried avoiding the smudged mirror, but her eyes betrayed her. She was immediately grateful she hadn't turned on the bathroom light. Even in the semi-darkness, the heavy circles around her bloodshot eyes, her gaunt cheeks, and pale skin stood out prominently. Her hair hung in heavy clumps. She used her fingers to gently separate the knots. After rinsing out her mouth again and blotting her face with a towel hanging from the metal rack, she opened the door and staggered back into the small dark room.

"Feeling any better?" Ronnie asked.

"A little. But I look just awful."

"I'll bring you my comb and brush. You can fix your hair. I also have a spare toothbrush and some mouthwash. If you feel up to a shower, I can bring you shampoo." She wrinkled her nose. "And better towels."

Lindsay lay back down. The dizziness had ebbed slightly, but not the nausea. She propped herself back up, reached for the glass, and shakily picked it up. Ronnie helped her. Lindsay drank nearly half, smiled her thanks, then lay back. Her throat had become scratchy again. "Where...am I?"

Silence. The white clouds above the girl's head showed prominently among the black puffs. Ronnie was obviously scared to death. "I ... was told to help you, but not tell you anything. I hope you won't be angry with me..."

"Of course not." Where was C.C.? What had happened? Was *he* involved in this? *Don't be ridiculous*. He had nothing to do with this. He was trying to take her away, not let her be drugged and brought here. Hopefully they hadn't hurt him. Fears rocketed through her. No. They wouldn't. They couldn't. They'd already killed Momma. They wouldn't dare– *Stop this and try thinking rationally.* "Did they threaten you?" she asked uneasily.

The girl didn't reply, but Lindsay could easily feel her tension. Then a bright flash of Ronnie doing a lap dance flared in Lindsay's mind before ebbing into darkness. Lindsay nearly smiled. Her powers were coming back. "You're a dancer?"

Ronnie's eyes widened. "How did you ... who told you?"

Lindsay shrugged. "You look like a dancer."

"I hope that's a compliment."

"You're very beautiful."

"Thank you." Blues and greens practically covered her head, but the whites and blacks did not diminish.

"You work downstairs?"

328

Ronnie paled and stood up. "Listen, honey ... *please* don't do this. You don't know ... the people we're dealing with ... they–"

"I know. They're dangerous."

Ronnie sat back down. Lindsay saw another flash, this time of Ronnie talking to a short, mousy-looking man with slicked-back hair, and saying, *"All right, Al."* No doubt that same guy C.C. had... Lindsay blinked. *I'm hearing voices now?* Her powers were obviously growing. Was it because of the drug they'd given her? Or was her fear pumping adrenaline through her system and charging up her abilities? Whatever it was, Lindsay had to use it. She didn't want to stay in this room any longer than she had to. She also had to find C.C. "How long have you been working for them?"

Ronnie shrugged. "A year, maybe."

"You seem very bright. Why do this at all?"

"It pays well. Beats waiting tables."

"I'm sure you can find something better."

"I make two, sometimes three hundred a night. All I have to do is take off my clothes and dance over some horny guy's lap." *And avoid Slick Al's slimy hands.* She smiled uneasily and shrugged.

Lindsay tried not to betray surprise at 'overhearing' Ronnie's thoughts. "Does Slick Al treat you well?" she asked. "Other than trying to put his hands on you?"

"He treats all his–" She jumped up from her chair. "How'd you know?"

Pulse hastening, Lindsay perked up. If she could get that Al person up here, she might be able

329

to find out a few things. She might even be able to find out about C.C. "Ronnie, do me a big favor. Tell Slick Al I'd like to talk to him."

She backed up. "Listen. You don't know what you're—"

"I'm sure Slick Al can give me a few minutes of his time."

Her jaw dropped instantly. Her colors turned a stark white.

"You're ... *really* weirding me out, lady..." She bolted for the door, pulled it open, dashed out, and slammed the door shut behind her. The sound of the lock clicking outside echoed loudly.

Lindsay lay back on the bed, closed her eyes, and willed her heart to settle down.

***

Feeling superior once again, 'Slick Al' Solo led Cross down the hall to the rear of the club.

Jerks like Cross had irritated him all his life. The tall, good-looking types that thought their shit didn't stink – they were all cut from the same mold. Al liked it when they screwed up and had to chow down some serious crow. It proved the world wasn't quite so fucked up.

Al ran three clubs, owned rental properties, and boasted more than thirty employees and three dozen hot babes. Cross was just an errand boy about to bite the big one just as soon as he'd finished going on that wild goose chase for Jo-Jo. So who was the schmuck *now*?

"You've got twenty-four hours," he told Cross. Then he unlocked the metal door. "So does your girlfriend."

Cross turned to face him. "That's not much time."

"Then I suggest you stop flapping your jaw and move your ass."

"And once I find the money?"

Al shrugged. "You and the girl can go."

"Just like that?"

"You got my word."

Cross moved closer. "You know what I think of you and your word."

"You ain't exactly in a position to argue, are ya?"

"If I find out anything's happened to her while I'm gone..."

"You're wasting time, cop."

Cross suddenly smiled. "*Now* I know what's bothering me."

Al didn't reply. He could feel a smart-ass remark coming on. He'd seen that smirk too many times before. And then Cross opened his mouth to confirm it. "You look like you're actually getting *shorter*. Forget your grownup lifts this morning?"

The hot wave surged through him, scalding the blood running through his veins. He wanted to pull out his piece and blow Cross's head off. He fought down the rage. Cross wouldn't be around too much longer. There was no need to show weakness at this stage. He tapped the face of his Rolex and immediately felt the calm rushing back. "Clock's ticking, cop."

Cross's index finger shot out, poking Al in the

331

chest and shoving him into the paneled wall. A sharp pain danced up Al's spine. His knees nearly buckled. Using the wall for balance, he grunted back into a standing position. "Just remember what I said about hurting the girl." Cross gave him an icy stare, and Al could see the madness in there, the fury. "Got it?"

Al pushed himself forward and growled, "Fuck you, Cross. Just remember, no money, no girl. Twenty-four hours, and she's a dead girl. *You* got it?" He jerked his clothes back into place and smoothed his hair as he stared Cross down. *You're one fucking big bad walking dead man, and I'm gonna be right there when your fucking ticket's punched.*

Cross brought up his index finger again and pointed it at Al's face. Then he went outside and closed the door behind him.

Al massaged his stinging chest. He glared at the door and thought about pulling out his piece again. *Asshole. I can't wait till your time's up.*

He went down the dimly-lit hall to see how his babes were doing. He needed a little loving right now. Babes were good to be with when a man needed to kick a little stress. Eva would do. Eva had a rack on her that would choke a horse. Her legs were perfect and went on forever.

He hurried down the hall, where the thumping of the juke and the cries of contented male customers reminded him how much money he was making. Lap dancing really put his ass in the gold. Take a dozen hot babes and pay them to dance for some horny jerks. Dump a fraction of those profits into his own personal account and he had that vacation home in Maui paid for in six months.

Ronnie passed him on her way to the dressing rooms.

Al froze in mid-step. Bitch was supposed to be upstairs, watching Cross's girlfriend. What the fuck was she doing down here? He grabbed her by the elbow and spun her around. "What the fuck you doing down *here*?" *Damn.* Looked like someone had scared the shit out of her. She even shook a little. "What the hell's going on?" He was the only one allowed to intimidate his dancers.

"I-I was just ... I had to ... I'm just–"

"My office. Right now."

"B-But–"

"You want me to drop-kick that fine ass of yours down the hall?"

Without another word she followed him back to his office.

***

Al sat down at his desk and lit a cigarette, watching Ronnie tremble as she stood in front of him.

She knew better than to sit down. No one sat unless he invited them to. It was good she was scared. She fucked up, and her ass belonged to *him*.

She reached up with a shaky hand and pushed back that golden mop. She sure was a hot-looking number. He'd wanted to nail her ever since she started working here. No go, though. The bitch kept putting him off. Thought she was better than everyone else. That was a hoot – a lap dancer thinking she was better than everyone else.

"So what happened? You were supposed to stay with her. You ain't with her, you're with me. Why're you here when you should be up there?" He pointed to the ceiling with his cigarette.

She pushed more hair away from her face. "She wanted ... she wanted a comb. And a brush. Her hair ... it's a mess. I told her I'd bring her–"

"You were told to stay there until I sent someone else to take your place."

"I know, Al ... I just ... I guess I needed some air..."

"You came down here for *air*? You saying there ain't *air* up there?"

She looked like shit. Couldn't have the customers seeing her like this. No one would fork over money for a dancer looking like shit.

"Al ... there's something ... she isn't right." She shivered, rubbing her forearms like she was on the juice.

He'd had problems with dancers before. Whenever they showed the signs, he fired them on the spot. When they were on the juice, they just didn't move right, didn't look right. But this bitch had never had that trouble before. So what the hell was going on? "You'd better start telling me what ain't *right* about her."

"She ... she did a number on me..."

"Define number."

"I ... can't explain it. She figures stuff out."

He stubbed out his smoke. This bitch had run

334

her mouth and let something slip. Now she was scared. He didn't care if Foreman knew anything she wasn't supposed to. She was scheduled to be dusted anyway. But if this airhead had run her mouth, he was tempted to let them do her right alongside Foreman. Couldn't have a dancer with an uncontrollable mouth, could he? "What did you tell her?"

"I d-didn't t-tell her ... *any*thing."

"What the fuck happened up there?"

"She just looks at you and ... and ... figures stuff out."

He got up, circled his desk, and slapped her across the cheek. She gasped, twisting around to avoid another blow. "*Pl-Please*, Al ... *don't* ... I didn't ... I didn't tell her *anything*–"

"I find out you did, your number's up." He went to the door. "I'm gonna check on this right now. You stay here. I'll be right back."

She didn't reply, just stood there shivering, her hand covering her cheek.

Goddamn bitch. He slammed the door behind him.

Chapter 27

The Mustang dozed behind the block building, in the gravel lot facing a privacy fence.

Murphy probably brought it here after dropping Lindsay off somewhere else. C.C. knew he couldn't just stand here, trying to figure it all out. There wasn't time. He had to get moving *now*.

His keys dangled from the ignition. Lindsay's handbag still lay on the floor. He opened the driver's door and slid in behind the wheel. Before starting it up, he checked the console between the seats. His Beretta PX4 lay inside, as always. He picked it up, dropped the clip in his lap and examined the barrel. Clear. He unloaded the clip. The bullets appeared undisturbed as well. Mindful of his bad hand, he reloaded it, jacked one into the chamber and put the gun back.

He picked up Lindsay's purse and opened it. He couldn't be sure, of course, but it didn't seem as if anyone rummaged through it. Why would they bring the car here and not touch anything? The answer was simple. He was on their payroll. Had been for months. Now even more so, since they had Lindsay locked away somewhere to make sure he did his job.

A blistering knot of heat flared up, settling between his shoulder blades. Bad enough they'd already killed a hooker to ensure his cooperation. Now they had Lindsay, and if he didn't find that money, they wouldn't hesitate to kill her as well.

But would they release her if he returned the money? He had no idea. These people weren't known for their honesty or sense of fair play. But what choice did he have? He couldn't very well call their bluff.

Forcing his mind on what lay ahead, he fired up the Mustang.

In spite of heavy traffic, he reached the Paradise Inn on Goldenrod Road in just half an hour. More than a dozen vehicles filled the small gravel lot in front of the drab-looking gray block building.

Jack Santella came here frequently and thought nothing of doling out coke and other illegal stuff to his old college chums. It was their haunt. Several of them – including Jack – had been arrested here in the past for drunk and disorderly and other assorted misdemeanors.

It was a good place to start. Once he found that money, he might have enough time to look for Lindsay. He could also use the money to bargain with. They might even be willing to make a trade for it.

The suitcase had been missing since Friday night. Whoever had taken it had plenty of time to hide it or spend it. Hiding it would be much easier and safer. Stealing a large chunk of money would not stay secret very long. Once the word got out, it spread fast. Someone who found a lot of money would usually immediately buy things and treat his friends to drinks and outlandish gifts. When some jerk suddenly turned philanthropic with his friends, they talked. And when they did, everyone listened.

The crowd sat at the bar and half a dozen tables near the windows. Men in suits filled five barstools and three tables. No one looked familiar, but any one of them could be working for Santella or Lanza. If they wanted to keep an eye on C.C., this would be a good place.

Tall, red-haired and slender, Eileen still looked good in spite of five kids, four failed marriages, and more than fifty years of life. C.C. had been here a few times before and trusted her more than anyone else for information. She'd been working here since the place opened ten years ago. She saw and heard everything. She came right over, polishing a glass. "Where ya been hiding, baby?"

"Here and there. How've you been?"

"Still kicking. What happened to your hand?"

"Got between two female alligators at feeding time."

"Gotta be more careful. We females get crazy when we're hungry or horny."

"Is there a difference?"

"We're meaner when we're horny. What can I do ya for?"

He slipped a ten-spot across the counter. "A little info."

She pocketed the ten and thumped her bony elbows on the counter. A whiff of lavender floated his way. "Ask away, baby."

"Were you here Friday night?"

"Came in after lunch – two, two-thirty. Who ya looking for?"

"Some college kids."

"Three or four of them were here till late."

"How late?"

"Till I threw 'em out. They were acting even stupider than what I usually tolerate."

"Recognize any of them?"

"One or two. But I don't know their names."

He slipped her another ten. "You sure?"

She pushed it back. "Baby, those are nice'n all. Half a dozen more might even get me that pair of fancy pumps I've been wanting. But they won't put a name in my head that ain't there."

He pocketed the ten. This would be harder than he thought.

"Sorry, baby." She patted his arm. "And stay away from those gators, okay?" She hurried away to tend to another customer.

"Well, if it ain't my old friend that likes kicking his buddies in the ass..."

C.C. caught a strong whiff of Aqua Velva and turned. The man wore his usual attire of black dress slacks and snug-fitting polo shirt. His dark-brown hair was covered with mousse and combed straight back, his goatee as perfectly trimmed as always. Three gold rings decorated the fingers of each hand. A gold necklace glittered around his neck. Pockets Sheldon sat down on the next stool.

Eileen brought over a frosted mug of Guinness and placed it on the table. Pockets just looked at it. "It's on me," C.C. said, handing money to Eileen before she walked away.

Pockets picked up the mug. "Whaddya want?"

"Your help. And I need it fast."

339

Pockets drank some Guinness and sat back. "And here I was, thinking you felt really bad about marking up my fine ass and wanted to make amends."

"Sorry about that," C.C. said, trying to move things along. Pockets needed his ego stroked before he'd start cooperating. "I went overboard."

"You did *that*, all right. It sounds good, hearing you say it, but it still doesn't take the sting out of–"

"I really don't have time for this." He'd already been here twenty minutes and had found out very little.

"Time for what?"

"Remember the lady I suckered you with Monday afternoon?"

"Tall, skinny, nice hair, and big brown eyes. How could I forget?"

"She's in trouble."

Pockets had more Guinness. "Who's involved?"

C.C. didn't reply. Pockets wasn't exactly the world's bravest man.

Pockets reared back slowly. "I'm beginning to smell shit, Cross. I mean heavy-duty, foul, sick-to-my-stomach crap." He sucked down one last belt and got up. "And one beer just ain't worth this favor of yours."

"I didn't even tell you–"

"When a gorilla like you is afraid to tell a stooge like me what's going down, it can only mean trouble. And to me, trouble means a handful of folks I'm not wild about coming after my ass. I'd like

340

your toe-print to heal before I find my ass on a slab."

C.C. didn't reply.

"Thanks for the beer." Pockets rushed outside.

C.C. followed him to the black Corvette parked out front. "Just hear me out, all right?"

Pockets no longer wore his same cocky expression. He was obviously scared. "We're talking some bad dudes here. You think I wanna end up dead? Or worse, find my ass in a *cell* with one of those animals?"

"That girl's gonna be dead if I don't find something in twenty-four hours."

"I hope you find it, then." He pulled the door shut and rolled down the window. "Like I said, I don't wanna end up in a *cell* with one of them."

"Just one or two questions?"

Pockets gave him the finger as he fired up. He backed up and spun gravel.

C.C. watched the beautiful sleek car pull out onto Goldenrod and head north. He glanced at his watch. *Another fifteen minutes shot.* Where could he go now? What could he possibly do when he'd just encountered two dead ends? Frowning, he turned and gazed absently at the front window of the Paradise, realizing two things simultaneously. Pockets had said the word 'cell' twice. Not once, but twice. And the two men sitting at the table by the window watched him without making it obvious. For their benefit, he shook his head and shuffled back to the Mustang. He got in it, fired up and pulled out, heading south.

As soon as the building was out of sight, he pulled out his cell and punched in Pockets' number.

Pockets answered on the first ring. "What kept ya?"

"I had to make it look good."

"Those two sitting near the window could work for Big John."

"Both around forty? Styled hair? Business types? Possibly."

"And since we're not positive, it's best not to take chances."

"Right about that."

"Whaddya need? And by the way, it'll cost ya a hundred."

"You tell me what I need and I'll give you *two* hundred."

"Sounds good. Let 'er rip."

"Hear anything about a suitcase of money walking?"

"Like around this past Saturday?"

"Close enough."

"Heard *some*thing went down back there."

"Were you here?"

"One of my many lady friends said some college kid hit on her and she couldn't get rid of the little shit. He was trying to show off for his idiot friends. She said they were all young. Early twenties."

"Anything else?"

"She said the kid coming on to her was Hispanic. Good-looking but a real dork. Obsessive about his hair. Full of himself. Couldn't hold his

342

beer."

"Alvarez's kid, maybe?"

"She said he was talking big. Mentioned his old man a couple times."

"Anyone else there?"

"Another kid, pals around with Santella and Alvarez. Spends time with Solo."

"The Calvin kid?" C.C. asked, suspecting it was Paul Calvin, the Rollins College grad who did odd jobs for Solo to support his coke habit. Calvin had been arrested for possession at least three times in the last year, but was always bailed out before OPD could ask him any questions.

"She was pretty sure he was stoned. Said he was sweating, sniffing and sloppy."

"She describe him?"

"Brown shoulder-length hair, glassy eyes. Medium height and skinny. Said his hair was messy and looked like it hadn't been washed in quite a while."

"That's Calvin."

"Anything else?"

"I owe you big-time." C.C. pocketed the cell. He made a U-turn at the Lake Nona turnoff, went back north, pulled onto the Beeline, and rushed back to Orlando.

Paul Calvin and Solo. *Money, my ass. One of those idiots had lifted a shipment of cocaine.*

***

Cursing softly, Al Solo slowly ascended the stairs.

Babes. They really made a guy's blood boil. He

didn't want to deal with a babe not long for this world, but sometimes he had to bite the bullet and jump in. He should be used to this. Anybody handled babes, they always ended up knee-deep in shit. But he needed to set her straight – just in case she wanted to freak or do something stupid. If she went apeshit and jumped through the window, he'd have to do a shitload of explaining to the cops – and especially to his bosses. Jo-Jo didn't tolerate shit happening in any of his clubs. He'd blame Al and wouldn't accept any sort of excuse.

Al couldn't blame him. Newshounds would be all over something like that, and talking to reporters was no good. They were assholes – always looking for ways to make themselves famous. And the cops always wanted to nail somebody's ass. Jo-Jo had a few cops and a slew of high-profile officials on his payroll, but it was always a good idea to be extra careful and avoid getting thrown into stir.

Things had to stay quiet – especially since that moron Calvin had found Jack Santella's shipment outside the Paradise Friday night. Stupid of Calvin to take it in the first place, but he was totally wasted and didn't know any better. He'd gotten straight after his three-day binge and called to tell him what he'd done, but it was *way* too late by that time.

Al had originally wanted to tell Calvin to return it. Just rent a car under a fake name, take it back to the bar, and leave it in the parking lot. Make an anonymous call and forget about it. Calvin would be in the clear and wouldn't have to worry about someone coming after him with a chainsaw.

Then Al got the call from Big John. The orders were simple and direct: Cross was going to find the missing shipment. Cross – the smart-ass cop who'd been trying to put everyone away – but mostly Al himself. That's when the ultimate plan came to him like magic. Al had a stolen shipment of coke and a suitcase filled with money, and a perfect way of getting Cross out of the way. No way Cross could find that shipment in twenty-four hours. Even if he did trace the shipment to Calvin, he'd be much too busy reporting his progress to Jo-Jo to know Al had already made plans to move it.

Calvin was a mess to begin with. If he talked, he'd lead Cross to a dead end. Al had plenty of time to pick up the shipment from his apartment house on Holden Avenue. He planned to do it before he went home tonight, then wait a day or two before 'finding' the shipment. By then, Cross and the girl would be dead, and Jo-Jo would be eternally grateful. And if Jo-Jo *wasn't* grateful, Al would still have the suitcase of money to dispose of any way he pleased. Two million added to what he'd already accumulated would buy a decent place in Maui.

Switching off his grin, he unlocked and opened the door. The Foreman girl lay in the bed, watching him. Not bad, but washed-out and pale – possibly from being knocked out and manhandled. Not much in the boob department, either, but she had great hair. Great eyes, too – big and almond-shaped. The kind that locked onto you and made you self-conscious. That was probably what happened with Ronnie, the big mouth.

The girl propped herself up. Those eyes stayed on him and didn't miss a lick. Al had no problem zoning them out. He'd been in the business much too long to let a pair of great eyes fuck up his head.

"Ronnie said you two had a nice little talk." He could sucker any bitch as long as the element of fear was present. Right now, those eyes told him she was ready to shit her drawers. It wouldn't take much to get her adrenaline pumping.

"We didn't talk *that* much," she said in a soft voice. "I just said how I'd like to clean up a little. She offered to bring me a comb and brush and maybe a toothbrush and some mouthwash."

This just didn't smell right. The bitch was obviously hiding something.

"She didn't tell you anything else?" He sat in the chair. "Didn't say where you are? Why you're here?"

"Why *am* I here?"

"Don't worry, you'll be leaving soon. Once your boyfriend does what he's supposed to, you're free to go."

She paused and looked at him like she was looking through him. Then she said, "Why was it necessary to bring me here?"

He shrugged. "Insurance. Your boyfriend can be stubborn."

"Why was I drugged?"

"I know that was, um, uncomfortable and all, but sometimes the hired help gets overzealous. They went overboard. Sorry."

"They didn't think they could bring me here

346

without drugging me?"

This bitch was much too smart. Too damned bad. He wasn't going to regret putting her lights out at all. "It made it easier for them, I guess. Like I said, they get carried away."

She lay back down.

"You want something to eat?"

"No."

"So. There's no other reason why Ronnie left you alone?"

"Like I said, we didn't talk much."

She was definitely holding back. Just too damned nervous. That could be because of the situation, but he knew he couldn't chance anything. He'd keep her here until it was time, then have Murphy and Landon come back, knock her out again and take her somewhere to dump her.

All he cared about for now was keeping her quiet until tomorrow. As for Ronnie ... she had to know how badly she'd fucked up. Without another word, he got up and left the room.

***

The Church Street Oyster House had been doing its usual booming business for the last hour.

Tourists and locals filled every available table and barstool, sucking up steamed clams, crabs, oysters, and beer, just as quickly as it was placed in front of them. The men's room bustled. Men in shorts and tank tops whistled at the urinal while others belched, farted, or worse.

Lenny Alfredo found a vacant stall, slammed the door behind him and latched it. The stall made him gag. Nothing more disgusting than the men's room in an oyster bar. This place was even worse than the Wal-Mart bathrooms he'd seen. Graffiti covered both walls, the door, and portions of the cracked yellow tile behind the toilet bowl. Someone named *'Pokie'* said he could *'rock any time, any day, any way,'* and gave two phone numbers and his cell. Someone else had written, *'Cunts suck.'* Lenny shook his head. Why did people have to be so nasty and mean when they took a dump? Maybe they had irritable bowel, or a bladder problem. They certainly didn't have any self-respect.

Sitting on the seat was not an option. It looked like somebody had missed completely or purposely tried to coat the rim. Probably Pokie, while scrawling his nasty message. Some guys just couldn't multi-task.

Three hundred bucks so far, and he hadn't even been here an hour. No wonder this was his favorite money store. He pulled the cash from the wallet he'd snatched on his way over and counted it. Three hundred in tens and twenties. Good deal. He peeled off two hundred and stuffed the rest back in the wallet. The man would go apeshit trying to remember what he did with two hundred bucks.

Elbowing three oldsters waiting for a urinal, Lenny left the room and went back out into the hectic eating area. At the center table, a family of five sat, eagerly devouring their meal. A husky bald man and his tiny wife, a pudgy boy around fifteen, a skinny brown-haired babe a little older, in a tight tank top and jeans, and another pudgy boy around

348

ten. The driver's license said Hector J. Wilson, the owner of the wallet, was from Westerville, Ohio.

Just as Lenny was about to pass, he stopped abruptly and bent down. When he straightened, the wallet appeared in his hand. He handed it to the man, who was busy sucking down a fistful of steamed clams. "Yours?" The man's mouth was full. He nodded and grabbed the wallet with a chunky, butter-smeared paw. "You're welcome." Lenny smiled politely. The daughter looked him up and down. Especially down. *Oh boy*. Hector and his wife would soon have major issues with their teen daughter and her raging hormones.

Lenny decided to leave. Five hundred in one hour was more than enough. He didn't want to appear greedy. He opened the entrance door. Someone stood there, blocking his way. Cross again. "Man, you showed up at a busy time." He tried squeezing by. "Good luck finding a table."

Cross grabbed him by the shirt and yanked him out onto the street.

Lenny regained his balance, straightened, and fixed his crumpled collar. "Can't you take bad news like a *normal* human being?"

"Do I look like I want a fucking *table*?" Cross snapped.

Lenny brushed off his sleeve where he'd bumped into the building. "Can't you get the police force to cough up some jack for counseling sessions?"

"Don't have the time."

"Whaddya want? I thought that last job I did

349

squared us."

Cross appeared more irritated than usual. Something was definitely bothering him. "I need a little info." Cross handed him a ten.

"That it? A lousy ten-spot?"

Cross sighed, reached into his pocket again, and pulled out another ten.

"That it? Another lousy ten-spot?"

Cross glared.

Lenny shrugged. "Figured it was worth a try."

"I don't have time for this."

Lenny pocketed it. "Then I guess you won't wanna talk over coffee."

"Just one simple question. Paul Calvin."

Lenny figured it might be something like this. What he'd heard on the street a couple of days ago told him there'd soon be fireworks. Too bad Cross was mixed up in it. "He's a wreck. A walking zombie. With the shit he sucks up? His brain's gotta be a slab of Swiss cheese. Works for that shithead, Slick Al Solo. Odd jobs, mostly. Pissing-around money."

"I know."

"What *don't* you know?"

"Where he is."

Lenny shrugged. "Probably with Slick Al."

"What does he usually do for Solo?"

"You don't know?"

"I *thought* I did, but something came up and I'm not sure about anything anymore."

"This about that gi-normous chunk of money he found?"

350

Cross froze. "You *know* about the money?"

This didn't make sense. Everyone knew about it. "It's all over town."

"Son of a bitch."

"Calvin also found a shitload of coke with it – or is that something else you don't know about?"

Cross looked like he was about to faint. "I *knew* that weasel Solo lied to me."

"Calvin's got diarrhea of the mouth. Especially when he's high. Thing is, he's always so fucked up, nobody believes what he says."

"Damn..." Cross leaned against the brick wall.

"You're not taking care of that finger, are you?"

"Forget the damned finger. More important things going on."

"You have to find that money? Or the coke?"

"Yeah."

"Who's the stuff belong to?"

"Guess."

Had to be Lanza or Big John. It was their turf. Calvin was hitting the big leagues and probably didn't even know what he'd done. "Calvin must've been seriously comatose to take it in the first place. If I were a betting man, I'd say he's keeping pretty close to Slick Al. He's crazy if he thinks Solo will protect him."

"Solo looks out for himself. But he wouldn't want Calvin out wandering around. Not while that shipment's up for grabs."

"Solo's got a few rentals in that area. Know where they are?"

Cross scratched the back of his neck. "I know about that building on Holden. He also owns a couple of flea traps on President's Drive."

"One of Solo's girlfriends manages his places. He likes to stop in pretty regularly and get his ashes dusted."

"Any idea where her office is?"

"None. But since he only owns three or four places, it shouldn't take you *that* long to find Calvin."

"Like I said, I don't have much time to do this."

"Wish I could help."

"Wish you could, too."

Chapter 28

Ten minutes after the scary little guy had left, the door opened slowly.

Lindsay sat up on the bed. It was Ronnie. Lindsay relaxed a little, but as Ronnie drew closer, Lindsay covered her mouth. Ronnie's eyes were bloodshot, her hair a mess, her lips swollen. The left side of her mouth dripped blood. Dark droplets pitted her chin. "My *God*." Lindsay couldn't hide her shock. "Is there something ... anything ... I can *do*?"

Ronnie slumped in the chair. She blew her nose with a wet Kleenex and coughed. She was having difficulty holding back her tears. Her hair hid her face.

"Who *did* that to you?"

"Al. Who else?"

Lindsay cringed. "He's done that *before*?"

"He ... got carried away this time."

This time. Lindsay had been right in her suspicions. But it made no sense.

"Didn't you tell me you're a dancer?"

A nod.

"And he did that to you anyway?"

"He uses a phone book. It really hurts but doesn't leave bruises. He doesn't want his dancers showing bruises. He's usually more careful, but ... when I wouldn't tell him what he wanted to know..." More tears. She sniffed, then turned to Lindsay. "What ... what did you tell him?"

My God. He told Ronnie the same lies.

Lindsay had been right about him. He *was* scary and evil. The deep-red blotches swimming above his slicked-back hair had told her everything. "Ronnie, I didn't tell him *anything*."

Ronnie pushed some hair away from her smeared face. Her eyes glistened. "*Nothing*?"

"I told him you went to get a comb and a toothbrush for me."

"You didn't ... you didn't tell him that I told you where you are? Or why you're here? Or anything else?"

"He lied to you, Ronnie. He's a very bad man, and he's going to kill us."

Ronnie cringed. "He ... *told* you that?"

"Ronnie, listen to me. We've got to get out of here."

"I can't believe he actually told you something like that."

"He didn't have to."

"Then how ... how do you know?"

"I can read people."

"*Read* people?"

"I can tell when they're lying." She hoped that would suffice.

"How? How can–"

"We don't have much time. But please believe me. I can tell things about people without having to listen to them."

"That's why ... why I left the room. You really scared me. Please tell me how you can do it. I need to know. *Please*?"

Maybe after a quick demonstration, they could get out of here. "Tell me something about yourself. Something personal. Anything will do."

"Anything?"

"Just tell me. It doesn't have to be true. I'll be able to tell."

"I still don't understand..." She wiped her eyes. "Okay. I'm twenty-five years old and my birthday is in May." Tiny red wisps quickly appeared above her head.

"That's a lie."

Ronnie blinked. "How ... did you *know*?"

"I'll tell you later." Lindsay got up. "We have to get out of here."

"Just leave?"

"We don't have a choice."

"But ... I *work* here. And I look like hell. I need to fix my face and–"

"Ronnie, if we don't get out of here in the next couple of minutes, we're both going to be dead."

***

Al had a bad feeling about sending Ronnie back upstairs after knocking her around.

Babes had to be handled carefully. They had an irritating habit of talking to one another. When one got the shit beat out of her and then spilled her guts to another one, they were liable to put their pea brains together and plan something. And this definitely wasn't the time for surprises. Anyway, things might move along much better if two of his boys bundled up the Foreman girl right now and dumped her somewhere. It was senseless to keep

355

her upstairs. They'd need that room in a few hours, anyway.

He stubbed out his smoke and picked up his cell. The low-pitched voice answered on the second ring. "Yeah, boss?"

"Billy, I want you and Mongo Man to do a little errand for me."

"Right now?"

Al gritted his teeth. What the hell was wrong with these punks nowadays? They had no problem standing at the door and collecting money, but when they were told to do something different, they went totally stupid. "No, I meant next Christmas. Yeah. Right now."

"Who'll take care of the front?"

"I'm the boss. I can handle that."

Silence.

"What the hell's the problem?"

"Mongo Man ... he ain't back yet."

If those steroid freaks weren't good at keeping the customers in line, Al would have no use for them. "Asshole's supposed to be out front with you. Why isn't he there?"

"He ... went to take a leak."

"How long's he been gone?"

"Just a couple minutes."

Al groaned. Every time he turned his back, these morons tried fucking with him. "The truth, Billy..."

"Maybe ten minutes."

"Ten minutes to take a *leak*?"

"Maybe he had a problem..."

356

Al snorted. "Yeah. The idiot probably got confused."

"Huh?"

"When he went in and saw the urinals and the crappers, he probably couldn't decide which he oughta use first. Don't strain your brain. *I'll* find him. If he's trying to hump one of those dancers again, his ass is mine."

"Boss? You still want me to do that errand?"

"Listen and listen carefully, okay? I want you to stay right there. Do what you do best – keep your mouth shut and take money. Got it?"

***

Ronnie pressed her ear to the door.

"How do we get out of here?" Lindsay whispered close behind her.

"The back staircase leads downstairs to the dressing rooms and the offices behind the bars and lap dancing areas. There's another short hall that takes you to the rear exit."

"When do the customers come up here?"

"Usually around midnight, when we finish up downstairs. Anyway, it's much too early. We've got plenty of time. I have a car in the back lot."

"Are there attendants?"

"Only in the front. The parking in back is just for the employees. Once in a while, one of the bouncers or barmen goes back there for a quick smoke or joint. If we can reach my car, we can get away pretty easily. The lot goes around to the front, but it's always such a madhouse out there, no one'll notice us."

357

"Do you have a cell phone?"

"In my car. Is there someone we can call?"

She didn't know C.C.'s number. But right now she didn't want to worry about that. "I'll figure something out when we get out of here."

Ronnie listened for about another minute, then eased the door open.

The dimly-lit hall revealed no one. The heavy throbbing of the juke downstairs echoed up the stairs. They tiptoed down the hall and quietly descended the stairs. When they were about halfway down, a huge shadow slowly darkened the area of the landing.

Ronnie froze, nearly tripping. Lindsay stopped dead behind her. A huge bearded man in a tuxedo appeared at the foot of the stairs. He was about to walk right on by when he suddenly stopped, turned his head, and stared up at them.

***

Her lithe, half-naked body beaded with sweat, Judi finished her dance.

After collecting the five-dollar bills dangling around her chain belt, she folded them and stuffed the wad into her tiny clutch. Then, draping a towel around her neck, she left the crowded, sweat-filled room and glanced at her watch on her way to the dressing rooms. It was getting late, and she had to hurry home. Otherwise, Mona, her 'material girl' babysitter, would slap her with an hour of overtime again.

The huge hulking figure of Mongo Man appeared halfway down the hall. He was staring up the staircase. Judi's pulse pounded. Just what she didn't need right now. At least her customers slipped money down her belt for the privilege. The bouncers did their pawing and drooling for free.

Maybe I can slip past him this time. She opened her clutch, found her keys underneath the wad of cash, and hastily tried unlocking the dressing room door. Luck was not on her side. She was jittery from the last six lap dances, and in her frenzied state, her fingers had turned worthless. The keys dropped to the floor. *Damn.* She quickly bent over and scooped them up. When she straightened, she was staring at his massive chest just two feet away. His small glossy eyes took in her silicone breasts. The drool, as usual, had gathered on his lower lip.

"Want me to get that for ya?"

"N-No ... it's all right. I can manage–"

"No problem." He took them from her shaking hands and approached the door. Judi watched him nervously and wondered how she was going to shake him this time. She knew he wasn't as stupid as he looked, but that didn't matter. No girl in her right mind wanted a drooling King Kong smothering her.

The door clicked open. Grinning, Mongo Man held out her keys. Careful not to touch him and give off any false vibes, she took them. Now all she had to do was slip past. At least he wasn't blocking the door this time.

His cell beeped. Her heart slid right back down where it belonged. His eyes still fixed to her boobs, Mongo Man brought out his cell. He immediately stiffened. Slick Al, no doubt, probably wondering where he was. Judi sighed. *Thank God for small favors.*

Twenty feet behind him, Ronnie and a tall, skinny girl appeared from upstairs. Even from this distance, Judi could tell something was wrong. Ronnie looked a wreck. The two girls glanced in their direction, then hurried down the hall.

"Yes, boss... Yes, boss ... I'm there now... Ya want me to go *upstairs*? Well yeah, I heard ya, but I just saw 'em ... on the stairs... Sure thing, boss. Right away." He pocketed his cell and spun around.

Judi didn't like the looks of this. She also didn't like how Slick Al batted the girls around and treated them like his slaves. Judi liked Ronnie. If they needed to get away, they could probably use a little more of a head-start. She dropped her keys again. "Damn!"

Mongo Man turned back around. She smiled sheepishly. "I'm *so* clumsy today." Then she reached up to push back her long black hair away from her face.

Mongo Man bent over, picked up her keys, and handed them to her. "Thank you." He'd started drooling again.

"Who *was* that?" she asked in a soft voice. "On the phone? I didn't by any chance get you in *trouble*, did I?"

"Shit, shit, *shit!*" Suddenly remembering, he spun around and lumbered down the hall.

Hopefully, Ronnie and her friend had gained a little distance. Judi ducked inside the dressing room,

360

pulled the door shut, and locked it.

361

Chapter 29

At seven o'clock, the huge parking lot of Babes Galore screamed in chaos.

A long line of vehicles sat from the Orange Blossom Trail turnoff to the front entrance, waiting nearly a quarter of a mile down the private road. Cars, pickups, and SUVs filled the front lot from the first row to three-quarters of the way back, where a grove of pine trees separated the property from the main highway.

Dwarfed by two monster trucks in the last row, C.C. waited tensely in the Mustang while going through the scenario once again in his head. Paul Calvin lifted a shipment from Jack Santella's Charger, got scared, then told Solo about it. Solo, being the opportunistic weasel he was since the day he was born, conned Calvin into bringing the shipment to him. But instead of returning it, Solo had hidden it for himself, and to save face with Lanza, he'd sent C.C. on this wild goose chase, all the while keeping Lindsay's life hanging in the balance.

Neither Santella nor Lanza knew what Solo was doing. C.C. couldn't tell them what was going on. Hoods stuck together. They'd never believe the word of an undercover cop.

No sense wasting time gallivanting all over town, looking for something Solo had stashed. There had to be some way of getting Solo to lead him to it. There also had to be some way of finding

Lindsay. He wanted to go back inside and interrogate Solo the old-fashioned way, but since the place was crawling with gorilla-sized bouncers, he wouldn't get very far. And anyway, any aggression on his part would endanger Lindsay. But there had to be a way.

C.C. got out of the Mustang and squeezed through the narrow, jagged lines of parked cars. A large warehouse sat in a pine grove directly behind the club. C.C. had heard rumors that some of Lanza's coke was cut and packaged in one of his warehouses. He didn't think Lanza's men would be stupid enough to do it so close to the club, but since C.C. didn't have anything else to go on, he decided it was worth a try.

He cut through the solid line waiting for the only available space in the front of the lot. At the entrance, two bouncers took money from the long line of anxious customers. Behind the building, three dumpsters sat directly behind the rear door. To the right, a small parking lot of maybe a dozen vehicles sat unattended. C.C. squatted down between two dumpsters and surveyed the scene.

Several rides sat in front of the warehouse – an Audi, a BMW, a couple of older sports cars, and two top-of-the-line, tricked-out pickup trucks. There were no windows in the warehouse. The small frame of glass on the metal door was black. If he could reach the building unnoticed, he could use his penlight and check out the place in just a couple of minutes. A camera was bolted to each corner of the club, just under the roof overhang. The two in front were pointed at the front lot, the others at the walk leading to the warehouse. He'd seen their operation and knew someone was always watching the monitors, but decided to chance it anyway.

Before moving away from the dumpsters, he listened for another minute. Nothing but the muffled throbbing of the jukebox inside the club. The throbbing suddenly grew in volume, then the sound of a door slamming shut muffled the throbbing again. He heard swift footsteps crunching the gravel, followed by a car engine firing up and spinning out in gravel. A late-model, light-blue Camaro rushed his way, a blond woman behind the wheel. The car shot past, slowed, and turned left at the corner, toward the front lot. He caught a glimpse of a passenger through the rear window of the Camaro.

Another door banged shut. He ducked behind the dumpster. Footsteps rushed toward the vehicles parked in front of the warehouse. C.C. risked a peek. Murphy slid behind the wheel of the BMW while Landon, talking busily into his cell phone, got in the passenger side. Murphy fired up, slammed it into gear, and tore out of the spot.

***

The front lot of Babes Galore screamed with headlights, growling engines and traffic sounds, but C.C. could distinguish the blinking taillights of the BMW struggling through the solid line pouring in.

Camouflaged by the darkness of the pine trees, he kept low, using the parked vehicles for additional cover. By the time he reached the Mustang, the BMW had squeezed its way to the entrance. Tossing gravel, it tore out into the heavy traffic and headed north.

C.C. jumped behind the wheel of the Mustang. His keys were already out, but in his agitated state his aim was off. It took what seemed forever to slip the right key into the ignition. He finally fired it up, slammed it into gear and jolted out of his space. In spite of the traffic, he maneuvered the sleek car in and out of lanes, slipping through a red light, losing some of the congestion and gaining distance. The BMW's taillights showed about a block ahead, brightening and dimming as Murphy rode the brakes.

A beep coming from the floor in front of the passenger seat made him jump. Lindsay's handbag. Keeping his eyes on the traffic ahead, he grabbed the bag and dropped it in his lap. Three vehicles ahead, the BMW swerved into the passing lane, then fell behind a procession of slow-moving vehicles in the right lane. C.C. gunned it, cutting off someone in a Dodge Ram hauling an ATV. Ignoring the angry protest of a horn, he gained more distance.

The BMW's taillights showed again. The light changed. Murphy sailed right on through. C.C. tried squeezing through as well, but the vehicles in front of him slammed to a stop. Before he could swerve into the oncoming lane, a heavy flow of approaching traffic forced him to jam on the brakes. His nerves quivering like frayed cables, he fought to stay in control. *Don't lose it. They can't get far in this traffic*. He took a deep breath, focusing again, then rummaged through Lindsay's handbag.

365

Lindsay's cell beeped again from inside the bag. He snatched it up and put the bag back on the passenger seat.

A heavy thump on his window made C.C. jerk his head to find a huge bearded guy with one thick black eyebrow and a pronounced scowl on his bulldog face motioning for him to roll down the window. C.C. rolled it down. "Problem?"

"You cut me off back there, asshole."

"Yeah, I did. Sorry about that." He made a move to close the window.

The guy reached in and tried grabbing C.C. by the throat. A heavy puff of whiskey and B.O. rushed into the cab. C.C. pushed the big, hairy paw away. "I'm a cop, fella. On a case. Let it go."

The scowl turned into a sneer. "You're a fucking cop? Let's see a fucking badge."

I don't need this. C.C. opened the console, pulled out the Beretta and held it up. "Don't seem to have my badge with me. Will *this* do?"

The big man spun around and raced back to his vehicle. The light changed. C.C. put the gun on the seat and joined the flow.

***

Her face a taut mask, Ronnie jerked the powerful car onto the main road and wove recklessly through the heavy northbound traffic.

Her hands shaking, Lindsay fumbled with her seat belt. She hoped they wouldn't be killed. But they had no choice. They had to get away. Death faced both of them back at the club.

That scary Slick Al guy made her think of

366

Hannibal Lecter and other sickos she'd seen in movies. He hated everyone, envied everyone. He terrified her even more than the man who'd killed Momma. But now she faced something even scarier and more difficult than anything else. She not only had to help Ronnie out of this, she had to find C.C. and somehow make everything right. And that meant doing something she never thought she'd ever do. She had to forget about Maisie and about the man who'd run her over – and the League. She had to turn a blind eye and just let things go. Despite her feelings, her beliefs, she had no choice. She was responsible not only for Momma's death, but also for killing the man who'd murdered Momma. She'd endangered Ronnie, C.C., the lives of everyone they passed on the highway, and everyone else she'd come across since the night she'd held Maisie's hand and watched her die. It was wrong to run away, and it was unfair to have to. It would change her forever, but she saw no other way.

Dad had been right all along. The world was indeed dark and frightening, filled with bad people who did bad things. But Dad was wrong about one very important aspect of all this. Not only did a person have to be brave to stand against the bad guys, sometimes sacrifices had to be made. And those sacrifices oftentimes included other people. Was she prepared to sacrifice others in her campaign? She made a vow to herself at that moment. If she got out of this, she would never endanger anyone else's life again.

She turned to Ronnie, who gripped the wheel as she careened past other vehicles. It was time to concentrate on survival. "Any idea where we're going?"

"Doesn't matter." Ronnie cut in between a van and an SUV, then swerved into and out of the turning lane. All the while, she kept glancing in her side mirror. "We lucked out with Mongo Man, but he probably told Al he saw us."

"*Mongo* Man?"

"That big ape at the foot of the stairs."

The remorse came back, stabbing her harder. Lindsay felt so sorry for Ronnie. And for C.C. But especially Ronnie, who was a total wreck. She could barely keep her hands on the wheel.

If only I hadn't brought her into this... If only I'd asked C.C. not to stop for that police car... If only Momma hadn't come home yesterday–

"I feel *so* bad for getting you involved in this," she said, nudging away the growing panic.

Ronnie didn't take her eyes off the road ahead. "I've been on Al's shit-list for quite a while. He really doesn't need much of an excuse to bat me around."

"How'd you get on his list?"

She shrugged. "I wouldn't put out."

Lindsay *was* right about him. The hatred, the envy. The lies. He was a psychiatrist's dream, and society's nightmare.

Ronnie snuck a quick glance in her direction. "You can't blame me, can you? I mean, look at the guy. He reminds you of Squiggy on *Laverne and*

Shirley, only with better clothes and the manners of Charles Manson. What girl in her right mind would want that?"

"Do the other girls feel the same?"

"A few let him have some just to make him happy and to get him off their backs. The girls he lusts over can get away with a little flirting. They think that if he hopes he'll get lucky, they're off the hook. So far, it's worked. I made my big mistake when I told him I wasn't interested. If I wasn't such a good dancer, Al would've kicked me out long ago."

"But he beat you up anyway."

"He goes crazy when he's pissed. He's scary for a little guy."

"Yeah. I already figured that."

"I know." Ronnie slipped though a red light and switched lanes again. "I'm still trying to figure out how you can read people."

"I'll tell you when we get out of this." She had to think of something. If only she knew where C.C. was – and whether he was still alive. C.C. *had* to be alive. She couldn't imagine surviving this without him. She took a deep breath. "You mentioned a cell phone."

Ronnie pointed to her console. Lindsay opened it, reached in, and pulled it out. She held her breath and punched buttons.

"Calling someone who can actually *help* us?"

"I'm trying a long shot."

Ronnie glanced at her side mirror again. "Uh-oh..." She stiffened in her seat. The Camaro bumped the shoulder.

Lindsay stopped punching in the number to her cell phone. "What's wrong?"

"That BMW bearing down on us looks awfully familiar."

Lindsay twisted around. "You've seen it at the club?"

"It belongs to Al. He lets his bouncers use it to run errands."

It was getting dark. The shiny black windshield of the vehicle behind them reflected wavy slashes of white from the passing street lamps.

Lindsay closed her eyes and focused. The faces of two men appeared amidst the blackness in her mind. The two cops who'd stopped her and C.C. sat in the front seat of the BMW. They weren't wearing police uniforms this time.

Lindsay opened her eyes and focused on Ronnie's cell phone, frantically pushing the buttons.

***

Whipping around a gold Buick with handicap plates, C.C. glanced down to see a missed call displayed on Lindsay's phone. With the number on the screen, he pressed the call button and waited as the number rang. Lindsay's breathless voice came on a second later. "C.C.?"

"Lindsay!" A hot wave of relief washed heavily through him. *Thank God*. She was all right. "Where are you?"

"We're on the Trail, heading north."

He tried a long shot. "You in the Camaro?"

"Yes. Ronnie and I managed to—"

"I'm right behind a black BMW driven by the two goons who kidnapped us."

"Those guys are after us!"

"I know."

"What'll we do?"

"Try to use the lights to your advantage. If you can, squeeze through red and play it by ear. Don't worry about the rules of the road. You've got two psychos after you. Just try not to hit anyone. I'll do my best to stay behind them. If I get a clear shot, I'll try to shoot out their tires. Do your best to keep as many vehicles between you two as you can."

"Are you all right? I mean, did they hurt you or anything?"

"I'm fine. Worried about you, though. Who's the blonde?"

"She's one of the dancers at the club."

"How's she holding up? She's not freaking, is she?"

"We'll be okay for a little while."

"Just watch the traffic, try to keep as many cars between you and those bozos as you can. They're liable to try anything."

Another yellow light. Since he was more than half a dozen vehicles back, it wasn't possible to make it through. "Hang on. Do whatever you can. I'm about to hit another red. I'll do what I can to get up there, but I've got to sit tight for right now."

The flow went on through, stopping one row short.

Lindsay's voice jumped sharply as she shrieked, "Oh, no!"

371

"What's wrong?"

"They're *beside* us!"

***

The BMW crept up on their left. The window eased down. Something black and tubular-shaped extended from the cab. A gun.

"He's ... got a *gun!*" Ronnie jerked in her seat. The Camaro swerved, nearly sideswiping the white Saturn beside them. A horn blared. "Wh-What'll we *do*?"

"C.C., they've got a gun." A hot bubble encased Lindsay's head. Her voice sounded muffled and far away. The phone in her hand had become a heavy block of ice.

"Any way you can turn off somewhere?"

"Too much traffic."

"No holes anywhere?"

She glanced to her right. "We'd have to cut in front of the Saturn we almost sideswiped."

"Do it."

The gap wasn't even half a car length. Ronnie couldn't possibly fit the Camaro in there without pushing them off the road.

"But there isn't enough–"

"Just *do* it!" The alarm in C.C.'s voice sent a heavy sheet of ice sliding down her back.

Without hesitation, she said, "Pull in front of the Saturn *now*!"

Ronnie opened her mouth to protest. As if in a trance, Lindsay watched her own right hand grabbing the wheel and giving it a hefty yank.

A loud *boom* roared somewhere to their left.

372

The Camaro dropped sharply on the driver's side and skidded. Jerking in her seat, Ronnie fought to correct the skid. A protest of brakes squealed to their right, then behind them, then in front. A symphony of blaring horns surrounded them. A loud crashing noise thundered behind them.

The Camaro fishtailed, spinning around. The night quickly turned into a maze of gooey colors. A blur of white slammed into them on Lindsay's right. Lindsay reached out to grab onto something. The cell phone jumped onto the dash, then slid over to the other side. Ronnie let go of the wheel and screamed. Thick sheets of white and black surrounded Ronnie's shoulders just before her head thumped against Lindsay's left arm, slamming Lindsay against the door.

A street lamp rushed toward her. Chills scurried up her spine. A sea of multicolored lights exploded before her. The dashboard reached out for her face. Blackness followed the harsh slam into her forehead.

PART VIII - FRIDAY & SATURDAY
Game Over

Chapter 30

A sea of white.

Fear? No. A room with white walls. A white door. A white ceiling. White sheets.

A hospital room.

Lindsay closed her eyes and the images thundered past. A cop car, its lights flashing. Two large men in blue uniforms. C.C. walking away. A BMW. A lowered window. A gun. A loud boom. Ronnie screaming. The cell phone sliding across the dash. The street lamp rushing toward her. The dash slamming into her face. Darkness.

Her forehead buzzed with a light numbness. She wanted to touch it. Her arm weighed a ton, but she forced it upward. A heavy tingling started in her hand, moving into her shoulder. It stopped, then became a distant throbbing. A huge bandage covered her forehead. Her arm dropped to her side.

The effort made her shoulder ache. She must have banged it on the door when the Camaro smashed into the street lamp. She shifted her position just a little, and her right side flared up in a warm rush of pain. Her feet and ankles began tingling. She tried looking down at herself, but her chin caught on something. A neck brace.

Did I break my neck? She turned her head

374

slightly – to the left, then the right. It ached, but at least it functioned.

She was alone in the room. A stack of equipment covered a table off to her right. The drapes were partially open. Strands of gleaming brightness told her it was probably late morning or early afternoon.

The door opened quietly. C.C. appeared in the doorway. When he saw she was awake, he came right over. His smile appeared awkward. She could tell he was forcing it. *I must look really bad.*

Her looks didn't matter. She was glad to see him – to know he was all right, that they hadn't done anything to him. She was also glad she wasn't in that dark, musty-smelling room anymore.

The bandage on his hand looked fresh. He sported no other bandages or bruises that she could see. And the blues and greens floating above his head gave her hope. So why did she feel something was very wrong? And why did several white patchy puffs appear above C.C.'s head when he sat in the chair beside her bed?

I've lost something. A leg. Or an arm. But it can't be a leg because my feet ache. She took a quick inventory. Everything seemed to be where it was supposed to be. "Am I ... all right?"

He nodded. The white vanished. No red. Good. They were off to a fine start.

"I'll be able to leave soon?"

"They're still waiting for the lab results." Still no red or white. "Just minor bruises. No internal damage. A slight concussion from when you hit your head."

My God. Poor Ronnie must be even worse. Maybe not. She might have escaped serious injury when she was knocked into Lindsay. Lindsay hoped so.

"What's the neck brace for?"

"The collision jarred your spine. They were worried about cervical fracture. To be safe, they left it on while they did their tests. They said they'll take it off as soon as you–"

"How's Ronnie?"

The white clouds reappeared. He said nothing.

"C.C.?"

He sighed. "It looks like I'll be able to take you out of here–"

"Is she all right?"

Blackness showed among the white. *Oh my God*. She gasped. "Ronnie ... is she ... *dead*?"

C.C. looked down at his lap.

"*No!*"

He shifted in his chair. Still looking down, he said, "There was ... massive internal damage. A truck slammed into you and hit the driver's side..."

She didn't hear the rest. The hot tears filled her eyes, her entire being. They were tears of sorrow, of anger, of regret ... but mostly anger. For Ronnie, for Momma, for Maisie ... and for everyone else who'd suffered because of all this.

She turned on her side. The tears dropped silently onto the pillow. Silence was good. Silence and nothingness. It sounded so wonderfully peaceful. She prayed for sleep to take her away. She vaguely heard C.C.'s voice off in the distance, but ignored it. It was part of the terrible place she was running away from. A horrible place where people lied and killed one another. Thankfully, peace came quickly, nudging her gently away.

***

She didn't know how long she slept or how much later it was.

But she didn't care. She was just glad that they took off the neck brace and told her she could leave. Her forehead bandages were replaced with a much smaller one. And thanks to the meds they'd given her, her injuries didn't hurt nearly as much.

C.C. helped her out of the wheelchair. The morning was warm and muggy, but that didn't matter. She felt one hundred percent better. She'd escaped the cold, antiseptic building and was once again taking in fresh air.

Fighting the dizziness, she forced herself to stand. It took two shaky tries, but she managed. It was time to get her life back. She wanted to have a long, warm shower, fix her hair, and get back into fresh clothes. She didn't know if she'd be able to do any of those things before someone else came for her, but she had no intention of living in fear anymore. They'd taken away her fear along with everything else.

C.C. helped her into his Mustang. He was very attentive, treating her like delicate porcelain. She appreciated his efforts, although it seemed a tad much.

They were soon on their way. She had no idea

where they were going. It didn't matter, did it? Where could they go where it would be safe? Where they wouldn't be followed?

Witnessing a crime had ruined her life. Momma was dead because of it. Also a sweet young woman named Ronnie. Lindsay could have prevented all this from happening, but she hadn't. She'd pursued her silly child's idea of good and bad, of black and white, of crime and punishment. She remembered the vow she'd made to herself in Ronnie's Camaro. The suffocating blackness of despair slammed into her. The tears came back. She covered her eyes with both bandaged hands.

As she cried, she felt the car slowing down. C.C. put it in park. He didn't say anything. She figured he wanted to help, but didn't know how. Then, in a soft voice, he asked, "Anything I can do?"

She fought back the sobs and shook her head.

"I've got my flask with me."

"You know I hate whiskey. Besides, I'm on meds. Maybe later, when I care a little less..."

"Lindsay, look at me."

She couldn't see anything through her tears. She felt him gently taking her left hand and putting something soft in her palm. Tissue. She used it to blot her eyes, then blew her nose. She handed it back.

"That's okay ... you keep it."

Incredibly, she found herself smiling. Thank God for this man. If it wasn't for him...

"You did what you had to do," he said.

"And look what happened." The anger rushed back hotly. She wanted to stop it, but decided not to. She deserved to be consumed by anger. It somehow seemed fitting. And it was the only thing that made sense.

"Stuff like this happens when you're dealing with–"

"Animals. They're animals, C.C. No. I take that back. Animals kill to eat or defend themselves. Those horrible people kill because they like to and because they're too stupid to fix their problems any other way. Animals are much more humane."

"Maybe so, but–"

"I was naïve. A silly child. I know that now. I also know that there's no room for truth or honesty in this world."

C.C. sighed and rubbed his eyes. "I ... don't like hearing that coming from you."

"It's true, isn't it?"

The sadness taking over his face made her hate herself for putting it there, but circumstances beyond her control had made it that way. "You know I'm right."

"You're the nicest, most honest person I've met in a long time."

"Momma's dead. I killed a man. *Me.* The nicest, most honest person you've met in a long time *killed* a man. Ronnie wasn't even *involved* in this. All she did was sit with me in a room for ten minutes and help me to the bathroom. Now she's dead."

"And none of it was your fault."

"Then why do I think it is? If I hadn't been so

379

bullheaded about doing the right thing, Momma would be *alive*, C.C. So would Ronnie."

C.C. ran a hand through his hair. "You're old enough to realize that life doesn't always happen the way it should."

"Why does it have to happen the way those jerks want it to?"

"It all boils down to who they are and what they are and what they do when they're threatened. You helped an old woman. Don't beat yourself up for that. And *please* don't change because of it."

The rage took over, plowing relentlessly through her. A giant mass of heat flared up in her core. Tongues of flame tore into her extremities. She cringed at its power, gritting her teeth until it subsided.

When she opened her eyes, they were wet. Her cheeks were hot. So was the back of her neck. Her scalp tingled. Her hands had become sizzling, white-knuckled fists. But the moment was far from over. The mass of heat had decreased in size, but not in intensity, as it settled somewhere in the pit of her stomach. "C.C., they *killed my mother!*" The words tore like hot coals from her throat, sending shivers down her spine. The tears burned like acid. "Momma's *dead! Dead!*"

C.C. wrapped his arms around her and held her close.

***

Later, after he'd given her more Kleenex and some time to repair her face in the visor mirror, she felt as if she'd just run a mile.

380

Her joints ached, and her limbs throbbed. But somehow none of that mattered right now. She was concerned about the rest of her life. It didn't even matter how long or how short it was. Only what she did in the time she had left. "So what's next?" she asked. "Who are they going to send for us now?"

"Lindsay, listen–"

"I want to know. I really do. I've already dealt with one of their killers, two of their bad cops, and a psycho club owner. What's the worst they can do? Kill me? They already tried that. So what's next?"

"Lindsay–"

"Who's *doing* all this?"

He went silent.

"Is it that Lanza guy?"

He still didn't speak.

"Isn't he the jerk who ruined your career?"

C.C. sighed. "He's the one who ordered me burned."

"I want to see him."

He stiffened. "Now why in heaven's name–"

"C.C., take me to him."

"Why would you even want to get *close* to him?"

"I want to look him in the eye and tell him exactly what I think of him."

"You think that'll change anything?"

She knew it wouldn't change much at all. But she also knew she had to do it. The vow she'd made to herself had been stupid. It didn't matter – not to them. They couldn't care less that she'd vowed to change her ways. All they cared about was that she'd threatened them. They'd send someone after her even if she decided to live out the rest of her days in a convent.

Something had to matter. Something had to make them realize they were wrong, that life was not a game. And that it wasn't something so cheap and insignificant that it could calmly be eliminated with a quick phone call. Otherwise, what was the point of living at all?

"I want him to see my face. Then maybe he won't be so quick to want us dead. I want him to tell me how he can sleep at night after he just ordered one of his psycho friends to kill my mother."

"Doing that will only make things worse."

"How can this get any worse, C.C.?"

He didn't reply.

"I want him to know how I feel. He might kill me right there, but before I die, he's going to know who I am and how I feel."

"Lindsay, he's a mob boss. A businessman. He doesn't *care* how anyone feels. He does things his way. You honestly think anything you say will matter to him?"

"It'll matter to *me*."

"I don't know if you can even get *near* him..."

"Do you know where he might be right now?"

"Maybe, maybe not..."

"Can you take me to see him?"

He shifted in his seat. His colors had turned solid white. She felt guilty for scaring him, but there was just no other way. Even if Lanza killed her, she had to do this. Her pulse raced. Her mind was made up. "C.C.?"

"It'll be tricky..."

"Does that mean you *will*?"

He just sighed.

"C.C., if you don't help me find him, I'm going to get out of this car right now, flag down the first taxi I see, and have him take me all over Orlando until I track down that nasty, cold-hearted monster."

Chapter 31

Big John Santella easily sank the twenty-foot putt. "How about that?" An easy grin stretched his heavy features. "My mind must be on my game this morning, eh, old man?"

Jo-Jo wasn't in the mood. But it wouldn't accomplish anything to bitch in front of Solo, who stood off to the side, doing his best to stay in the background. "*Paisano*, sometimes gloating's good for the soul. This ain't one of those times."

It took great effort not to toss his putter. That would be undignified. Jo-Jo prided himself in his dignity. He'd finished the last hole with a six. Would've been a four, no thanks to that damned Solo showing up like a bad cold. Right now he stood there like a dickhead, smoking his cigarette.

Solo had no class. He'd brought the way of the streets down to Florida with him. Luckily he knew how to run strip clubs, so at least they could keep him out of their hair. Let the little shit get into his scrapes and push the broads around, if that's what it took to make him feel like a big man. Just so he didn't show up like a dirty penny and make a nuisance of himself. Like now.

But he'd shown up – which told Jo-Jo something was wrong. Worse, he'd shown up on the fifteenth hole. That was when Jo-Jo's game started falling apart.

Jo-Jo handed over his putter and some twenties to his caddie and accepted a hand-rolled cigar from

Big John. "Now that the game's over," he said, giving Solo a quick glare, "you can tell us why you're here instead of running our clubs."

"It's about that bit of business the other day," Solo replied a bit uneasily.

"You saying you came to tell us you've found the missing shipment?"

"I might have a good idea where it is."

Jo-Jo stopped walking. Something didn't sound right. "Cross was supposed to find it by yesterday evening. This is today. He's late."

Solo grinned. "He fucked up and I was forced to take matters into my own hands."

"You got Cross somewhere?" Big John puffed on his cigar.

"I've got my best men looking for him."

"What the hell happened?"

"Some trouble ... at the club."

"What's this have to do with Cross?"

Solo kept shifting his weight. He looked like he had to take a leak. "Well, Jo-Jo, the girl–"

"What about the girl?"

"Like I said, there was trouble."

Jo-Jo was getting a bad feeling about all this. Things had been going wrong all week. If Solo had fucked things up worse, Jo-Jo was going to send him back to New York in a shipment of small boxes. "You still got her, right?"

Solo swallowed noisily and took a step back. "Uh..."

"What the fuck's *that* supposed to mean? You got her or what?"

"Well, Jo-Jo, I *sorta* got her..."

"What's the fucking problem here? You *sorta* got the girl. No word from Cross, and we still don't have the shipment. What the fuck am I supposed to tell Biloxi?"

Solo looked a little pale – as usual when faced with pressure. Jo-Jo liked that. It gave the little shit some humility. He kept scum like him around for jobs he didn't want his good men doing. When they fucked up and turned into an embarrassment, it was time to flush them. "Well?" Jo-Jo asked. "You wanna tell us what we're supposed to do?"

"I think I know where the stuff is," Solo said, finding his voice.

"Is it on its way up to Biloxi?"

"Not yet, but–"

"Then it don't matter if you know where it is. Yeah?"

"There's a little problem getting to it. I think I might be able to find it this afternoon."

"If you know where it's at, go get it," Big John snapped. He suddenly jerked around to his right. "What the *fuck*?"

Two figures – a man and a woman – emerged from the row of tall pine trees bordering the fairway. They were walking toward the green. As they drew closer, Jo-Jo could make out the man. It was Cross. His companion, a tall, skinny young chick, limped along beside him. Her forehead and hands were covered with bandages.

"This is a *private* club," Jo-Jo barked as they drew closer. *Sfachim* must have knocked a few screws loose in the last couple days. He had to be nuts to come here without permission. Jo-Jo already had his cell out. "I can have security out here in one minute."

"I can do better than that," Solo said, shoving his hand inside his jacket pocket.

Big John took a step toward Solo, dwarfing him. "I see a gun when that hand comes out, you're gonna have to learn to wipe your ass with your other hand. Where the hell you think you are? Beirut?"

Reddening, Solo lowered his hand to his side.

Cross and the girl kept coming. When they were less than twenty yards away, Cross said, "This isn't my idea. It's the lady's."

"Tell your *lady* she's got some pretty foolish ideas," Jo-Jo said. "Or don't she listen?"

"She listens real well, but when she wants to do something, you can't change her mind."

"You're the man. You can't change her mind for her?"

"I've tried, believe me. Since we're here, why don't *you* see what *you* can do? She might listen better if it's coming from you."

"Girl, you shouldn't be out here. Not without a hat, anyway. Too much sun is liable to burn that pretty skin."

"You're *worried* about my pretty skin?" she said in a soft, low voice.

The animosity coming from her was thick enough to cut with a knife. Jo-Jo had a feeling this was the Foreman girl. The one with the big mouth.

387

How she'd gotten away from Solo was one thing. Why Cross brought her here was another issue entirely. It was time to get them off his property. Peacefully, of course. There were guests in the area, and they'd paid big money for the privilege of being here. "You were supposed to find something for us. That why you're here? To tell us you found it?"

"Lindsay wanted to meet you."

She hadn't taken her eyes from him. The animosity remained in the large brown eyes. This was one pissed-off woman. But Jo-Jo was in charge. The sooner everyone knew that, the better. "You need to go back where you came from. This ain't the place for you or your friend."

"And where should we be?" she asked.

"You're trespassing. I can call security, or I can call the cops. It don't matter to me. Either way, you two get hauled off while me and my friends go back inside and have our brunch, relax and enjoy the sunny morning."

"You really don't like people, do you?" the girl asked.

"How's that?"

"You don't care if they live or die."

What the hell is she talking about? I don't need this. First, Solo comes out here and fucks up my game. Now this. I need to be home, taking a stroll around the house, enjoying the gardens, the lush scenery. The peace and quiet. Maybe even pick a flower for Madeline and lay it in front of the statue at the shrine.

"I don't know you, girl. You show up on my

property with this cop who's supposed to be doing a job for me. Now you're asking weird questions. If I were you–"

"My name is Lindsay Foreman. My mother's name was Dorothy. She was forty-four years old. She was very bright and intelligent and liked to laugh and have fun. Now she's dead because of you and your stupid *games*." Her rage grew as she drew closer. She trembled, nearly stumbling. Her big brown eyes filled their sockets. Her pale skin flushed. A corner of her mouth quivered. He'd seen that sort of expression many times before.

Jo-Jo suspected her bandages had something to do the "trouble" Solo had mentioned. Solo's plan to have Cross retrieve the shipment probably backfired and the girl had gotten hurt. A quick glance told Jo-Jo he was on the mark. Solo looked like he wanted to bolt into the bushes. So what was all that nonsense about Solo knowing where the shipment was?

"Sorry about your mother," Jo-Jo told the girl.

"I'll bet."

He shrugged. "It's tough, losing a parent. Life's tough – even worse without your parents."

"Are *you* a parent?"

"Course I'm a parent. I have two daughters and six grand–"

"If you really *are* a parent, you ought to value human life more."

He turned to Big John. "What's she talking about?"

Big John shrugged.

"Solo?"

Solo shrugged uneasily and glanced at the bushes again.

Jo-Jo positioned his thumb over the correct button on the cell. The slightest pressure and security would be here in a flash. But first he wanted to know about this girl's mother. After this mess was taken care of, he and Big John were gonna haul Solo into the nearest vacant room in the Club and find out just how much the little *stronzone* had fucked up. "Speak plain, girl. I don't know what you're driving at."

"You killed my mother." The words came out venomously. The girl's bandaged hands had curled into fists. Her body shook. "You paid one of your killers to come after me, but my mother got in the way, and now she's dead. She got in the way because she came home for lunch instead of staying at work. Now she's dead. She really deserved to die because of that, didn't she? You're a cold-blooded, nasty, ignorant old man. I hope you—"

"Wait." His thumb pressed the button. "I don't know what you've been smoking, girl. I know nothing about your mother getting killed."

"You paid a man named Radner to kill me. My mother came home when he was in our apartment, so he killed her. Then you sent two more killers after me, but I got away, and a girl working at *that* dirty little man's club helped me get away. She's dead because of him, and I came here to tell you about it."

The girl was obviously speaking the truth. A

390

damned shame, though. Jo-Jo couldn't side with her against a colleague. Solo was a *stronzone,* a walking pile of sludge, but still a colleague. It was proper to let a colleague defend himself against such serious allegations. "You know what this is all about?" he asked Solo.

Solo shrugged. "I don't know what she's talking about, Jo-Jo."

"He's lying," the girl said.

"Who you gonna believe, Jo-Jo? Some trailer trash slut? Or one of your own men?"

Solo had a point. Jo-Jo didn't know this girl from Adam. Solo had been running the clubs for several years now. Ran 'em good, too. "You have proof of what you say, girl?"

"He knows I do."

She stared at Solo, who stared right back at her. Definitely something between the two of them. Solo had nothing to do with Radner. Solo wouldn't know how to handle a high-priced persuader. This girl had problems, sure, but Jo-Jo couldn't be bothered. Accidents happened all the time – especially when people showed up at the wrong time. But that wasn't his problem. He couldn't be responsible for everything that went on, could he? "Listen, girl–"

"Miss Foreman."

Where the fuck was security? "Like I said, I'm sorry your momma–"

"You don't care that my mother is dead. You just want us to leave so you and your friends can go inside and have your coffee and talk about who you're going to do away with next. That's what horrible people like you do."

She really had balls, all right. Seemed an awful lot like his eighteen-year-old granddaughter Alicia. Especially the defiance. Madeline would even agree, if she was still alive. But this wasn't the time or place to show her stuff.

"Cross. This girl ... she know who she's talking to?"

Cross nodded.

"She know how people usually treat me?"

"I don't think it matters much to her right now."

"Girl–"

"*Miss Foreman.*"

"People don't walk onto my property uninvited and have the brass *cojones* to call me a liar – especially to my face."

"Maybe if more of them did, fewer of them would die."

"*Huh?*"

"Maybe if you saw the faces of your victims once in a while, you'll be less likely to play your games with them in the future."

"Cross, what the hell's this all about? Ask her what this is about."

"Give her a minute. She'll tell you. She's on a roll."

Still looking at Jo-Jo, the girl said, "I want you to see my face and remember it. When you killed my mother, you changed my life forever."

"Like I said, I know nothing about–"

"All I did was help an old woman who was run

392

over on the highway and left for dead."

Jo-Jo glanced at two security wagons emerging from the office area on the other side of the building. *About damned time.*

"I went with her to the hospital and held her hand while she died."

"That was, um, good of you to do that–"

"I didn't do it because it was *good* of me. I did it because no one else cared. Especially the jerk who hit her. Does that seem right to you, Mr. Lanza? Does that seem okay that someone can run over an old woman and just leave her lying there?"

"Well, no, that was pretty damned–"

"How did Madeline die, Mr. Lanza?"

His cheeks grew warm. His pulse fluttered. *What the hell's going on?* "Listen, girl ... Miss Foreman–"

"How would you like it if your wife was run down and left on the highway?"

How the hell does she know Madeline's name?

"My *wife?*"

"And how would you like it if the only person who stopped to help her became the target of a bunch of psychos?"

The security wagons pulled up behind Jo-Jo and squealed to an abrupt halt. Four guards jumped out and rushed over to Cross and the girl. As they approached the girl, she said, "The next time you're home and walk out back to your shrine to pray, remember the name Maisie. That was the name of the old woman. I don't know her last name because she didn't have any friends when she died. I was the

393

only friend she had."

Jo-Jo no longer felt the ground at his feet. The cell slipped from his hand and dropped silently to the trimmed grass. His body had gone numb. *What's happening here? The shrine. How the hell does she know about the shrine?*

"Wait!" he barked at security. "Let them be."

***

The man everyone called Jo-Jo Lanza cautiously approached her.

He didn't look like a mobster now, just a confused old man in baggy shorts and a crinkly red cap who'd just heard something strange. He seemed so vulnerable and small that her anger gradually subsided. He was responsible for Momma's death – that would never change. His colors told her he didn't know, but the fact that he'd paid a man to come after them made him accountable.

The image of the statue had flared in her head earlier, becoming crystal-clear right after Lindsay had seen the woman's name. The old man had then appeared in his navy-blue housecoat, watering plants around the shrine. She didn't understand how a man who dealt in violence and death could be religious, but his reaction told her he was.

"My shrine," he said in a soft, uneasy voice. "How ... did you ... *know?*"

"It's in your yard. There are gardens around it, and flowers. It's really very pretty. My mother loved flowers."

"But how ... how did you *know?* There's a fence surrounding the property. And a locked gate.

394

And guards. No one can get in without–"

"I didn't have to get in."

The white swirls flowing above his cap thickened. He glanced up at the sky. "Then ... how did you *know*?"

"The lady I helped." Lindsay was relieved she now had the chance to talk about her. This old man was bad. He employed bad people to do bad things, but he deserved to know. He was a large part of this, too. "Maisie was very special. She gave me a gift. I didn't know what it was at first. I actually thought it was a curse. Sometimes it was. But other times ... other times it helped me."

"What ... sort of gift?"

"I can tell when someone is lying, and when someone is telling the truth. I see fear, and I also see death." She glanced at the terrible little man standing near the bushes, his face taut and bone-white. His colors, a heavy mix of reds, whites and blacks, hovered close. "Right now, I know someone's been lying to you. He's standing right behind you."

Lanza didn't turn around. His tired expression told her he knew who she was referring to. "Lying about what?" he asked.

"I don't know exactly, and I surely don't want to. It's about the car that ran down Maisie."

The other man – the big one with thick dark hair – came closer. The security guys had returned to their vehicles. Solo had slipped behind the bushes and took off running up the paved path.

Lanza didn't seem to notice. "Go on," he said

softly.

"You wanted C.C. to look for something for you. That nasty little man has had it all along. He was going to have me killed. He hates C.C. and wants him dead. He was going to tell you he found what C.C. was looking for. In doing that, he thought he'd look good in your eyes."

Lanza's tanned features grew taut. "Anything else?"

She'd seen two large leather suitcases. One was filled with money, the other sacks of white powder. She saw no reason to mention it. It would upset these two men. She didn't want to be around when they were upset. Lastly, she didn't want anything else to prolong this. She was tired and wanted to lie down. "That's all," she said.

Lanza stared at her. Green and blue splotches appeared within the white swirls floating around his head. He snuck another quick peek straight up as if he thought something would fall from the sky. Words from a prayer entered his mind, then vanished. "I believe her," he told his friend.

"Sounds reasonable, old man."

"The fact that Solo just made tracks like a scared rabbit should also tell you something," C.C. said. "Plus another minor detail you two should know."

"What's that?" the big man asked.

"This girl never lies."

Lanza didn't take his eyes off her. "I'm still wondering how she knows about my statue," he whispered.

"She knows a lot," C.C. said. "Just try keeping something from her."

"A bad habit," the big man said, staring coldly at her. "Knowing too much can get you–"

"Stop that kind of talk, *paisano*." Lanza made a quick sign of the cross. "This young lady ... she's special ... and not to be messed with."

The big man said nothing.

"Punk made suckers out of both of us," Lanza said. "*He's* our problem."

"Only one way of keeping this quiet, old man."

Lanza nodded. "Boy's been working too hard. He needs a long vacation."

"Guess this is as good a time as any." A puff of black exploded from the big man's broad shoulders. He produced a cell and punched in numbers.

"Just make sure we find out a few things first," Lanza said.

The big man walked away, talking rapidly into his cell.

Lanza remained staring, his colors a mix of whites, blues, greens and turquoise. "You've done us a big favor, young lady," he said.

Her anger had vanished. She found that she could no longer hate him. He was just a tired old man betrayed by one of his own. She found it somehow reassuring that even with all his wealth and power, he could be just as vulnerable as everyone else.

"Anyone who knows me will tell you I pay my debts," he said. "So ... how do I repay you?"

"Is he serious?" she asked C.C.

C.C. shrugged. "I guess now's a good time to find out."

"Try me, young lady."

"All right. Take C.C. off your payroll."

The old man sighed heavily. He glanced upward one last time and nodded.

"Thank you." Her back began hurting and her feet had turned tingly again. She really needed to lie down. In a hot tub first, then a nice, soft bed. "Let's go," she told C.C. "I'm kind of tired."

"You remind me of one of my granddaughters," Lanza said. The beginnings of a smile touched his lips. "Her name's Alicia. You don't look like her, but you're alike. The same sass, the same defiance. Any Italian in your blood?"

She shook her head and turned back to the woods.

"You can go out through the front, with all the other guests," Lanza said.

"Thank you." They started up the walk.

"Is that all you wanted?"

She turned to face him. "I can ask for something else?"

"As long as it isn't as expensive as that first request." His colors remained blue, green and turquoise.

"If it's not too much trouble, I'd appreciate it if no one else comes after me again."

The old man chuckled. "Young lady, as long as I'm around, as long as my outfit is running things, you won't have to worry about that."

Chapter 32

C.C. was silent as they descended the paved road fronting the country club, where he'd left the Mustang.

Lindsay welcomed the silence. She was exhausted. She hadn't had a painkiller in several hours and badly needed one. She didn't know if she was proud of herself for what she'd done back there or just relieved the ordeal was over. Probably both. Confronting those men was necessary – a way of interrupting their stupid game, of telling them how it affected people. It also made her realize how precious and fragile life really was.

Everything seemed so temporary – as if life itself was nothing more than chance. She'd read stories about the people working in the World Trade Center who hadn't gone in the morning of 9/11. Some were on vacation, while others were trapped in traffic or called in sick. Still others were detained at the barber shop, or the dry cleaners. Dozens of people were alive simply because they weren't where they were supposed to be during that one horribly tragic morning.

If Momma hadn't come home during her lunch hour ... if Maisie hadn't walked along that stretch of Colonial Friday night ... if I hadn't gone to the mall that night...

Chance. There was no other way to describe it.

As C.C. got on the Turnpike and joined the heavy flow that would take them back to Orlando,

Lindsay opened her handbag, found her meds, twisted off the child-proof cap, and dry-swallowed two. Luckily, they went down easily.

"Are you all right?" C.C. asked.

It was nice, having someone in her life who cared. She couldn't imagine going through any of this without him. "Just tired and a little achy."

"You have any idea what you just did back there?"

"Other than taking you off their payroll?"

C.C. shook his head. His colors swirled around restlessly. The only shade she didn't see was red. "Because of you, I can do my job again. And you no longer have to worry about anyone else coming after you."

"But he'll still buy people, corrupt them, and make them do bad things."

"That's what he does. By the way, did you tell them the truth?"

"About what?"

"When you said all you knew was that Solo had been lying to them."

"He *was* lying."

"That's not what I'm asking."

She stared at the road ahead. She wanted this to be over – finished. She had enough of those idiotic games to last a lifetime. But C.C. had asked her a question. She decided to tell him what she thought he should know. "I saw two suitcases."

"Anything else?"

"No."

"You sure?"

"It's all I saw. All I wanted to see."

C.C. didn't say anything, but white splotches quickly appeared, smeared with thick black bands.

"Can we ... not discuss this anymore? I want to forget it. Forget everything."

C.C. was silent for a while. She looked over at him and saw his mouth curl in the corners when he said, "You definitely put the fear of God into Lanza."

"I don't know about *that*..."

"You saw his expression when you mentioned his wife's name. His shrine. I was almost certain he'd wet his pants. Don't you realize how paranoid and superstitious these mob bosses are?"

"I'm only interested in how badly they treat people."

"Lindsay, you're not going to change anyone – especially a rich old man who's been getting his way the last forty years. But what you did will probably get him thinking."

"About what?"

"Death. God. Miracles. Special people with special gifts. Lanza is a God-fearing man. He'll probably think of you a lot in the next few weeks. He'll also think of his granddaughter and his dead wife. And the next time he walks outside to visit his shrine, he'll see you. If that's all it takes to make him a little more appreciative of human life, then you've done this city a great service." C.C. went back to his driving. His colors had dimmed, but the strands of gray cropping up among them told her he was nervous about something.

401

"There's something on your mind."

He laughed. "It's impossible keeping things from you, isn't it?"

"You won't have to if you just talk to me."

"I've been checking into something the last couple of days. My sergeant heard about everything when he came back from Miami. He gave me a few days off, so I decided to do a little investigating while I was waiting for you to recover."

"Investigating?"

"It's about Maisie."

***

Just off the Orlando exit ramp, less than a mile past the loop crossing South Orange Blossom Trail, a narrow two-lane road turned onto an uneven dirt path leading into a large overgrown field.

Behind a clutter of rundown concession stands, a row of weather-beaten travel trailers rested quietly in a grove of oak trees. Beat-up pickups, SUVs, and ancient station wagons sat between them. Picnic benches, lawn chairs, swings, and teeter-totters cluttered an area off to the side. Half a dozen elderly men and women sat at the picnic table, drinking from white mugs. Two men played checkers while another shuffled cards. An old man wearing a tattered straw hat, a loose-fitting sweatshirt, baggy gray trousers, and tennis shoes relaxed in a rocking chair, a curved briar pipe stuck in a corner of his mouth.

C.C. parked in front of a dilapidated travel trailer. "Carnival people," he said, switching off the engine. "This is where they live when they're not

402

traveling."

"How do you know about them?"

"I'm a cop. I know a lot of things."

"I ... have a strange feeling … about this place," she said. Maisie had been here. She could sense the old woman's presence in the grove of trees beyond the travel trailers.

"I figured you would." He pushed open his door. "Let's find out if you're right."

The group at the picnic table abruptly got up and hurried inside the nearest trailer.

C.C. and Lindsay approached the old man, who pushed himself up from his chair. He scowled at C.C. "You again?" he said in a high, raspy voice, then turned toward the trailer behind him.

"I told you I'd be back."

The smoke rising from the old man's pipe grew thicker. His eyes shifted to Lindsay. A wisp of white appeared just above the straw hat.

"I also told you I'd bring someone this time," C.C. said. "Someone you'd talk to."

The old man said nothing. He took another step toward the trailer.

Lindsay could tell these people didn't like strangers. She hoped she could gain their confidence. "My name is Lindsay."

The man still didn't speak.

"Does the name Maisie ring a bell?"

The man stopped edging toward the trailer. "Don't recall ... that name." A heavy reddish hue appeared just above the loose folds of the hat.

"Why are you lying?"

The old man stiffened. His eyes, small chunks of coal, were barely visible among the wrinkles smothering them. He grabbed the bowl of his pipe. "Ain't nice, calling an old man a liar."

So much for gaining their confidence. "Even if he is?"

"And ya know this how?"

"I see it."

He pushed the brim of his hat up an inch or so. "How?"

"Maisie's gift lets me see lies. And hatred. Sometimes I even hear voices."

The man didn't speak.

"You knew her, didn't you?"

"Leave us. Forget about it."

"Maisie won't let me."

His eyes grew. "Tell this ... Maisie–"

"She's dead."

The old man stood quite still. His colors turned dark. "If she's dead ... how can she–"

"I don't know. I only know she's been with me ever since."

"She's ... *with* ya?"

"I haven't been the same since she died."

"She gave ya the hex?"

"It's not a hex. It was her gift to me. I was with her when she died."

"How'd she die?"

"She was struck by a car."

He stared at his pipe as if he was trying to put it all together. "And ... you were with her?"

"I didn't want her to die alone."

The old man raised his face. Lindsay could see the sadness in his eyes, his features falling. His colors grew thicker. The black was laced with gray, and wisps of silver. "Her life ... was not happy," he finally said.

"Tell me about her."

The old man pushed up his hat another couple of inches.

"Please?"

"Then will ya leave an old man in peace?"

"I promise."

He shuffled back to his chair and collapsed into it. "She came from Europe as a young girl." A catch in the old man's throat had softened his voice. "Romania, we think." He slouched forward and fiddled with his pipe. "Her thick black hair turned blue in the sunlight. Her eyes, a silvery gray. They glittered, made ya feel ... warm inside..."

The old man sat there, remembering. Nodding as the memories became clearer. "She joined up with us in New York and stayed with us when we came down here for the winters. That was about sixty years ago, I guess."

He turned silent again, his colors blue and green. Dark knots of smoke squirmed heavily out of the bowl of his pipe. "She could somehow see into people, feel their joys and sorrows. Touch them and see their destinies. She saw and felt mostly death and sadness. She tried putting it in a dark place so she wouldn't be able to find it, but she couldn't for very long.

"She had no family, never spoke of anyone

405

close. Whenever someone asked her, her eyes went dark – like a candle when ya blow it out. Sometimes she'd go off by herself. She liked the woods. You could always find her there, wandering around. She loved animals, talked to 'em just like she was talking to one of us. She performed on horses and elephants, even worked with the lion tamer a couple times.

"One day she fell for a banker who'd come to see the circus, and left without a word. Didn't see her for years, but we all knew she'd come back. The dark in her kept happiness from getting too close. Just like the rest of us, only with her, the darkness was worse.

"Some say she lost her new family – possibly a fire. Whatever it was, it was bad. She came back but was never the same. The light in her eyes had gone out. She was no longer young, no longer beautiful, but she still had her gift. She read fortunes, told people things. She told them good things because she didn't want them hearing the bad. When bad things happened, they came back angry, wanting their money back. She told them the truth from then on, and they left her alone.

"She wandered off again one day a few years ago and never came back. We never saw her again. Some said she took to the streets. We think she no longer wanted to be around people because of what she saw."

Sighing brokenly, the old man grunted out of his chair, turned stiffly to the ramshackle travel trailer behind him, and slowly climbed the steps.

C.C. was silent as they got back on the main highway.

Lindsay greatly appreciated the effort he'd made to track down the old man. "It must have taken a lot of time."

"Not that much. Like I said, I had some time to kill."

"I appreciate it anyway."

"Did it help?"

"Her life was so sad, so tragic. She had such potential. I guess ... I guess I wanted a happy ending."

"You knew the ending."

"She didn't start out that way."

"We all start out the same. Life beats us up in thousands of different ways."

"She had such a special gift. She could've helped so many people."

"How?"

He was right. Lindsay also had the gift. Could it save Momma or Ronnie?

"Why'd you want a happy ending?" he asked.

She turned away and watched the houses and businesses they passed as they went north. People walked into restaurants and came out of car dealerships, each going on with his own individual existence. Everyone had a destiny, a purpose. "I don't ... want to end up the same way," she said softly.

"What makes you think you will?"

"I have Maisie's gift. It destroyed her."

407

"She let it."

"Maybe she didn't have a choice."

"We all have choices."

"Maisie chose to leave the circus with a man who loved her. Look what happened."

"She gave up. *That's* what happened."

***

Twenty minutes later, they reached the intersection of Colonial and the Trail. C.C. stopped at the light. "Back to your apartment? Or do you need more time?"

Dark images swept by. The living room sofa, where Momma had died. The carpet in front of the sofa, where Lindsay had killed a man. She had to face going into Momma's room, knowing Momma would never be there again. Going through Momma's things. Their family photos. She knew she could do it. She'd survived so many horrible things, she was confident she could face anything.

"I think I can go back now." She didn't even sense fear or apprehension in saying it that time. "But there are three things I have to do first. I want to go back to the Presbyterian Church, where I first found out about Maisie. I want to make arrangements for some type of service for Momma."

"Was she religious?"

"She stopped going when Dad left us. I still want a service for her. I'd also like to have a service for Maisie and Ronnie. Maisie's like an old friend. She helped me through some tight spots. Ronnie saved my life. I owe her as well. I know this

408

probably doesn't make much sense to you, but–"

"It makes a lot of sense." Thick blue and green strands shimmered around him. "We can do that whenever you like."

"I think I'd like to do that first."

"Then what?"

"I have to stop by the police station."

He scowled. "You *still* want to do that?"

She shrugged. "When all this first happened, I promised Maisie I wouldn't let her down. What's different?"

"The difference is, no one can touch you again."

She blinked. "No one?"

"You know what I meant."

She smiled. "Good, because when I start feeling more like myself, I'd like to get to know you better."

He pushed a hand through his hair. Wisps of white appeared near him. "I'm ... more than ten years older than you."

"I've aged a lot in the last week."

"What about my track record? I'm not exactly the world's greatest catch."

"Who said *I* was?" Then she leaned over and kissed him.

She had no idea she was going to do that – it just happened. She was glad it did. And going by C.C.'s somewhat shocked expression, as well as the bright colors jumping around him, so was he. She'd thought about doing that for a while, but since so many other things were going on, she'd put it on hold. But now that she'd finally done it, she was pleased to discover that it felt good. And so did she.

She didn't know if there was enough between them to build on, or even if it would last. She liked C.C. very much. His colors told her he liked her, too. They'd shared a lifetime of memories in just days. He'd been there when she needed someone. She was glad she'd been able to help him when he needed it.

She hoped her life would not be unhappy or tragic. She thought she might be able to make the decisions Maisie should have made as a young woman. And with the help of the colors, she'd know which path to follow, from now on.

The light changed. His face flushed, C.C. forced his attention back to the road. "Uh ... what was that third thing you wanted to do?"

"We have to go back to Sarah's. I have to pick up Marvin."

THE END

ALSO BY DAVID BERARDELLI

THE APPRENTICE
THE WAGON DRIVER
STEPPING OUT OF MY GRAVE
ESCAPE CLAUSE
FATAL INNOCENCE
THE FUNNY DETECTIVE
JUST A SIMPLE ERRAND
WORKING FOR A MOB BOSS
AND DARKNESS FELL
AFTER DARKNESS FELL
IN ANOTHER REALM
BEYOND RECOGNITION
LOOKING FOR A DEAD GUY
THE NIGHTMARE COLLECTOR
HIDDEN
BEYOND GUILT
A RIPPLE IN TIME
HUNTING THE TALL BLONDE
AWAKENED
THE PLANNING COMMITTEE
WINTER SCENE

www.ingramcontent.com/pod-product-compliance
Lightning Source LLC
Chambersburg PA
CBHW011652010726
47499CB00010B/3227